THE FATEFUL FEW

Alan Friggieri

The characters and events portrayed in this book are fictitious. Any similarity to real persons, living or dead, is coincidental and not intended by the author.

Paperback edition ISBN-13: 979-8370262845

Cover design by: Alan Friggieri
Cover photography adapted from Fía Yang (fiayang.com)

For anyone who has ever been unsure.

"My whole life, people have told me who I am; what I am and am not capable of... I'm the only one who knows,"

For Sarah, without whom I couldn't have done any of this and for whom this book has been such a part of our lives for the last few years. I love you with all my heart.

For Sophia, from Dad. Put this book back on the shelf right now - it's full of rude words and scary stuff! But, because I know you'll at least read on until the end of this bit: know that this book contains an important story that for a long time was my dream to tell, and I hope it has a positive effect on those grown up enough to read it. I hope you remember to follow your dreams. I love you with all my heart too.

CHAPTER 1

Look! Up in the sky!

Steve shouldn't be here. What's more, today is one of those days when, deep down, beneath his authoritative crew cut and self-assured moustache, he doubts he is really fooling anyone. And those days are happening all too often recently. To anyone who cares to look in his direction, Cpt Steve Blake's US Air Force career would look like a steady and gravity-defying upward fall. He remembers his dad, in response to hearing that the cream always rises to the top, proudly and sagely rebuking, And Some Shit Floats.

For the last year, Steve has been stuck three days a week, a hundred feet below ground in Montana, in a tiny pill-shaped capsule, staring at the same digital displays, crowbarred into a panel of antique dials and switches. The only way out is through two stages of metal and concrete blast doors leading to an elevator shaft, or through a tiny emergency escape hatch in a back corner. The only contact with the outside world is a one-way phone line to the control building, or if a command were to come over the radio, which nobody wants. His only company is his launch deputy, Lieutenant Hanson. The less said there the better. Steve and his deputy are only here because, when the system was designed in the 1960s, men were more trusted than computers. There are two of them because one man cannot be trusted not to make a mistake. The fact that Hanson is a woman leaves Steve grasping for the punchline to this joke. Come to think of it, maybe someone has cared to look in his direction after all. A quarter of the way into his nuclear alert tour, Steve wonders whether he is losing his mind. He takes a sip of coffee from his Thermos—no cream. The taste bites.

As he swallows away the bitterness, the little rectangular display that only lights up in training drills now suddenly springs to life, flashing three letters in front of Steve's blinking eyes. Before he takes control of his speech faculties, the words, "E.A.M. inbound," tumble out of his mouth.

From this point on, the procedure has already taken over their actions and words. They couldn't diverge if they wanted to, so ingrained is it into their muscle memory. Steve and his launch deputy are already pulling down their respective codebooks when the echoey sound of the Emergency-Action Message hisses into the two-man command capsule. Androgenous and delivered with a professional stoicism completely detached from its consequences, it could have been delivered by a robot.

"Zulu-Uniform-Juliet-Tango,"

There's no room for thought, barely room for breath in the capsule. Within seconds, Steve and his deputy have decrypted and authenticated the message and are cross-referencing the war plan. This is not a drill.

"Crowd Pleaser,"

So rehearsed are their responses, he can't even tell which one of them said that, but it doesn't matter. They both know what it means. The two officers have just been given the order for immediate release of their entire arsenal; ten Minuteman III nuclear missiles.

"Enter launch code," he orders, definitely him this time. The readout on the display confirms the radioed launch order.

"Target selection complete," Hanson intones robotically as she reads from her monitor. She'd be suited to delivering the E.A.Ms. "Time on target sequence complete," she continues, "Yield selection complete,"

The countdown has begun. *This is it.*

"Alright, Missileer, this is our time," he

says, this line only privately rehearsed. Steve manages to project his voice over his shoulder (as unnecessary as that is in the poky command capsule) and give the order to "Insert launchkey,"

Destiny is calling, and instinct answers, he thinks.

"Enable missiles,"

Clack-click, clack-click, clack-click is the answer as one after another is enabled. Each 350 kiloton intercontinental ballistic missile is just a small yellow bulb on a dashboard, flicking on at the President's command.

"Captain," he hears, still holding the launch key at *Set*. His deputy will be doing the same, waiting for his order to switch to *Launch*, wondering why he's not given it. "Captain?"

The brakes are coming on. For the first time in his career, the brakes are coming on in his head. The procedure squeals silently.

"Wait." he says.

His training tells him *no delay*. The order is clear, and can only be given by the President as Commander-in-Chief. Steve's is not to challenge. But nuclear war—*World War*—is the other side of that key-turn. And he knows the stories. The first near-apocalypse was in '79, when someone left a training tape in the early warning system monitors. Four years later, in 1983, one Russian's niggling feeling averted Armageddon when Russian systems actually showed incoming

US missiles. The Russian duty officer, Lieutenant Colonel Stanislav Petrov, went against protocol, deciding not to act because his gut told him it was a glitch. He was right, and he saved the world. But this is different. This is a direct Emergency-Action Message, triggered by the President. But what if the President's intel was wrong? What if he was acting on a glitch?

"Captain?" Her grating voice is more urgent and verging on insubordination.

“Get Wing Command on the line,”

Maybe World War III has already started. It would take up to thirty minutes for the warheads to reach their destinations on the other side of the globe. Just a handful of minutes before they reach their first target. *What's already in the air on its way to us?*

There's silence while his deputy hangs on the phone, punctuated only by Steve’s own heavy breathing as he tries to deepen and slow his breath, to get in control now that his heart is thudding. He finds he can't tell whether his fingers are gripping the key or the key is gripping him. Either way, he can't move. That tiny movement, turning the key to the launch position, would change the entire world forever. Millions of lives outside of this buried capsule, gone with the flick of the wrist.

“No response from anybody, Sir,”

He just stares blankly; not at her, he hasn't

looked at her once and can't; at the key in the slot, between his fingers.

"Sir," she goes on, "The order is clear, sir. The codes check out. The war plan matches. The targets are set. The missiles are enabled,"

He looks at her now, her severe features accentuated by the primary coloured lights on the panel in front of her.

"Why is there no answer? Why isn't control responding?"

"Sir, we have to follow out the order. We already breached protocol by calling. We should have launched by now,"

He hates to admit it but she's right. For all they know, China—or whoever—has already fired and, by delaying the US's counter strike, he's ensuring their own defeat.

"Lieutenant, the order is Crowd Pleaser,"

Crowd Pleaser—the most catastrophic war plan in the book; the one no-one thought would ever be used; the dusty one at the back, added in paranoid fervour or intellectual self-gratification.

"Captain, you need to turn your key,"

"Try the line again," he orders, "What if something went wrong and there's been a mistake?"

"Then protocol is that the updated order would be issued via a secondary E.A.M., Sir,"

"I know the protocol, Lieutenant!" He barks, "Make the call,"

The look she gives him says *we don't have time for this*, but she does it anyway, hand still on her launch key, not giving up on proving him wrong.

"Fuck," he mutters to himself as she sits there, stoney eyes staring back at him, on a silent phonecall.

Samantha. I'm sorry.

"On my mark, rotate launch keys to *Launch*,"

I shouldn't be here.

* * *

At the exact moment the nuclear missile launch is ordered, the President of the Free World tweets, "Big fat dose of truth on its way to N Korea. You made without a doubt THE WORST DECISION today. Nukes. Very bad." It is coming up to 2:30am in Pyongyang, nearly four hours before sunrise there.

Before newsrooms or war rooms can get a grip on reality, smartphones are aimed at the skies over the state of Montana, home of the United States Air Force's nuclear weapons programme. The first visual confirmation comes from a thirteen year-old named Carl, who loves superheroes and strawberry swirl ice cream.

His love of superheroes and comic books was how he survived the hardest years of his life, and it all began with one square box, one panel, in a comic book. A ferocious missile, accompanied by the roar of a hundred stampeding stallions in Carl's mind, as it tore through the pages, dragging storm clouds and fury in its wake. But, in that moment, on the brink of destruction, all the world needed was its hero. In the face of a 550 megaton nuclear warhead, *his* winning smile and bulging muscles told the little reader not to worry. Carl knew Superman had everything under control; that while some dark and scheming villain was plotting the world's end, it wouldn't matter as long as he kept turning the pages of his comic book.

Now, thousands of pages later, the sky is clear of superheroes, because they aren't real. There's no-one coming to the rescue.

He's on his way to Yellowstone National Park with his foster parents when he captures a photo of the moment on his phone: ten white plumes stretching from the horizon to the clouds above, like the toppling columns of an ancient temple. No saviour. He tweets the photo in reply to @POTUS, along with the words, "FUCK YOU".

Just as Carl was beginning to feel like he's found a family, he realises they won't even reach the park gates.

* * *

Steve has opened the blast door and is stepping into the steel tunnel when he hears the pistol cocking behind him. The sound of it cuts through the blaring alarm and hits him in the back of the head like his deputy has already pulled the trigger.

"Do not step outside of this command post, Captain," Fear and self-preservation hold Steve in place. "Sir, do not abandon your post,"

Steve closes his eyes. "Stand down, missileer,"

"Sir. Do not abandon your post,"

From the other side of the command capsule, the cocked pistol still drills through the electric recycled air into Steve's skull.

In the tunnel junction, the lights above Steve's head flicker and the entire base suddenly shakes. The only thing that can make that sort of impact down here, buried in a steel casket a hundred feet underground, is a direct strike on the base, which he will soon discover when he is vapourised. Now comes a sickening and guttural shudder as the earth groans and metal screams. Steve loses his footing and the lights go out completely. In the pitch black, the wall slams into Steve's left shoulder and the air is sucked out of his lungs, sending him to his backside. Before a single thought crosses his mind, the emergency lighting pulses into being, bathing everything in a hellish red. Everything is thudding and ringing, Steve's head feels like it is going to explode, his shoulder may well have done so already and his heart feels five times too big, threatening to burst his chest with each pounding. It must have been a near miss. His straining lungs find air and he clambers back to his feet.

"Are you okay? Where's that draft coming from, is the wall breached?" Steve finds himself shouting over the ringing in his own ears. Hanson must not have heard him so he shouts again as he trips into the capsule. "Come on. This area isn't safe now. Who the hell are *you*?"

Where did she come from? Steve must be losing his mind, he thinks. *No-one else could be down here.* Hanson and the other woman are completely ignoring him, chattering indecipherably to each other. It's as if they don't care that the world is ending. *Oh, Samantha, what the fuck am I doing here?* "We have to get out of here. Let's go." He knows they aren't following, but no-one could say he hadn't tried. As he hurdles back out of the capsule, Cpt Steve Blake runs face-first into something thick, metal and immovable. Unconscious, the last thing he feels before the end of the world is a perfect sensation of floating.

* * *

Despite the space between them in the steel and glass box somewhere in Virginia, Cassandra feels cramped with four American military men and their barely tolerable egos. The dully-lit funicular lift clunks steadily into the bowels of the damned facility below. The vacuum of silence in the air makes her feel dangerously conspicuous; the only one without a military rank, the only woman, the only person of colour, the only person who shouldn't be here. Standing in a corner of the 4-metre carriage, the brief silence afforded them as Lieutenant General Hilton tries to unlock his iPad is the first moment she has to contemplate what she's just heard.

They—senior leaders from US military forces, and her—were at a joint security service meeting at a military installation in Virginia. In the room were General Fletcher, the Chairman of the Joint Chiefs of Staff; Lieutenant General Hilton; Admiral Astor, the Vice Chief of Naval Operations; and General Raymond "Death Ray" Lorre, Chief of Space Force Operations. On screen were the chiefs of the Air Force, Marines, Coast Guard and National Guard. Cassandra was taking notes on behalf of her supposed boss at the NSA, who sent his apologies at the last moment, due to unforeseen circumstances. Cassandra is essentially in the role of a glorified secretary, with top tier security clearance.

The meeting was turned upside down when, awkward and shrill, the theme to The Simpsons burst into the meeting from Fletcher's trouser pocket at the head of the table. Cassandra shouldn't know of the personalised ringtone, set by his son and which he has been unable to correct. But that's the least of the things she shouldn't know. One other thing she knew before any words were exchanged: Fletcher's fourteen year-old son Eric knows only to call this number in a life-or-death situation.

At first embarrassed by the intrusion, Fletcher answered the call. Then, his pink cheeks reddened and embarrassment turned quickly to anger, bleeding from his face to his entire body. When anger became disbelief, his shoulders dropped. For a split-second, there was an almost imperceptible flutter of despair in his watery eyes before his loosening bottom lip was firmly buttoned over with stiff, bullish machismo. Somehow, US intelligence has gotten so bad that a five star general gets front-line updates from his 14 year-old son.

"Gentlemen," he said, forgetting Cassandra, "We have ten minutes to save the world," Cassandra had never seen such an explosion of energy from the weighty man as he bounced to his feet, the wheeled chair careening out from behind him, "This is not a drill,"

In the lift, Hilton has finally unlocked his iPad.

"We have ten Minuteman III warheads on course for ten different targets," He announces as chunky cogs bring their descent to the secret war room, "A.D.A. are calculating likely targets,"

"There's no need," Gen. Fletcher isn't looking at anyone. His gaze is fixed at the far end of the lift floor as if boring out the path ahead of them. "It's Crowd Pleaser," he says.

"Excuse me?" asks Death Ray, knowing when not to feign knowledge.

"I know this war plan," Fletcher says, "Crowd Pleaser is the worst case scenario. The ultimate reset button." For all his bluster, Fletcher usually cuts straight to the point first, but he's holding something back. He blinks for the first time and looks at his wristwatch, "We have less than seven minutes before DC is lost,"

Cassandra's head is spinning.

"*This* is a war plan?" Says Astor, asking the same question Cassandra is thinking.

"We have plans for every scenario, Admiral," Fletcher replies, "Including successful enemy invasion,"

Hilton is still looking at his iPad, the screen giving his face a pallid luminance, "We have three forced re-entry opportunities on the way to Washington, which would yield the least structural damage and immediate loss of life --"

"-- But either way," Astor cuts in, "The fallout will be catastrophic, with radioactive debris spread for miles,"

As Cassandra listens, she roots her feet into the ground to subdue the shaking in her knees, but she can't hold the tremor in throat. She remains silenced. *How could even the US be so foolish for this to be considered a war plan?* And the exit strategy is to shoot down the first nuke over a less populated area. Cassandra feels like screaming. *What good is a bloody emergency base if it takes so long to reach?*

Unflinching and evenly voiced, Fletcher speaks as a man whose mind has already leapt forwards into the cavern below, "You don't need to tell me that, Admiral," he says, before directing his voice to Hilton without moving an inch, "How soon before the first re-entry point?"

"We just missed South Dakota, Sir. Iowa's next—in 27 seconds. Population: three million. Estimated immediate fatalities: two- to four-thousand."

"What are we going to do about the other nine warheads?" Death Ray asks, but they all already know the answer, and it's not good.

As the funicular continues its descent, the concrete wall on the other side of the glass front suddenly vanishes upward. At first, there is only inky blackness until they are brought below the height of the large white lights suspended on wires from the abyss above. Further they descend, the passengers silently absorbing their new environment, into the area of light, until the ground is visible, lit from above and by flood lights as if it were a football stadium inside a mountain. The central focus of the lights is a series of large screens above a bank of control panels and monitors, operated by three seated men in boiler suits.

It's not a smooth arrival as the funicular bumps into its dock and locks into place before the heavy reinforced glass front cranks across to release its cargo of passengers.

At the control station in the centre of the room, Fletcher, Hilton, Astor, Lorre and Agent Cassandra Bryce stand behind the three technicians and glare at the metre-squared radar map of the world. No secret answer jumps out. Red dashed lines trace from Montana to the cities once secretly chosen for obliteration by a gaggle of grey-haired white men. The *bogey* on which they all focus continues its red dash across the green map toward the outline of Washington DC.

For obvious reasons, the best defences against Intercontinental Ballistic Missiles are offshore, before the threat would reach US airspace. If those fail, the last line of defence is THAAD, the Terminal High Altitude Area Defence system deployed at key sites actually on US soil. It is a blunt instrument and the ultimate testament to Americans' predilection for shooting things. Shoot the airborne warhead to detonate it in the low atmosphere or bring it down to bomb somewhere else before it reaches its target. Even so, THAAD was conceived as a defence against *foreign* attack, allowing twenty to thirty minutes to bring the system up to speed and launch. Hilton's *re-entry opportunities* have thus quickly became moot and Iowa, followed by Ohio, escaped oblivion. THAAD's Surface to Air Missile unit in Washington DC, however, is ever-ready at an *Elevated* threat level poised for any order.

"This is our last chance, Sir," Hilton's voice echoes around the cavernous war room.

"Then fire everything," returns Fletcher. *Fucking Butch and Sundance, these two*. Hilton taps his iPad once with his index finger. That is all it takes. The SAM unit based on a high roof somewhere in Washington DC releases all six of its anti-missile missiles.

None of them are essentially bad men. They are entirely capable and well experienced military and naval professionals, and whatever Space Force is. What bothers Cassandra is that, even during the final brief moments of the world as we know it, they're acting like it's a film. That their behaviour is a psychological defence to the enormity of the situation is little consolation. Her colleagues at Vauxhall and across the globe; her family; her few friends; the lives of everyone on the planet deserve more; and no-one is asking the obvious question: Where is the president?

* * *

Lieutenant Ademola stands in the early afternoon sun, south of the Visitor Center entrance and watches the queuing throng of tourists. Among them, is a particularly well-behaved group of a dozen green blazered school children of around his middle son's age. From the number of blonde plaits and the sound of the mature chatter, he figures Swiss. Their teacher is a prim white lady in a tweed jacket and pencil skirt. She moves like a ballerina, gliding more than walking. As Ademola watches, she initiates a friendly conversation with a small boy at the front of their group who's a little ruddier than the rest. His black shoes aren't quite as shiny and his white shirt a little off-white. She bends to one knee to tie the munchkin's shoelace and a strand of mousey blonde hair slips from her up-do to settle in front of her face. With an effortless grace, she tucks it back behind her ear with her left hand and breaks Ademola's heart. A wedding band. Her cool-blue eyes flash him a glance as she gets up and he thinks he must have been staring. His Glock 22 is getting heavy.

"Hey, pal," a smiling Brooklyn quarterback by the looks and sound of him, with his Latina girlfriend, has approached him.

"Good morning, sir," Ademola returns.

"Jus` wanted to say I think you guys are awesome," the guy pats him on his arm, "Keep up the good fight,"

And with that, the couple turn together to join the queue. The girlfriend loops her arms around her boyfriend's bicep and leans her head on his shoulder as they walk. It happens at least twice a day now and it makes him feel good about what he's doing with his life, despite the criticism from his brother.

"Thank you, sir," Ademola says after them, "You have a great day,"

The Swiss lady and her class are out of sight. He breathes out slowly through his nose and consciously relaxes his shoulders to ease the tension. He still has a long day ahead patrolling Capitol Hill.

Ademola's ill-fated attempt at relaxing is nipped in the bud by the harsh static of an incoming call on his lapel radio. But the message is cut off.

Over on the sidewalk, a toddler is tugging at his mama's shorts but she's more concerned with her phone. He insists, "Mommy! Look! Up in the sky!"

The mother looks shocked about something on her phone, covering her mouth with her hand. Ademola guesses she's received some pretty terrible news. She turns her head to look up, shielding her eyes from the sun, to see what her son is pointing at.

Ademola's radio crackles again. "All units: 10-89. Repeat: 10-89. Clear... everybody. Evac the lot. I... God Bless,"

"I need more detail than that. Over"

He gets no response from Control. Spinning, he sees his team dotted around the area. For a brief moment, they're all looking to each other to make sense of the situation. Then, Ademola sees Taylor following the gaze of the mother and her child. More and more people look up to the sky. Ademola's personal phone starts buzzing in his pants pocket.

He turns around and looks up, as six missiles launch from a roof to the South East, straight up.

* * *

This is totally illogical. Cassandra and the room of men have just watched the radar as, one-by-one, the SAMs seemingly struck the first warhead to no avail, which continued remorselessly towards DC. For nearly a minute, the warhead progressed at an increasingly slow and irregular velocity and is now just hanging there on the screen, a red triangular *bogey* pointing menacingly at its target.

It's beginning to feel like someone is

playing a sick game. Cassandra's fears constellate into the gut-wrenching image of one man's face, for no reason other than the guilt that still haunts her, that she failed to catch him, that he will always be out there, plotting, pulling strings, destroying lives.

The seven male occupants of the top secret, underground war room have become impotent and baffled spectators. Cassandra feels just as hopeless but there is little new about that for her. The black trouser suit of a NSA intelligence captain is just one more in the long line of observer roles to which she's been condemned. Too often, she can only watch, record and report; keeping the powerful in power, keeping certain weapons out of the wrong channels and the money flowing through the right ones. Now, so distant from the real world above, watching the beginning of the end in a bunker, she can't help her mind being drawn to her greatest failure; the last time she did more than just observe; the op that nearly ended her career; the op that saw her friend and informant, Ali, headless on a rug, and her boss' favourite employee with a kitchen knife in his ribcage.

She used to imagine a vast and steady radar, just like the one in front of her now, sweeping over the land, gradually eliminating hiding places as each piece of data fed back. Now she just sees bodies.

Suddenly, Fletcher slams his red, meaty palm down on the radar display, "Blast!"

The three technicians almost jump out of their seats and begin scrabbling at their keyboards. The primary bogey, the missile heading for DC, has just disappeared from the screen.

"What the hell is happening out there?" Fletcher appears volcanic.

Hilton takes half a step forward, his stooping figure crowding the small corner of the war room even further, "Do we have impact?"

"Negative, Sir," returns one of the technicians.

"No impact, Sir," confirms another.

Fletcher is about to erupt; his neck looks ready to burst his collar.

"You," Astor intervenes, reading the closest technician's name, "Davis, what is the most likely reason for this type of read-out?"

"Literally none, Sir,"

"Something must be wrong here," says another technician, pushing buttons and looking around frantically. This much stress causes mistakes, Cassandra knows.

"Okay, so what about the other ones?" asks Astor, who Cassandra is counting on to get this on track, "Those--"

"Confirm the status of the other bogeys," Hilton interrupts but at least he's on the same page—they need to focus on what they know, and what they can do.

After a barely tolerable few seconds, made less tolerable by the news, they get their confirmation: the other nine nuclear warheads are still rocketing towards their targets.

"London: T-minus eight minutes thirty-seven seconds. Berlin: T-minus eight--"

"Get the boys at *Andrews* on the line," orders Fletcher, cutting off the radar operative. He has no desire to know how many minutes and seconds it will take for the world to crumble. He no doubt already knows. He does, however, as they all do, desperately need to know what's happening over DC. Looking at another of the blips, Cassandra can only hope that the Royal Navy has something better up its sleeve than its single counter-narcotics and humanitarian vessel patrolling the North Atlantic.

* * *

For a long time, Royal Air Force Flight Lieutenant Spitelli has counted on a one-way mission. When the call came, he thought it was a drill, just like everyone else, and, even after the truth of it was made clear, the reality itself didn't begin to dawn. There's no way the reality of nuclear war can settle in—it's too vast a concept, too many lives, too big. His own life ending, however, was something he had rehearsed over and over. He felt no shame in taking the mission, no hesitation in volunteering the second he and his colleagues were scrambled into the hangar. He was totally focussed putting on his flight suit, calmly stepping into his cockpit, exhaling a measured breath as he put on his helmet. Death had been a weary co-pilot for too long and now He was curling his boney fingers around Spitelli's hands on the control stick. The bargain was complete. So why the ball in his throat?

Everything about being strapped into the cockpit of a Typhoon fighter jet is singularly focused ahead. It envelops Spitelli. The control stick is between his thighs, everything below his knees embedded into the guts of the machinery, and his eyes on the heads-up display in-front. At full throttle through the darkness, G-force leaning into his chest, he tracks the bogey as it approaches from the mesosphere, above ordinary radar, from the West. Wales is somewhere below. His heart flutters with adrenaline. It feels like sneaking up on the seeker in a game of hide-and-seek.

His MBDA Meteor missiles are meant for out-of-visual-range combat but he's going to get really close. He's going to stare death in the face and whisper its name. If he can detonate the warhead at his maximum altitude he will save the population from the fireball and fallout. He'll die a hero in their eyes. After the evacuation, they'll have a parade, maybe a full-on festival. Maybe that's the thought that's making him sick.

Spitelli's radio crackles, "Quebec-Charlie-Yanky. Come in, Oberon" He tries to block it out. "Oberon, confirm status. Over," Command wants to know what the hell Spitelli thinks he's doing. "Ober--"

Spitelli, call-sign Oberon, switches off his radio.

His radar tells him he's within visual range before he catches a glint of metal in the starlight. The W-78 warhead, the payload of a Minuteman III Intercontinental Ballistic missile, is on his twelve. Beyond how impressive the hardware is, there's a kind of beauty in the serenity and inevitability of its silent swan-song. For a second he considers gliding straight into its embrace, but decides to stick to his script. He'll be the only one in the world with a seat this good.

The ball in his throat remains but the tears are stuck somewhere. Not even the sheer beauty of the night, his rage, all the tears he's shed before, the finality of it all, and his sadness are enough.

"Target engaged,"

Straight and true, his missile rumbles through the night sky toward the nuke. As his gaze reaches the warhead, an illusion of light and shadow forms a human-like image. It's there for a split-second.

The explosion burns so bright it turns

night to day. But no sooner than that, darkness returns. The missile struck perfectly but the impact is cold and underwhelming. There is no nuclear death, no armageddon. The nuke was a dud.

Spitelli and his Typhoon hurtle forwards and pass beneath the blast as it cools. For a brief moment, as he flies under the waning explosion, he could swear there was someone in there. When he checks his rear view, there's only smoke. He does two more flybys but sees nothing.

Spitelli gestures across his chest, to his forehead and down to his core, doing something he hasn't done for fifteen years, making the sign of the Cross.

* * *

Daniel Takei does not run with the others, because he knows what comes next. It's rooted in collective memory, the cultural unconscious. He chooses another path. He knows they can't run far enough. Instead he peacefully places his palms together in silent, sectarian *prayer*, a thanks for an adventurous, loving and colourful life, and looks on. The sun is about to rise but, in this part of Tokyo, diligent workers were already starting their day thirty minutes ago. Takei is here for another reason, which is now totally inconsequential. He makes his peace with that too.

He stands across the street from the Tokyo Metropolitan Government Building and watches the warhead stream towards it. It must be an impact detonator. As it passes directly over his head, a sudden, deafening explosion knocks him to the ground. The world shakes and it seems that every window shatters. A piercing siren screeches, dizzying Takei to the point that he almost doesn't see the traffic light falling towards him before diving to the ground and rolling out of the way. Everyone else is on the floor too, some people are face down and not moving. Blood trickles over his lip, down his neck, around his ears and hands. He realises the screeching is his own ears ringing.

He gets up onto one knee and sees the warhead crashing through the top of the building between its two towers, toothless-looking with their blown-out windows. It feels to him as though time has stopped. Suddenly, a blinding white light bursts from behind the building, casting it in silhouette and throwing its long shadow over the street. In its final moments, Tokyo appears to be a macabre shadow puppet theatre. Getting to his feet, still deaf and half-blind, Takei stares into the shifting light.

The congregation of spectators is beginning to do the same, gazing dumbly and uncomprehendingly at something both terrible and beautiful. The source of the light is ascending behind the building, forming new shadows and shapes through the lattice of glassless steel and concrete. As it rises into view above the building, one by one people begin climbing to their knees, some with their hands over their mouths, others with hands in the air as if receiving blessings. Even Takei finds himself silently mouthing *my god.*

Although the warhead is at the centre of the light it doesn't appear to be the source. It continues to float up and up, taking the light with it and then, like the flip of a switch, it is gone. No more bright white light, just a crowd of people, mutely reeling in a March dawn. Only five minutes ago, this had been a routine weekday morning.

He picks a shard of glass from the back of his hand and drops it to the floor. He hears only ringing as he watches it mutely shatter on the sidewalk. He dusts himself off, takes his phone from his inside jacket pocket and is about to compose a text to Control when he looks up one final time at the sky. At that moment, that tiny black cone appears to pierce the blue from outer space, growing in size as it falls back to Earth, the warhead has returned.

* * *

General Fletcher hangs up the phone

to Joint Base Andrews, who are responsible for the THAAD unit in Washington. It's confirmed: although the Washington warhead was undisturbed by their anti-aircraft missiles, shortly after clearing the collision zone, it stopped and vanished. Listening to the call, Cassandra overheard every theory from Chinese holograms to ISIS sleeper-agents.

With the technicians back at their control panels, Davis speaks up, eyes still glued to his monitors.

"Similar reports are coming in from Britain, Germany, India," he swivels his chair to face his commanding officers, "All attempts to intercept or mitigate the warheads were ineffective, but then they apparently vanished without a trace,"

One of the other technicians passes Fletcher a headset plugged into the control panel, "Sir, it's the President,"

Cassandra observes, through Fletcher's imminent rage-induced coronary, his attempt to sound genial. He is not this President's biggest fan.

"Mr President... No, of course I don't believe it was you, Mr President... Of course, Sir. Yes, I know you're in Bedminster... I wouldn't suggest for a moment that it was the Russians, Sir, nor anyone for that matter, until we have solid evidence, Sir... Understood, Mr President...

What a fucking asshole," Cassandra assumes the call ended before this last utterance. "Well," he says, and then exhales deeply, while his entire body transforms from quaking volcano to exhausted, middle-aged veteran. "The good news is that at least eight of the ten Minuteman warheads appear to have never detonated. We're still waiting for any intelligence from Beijing or Tokyo," He removes the headset and pinches the bridge of his nose in an effort to continue. The others look on. "The bad news is, the launch codes were hacked and literally no-one has any idea what just happened,"

"Someone knows, General," says Lorre, the Death Ray.

This will be on all of them. There should have been alarm-bells ringing throughout the international intelligence community before today but there was not even a whimper. She looks deeply into the world map displayed on the wall of monitors and remembers the last time she got it wrong.

* * *

The alarm is still blaring when Steve wakes. Utterly piercing, it feels as though it's boring a hole in his face. As he gets his bearings, he realises he's lying on his back. The red and black blur in front of him gradually comes into focus, forming a dull woman's face.

"Captain," Hanson is on one knee, her hand on his right shoulder. His left shoulder still throbs and his nose is in agony. He can feel his face swelling and warm sticky blood in his moustache.

"Oh God, my *node*," he complains, failing to say *nose.*

"It's broken, sir," scooping her arm under his back, "let's get out of here,"

Hanson helps Steve to his feet with reassuring strength, despite the fact he can do it himself.

"*Dank* you,"

He takes a moment to survey the dreaded scene, bathed in red emergency lighting. In front of them, he identifies the culprit of his broken nose and recently unconscious state: the eight-ton steel-and-concrete blast door to the elevator, designed to withstand a nearby nuclear explosion has been blown out of the wall and is lying in the tunnel junction. He has to get out of here.

"Come on," he calls, sounding as commanding as he can muster.

"I've already tried the phone again, sir. Zero response on any line,"

"NBC and *redpiradord* on. I'm going *do dee adth*," he needlessly tells her to put on her respirator and that he's going to try the emergency escape hatch.

They awkwardly trip and hop into their protective suits and strap on their respirators. Steve has done this countless times in drills but never with a broken nose and injured shoulder. He turns his back from his deputy so he doesn't have to know if she sees his clumsiness. His face must look a joke right now.

When their gear is on, the respirator mask allows him to forget about how his face looks. At the far end of the command capsule, Hanson stands by the emergency hatch and awaits her Captain's nod of approval. Steve isn't about to do that.

"*Dep adide,*" he says. He wants to tell her this reccy is on him but moving his face hurts too much.

He once thought he wouldn't screw Hanson if they were the last two people on Earth. Now he wonders what it will be like to stand in the centre of a nuclear crater together, and whether Hanson has any respect for him at all.

Halfway up the escape tube, he realises his heart has not stopped pounding since his fingers were on the launchkey. Inside the respirator mask, a bead of sweat hangs on his brow and drops. There's a procession down his back and his hands are clammy in the suit's gloves. He continues his ascent to the unknown, rung after rung, his respirator amplifying the sound of his laboured breath, the sound of his boots on the metal rungs echoing.

When the hatch is within reach, he reaches for it, but the captain realises something odd. If a nuclear warhead has detonated on the other side, the hatch should be throwing off substantial heat. He disarms the hatch door and swings it open, and is momentarily blinded by light. Slowly lowering his hand from his eyes, Steve squints into a spring morning.

As he clambers out of the hatch to freedom and gets to his feet on the cool gravel, he can't help but let out a short burst of laughter. All along the horizon is clear. Then it hits his back: burning heat and the crackling of a dying fire. Turning, he faces the pitiful sight of what was once the launch control support building, sitting almost directly above the control capsule a hundred feet below. He regrets his idiotic laugh. Thick smoke is still rising from the demolished building, no chance of any survivors. The explosion was so powerful, the far end of the building is a crater, it blew all the gravel away from the perimeter of the building and charred the ground. The building was designed to be as non-flammable as possible but a number of fires still rage. Steve's knees feel loose above feebly rooted feet.

Hanson runs past him in her protective gear, towards the building. She was supposed to have waited below. Pushed back by the heat, Hanson stops where the door used to be. Steve knows they can't do anything here; they need a getaway plan.

He has taken only a few steps forward when Hanson silently collapses to her knees. He breaks into a jog and stops behind her, crouching.

He says her name but she ignores him. Her shoulders convulse and she makes an odd sound like crying. He thinks he hears her say something and tries to ask her to repeat it but he realises she *is* crying.

"Danny," she repeats.

Steve puts two and two together as he adjusts to the revelation of Hanson's heterosexuality. *That guy?* Danny is -- *was* a second lieutenant who had begun his tour around the same time as Steve and Hanson. He always seemed a bit of a drip.

He puts his hand on her shoulder so lightly she probably doesn't feel it, "I'm *dorry*. I --"

She isn't listening again. A long silence follows in which Hanson appears to pray and Steve falls back on his haunches. He finds himself staring at flames that seem to not die and follows the smoke up into the sky, wondering where the warheads are now, how far along their orbital courses to their targets, what distant deaths are being tolled, what wars being fought and at whose wills.

Hanson breaks the silence. "They're all gone," she announces unnecessarily, "What the hell happened here, Sir?"

It is baffling. Steve feels curiously little for the horrific death of his colleagues. Instead, he finds himself wondering what lies ahead for him if he goes AWOL.

From his low position, he can see under the smoke. Scattered amongst the charred pieces of roofing tiles, masonry and twisted metal lie the debris of desks, chairs, computers and other office equipment. Steve notices a couple of broken picture frames, the glass shattered and the photos turned to black curled paper. Then he starts to see the bits of bodies. He quickly averts his eyes. It's not something his stomach can take right now. *What happened?* None of this makes any sense.

"I..." he struggles for words. All his training has to have been for something. He is the missile combat crew commander here.

It's then that Steve's mind is drawn back to the broken roofing tiles and metal beams. They are only inside. Nothing at all from the roof is on the sooty ground around the outside of the building. He pulls off his respirator and pulls back the hood of his NBC suit. This was no nuke anyway. Hanson turns to look at him and does the same, although he suspects she has more self-destructive reasons.

Looking back into the flames, Steve's heart rate is finally beginning to come under control. Some of them are still in their chairs, Steve realises and he tells Hanson as much. They couldn't have known what hit them.

"But," Hanson wipes her face with the back of her gloved hand, "how could all the watchmen... the radar... let this happen?"

Looking for the guards who should have been patrolling the exterior, he finds his answer protruding from under the rubble surrounding the ruins. *What was* he *doing so close?* Something drew in the guards before the bomb dropped.

After another silence, "Cpt Blake," her puffy, wet face turns fierce, "I'm going to find who did this and I'm going to kill them,"

He believes her.

CHAPTER 2

Memories, dreams, reflections

Ashley Kindle finally plucks up the courage to look at the little bottle of pills on her nightstand. She shouldn't have them. If he finds out, she's dead. He could be watching right now. She's always being watched. That's why she hasn't left her safe-zone around her bed in three days, why she hasn't left the bed itself in seventeen hours. The digital clock, next to the bottle and the small lamp that lights the room, tells her it's 02:03 Mar 21. She smells and she needs to wash but it's twelve exposed paces to the washbasin and thirteen and a half to the shower. She's been fired from her job at the computer store by now for sure. She should flush the pills down the toilet and look again, for the fifty-first time, for the substitute pills the Professor gave her. Not the dirty shit her doctor prescribes. They made her fat and shaky. They made her feel all groggy and weird. The Professor's pills though, they make her feel calmer, which is all she really needs. And he said she shouldn't. He told her to get rid of her old pills, made her flush them as he stood over her like a strict father, the beautiful fucking monster. He is her salvation but she is so desperate for her old pills. Hey. Deep breaths. Ashley runs her fingers through her greasy hair, rubs her mouth and tries to sit up a bit. Her mouth is dry and there's a glass of water right there with the pills. She can't remember when she found the secret old pills or got the water. Maybe it wasn't her.

"Hello?"

No-one else is here. Just the watchers. The little red light on her webcam blinks. *Hey, I've got an idea.* She heard recently at a meeting that microwaves can spy on you now. There are some real crazies at those meetings. Her laptop peaks out at her from halfway down the bed, under the covers; the laptop that hacked the President and the launch codes, connected to the headset that delivered the Emergency-Action Message. There's no better way to show your devotion than to start armageddon. But something went wrong. Everyone's all still here.

She feels the choking need to cry but can't.

"Oh God, what have I done?"

She knows she needs to pull herself together, this is her illness talking but the Professor says she isn't really sick. As usual, she doesn't know what to believe. *Hey, why don't you fucking kill yourself?* Ashley grabs the pill bottle and unscrews the cap. "Just a couple," she tells herself, "Let's be sensible here," She takes her pills and downs the water, desperate but achingly hopeful for the numbness they promise.

Last time she started her meds again after a break, it took four days for them to start making a difference, but she's worse this time. It's going to be a while. As she imagines the pills dissolving in her stomach, spreading their contents inside her, she wonders again whether the Professor thinks she's stupid. She's smoked enough joints to know the brown pills he's given her are weed but she's grateful for them nonetheless. If only she could find them. She slides open the top drawer of her nightstand and rummages past tissues, tinfoil, headache pills, the detritus of life. She finds something else she's longing for as the smooth glass bottle of vodka takes its place in her hand, "Just to take the edge off,"

Just another shot to quench the burning from the first and then she puts the bottle back in the drawer and closes it firmly.

From her distressed bed, something incongruous catches her eye across the room, poking out from a pile of clothes. It looks like a blue plastic propeller. *Shit, what's that?* Whatever it is, Ashley just feels like it shouldn't be there. She needs to get rid of it and she gets the sense she was supposed to have done so already. She bites her lip and scrunches the damp bed sheets in her fists. If she gets out of bed, she'll be watched wherever she goes. They've been following her since she was little, gathering information on her, building file after file.

Ashley got into hacking so she could figure out what they're doing but, after all these years, she hasn't got her answer yet. Whatever they're planning for her, it's more secure than the nuclear launch codes. Worst of all, she knows that doesn't make any sense.

She's totally on her own. Trapped by her own mind. She practises the mantra her therapist gave her, more words recently forbidden by the Professor. Telling herself and the room, "I am Ashley Kindle. I am--" she closes her eyes to focus, "I am Ashley Kindle. I am unwell but I will get better. My thoughts do not own me. My past does not own me," She opens up her laptop and taps a shortcut key to run a pre-recorded video of herself sleeping. This will only keep them fooled for so long so, if tonight's the night they abduct her, she's going to have to move quick. Ashley Kindle slips her naked, stubbled legs from under the sheets and out of the bed. She shivers and the hairs on her arms stand up on end. "I am Ashley Kindle," she repeats the mantra, focusing on how it feels to form each word, the breath that leaves her lips, her stomach rising and falling. As she sits on the edge of the precipice, the room begins to spin and she wants more than anything to get back into bed. But she has to get rid of that thing in her room. She takes another deep breath, "I am unwell," and places her bare feet on the cool, thick rug, "but I will get better,"

It's now or never. She stands and is hit by a mega headrush and sways a little on her feet. She pulls an elastic band from her wrist, scrapes her thick black hair into a ponytail and kicks the clothes off of the thing on the floor. Squatting wide and menacing on four contorted legs, the drone looks like it's been discovered in the middle of some dark act. Ashley feels sticky and disgusting just looking at it. Reminding herself that it's just another plastic toy, she dresses in the jeans and hoodie that had been covering it. On the floor, she spots her iPod, with her earbuds already plugged in. Another method for staying on top, she inserts the earbuds and selects a tried and tested playlist. She leaves her mobile behind—too easy to track.

By the time she reaches the front door of the apartment block, she's feeling much more like herself. Sometimes that's all it takes; to get up, stretch her legs, listen to some music and get outside. Other times, outside is a swamp of old fears and memories threatening to pull her under. Tonight, she's lucky. Ashley doesn't bother removing the parking ticket from the windshield of her beat-up old Ford before throwing the drone on the worn blanket on the backseat and getting in. Littered with cigarette butts and empty bottles, her car is warm with familiarity. It's been a refuge as many if not more times than her dishevelled bed.

In a silent ritual, she kisses two fingers and touches them to the faded photo of her mom on the dash before turning the key in the ignition. When the engine eventually starts, a light flashes to warn her she's low on gas; sometimes, when she gets confused, she loses hours, whole days even. If only this drone could vanish just as easily -- *What are you doing?* -- but it's just a few miles from her apartment in Helena, Montana, to Spring Meadow Lake, and the escape from her dread.

* * *

As the carriage conveys the Professor to his destination, the land and trees on the other side of the window dissolve from one form to another. Mountains rise and fall and rise again, trickling streams tumble into foaming rivers, open plains become rocky edifices through which the locomotive bores a clear path. The accompanying swell of nostalgia for a romanticised idea of the land and its past is inevitable yet deeply pleasing. He imagines goatherds tending their flocks and smoke billowing from the chimneys of the little wooden houses. He chooses Mozart for his companion, another inevitability. Music is essential. Years of training, analysis and supervision have made him all too aware of the deafening nature of *the unspoken* between others.

There are not many other passengers but there are enough that, were he to listen, it would not be long before the desire rose up to -- no, he lets go of the thought and lets it float gently away; a fallen branch on a stream. There is a woman three rows down, however, who is bombarding her travelling partner with a perfectly paced and inane conversation. The pace is expertly maintained—not through conscious will, but through a lifetime of practice nonetheless—to camouflage another level of barrage, a mostly unspoken yet violent deluge. *Externalisation, projection*, she throws out in every direction as if to say, "*Do not make me think,*"

If the Professor were not to block it out, the strength of his perception—or rather the diminishment of his blinkers—is such that he would hear her silently shouting, "*I cannot see the truth of my experience!*" The woman's ego is understandably defended against her truth for, to face it unguided would eventually result in complete mental breakdown. If, however, he were to allow it, the desire might rise up to walk down the carriage to where she sits, shake her by the shoulders and tell her firmly and precisely what she has really been spewing; why she is the way she is; to penetrate her defended psyche and reveal to her what exactly she has been saying to him. Of course, he won't. He won't tell her that it all stems from the unremembered abuse she suffered as a child. He would never do such a thing.

She must seek help from a professional such as himself, to guide and support her to look deep enough within herself to find the truth, before it is too late. Without a fresh adult trauma, however, it is unlikely she will do so. Sadly, the probability of anyone embarking on such a journey and making meaningful progress is pitifully low. She is another human being with a broken soul and this is the great tragedy: mental ill-health caused by childhood trauma, created and proliferated by a sick society caught in an almost unbreakable cycle. It is something of which Professor McAvoy is not currently seeking a reminder.

He looks back out of the window, beyond the old man in the glass, at the distant pines across the verdant pastures.

When the train pulls into the tiny station, he is the only passenger to alight. As he removes his headphones, a chilled breeze whispers along the side of the carriage around his neck and ears and Professor McAvoy welcomes the unseasonably crisp afternoon. He's held here for a moment as the train drones away down the line and he remembers himself as he was when he was here last—in 1980, a student, still believing he could really improve the world through psychiatry. The station has changed little and the mountains standing over it are eternal. He has no reason to believe the place he must find, which is an hour's walk into the wilderness, will be any different to as it was then.

He has four hours until the next train south, continuing his way to meet a prospective patient.

The last few days and their near cataclysm have drained him of his finite vitality more than the previous month. As such, he wants little more in this moment than to clear his head of the young American seductress who started it. Her ability to so greatly yet so prematurely accelerate events has frayed his nerves. *Of course* one could not solve the great puzzle of the relentless cycle of human trauma so bluntly. He never should have allowed her that moment. The many ways in which things could have gone horribly wrong don't bear thinking about. *The recklessness of it.* It was in her to rush, to fumble and flicker, not owning the effect she has, sometimes willfully ignorant, sometimes entirely unconscious, of the damage she causes. He would need to show her a lesson.

She would be in bed now, feeling dirty after a long day, hair a mess, eyes heavy, body loosening, welcoming sleep. The Professor catches himself and smiles inwardly at his daydream. His more lofty colleagues might criticise him for working *in* the counter-transference rather than *with* it. They might be right but he gets results.

Treating individuals, however, is not enough and he is running out of time. The futility of treating one human being at a time to *break the cycle,* while wider society continued to perpetuate the problem plagued him from the beginning of his career, but it was later that his own breakdown set him upon realising his *fury* at it. It was around the time that he was consulting on the release of psychiatric in-patients at secure and semi-secure units. His thoughts began to constellate into the idea that, metaphorically speaking, society needed to be infected with the antigens of its own making—the severely mentally unwell—in order for it to gain awareness sufficient to see the error of its ways. The mentally unwell could not simply be locked away in secrecy. Of course, he would soon find that releasing these unwell individuals did nothing. Humanity's broad and deep collective defences are a tempestuous ocean compared to those little red boats of madness he set sail with his pen and official stamp.

The train of thought ends when the tension in his shoulders begins to burn. He wonders how long he has been standing on the platform looking like a lost fool. He inhales the scent of pine and grass, tightens the leather shoulder straps on his canvas bookbag and sets out to the end of the platform where he is faced with his first obstacle. Some committee of bright sparks has erected a waist-high chicken-wire fence. His hips creak just thinking about it. With a quick glance over his shoulder, he climbs over painfully.

The railway tracks navigate through a dense forest of pines where, beyond, through the haze of time and distance, the mountains are green, grey and blue. Walking along the tracks, feeling the crunch of ballast beneath his walking boots, every step feels a fraction closer to lost youth. As he progresses, he needn't search for familiar landmarks; instead a gnarled tree here, a rocky outcrop there whisper to him until he feels that the land itself is carrying him along. His journey becomes effortless and lifting, a gentle wind at his back. Eventually, he spots the clearing up ahead to his left and diverges through it. He has to crouch under needly branches that brush his heavily whiskered cheeks. He is halfway.

Following the sound of trickling water, he passes through successive curtains of light and shadow cast from the soaring canopy of pines.

The trickling becomes clearer as he rounds a mossy pile of boulders, which to him is a forest maiden's visage, framed by wild flowers, warmed by a golden crepuscular spotlight. The path steepens and the trickling sound begins to tumble and then to rush. The cool air clears his lungs and fortifies his chest and he pauses to hold onto that temporary, forgotten feeling as best he can. Holding the restorative feeling in mind, he finally nears that place for which he has been searching; his entire reason for this detour in his journey, perhaps the entire reason for the journey itself. Through the trunks and needles, he sees bright green grass ahead, undimmed by the gargantuan pines and is held at his throat by a wave of something that appears to emanate from the clearing. Before he has turned his attention to it, the feeling is gone, floating out behind him like an ethereal creature of lore.

This must be what it feels like to find somewhere one had thought only existed in a dream. He steps into the clearing and right in front of him is the ancient and secret gully, bathed in sparkling sunlight. He climbs down into the bowl-like mossy oasis, created millennia ago by a river having long since changed course. But he is old and not as steady as he once was and the moss is wet—his feet slip and he falls painfully, sliding on his side into the centre. He lies there and laughs to himself. It is such an unfamiliar sound that it makes him laugh all the more. Such a serious old man, reminded of his fallibility.

He removes his book bag and lies on his back, looking up at the clear sky, feeling the softness of the ground holding him from below and the glow of the sun warming him from above. He listens to the sounds around and within him and feels his heart beating through his back, thudding on the ground below. He takes one deep breath and then another.

The inextirpable nature of the cycle of trauma that holds humanity hostage has occupied Professor McAvoy's thoughts for years now but here, he attempts to understand it in a different way. His hope is to connect to that feeling he had so many years ago. He had felt such peace then, a kind of deep spiritual connectedness, as if everything was wonderfully simple and as it should be. He closes his eyes, continuing his deep breathing.

Gradually he travels back through time and finds a small, blond boy; himself. He is running through trees, the low ferns whipping his naked legs below his shorts and he is laughing triumphantly yet nervously as if being chased. He runs for a little too long and darkness has gathered overhead, trees blotting out the afternoon sun. He realises he is alone. Turning, he is totally lost and a panic builds from his ankles up. As he searches and the creeping panic reaches his knees and they threaten to tremble, he sees a breaking in the dense wood; a light that could be an open space. He tramples through fern and undergrowth to reach it. As he steps out into the light, warmth washes over him. Slowly walking around the gully, he knows somehow that he has *returned.* This place is telling him that this is where he is from, that he has some long, forgotten history here, as if, at any moment, little forest people will step out from behind the mossy rocks and trees and welcome him home. He sat on the soft, furry moss in the centre of the gully and rested his back on a smooth green rock. Young Terrence sat there, near motionless, for hours, watching the stream simultaneously pass by and remain in the same place. He was utterly, euphorically content as if he had found not only a missing part of himself but of all mankind.

He opens his eyes again. A chill shivers down his spine and he's made aware of the damp having seeped through his knitted jumper. Attempting to remember, to re-feel, is like trying to grab hold of the wisps of smoke from his father's pipe. The more he tries, the further the memory becomes. There's no stream here but the smell of stagnant water has been gradually gathering in his nostrils. It's as if this isn't the right place and yet it is. When he came here as a young man, he now realises, he mistook it for the place in his childhood vision. The realisation is annoying. It's not here. Now, the professor cannot tell whether that place in the vision was even real or just a dream. He knows only that this muggy little clearing is hollow in comparison. He sits up with a creak and hugs his knees. The damp has made its way through the seat of his trousers.

The rattle and whistle of a not distant train draws him out of any contrived reverie. This place, now and in his twenties, is a mockery, a pale misremembering, a mirage, set asunder from any peace it may have once had by the trappings of human progress around it.

He scowls at how much time and effort it takes to get to his feet and sling his bag back over his shoulders. He's going to have to sit through the rest of the train journey in cold, wet clothes like a sick old man who's pissed himself.

With one last look at the place, he reminds himself there can be no half-measures or imitations. To rend humanity's recovery, he must unlock and up-root the disease at its heart in a most dramatically alchemical way. Taking his small notepad and pencil from his pocket, he flips to a blank page and makes a note:

To begin anew, we must return to Eden, the archetypal Mother, and unity.

* * *

Jill Hanson drags the scene through her mind again and again looking for any trace of her quarry. Her dad used to take her hunting up in the mountains outside Dillon and they'd camp out, playing the long game, tracking a big bull elk from his prints, dung, antler marks. She could examine each telltale trace right under her nose, smell the earth, feel the same breeze as the animal, hear the same leaves rustling, feel the mottled sun on the back of her neck.

She and Cpt Blake have been put on leave and subtly ordered not to leave the state. Her brother's home in Helena, Montana, had to be both her camp and hunting ground. For some reason, Steve had asked her to stay with him, but Jill couldn't think of anything she wanted less than that sociopath's hospitality.

She glares at her brother's rifle over the fireplace to focus her thoughts and her determination. What was left of her crew suggested they'd been sitting or standing around when they died so they didn't see or hear the attack coming. It didn't trigger radar nor raise the alarm from the watchmen patrolling the grounds. Whatever it was was stealth or too small for radar. No way a hostile power could get a stealth bomber that far into US airspace. At least, that's what Jill has to believe. But the captain did say something useful; he noticed that the watchmen had been caught in the blast close to the building so they were drawn in by something; something suspicious but not obviously dangerous. It wasn't an inside job. It couldn't have been. The other useful thing Blake had seen was that the roof hadn't been blown off but had been blown down and out, suggesting the explosion originated on top of the building. Someone with knowledge of all their codes and war plans had managed to get a genuine E.A.M. to the command capsule and had destroyed the launch control support building, killing everyone inside, to ensure the order was carried out without any challenge. There is literally no way that should be possible. Unfortunately, the thought of what is *possible* or not keeps leading back to the topic that Jill is trying to avoid: As much as she hates to admit it, what happened that day screwed her brain.

Jill had been trying her best to rein in that selfish bastard captain and maintain some semblance of protocol and order when the ground shook and the elevator blast door exploded off its hinges knocking out the lights and raising the emergency system. Across the confusion and darkness, she could swear she saw a young, dark woman in jeans and a t-shirt, covered in soot and sweat. Time went haywire, one moment everything was slow motion and the next, things were jumping ahead. Suddenly the young woman was standing right in front of Jill demanding to know how to stop ten Minuteman III missiles that had already launched. Then, she was gone. Vanished into a puff of smoke. Was it the shock? Blake and Jill hadn't mentioned it to each other. She seemed so real. Better to keep it to herself and stick to reality. The illusion of a miracle woman isn't going to help her find the terrorist bastards who killed Danny and used the US Air Force as their pawns.

She gets up to make a coffee; her brother, Tom, will be back soon with her two nieces and will insist on doing dinner and looking after her. He seems to expect her to mope around eating ice cream from the tub and feeling sorry for herself so it's better to get as much as possible done for herself now before he arrives. The last thing she's going to do is crumble. Danny showed her so much about being alive—killing those responsible is her promise to him, not being depressed and useless.

When the doorbell rings, Jill nearly spills her coffee. She glances back at the rifle and then makes a note to herself that, when this is all over, she should probably talk to a professional about how she feels. But she has every right to be a little spooked; no-one visits in this quiet corner of town. She places the mug on the counter and silently steps over to the shutters. The doorbell rings again. Outside is a black woman in a pantsuit and sunglasses. Obviously an out-of-towner, couldn't look more like IRS if she tried.

* * *

Cassandra removes her sunglasses and gives Hanson the warmest professional smile she can muster after the ten-hour trip and two stopovers from Norfolk, Virginia, to Helena, Montana.

"Missileer Lieutenant Jill Hanson?" Cassandra shows her badge and passable counterfeit ID. "My name's Amanda Christchurch and I'm with the Office for Special Investigations," Hanson visibly tenses. "Is now a good time?"

"Sorry, yes, of course, ma'am. Come in," Hanson attempts a smile back and steps aside. "I've already given the FBI everything I know and my brother's family will be home soon,"

Nothing like a little added time-pressure.

"I'm sure, given the circumstances, you appreciate the need to be thorough,"

"Of course, ma'am. Please, take a seat,"

There's no computer in sight but Cassandra spots the outline of Hanson's mobile in her tracksuit bottoms as she sits on the couch. As Cassandra takes an armchair opposite Hanson, she also sees a coffee getting cold on the counter. "I hate a cold cup of coffee," she says.

Hanson springs to her feet. "Oh jeez, where are my manners?"

She's distracted but not symptomatic of shock and not so distracted that she appears chaotic or unable to focus. Quite the opposite. Cassandra notices Hanson glance at a rifle above the fireplace.

"Not a problem," Cassandra says.

As Hanson passes, Cassandra covertly slips a credit card sized device into the same pocket as Hanson's phone.

"Black?" Hanson's lips tighten. "I mean, with milk or?"

"Black's fine. Two sugars if you have any please,"

Cassandra detests coffee but builders' tea can be a little incongruous with American aliases. While Hanson pours the cafetiere, Cassandra slips another, smaller, bug under the coffee table.

"Why don't you start on the morning of the day it all happened, March 19th?"

Being the only two surviving crew members, Hanson and Blake need to be covered off and, at this stage, the most likely explanation remains that it was an inside job. As Hanson bends to hand her interviewer her coffee, Cassandra leans in to accept it with one hand and retrieve the planted NFC device from Hanson's pocket with the other. A little sleight of hand and a few seconds of proximity is all the device needed to clone Hanson's phone and all its contents. A part of her dreads finding anything on it. It's the part of her that longs for predictability. The part of her that has kept her in a job. In the past, she'd reached too high and been burnt. *Observe and report, Cassy, observe and report.*

After Hanson finishes talking, Cassandra projects stony expectation and silently searches her eyes. *Christchurch* already put Hanson on the back foot, arriving unannounced and allowing her to feel like she owes her greater courtesy. Now that the silence starts to look uncomfortable, Cassandra waits some more.

"You really want to catch these bastards, don't you, ma'am?" asks Hanson.

"Yes," Cassandra doesn't blink. "What's your theory?"

Her question takes Hanson by surprise. Clearly she hasn't been asked this before but, if Cassandra's hunch is correct, Hanson's distraction stems from her own investigation, fuelled by anger and maybe something else. She knows the feeling.

Hanson takes a steady, measured breath and the last gulp of her coffee, and opens her mouth to speak—just as the happy sound of the chatter of two little girls bounds up to the front door and it swings open.

"Aunty Jelly!"

Hanson's entire demeanour loosens as she hops up from the couch.

"Hey, girls! My friend here's just leaving,"

Hanson's brother, Tom Dean Hanson, steps through the door behind the two pretty little redheads.

"Yes, you ought to be going," he says upon seeing the suspicious woman in his home.

"Tom, it's okay," Hanson intervenes, leading Cassandra to the door as her brother steps aside, "Give us a minute,"

Outside, Hanson closes the door and they stand on the porch, "Have you seen the launch site?"

"Only photos. Not yet in person,"

"I think a bomb was dropped on the roof but it must have been a drone to be small enough not to be caught by radar or be shot down before it could release its payload,"

"I don't imagine there's a mobile or wifi connection that deep into the prairie,"

"So it was radio controlled,"

"Which means we need to be looking for vehicles within a reasonable radius of the site,"

"Yeah, not exactly. Look, I know a thing or two about radio. With a decent set-up, the operator could easily have been forty miles away,"

That's over a thousand square miles; an area the size of Cornwall. *Observe and report.*

Next stop: Missileer Captain Steven Blake. She's navigating a rented Toyota Prius through the leafy streets between pastel bungalows when her phone vibrates. She accepts the call without saying a word. After a second's pause, the voice on the other end begins with the authentication phrase, "Hello, is that Prithi Takeaway?"

"Yes, hello," she responds, "Would you like delivery or collection?"

"Neither. I'd just like to read you the menu,"

It's an update from one of her remaining friends at the Service, about a different operation; one officially long over, about which she shouldn't know anything, which ended in deaths, disgrace and a dead-end.

Engel Pfieffer, one of those dead, must have received another letter, posthumously. His name is like a hand around her throat. Alive, he was her last chance at catching one of the worst human beings to have ever lived; Number Three on the world's most wanted list. Despite the events of the last few days, her hope lives on that one day a letter will arrive at Pfieffer's address that explains everything, that helps her find the man she's hunting, who everyone else thinks is a ghost, and makes meaning of all the deaths. Maybe, in death, Pfieffer can still provide the answer.

* * *

It was *Op Turpentine*, 16:07 on 17th September 2014. Cassandra had been in Iraq five months, refusing to lose hope that she'd secure a lead. She liked to visualise a vast and steady radar sweep over the land, gradually eliminating hiding places as each piece of data fed back. She was looking for Ibrahim Muhammad Al-Nasser, Number Three on the world's most wanted list, strategist, recruiter and chief interrogator—an all-round evil bastard. If anyone within the organisation—and ISIS is an organisation—was suspected of faltering allegiance or thought not to be executing the strictest Sharia, they were sent to Al-Nasser or one of his stooges. They were all sadists, with their own twisted moralities, but he was particularly deviant. He was a meticulous breaker of men and rightly the most feared figure in that part of the world. Intelligence circles called him *Picasso Al-Nasser* because it was said he liked to flay his victims alive and display them in *creative* ways, offering private exhibitions to those he was about to question.

One day in January 2014, he had disappeared without a trace. Three months later, Cassandra was sent to find him or whomever removed him.

She waited in a small room at the back of the tea shop for her asset to arrive. Ali had been providing intelligence on and off for almost a year and was a trusted resource. Now in his fifties, he had been a university lecturer and a father but that was another lifetime. He was calm, thoughtful and cunning, with a wicked sense of humour. He had a disarmingly kind face: the turn of his eyebrows, his thick eyelashes, his natural smile. She hated the danger she'd put him in, that she'd manipulated his sweet nature and private need for recognition. He rounded the corner to enter the room and greeted her with a nervous but brave smile. Something was wrong—Ali was not a nervous man.

"I'm in, Cassy," he had a way of speaking up to her despite being at least three inches taller.

It had taken four months of coaching, determination and patience but Ali had pulled off the impossible, going far beyond what was usually expected of an intelligence asset at his level. He had infiltrated ISIS and gained the trust of the inner circle. From then on, if he were seen talking to a woman in public, they would both be dead. Unfortunately for Ali and Cassy, she was both a woman and the best at what she did.

She could not embrace him how she wanted and thank him nor pull him out while he still had a chance. Instead, she smiled, put her palms together in a gesture of thanks and said, "Congratulations, Ali. You're doing something incredible," she sat on a dusty cushion and he followed suit, "You have every right to be frightened but you realise you can't back out now? Any sign of hesitation and they'll kill you or worse,"

"I know, Cassy," he said, "I know," He was beginning to relax in her company. Then came the big news. "Al-Nasser wasn't murdered. He disappeared and they're all very angry and worried," He had more to say. Cassandra said nothing; he'd continue when he'd planned his words. "There is talk that he has betrayed them --" He trailed off a little, climbing the mountain of his own terror. She was his silent guide. Ali reached the summit and continued his report, "-- And stolen a powerful weapon,"

That was the last time she saw Ali alive. They decapitated him in his living room, in front of his family.

Four months later, at 09:13 on 8th January 2015, it was raining and Op Turpentine had led Cassandra and the Service to Munich. It was an understatement to say that Al-Nasser's threat-level was significantly amplified by the suggestion that he was on the run with a stash of plutonium. The powers that be had the unenviable job of weighing up the risks and benefits of a fast and light approach versus the full force of Interpol and the joint intelligence community. The risk of Al-Nasser wiping out the

European continent trumped all concerns and urged speed. The Service moved as soon as they had intelligence. There was also good reason to believe her boss kept Op Turpentine quiet in case they were wrong. The whole thing was set for disaster from the start.

She was sitting with two guys in a damp room furnished with not much more than three deck chairs and a bed covered in empty takeaway boxes. Their attention was fixed on a laptop displaying a thermal image of what lay behind some closed curtains in the block of flats opposite. On it, a hot yellow human form sat at a desk, barely moving, staring at a computer. On another laptop next to this one were feeds from half a dozen bodycams in various positions around the street, including the one that was approaching the target on the thermal display. The bodycam laptop carried the sound of the rain from outside to inside. On the other end of that sound was an earpiece. The wearer of that earpiece was turning left at the end of Jägerstraße onto Kardinal-Döpfner-Straße and walking along the pavement to a plain looking block of flats. It was Cassandra's decision for this to be run by a single operative. Armed teams more often than not ended with the suspect's suicide before they got as far as the apartment door.

The operative was on his way to a flat rented by a man who didn't technically exist, using the name Engel Pfieffer. As he examined the magnetic lock on the door from the street, he must have felt the cleansing rain pelt his face and the reassuring weight of the silenced Walther PPK on his hip, concealed by his black overcoat. Codename Zulu, he was SIS's secret weapon, or at least the one she knew about. He would silently enter the building and take the suspect by surprise, as quickly and quietly as humanly possible. Support teams were placed in the building opposite, two sedans on this street and another on Jägerstraße.

Despite Cassandra being one of the best field intelligence operatives of any agency, she had only had to use lethal force one night, many years before. It was something in which she took no satisfaction. For Al-Nasser, however, she had caught herself fantasising about the garotting wire, and sometimes, simply dropping something very large and heavy on his head. That wasn't satisfaction though—it was something else. She paused the thought—the greatest victory would be to see Al-Nasser, exposed, pathetic, powerless and standing trial.

There was a click-clack and the subtle sound of moving air.

"He's opened the front door and is entering the building," said the agent to her left, stooping over the laptop.

They watched Zulu's bodycam as he moved

through the murky darkness. The heat signature on the other screen didn't move. The speaker fizzed slightly.

"Zulu's reached the bottom of the stairs,"

The first step creaked and she heard a brief, electrical flickering. A movement sensor triggered the hallway light and after a flash of white, the whole scene burst onto the screen as Zulu began scaling the stairs.

The other guy spoke into his personal radio, advising Zulu, "He's still sat at his desk," he said, "Room at the end of the landing,"

The heat signature's form suddenly hopped up and moved out of sight.

"No, wait, he's getting up. Moving into the kitchen. Making a cuppa probably. Switching to camera two,"

The thermal imaging screen now showed the view of the kitchen window, where the curtains were also closed.

"Zulu's at the top of the stairs," continued the guy at the bodycam screen, "Picking the lock to Nasser's door,"

"We don't know it's him," corrected Cassandra.

She remembers the rain picking up, the sizzling spray on the windows making it harder to understand what she was hearing from the speaker. She consciously slowed her breathing as Zulu swiftly opened the door and got inside. The door clicked shut. She heard something like a foot dragging on carpet.

"He's blocking the door with something. Doorstop probably,"

The pit of her chest tightened and burned. Cassandra recalled the faces of ISIS's most recent victims, blown-up cars, bloody market squares, and Ali. She gritted her teeth at the intrusive images of dead school children covered in soot and rubble, and young women disfigured for life by acid. She focused this fire into a blade that cut through all other thought or feeling and willed Zulu to be as singular in his dedication. She felt her heart pounding against her damp blouse and, in her mind, the Walther PPK that would then be in Zulu's hands.

The kitchen was the last door on the right. Zulu was passing the room with the desk. The thermal display showed the white-hot kettle producing billowing yellow vapour that diffused into a rainbow as it cooled and mingled with the air in the room. The human form—possibly Al-Nasser—stood perfectly still, appearing to be waiting for the kettle.

As Zulu approached down the hall, steadily side-stepping, back to a wall, pistol out in front, the sound of man's humming grew louder. There was something familiar about the tune. As Zulu reached the door-frame and raised the pistol close to his cheek, his bodycam showed a mirrored cabinet in the bathroom opposite the kitchen. In the reflection, they saw their first glimpse of the other man. From behind, he seemed so vulnerable, the back of his neck soft and unprotected. While Al-Nasser is undoubtedly a monster, seeing him unguarded reminded her that even the most evil of men are ultimately fragile human beings like the rest of us. Then the humming grew louder and clearer.

"Bohemian Rhapsody," she whispered, half to herself.

Only a thin wall separated Zulu and the man in the kitchen. Exactly as the kettle began to whistle, screeching through the mic into the small room around them, the humming reached *Mama* in the first or second verse and he and the kettle duetted, dragging out the second syllable in an increasingly urgent and high-pitched glissando until Cassandra couldn't bear it.

"Freeze!"

The blurred form of Zulu spun around the doorframe, pistol held at eye-level. In that same instant, there was a scream of pain.

The speaker crackled, "Scheiße!" cried the suspect.

Zulu collapsed in the doorframe.

"Fuck that hurts,"

More frenetic motion, clattering and the splash of boiling water against a wall.

"Es tut mir Leid!" blurted the German voice

as its owner dived for the kitchen window. The three of them lent in close to the bodycam screen, trying to work out what they were seeing.

The suspect had gotten himself stuck with his arse and legs still flapping idiotically on the kitchen table under the window. Months of work on a fucking wild goose chase. This was not Al-Nasser.

"Report now," commanded a third voice on the line. The boss was listening in.

"Situation under control," replied Zulu.

It sounded like he was breathing through pain.

They watched as Zulu folded the man's arm up between his shoulder blades and pulled him back into the kitchen. He pushed him to the floor to sit down and, with one hand aiming the gun at his head, he threw some cuffs at him and told him to put them on. Grabbing something from the side, probably a dishcloth, he spoke into his wire.

"The paranoid arsehole rigged a nailgun to a tripwire. Shot me in the bloody ankle,"

That's when things went to shit. He must have been distracted as he considered whether to stymie the bleeding now or wait for the support crew. With freakish speed that appeared to them as a yellow flash across the thermal screen, the suspect sprung from the floor, clearing the few feet between Zulu and himself. His head was level with the pistol when there was a white flash and it was no longer a head. The back of his skull exploded in a hot puff, a splattering of colour in a wide arc. The body fell limp and his flopping head seemed to latch onto the pistol and pull down Zulu's body. The two of them slumped on the kitchen floor.

"Bravo Team, go!" the radio blasted.

Cassandra's guts turned to soup. They had a matter of seconds before Support swept into that flat.

"I'm not losing Al-Nasser," was all she could say.

She knew this man wasn't Al-Nasser but he was the only lead they'd had in months. Cover suddenly seemed an expendable luxury as she got up and sprinted out of the room, leaping down the stairs to get to street level and meeting Bravo Team as the plain-clothes ex-soldiers, medics and investigators ran into the building.

At the top of the stairs, they shared looks of disbelief. The legendary Zulu couldn't be dead, but he was. They found him with a kitchen knife in his stomach. It had gone up under his ribs and straight into his heart. As she was ushered out of the kitchen by forensics and clean-up, she blinked away the sight of the place, awash with bloody splintered bone and blobs of brain-matter.

This might have been the end of her career but it wouldn't be the end of the search for Al-Nasser. Dream-like prescience compelled her to the room in which the suspect had been working before he got up to make tea. She noticed on the way that there was a tripwire on the threshold to each room. Stepping over this one into the makeshift study, she was presented with a writing desk, a lamp and a low-spec, grimy laptop—nothing particularly interesting. It was when she turned around that she was struck by the suspect's "madman's wall". Floor-to-ceiling, corner-to-corner newspaper clippings, printed web pages, sketches, poetry, journal entries. The pattern was immediate: Oil spills, riots, looting, police brutality, growing share prices, political rallies and political scandals. She rifled through his desk, opening each of the three drawers. As she slid open the bottom drawer, she was faced with a pair of tits and a vacant glare. The stack of porn was as deep as the drawer and heavy as she lifted it onto the desktop. The usual shame associated with buying pornography in-person did not seem to apply to this guy. Perhaps the purchasing represented part of the thrill. No, that wasn't it. The magazines were old. One of them was dated 1997. The porn seemed pretty ordinary until something caught her eye in the bottom of the drawer. Compared to the other magazines, this one looked like it had seen a lot of use and had its own plastic protective sleeve. The significant factor being that this one appeared to focus on familial relationships. *Inzest* didn't need a degree in linguistics to translate. *The poor boy*. The other magazines were probably there as a distraction.

That was as far as she got before being evicted by a flood of forensics personnel. Her last chance at nailing Al-Nasser.

"Bit of a FUBAR isn't it, Bryce?" Her commander didn't ask her to sit down or put her at ease. Cassandra knew, standing to attention in *Papa's* glass office in Vauxhall, that the best course was to say as little as possible, for now. Sitting across from her in his two-grand office chair, he continued, "Spare me the details, just tell me you have the cave Picasso's hiding in,"

His face said he already knew the answer to his question, but he couldn't bear not to give her this one last chance. For him, the surrogate father role slid on like an old slipper. He played it with effortless force. As such, his disappointment was palpable. He tended to forget, however, that Cassandra was twice the age of most of his wards and never needed for a surrogate family nor benevolent benefactor. Unlike Zulu. Nonetheless, she played the game because it softened the blow for both of them. She maintained perfect eye-contact and broke the bad news with that look alone.

"In a year, what do we have? One of the best assets we've ever had, undercover in the heart of ISIS, is dead and your wild goose chase ends with a nutcase with the back of his head blown off,"

She didn't question why he said nothing of the death of the greatest secret agent in the history of the British Secret Service but Cassandra could see all too clearly where this was heading.

"We know he had contact with Al-Nasser, Sir,"

"Assuming you've not been following a ghost this whole time,"

"His flat, Sir," she said in her last-ditch effort, "There was absolutely nothing?"

"No, there was something," Papa slid an iPad across his legendary and anachronistic mahogany desk to Cassandra, "This was stuffed at the back of his pigeonhole—addressed to Engel Pfieffer and postmarked Buenos Aires,"

The iPad showed a scan of a handwritten letter. Cassandra read the German, translating in her head as she went:

Humanity is spiraling through a torture of its own doing. Spoon-fed trash by self-serving narcissists, war-mongers and profiteers, the people of the world roll over and wag their tails in ignorance. Greed, self-interest and vacuous populism only rot the soul and dampen the senses. Whipped into conformity by equal parts outrage and apathy, humans have become obliviously weak and supine. The great manipulation is not by populist figureheads, nor by those influencing mass perception from the shadows, but by the unconscious itself, distorted through the cycle of long-held trauma, that rots at the heart of all of them. God is dead and he was killed by man. Now is the time. Humanity needs to be reset. The rot must be cut out. I hear it crying out through unspoken anguish and I answer. Although you will not like the taste of the medicine, you will take it and you will heal.

It read like a manifesto but this was not like anything from any Islamic group. The reference to Nietzsche's *The Parable of the Madman* was particularly strange. Was the author a madman or masquerading as one? It just didn't seem right, as if contrived to confuse. *Gott ist tot; God is dead*; not *Allah.*

"But this alone is enough to keep the case going," she pleaded.

"This alone is the ranting of a lunatic who burned off his own fingerprints and boobytrapped his flat,"

That same day, the case was deprioritised and Cassandra was reassigned to her desk indefinitely. After a year of silence from Al-Nasser, evidence of the plutonium Ali had sacrificed his life to warn her about never came. It was a dead-end and a disgrace.

And now, after all these years, Ben calls her to tell her the letters are still coming. The first letter they found at his flat was followed by another. The Service kept up the rent, paid the bills but stopped short of posting any personnel at the site. The second letter was along the same dystopian lines as the first. It was followed by another one month later, and then another, and another, every month. No-one knew what they meant or who sent them. On the face of it, the letters all seemed like the ramblings of a paranoid delusional. They used phrases like, '*the watchers*', '*they*', '*them*', and threatened that something terrible was around the corner: '*the time is coming*'. Look a little deeper though and it was clear that they were too measured, coherent and structured. They had been designed to appeal to paranoid delusions but the author was not plagued by them. If this wasn't Al-Nasser, then Pfieffer had himself mixed up in some other very scary business.

It also became clear that Pfieffer wasn't the only recipient. Indentations in the paper revealed that the same letter, or versions of it, had been written multiple times, in English, French and Spanish. Whomever it was that was sending them at least felt like he had an eager audience.

Another letter isn't due until next week.

"Go ahead, I'm alone,"

"I shouldn't keep doing this," the young man's voice says, more annoyed than genuinely concerned, "Our author sent another letter—he's in New York,"

It's not Montana but it's the first time he's shown up in the US in six months.

"Okay, read it to me,"

He tries to remove any emotion from his voice as he begins,

"See where the world has arrived. We live on the brink. As one who knows, you must do your part. The time will come for you to take your place but you must be extra vigilant for you are always watched. This is the way for one who knows. You will push the reset button and, this time, the Rapture will be unstoppable and omnipresent. You will not hear from me for some time. Remain strong and remember the truth. Instructions and materials will follow. Watch for my signal,"

"Oh my God," she says, "Is he talking about the nuclear launch? Could he have sent it before the 19th?"

"Unlikely. It's first class, marked 20th March,"

"FBI on the case?"

"*Papa's* not having any of it. There's still no

evidence that the author is Al-Nasser—or anyone of note,"

A surge of adrenaline courses through Cassandra's legs before she realises she's speeding. If *Papa* won't do anything, she has to get to NYC herself. The interview with Blake will have to wait. As she squeezes the steering wheel and eases off the accelerator, she imagines the scruff of a thawb in her fists and laboured breath on her neck. She lands a knee to a pair of balls in her mind.

"Bryce?" Ben interrupts.

"What?"

"Before you do anything, you should know," he exhales, "*Papa* is calling a service-wide meeting tomorrow. He wants an in-person debriefing this side of the pond following your interview with the missileers,"

Fuck. Al-Nasser might as well be the Loch Ness Monster at this point. *But what if he* was *behind the nuclear launch?*

*   *   *

"The attack on the launch base was conducted remotely from within a 40-mile radius," Cassandra begins, "Its objective appears to have been to cut off the command capsule from the rest of the facility and eliminate the possibility of the launch order being challenged.

In this, it was successful,"

Sitting across from each other, Cassandra can see him doing the mental arithmetic.

"And the missileers?" Papa questions.

"That the US Air Force maintains the missileers as suspects is due to desperation," she concludes.

Cassandra and Papa are back in his office at Vauxhall. The black, fragile atmosphere infecting the entire building seems to emanate from this room, with this man. Despite Papa's personal motive, the mood he sets betrays a sense of culpability around the nuclear launch. It's a clear signal that events are neither in his control nor anticipated. If they were, it wouldn't have been Cassandra in Virginia.

He looks at her from the other side of his ominous desk like a man trying to maintain normal levels of eye-contact.

"Is that your entire report, Agent Bryce?"

"The *York Notes*, sir,"

His hands, breathing, facial muscles and posture are perfect. Just like her, he's hiding something. *Semper occultus*, she thinks.

"Sir," she begins, "Who has the kind of hardware that could do that to a nuclear blast door?"

His eyes narrow.

"Agent Bryce, why did you join the intelligence service?"

"Sir?"

"Answer the question,"

She wonders what kind of game he's attempting to initiate. Clearly, he doesn't want the *brand guidelines* answer so she answers as honestly as she can.

"To save lives, sir,"

His reply comes a little too quickly: "And how many lives have you saved?"

"That's an impossible question to answer, sir,"

After a long moment, he sighs and finally looks down, pushing out his expensive chair. As he stands, his wiry frame looms high and he walks with contrived aimlessness to the window behind his desk; a view over the Thames on a grey afternoon.

"I thought you wouldn't want the pomp and ceremony," he says, seemingly to the river.

When he turns around, he holds out a small white envelope. *A letter.* Her mind races. It's a thin, unmarked envelope with perhaps only one folded sheet within.

Wordlessly, she accepts the envelope, unsure whether to open it now.

"You can read it later," he offers, "I'm promoting you,"

The cacophony of alarm-bells in her head is deafening. Her heart climbs up her chest and, involuntarily, she begins to open her mouth. *A promotion letter?* He cuts her off.

"You've done an outstanding job and now I need you..."

"Gone," she interrupts, barely able to restrain herself. She accepted her career's premature plateauing long ago. She's Black, a woman and Munich left a permanent mark. A promotion now can mean only one thing: He knows she knows about Pfieffer's letters, and he doesn't want her digging.

Papa was the agency's surrogate father and Agent Zulu was the golden boy. There's no way Papa would have been able to let that go; he would have pored over every letter looking for clues, had operatives on the ground in every location from which the letters were sent. He knows something.

"Cassandra, you have my total respect," he sighs again but this time it's mock disappointment—a hint of a threat, "Please don't ruin this,"

She spoke too soon before—he doesn't want her gone. He's about to assign her to a desk here in London so he can keep her under closest surveillance, and on a short leash. Whatever operation he puts her on now, he knows it will take her full attention, while running no risk of her interfering with this case.

"I need to know I can count on you to run *Op Underpin* from here,"

Bingo. Op Underpin is the umbrella for all

MI6's covert activity in Afghanistan. That also means Papa knows the attack was not the work of ISIS.

Over the years, Cassandra has become highly adept at hearing and—crucially—maintaining the illusion of full attention, while her cognitive function is focused entirely elsewhere. Later she would be able to recall everything Papa is saying but, right now, she isn't listening. *Observe and report*.

Yet again, she's faced with her own impotence, turning endlessly on the spot—a cog in a machine whose only purpose is to balance the system. She tortures herself for the thousandth time over whether she could have done more in the months before 9/11. Even in those early days, she knew something wasn't right but she remained passive and carried out her duties. Others were handling it. Now, the world just came the closest to Armageddon it's ever been, and she was stuck in a bunker watching on a radar screen. She's hit by a spiral of nausea and the intrusive image of Pfieffer's knife running into her gut instead of Zulu's.

Looking at Papa, she knows he has no intention of catching Al-Nasser. As always, he'll want to sew threads of espionage through him and whichever group is backing him. He'll want to make sure they stay right where they are. After all, *better the devil you know*. This is exactly the kind of strategy that enabled 9/11 and will enable the next attack, and the next.

"Yes, sir,"

CHAPTER 3

Must... use.. powers!

Benjamin Ademola drops the wet razor into his holdall and rinses the menthol-smelling foam from his face. Opening the bathroom cabinet, he chooses his wife's favourite aftershave and sprays his neck. As the stinging settles, the smokey citrus scent reaches his nostrils. He half-smiles a bitter-sweet smile to himself as he sprays his chest and thinks of late evening snuggles after the three boys have gone to bed. He throws the aftershave into the holdall with the rest of his stuff and hopes the mistake he's about to make doesn't cost him everything.

He walks back into the bedroom and gets dressed; smart, navy pants, white shirt, black socks, black shoes. He draws a black tie from a hanger in the closet. *She'd hate that.* "Officer, Ademola, am I under arrest?" she'd pout. He opts for her favourite colour: peach.

Outside, he pops the trunk of his old silver Honda and stows his and her bags next to the full fuel canister. Getting into the driver's seat, he slips his phone onto the empty front passenger seat and sees he has three new notifications from the dating app. He quickly clears the notifications and decides his pocket is the best place for it. It's a long drive and he doesn't need the distraction. Today is the day.

Instead, he turns on the CD player and listens to their songs. As *Be Without You* fills the car, he pulls away from the sidewalk and tries to remember how he first met Barbara and decided he was going to marry her. They were both only fourteen.

He'd been invited to a barbeque over at his cousin's and his mom had been fussing over him all morning. His shoes were never shiny enough for her and his hair always too unruly.

"I'll shave this brown head of yours, Benjamin," she teased as she playfully twisted his ear, "If it weren't for how handsome you look when it's done all nice," and she pecked him on his crown.

A Jeep cutting him up at a junction jolts Benjamin out of his reverie. Slowing to a stop at the lights, behind the impatient driver, Benjamin looks ahead at the sky, holding his breath. It's been nine months since the act of God that everyone calls *3/19,* the day ten nuclear missiles were launched against the world. For some, turning things into a series of numbers, *9/11, 7/7, 3/19,* makes them easier to swallow; easier to put at a distance and move on from. It's a strange thing to Benjamin, *3/19,* because he feels that everyone except those poor souls at the nuclear base was so far removed yet so close to it. *The Lord giveth and The Lord taketh away*—and He can do so in an instant. To Benjamin, 3/19 is a reminder and a warning to the world: don't get too complacent. God is watching. It was like the Sword of Damocles was suddenly visible and quivering above mankind's head for that thirty-minute window.

He arrives at his destination and walks up the steps to the main entrance of the hospital center. He takes a moment to practice his bravest smile and mentally rehearses his way back out of the building. With every step into the hospital, his feet and shoulders feel a fraction heavier. He stands up straight and tries to walk a little faster. He does his best to take on a positive frame of mind, smiling at those he passes and holding the door open for people much further away than necessary. Benjamin needs to be strong now. What's awaiting him in that ward on the other side of the double doors is the same as every day for the last four years on different wards, at different hospitals.

He pulls open the curtain that shields where she sleeps. It never gets any easier. The sight of her lying motionless, tubes up her nose, into her hands and neck, the monitor by her side a silent warning that everything hangs in the balance. He wants to see her in her own clothes again, smiling, doing her makeup, her hair, trying on dresses to go out dancing. Barbara had the greatest, strongest love for life of anyone he'd ever met. Her warmth was infectious and her laugh made his heart sing. Now, she is a patient. She wears a hospital gown and does not move. She hasn't moved for four years. Neither does he for a moment. He walks over to her bedside and draws closed the curtain. His phone vibrates in his pocket again—that stupid app, the one Barbara installed on his phone, when she knew more than he did, and insisted the boys would still need a mom, that she wanted Benjamin to be happy. How cruel that felt of her at the time and still now. But he knows why she did it. He wishes he knew how to delete it. He thought ignoring it would have made it go away by now.

"Hi, Barbara," he says quietly.

She never stirs.

"This is it,"

He feels tears coming and chokes them back into a lump in his throat.

"We're going to see that sunset,"

Benjamin is about to begin pulling the needle from the back of her hand when there's a commotion on the other side of the curtain. Someone seems very upset and angry. There's no time for this. Benjamin needs to mind his own business and get the two of them out of here, but *Officer Ademola* tussles with *Grieving Husband Benjamin* and wins. Smoothing out a crease in Barbara's gown before he stands, he steps through the curtain and sees the driver of the Jeep that cut him up on the way here, arguing with a doctor.

* * *

Sitting at her desk, breathing the stale office air, Lucy thumbs through her mobile. She does her best to distract herself, but the screen hits her with a reflection of her own drawn face. She tilts the phone to cut herself out of view, squeezing it a little to overcome the shaking in her hand. It's been nine months since she woke up cold, naked and hairless, tangled in junk on the edge of Tokyo Bay, coughing up brown sludge and vomit. Nine months since she stared at the Tokyo skyline, crying her last tears, waiting for the mushroom cloud that never appeared.

If only she'd been awake to see it, that morning's sunrise is said to have been the most beautiful sunrise in living memory.

The night before it happened, she had

no idea how much everything was about to change. No-one did. She had started the evening adding social engagements to the calendar on her phone, colour-coding things for her, things for her boyfriend James and things for both of them. James was on a late shift at the hospital performing a long surgery so, when it got to eleven, she decided to power on through, stay up and see him. She pinched an inch of paper from the printer and spent the next few hours drawing a complete calendar including all of James' shifts, which she had stored on her phone, and re-doing their social plans, making sure they weren't double-booked and fitting in regularly spaced meet-ups with friends, even suggesting dates when James could see his friends and family. When she was done transcribing their lives to paper, she started looking on her phone for artwork to go on the walls, remembering that she and James had both said that's something they wanted more of. After about an hour of endless scrolling and only sending three links to James, she began looking at AirBnB for their holiday this year. After a few other little projects were worked on, she got up and walked to the kitchen. She tore the old November sheet from the fridge and replaced it with the new one she'd just done that evening, which had more colour-coding, ruled lines and clearer spacing. Next, she put the other months in the cupboard next to the fridge and threw away the old ones she found there from the last time she did this exercise. With her jobs done, there were a few final touches to make before James got home; shaving her legs and plucking her eyebrows. She finished everything and returned to the kitchen just in time for the front door to their flat to click open.

"You're up," he said with a broad open smile. James has amazing teeth; perfectly straight and symmetrical.

"I'm up," she returned, unable to hold back her glee, despite how tired she should have been. There was always something exciting about staying up for him that made her feel like a naughty teenager; like her parents were sleeping just upstairs.

Below his dark green parka, the trousers of his grey tracksuit were smattered with rain drops, which also dripped from the dark licks of his hair down his pale brow. As he put down his holdall and walked towards Lucy, from the kitchen, she playfully threw a teatowel at his head.

"Hood?" she teased.

"Nah," he mumbled through a crooked smile as he ruffled the teatowel through his hair. "You know, it's nearly morning,"

She asked, already knowing the answer, "Shall we?"

"Let's do it," he said.

"You move the sofa and relax, I get the hot

chocolate,"

A few minutes later, as they sat on the sofa across from the window, drinking their hot chocolate, they watched the first slow rise of burnt orange on the horizon pushing between the gaps in the silhouette of the London skyline. He put his arm around her and she rested her head on his shoulder.

"Look", he said out of the blue, "I just want to say -- I mean --" Lucy didn't know whether she should still be resting her head on his shoulder but it was so comfortable on his warm sweatshirt and she was so peaceful and sleepy now, and something in his voice was reassuring. "I'm behind you with whatever you want to do," he continued, "I wouldn't be where I am now if it weren't for you,"

"Oh, Jay," she said happily, as if to tell him he needn't say anything, lifting her head and turning to face him.

"No, I mean it. You were backing me all the way through my medical degree and training..."

"All those papers I wrote for you," she teased her usual tease. His wry smile turned into a mock scowl as if to say *don't go there*. "Where's my honourary degree?" she went on. In truth, Lucy's heart soared with pride in him and how much he's achieved.

"I'm serious," he said and then he did something unexpected. He put his mug on the floor and from seemingly out of nowhere, he produced a gold chain necklace with a twirling round pendant. As he held it in front of her and it began to slow and go still, she saw the pendant was an ornate miniature compass, beautifully and delicately carved.

"That's beautiful," she said as she raised her hands to hold it. "Thank you, I love it,"

"Wherever you go," he said, "You can always find your way,"

"I'm here now," she said, leaning towards him, "With you,"

She laughed and screamed as he grabbed her by the waist and threw her back onto the sofa.

She doesn't know how long she sat there in the muck of Tokyo Bay, after realising the nuclear explosion wasn't coming. Eventually, she couldn't bear her mind spinning its tyres in the mud. She had to do something and what she found to do was just keep going—as always. She looked around for something in which to wrap herself. She was covered in mud and her joints felt like hot metal pins were being driven into them from the inside. Stumbling over herself through the slime and trash, she found a rotten old rag and slung it over her hunched shoulders. As she clambered up some steps out of the bay, her bare foot slipped and a rush of vertigo threatened to undo her. Clinging on, with her arms wrapped around the rails, she reached street-level and it wasn't long before she was in a hospital bed on a drip being treated for exhaustion and the bends. The doctors and nurses called her Yamada Hanako, which one of the doctors told her is the Japanese for Jane Doe. *Identity unknown.*

Scrolling mindlessly through Twitter is the only way to ease herself back to the present moment, through the filter of a screen, not yet ready to look up at the world around her, where she'd see a sprawling PR agency office full of people her age, into similar things, from the same kinds of places, but who are nothing like her.

On Twitter, one ominous hashtag starts cropping up on her feed, but there's no detail in the tweets themselves. The hashtag is *#prayformedstar*. Lucy finally looks up from her phone, past the bays of desks, to the nearest pillar-mounted TV, of which there are half a dozen, stretching to the far windows. All the TVs are muted with subtitles on and show a variety of news channels, except one, which for some reason is always on a Dutch children's channel. Most of the channels are covering the G7 Nuclear Disarmament talks.

Just when the news agenda had finally moved on from 3/19 and its consequences, G7 came along, offering another constant reminder of Lucy's biggest fear. It literally hangs over her on screens. BBC News 24 has the usual panel of subject matter experts. Some sort of military defence expert looks exasperatedly at a Catholic clergyman who looks condescendingly at an eyewitness wearing one of those stupid t-shirts. When the neutralised warhead was uncovered in a Japanese family's frontroom buried under half their roof, the media went crazy for the handprint indentation on its side—*her* handprint she thinks. The official line is that it's a random indentation made on impact, but that didn't stop these t-shirts popping up blazoned with its image along with cringe-worthy slogans like, *Touched by an Angel* and *The Hand of God*. This guy's one has a rainbow and the words, *Never Again.* Suddenly a *breaking news* scene-change cuts off the clergyman mid-speech.

A grim-faced news anchor delivers a silent announcement on the muted TV. Several of the other news channels begin following suit, as the scene changes again to a live aerial view onto a complex of buildings. The chyron at the bottom of the screen reads *MedStar Washington Hospital Centre*, and Lucy realises that this is the news that was blowing up on twitter.

The camera focuses on a group of children running out of the main building with their hands behind their heads. *Hostages.* They dash to the dozen police officers stationed outside a large cordon. The adults must still be inside.

Lucy is catapulted back to 3/19, the last time every camera pointed in the same direction. Her head is full of screaming, of screeching tires, shattering glass, the cries, the alarms—the sound the world made as she tried to save it. Her mind does another somersault and she relives the fall; the fall that felt like an eternity, that burnt every hair from her skin, melted and combusted her clothes, vaporised her sweat and tears. The fall that landed her in Tokyo Bay.

By the time she realises she's digging her thumbnail into the flesh of her finger, she's left a painful mark. But it's not enough; she feels her joints freezing all over again. When you've been in survival mode for so long, memory loses its grounding in reality. By now, nine months on, it's become impossible to differentiate between nightmare and memory as she sees herself feebly *throwing* a missile with her bare hands—the tenth nuclear missile—as far as she could, before she finally gave in to exhaustion and *altitude*. Her will against gravity and everything that used to make sense, finally expended. Her own childishness felt like a physical object falling with her. Other times, when the vision hits her, *she* is the missile falling on Tokyo. She barely remembers how she eventually got home to London, stowed away inside the freezing landing wheel compartment of a jumbo jet maybe. Since then, the furthest she's gotten to flying is tripping up the stairs.

No more hostages leave the hospital. Lucy tells herself that the police know what they're doing. They're trained for this exact thing and they've got it under control. If rushing in solved anything, they would have done it already. They'll have an expert negotiator talking the hostage-taker down. Even if Lucy could get there, she would jeopardise everything by getting in the way. *But what if they get it wrong?* Who knows how many people are trapped in that hospital and what might be happening to them? Doesn't she have a responsibility to do something, to at least try to help?

She could walk into that hospital without fear of bullets. But that means nothing to the hostages. She imagines multiple armed men, with their guns at the backs of hostages' heads, and the massacre she could trigger with her arrival. Even if she can fly super fast unharmed, if she accidentally moves someone else too quickly, the inertia could break their back or liquidise their insides.

This is how expertly Lucy creates reasons for inaction. As much as Lucy tries to pull herself out of her head, it's both a planning ground and a refuge. As long as she keeps busy planning or dreaming, her mind is her domain. After all, it's better to win imaginary fights than to try and fail. The problem is, imaginary fights don't save lives, and they don't get you anywhere.

As a young girl, Lucy would play chess with her Grangran. She would sit thinking of her first move for as long as any normal kid would take to finish the entire game. She'd stare intensely at the pieces for agonising minutes as Grangran's patience slowly waned, and Lucy felt that she herself might go mad if she didn't stop thinking soon. But she couldn't. She had to know every possible move and pick the safest one. Beginning shouldn't have been too hard—there were only so many ways to start—but she couldn't make the first move until she'd thought as far into every possible outcome as possible. She hated that first move more than any.

"Make your move," she remembers her Grangran saying with her kind, smooth face and her sing-song Tobagonian accent, "The game is out here, not in your head,"

Lucy eventually gave up on chess. The unknown future of the game frustrated and scared her. She couldn't bear her own mind with it, turning every possible move over and over in her head. Maybe this is why, her whole life, she's never stopped, always keeping busy with one thing after another. But she was kidding herself to think it was sustainable. Flying headlong, without a plan for her next move, escaping her fears, anger, hurt; sooner or later, her luck was going to run out—and it almost did over Tokyo.

"Get out of your head and stop doubting yourself," Grangran would say.

"Shit," she says aloud to herself now. Life in the office continues, but she shouldn't be here. The least she can do is be there to offer her help.

As Lucy fast-walks to the stairwell, she runs through every possible outcome she can think of and they're almost all bad. She hangs onto the imagined good outcome as, taking two steps at a time, she pulls out her mobile to see where the hospital is. She'll count the number of times she's going to pass over water once she reaches the East Coast: first Delaware Bay, then another stretch of water and some place called Kent Island, then she'll be in Washington DC. Lucy reaches the door to the roof of the office building. When she opens that door, there won't be any time to pause. This isn't a world in which superheroes soar. People who jump from buildings hit the ground. For just a moment, she wonders how far she could fall before people would see her. Looking at the door to the roof, she imagines a straight line between herself here in Hammersmith and the hospital across the ocean. Now she hides her phone and glasses under some piping. *Deep breath.* She runs her hand through the short hair she can't get used to and bursts through the door. She needs the rush of adrenaline otherwise this questionable leap of faith isn't going to happen.

To fly is simultaneously an unbearably enormous effort and no effort at all. Her heart races, coursing adrenaline to every tingling, swelling nerve-ending in her body. Flying at great speed creates a kind of vortex around her that means air is extremely limited. Lucy has only a couple of minutes before she'll need to slow down at a low altitude to catch her breath. Sometimes, the fear of not being able to stop, and dying floating in space a galaxy away, pulls her out of it, sweating, panicking and wheezing for breath. Not this time.

Within seconds, she's skirting over the Atlantic, "Shit shit shit shitshitshitshit,"

Eyes dead-ahead, streaks of lights and darkness bend all around her. For a split-second, Lucy sees the vastness of space, a quilt of stars beyond, but then it is gone, as if her eyes had momentarily pierced the blue sky. Through the corner of her eye, visions of distant cities, people, trees and things she can't explain blossom in and out of the stream of colours. Now, as she slows to feel the air fill her lungs, the vortex around her body becomes tighter and will eventually disappear. She remembers the fear of what this would have meant as she raced to catch the missiles, their height above the world threatening to boil her blood and freeze her lungs from the inside out. Turning back to find breathable air would have meant the death of millions.

She focuses on what's ahead of her. If she can stay calm and collected, review the situation, she might be able to incapacitate the bad guy or guys before there's any harm done. Easier said than done.

By the time Lucy reaches Washington DC, she's having second thoughts again, but there's no point stopping now. She slows enough to see where she's going, looking for a news helicopter. When she sees it in the far distance, she tries again to put her doubts aside, hopes there can't be too many helicopters over Washington DC at any one time and pushes on through the clear sky.

From this height, a hundred metres or more above the helicopter, there's nothing to tell her this massive complex of buildings is a hospital but she soon sees clumps of armed police with their guns aimed at the main entrance to the building. She's found it. She's gotten lucky.

She picks an open window on the side of the building, takes another deep breath and propels herself down, past the helicopter and inside.

She stands in a lifeless cream and white corridor, surrounded by total silence. As she listens, she becomes aware of her own heartbeat and breathing. *I'm not too late*. She imagines the hospital on a normal day, bustling with people and noise. Her first footstep echoes down ahead of her calling out her presence. Now floating up off the ground she glides onwards silently. Recently abandoned hospital beds litter the sides, their sheets tangled, hanging to snare unsuspecting passersby. An IV stand and a white hospital-issue slipper lie across the laminated path.

A ferocious thunderclap tears apart the silence and hits her through the chest from the distance, followed by a chorus of screams, suddenly and unnaturally extinguished. Her own gasp of panic bounces back at her from the new, sickening silence. She's on the wrong floor. Lucy dives through the laminate floor, bursting into the level below and then through to the next in a diagonal course towards the sound. As she accelerates through plasterboard walls and glass, angry machine gun fire perforates its victims. Without stopping, she smashes through a door to the source of the sound. She sees nothing now but the singular man with a gun. She flies straight into him and grabs the barrel, crushing and twisting it in her fist. With the other hand, she takes him by the scruff of his sweater and flies him through the wall behind him. His head hits something metal and whips forwards. He doesn't make a sound as she drops him on the floor three rooms down from where he'd held the hostages.

She turns away from him to the trail of destruction she left through the ward behind her. At the other end of her broken path, bullet holes pepper the scene of the massacre and she finds herself unable to look down to ground-level and what she knows she will see there. Staring through the plaster dust, wires and shredded blue curtains that hang in the air, she sees her failure to act sooner. There is silence. But now Lucy hears a whimper, which turns into a cry.

In a heartbeat she is in that horrific chamber, scanning for movement. There are bodies in two rows where they had been kneeling in the middle of the room. Men and women, some nurses and doctors, patients, visitors. Beds, trolleys and other equipment have been shoved to the sides and in front of the only door, which Lucy had obliterated when she came through. There are more bodies broken out from the two rows; hostages that must have tried to escape, probably when the shooting started. The cry intensifies, drawing Lucy to a man—*alive*—crawling toward the refuge of an overturned trolley. Another sob turns Lucy around to see a female nurse sitting on the floor, propped up against a bed, clutching her bleeding arm. The nurse is looking at Lucy with wide, panicked eyes. Elsewhere, the body of a doctor, her back soaked scarlet with her own blood lurches as she lets out a pained and woozy groan. Lucy rushes over to where she lies and realises it wasn't her at all. Her body had been half supported by the legs of a large man arched over a bed, his back to her. As his broad back shakes and he lets out another groan, the doctor's body falls completely to the floor. Slowly, the man raises his head and Lucy sees that he is protecting a woman lying unconscious in the bed, hooked up to machines and a drip.

All Lucy says is, "Help me," as she runs over to the nurse. She tears the sleeve off her shirt and ties it around the now barely conscious nurse's bleeding forearm. She and the man find two other survivors. The rest is blood and tears.

* * *

Daniel replays the video for the fourth time. There it is, eight minutes into the YouTube video of the hospital, just before the gunshots: what sounds like an explosion that momentarily destabilises the news copter. He taps the screen of his tablet to fast-forward to the moment the SWAT team rushes the entrance. There it is again. He pauses the video and sits back in wonder, feeling the December morning sun beam through the blinds and warm his face. Nine months on, eighty percent of the Service is still full-time dedicated to 3/19 but not Daniel. He has one night here in his London flat before he ships out to Pyongyang. Already fully prepared for the trip, he's used the downtime to bring himself up to speed with the top headlines. He lays the tablet on his chipboard desk and rises from his creaky chair, walking towards the window and the memory of nine months ago in Tokyo. Closing his eyes, he feels the slats of light and shadow across his eyelids. It was early morning and he was walking to the Metropolitan Government Building to case a potential source. He heard the engines rumbling first, then a panicked murmur, followed by the screeching tires heralding the first military Toyotas and LAVs on the scene. As he turned, soldiers were already jumping out and barking orders at civilians. There, just as the world flipped upside down, he heard the exact same booming sound as the one on the video.

Still in that moment in his mind, his eyes closed, he removes his work phone from his dark navy chinos and commands the device, "Call Sloppy Sam's Pizza,"

"Sloppy Sam's—Where my twelve-inch meat feast is all you need,"

Daniel opens his eyes, "Jack, you can't say that,"

"It's fine, I can see it's you, Mr Takei," Jack sounds like he's pulled another all-nighter, but nothing quells that kid's zest for what he does, nor his schoolboy humour.

"I need the police files on yesterday's incident at the MedStar in Washington DC," Anywhere else, he couldn't count on police paperwork being done so promptly, but he knows them in DC.

He turns to his collection of weapons. On a magnetic sheet on the wall are displayed his bladed weapons from across the globe. Below them is a small mahogany and glass cabinet that houses his gun and ammunition collection. Strictly speaking, none of them belong to him.

"Gimme twenty seconds, Mr Takei,"

"That long? What, are you on your tea break?" Daniel smiles.

"Just finishing the last Custard Cream,"

As Daniel ends the call, he peacefully slides from the wall one of a pair of khukuri knives, the curved blade of the Gurkha. Truth be told, he has no idea how to use most of the weapons he keeps. They fascinate him nonetheless. He flips it in the air and catches it.

With the file now on his phone, Daniel remains motionless, holding the blade by his side while he reads the small glowing screen. His expression turns a little more grim. It's a story about retracted health care and a father needing someone to blame for his daughter's lost battle with leukaemia. It makes for a bitter read. According to the report:

...the shots exploded a nearby O2 canister momentarily incapacitating the suspect... The subject was deceased prior to arrival of first officer on scene... cause of death was suicide by laceration of left and right radial arteries in the wrist.

That seems unlucky. Not to mention the fact an exploding O2 canister wouldn't be heard from the news copter, and certainly wouldn't shake the camera. Whatever it was, it was outside and in the vicinity of the news copter. Daniel ponders the delicate curls carved into the khukuri's decorative wooden hilt.

Something's missing from the report. Upon re-reading the witness statements, he spots the omission: one of the witness statements. He rolls his eyes at himself for missing it the first time.

There are two statements from the conscious survivors of the massacre: a nurse and an off-duty policeman. Both mention a third person helping them, a woman, but there's no statement from her. Daniel punctuates the train of thought by flipping the khukuri in the air once more.

"Call George Yendell,"

"Danny Tanaka, long time no see," answers Daniel's friend at Washington DC Metropolitan PD.

"Just great, thanks, George, how are ya?" Daniel's US alias slots in with ease, "Things must be messy after yesterday at MedStar. Things good? How're the wife 'n' kids?"

"All good, pal. Listen, I can't stay long. Things are indeed a little messy. What can I do for you?"

"Sure, George. No problem. Look, was there an explosion of some sort immediately before the gunfire and immediately after SWAT stormed in yesterday?"

Yendell pauses and Daniel can virtually hear the cogs in the police captain's brain turning. "Maybe," says Yendell, "but it's very irregular,"

"Go on,"

Daniel hears Yendell close a door.

"Before he finished massacring the room, the perp was blown back through three walls,"

Interesting.

"And did you hear the big *boom* that can be heard on the footage from the news chopper?"

"Boom? No, couldn't say so. Maybe?"

Yendell's telling the truth.

"So you're thinking some sort of gas leak or?"

"Nothing of the sort. That's the thing: It looks like he was pushed—backwards through three walls," Yendell's voice becomes a little more animated as he gesticulates on the other end of the call, "And whatever it was, mashed up his carbine real good. There's a three-foot wide hole cutting right through the hospital to our guy,"

"A what?"

"It's the darndest thing—like someone drilled through the place,"

"Thanks for this, George. It's real helpful,"

That explains why the perp slit his wrists with a shard of glass instead of shooting himself. Daniel swirls the hilt of the knife, inverting it into the palm of his hand, and, with the same hand, picks its lover from the wall.

"Sure. It's weird, huh?"

"Yeah, weird. One other thing," Daniel probes deeper, "How many walking survivors were there from the massacre?"

"What's this about, Danny Tanaka?" George is still friendly but he senses a criticism coming and he can't face having made another mistake in front of *The* Danny Tanaka. Daniel needs to be careful now not to trigger his defences.

"There's no statement from the third survivor, the woman helping the nurse and the police officer," Daniel begins dancing the two knives around each other, never quite letting them meet.

"Well, the report's right about that,"

"But they both mention someone else helping them,"

"Well, they weren't that specific and you

gotta remember these situations, they happen very quick and stuff gets hazy. If there *was* someone else, they pretty much vanished into thin air,"

"So there's no description?"

"Sorry, pal, but I really don't think it's a big deal and if my officers sensed there was anything to it, you can bet they'd have an artist's sketch and the works,"

"Okay, thanks a lot, George. We gotta get together and do that barbeque soon, right?"

"It's the middle of winter,"

"Oh yeah," *Oops*, "but I mean, you know, we're busy guys,"

Daniel throws the knives, one after the other, back up onto the magnetic sheet where they ring out as they connect. He realises now that whatever happened at MedStar is part of a much bigger picture. Nine months ago, Bryce called Daniel from her flight back to London and posed a riddle. *What kind of hardware could push an eight-ton steel and concrete blast door off its hinges without leaving a trace of explosive or machinery?* Perhaps the same thing that burst into a hospital and pushed a hostage-taker through three walls. He needs to share this with Bryce.

*   *   *

It's been nine months since 3/19; nine months since Cassandra uncovered the true identities of both Engel Pfieffer and Al-Nasser; but also nine months since any meaningful progress. If she took what she uncovered to Papa, he would have it swept under the rug and have her kicked out for good. To make matters worse, her attention is more divided than ever—the situation in Afghanistan has been escalating, with more civil unrest being met with police and now military violence. She knows she has to build the entire case on her own until it's too big to be covered up.

When she returned home after Papa reassigned her to Op Underpin, she found that she was being tailed. Whatever she'd done, she had really rattled him. Papa knew that one tail was insufficient, but it sent Cassandra a clear message. The only message Cassandra cared about, however, was that whatever she'd been doing, she was onto something big enough to spook Papa. If it had anything to do with the nuclear launch, she had to find out. She had to go back to the letters and back to Pfeiffer. It would mean going against Papa and dredging up history she'd rather forget, but anyone who could take control of America's nuclear weapons couldn't be allowed to try again. She couldn't let it go.

In her flat, now no doubt full of bugs, all she had was a cheap burner phone, a VPN to mask her internet use and some memorised phone numbers. One of those numbers was still an active asset; a hacker named AliasAnon, aka Jeremy Porter. Later that evening, AliasAnon had come through, sending the whole Op Turpentine file to her on the burner.

It was a painful read. On page 47 was the ID card of the man who killed Agent Zulu: Engel Pfeiffer, aka Otto Fleischacker.

It turned out Otto had a long and troubled history of mental health problems. He was already in juvy at fourteen but it wasn't until he was sixteen that he was diagnosed as paranoid schizophrenic. He'd been in and out of institutions ever since.

Cassandra thought back to the porn stash and couldn't help feeling pity. She supposed the young offenders institution wasn't the start at all. There would have been signs in his grades, changes in his behaviour. He probably found himself in detention for "emotional instability" or "lashing out". Things would have gotten worse until he first got caught crossing a line with the law. How different this boy's life could have been. She remembers his last words to her, or anybody: "I'm sorry,"

It's not your fault.

She trawled through his in-patient notes.

Papa would have gone to great lengths to understand the man who killed Zulu. She wondered how it felt having his number one operative killed by a no-body.

Otto's notes showed no sign of improvement in his mental health but, as if out of nowhere, there was an official psychiatric discharge form in 2014. The system had already failed him in many ways but his release was the ultimate failure. It was shortly after he was discharged that his address was raised as a lead in her search for Al-Nasser.

How could anyone in their right mind discharge this person? She asked herself. She punched the discharging physician's name into Google, and that's when everything started unravelling.

Professor Terrence McAvoy's name was utterly meaningless to her but his *face* was something else. Staring back at her from under a heavy, dark brow, framed by a thick salt-and-pepper beard were the beady grey eyes of one of the most evil men on the planet. At first, it didn't compute—a psychiatrist with Al-Nasser's face. Then, the chaos all tumbled together like a shifting kaleidoscope, suddenly forming a dreadful picture. Papa was right—Cassandra had been chasing a ghost this whole time; Al-Nasser was a legend, a fabrication. In his years of activity, there was never any actual evidence of his infamous techniques. The *stories* of savagely mutilated bodies, dissidents flayed alive and his macabre exhibitions were just that. She felt cheated—a fool. The ground beneath her feet began to crack. Everything she had thought was so crucial, her painstaking hunt for Ibrahim Muhammad Al-Nasser—Number Three on the world's most wanted list, strategist, recruiter and chief interrogator—was a fool's errand. She'd played right into this man's carefully fabricated persona long after it was even useful to him.

Perhaps only a shrink could execute such a gut-wrenchingly effective legend, exploiting hundreds if not thousands of people's nightmares. But there must have been a simpler way to get to the plutonium he so desired. He must have enjoyed the horror.

Eventually, she realised she'd not been cheated of anything—she had just pulled off the monster's mask. The kaleidoscope twisted again, reforming all her confusion and regret into a laser-like determination.

Of one other thing she was certain: Papa knew. Anyone reviewing Otto's file would have done exactly as Cassandra had done and quickly come to the same conclusion upon seeing McAvoy's face. Papa knew Al-Nasser was McAvoy, he knew he was communicating with Otto, presumably as the author of the letters, and he knew everything could have been avoided if they'd brought McAvoy in years ago. McAvoy was at large because Papa convinced himself that his great chess game was all going to plan. And in doing so, he'd sentenced Zulu to his death, risked global nuclear war and thrown Cassandra under the bus.

In the days, weeks and months that followed, she learnt all she could about McAvoy. Sometime in the early 2000s, Professor Terrence McAvoy started to unravel. There are no detailed notes of what he did but he had since been struck off and a record of the proceedings, which were conducted in his absence, was publicly available online. The report stated that he had an increased number of sessions with his supervisor and then an abrupt ending. This supervisor, Professor Mendelssohn, is a stalwart for his oath of confidentiality but Cassandra gathered from the report that McAvoy was more or less forced into a sabbatical before going AWOL and then he was struck off. AliasAnon discovered that, in 2009, McAvoy withdrew all his funds, caught a plane to Panama and vanished. That is, until he became Al-Nasser and the first grainy image of him in Iraq arrived back at Vauxhall in 2012. The rest, she already knew. He quickly rose through the ranks of what would soon become known as ISIS, his apparently horrific brutality earning a reputation and nickname that went global. Then, in 2014, he disappeared again with ISIS' suspected secret weapon—stolen plutonium. *What did he want the plutonium for if he was planning to hack the nuclear launch codes?* She asked herself. It didn't make sense.

All she had from 2014 to now were the letters to Otto and their postmarks—maybe something happened to the plutonium during that time, or he discovered how difficult it is to create a working bomb with it.

Today though, something finally shifted after all this time. This morning, her old colleague, Agent Takei, took a calculated but significant risk. He made a delivery that she hopes will finally offer another clue in the hunt for McAvoy.

She was starting out on her morning run, while her solitary tail tried in vain to covertly observe her from twenty metres behind. As Cassandra stretched by the little brick stepway from her road into Victoria Park, she inwardly rolled her eyes at how much Papa must be spending on her. Invasive surveillance doesn't come cheap and to avoid a papertrail, Papa's either pulling in a favour or paying for this little spy op out of his own pocket. The bugs in her flat and on her devices were most likely being monitored by AI, algorithmically searching for misbehaviour. Her tail barely looked old enough to drive; a junior recruit still on probation. While stretching, Cassandra saw that a loose brick on the stepway had been pulled out by a centimetre. It was imperceptible to anyone not looking for it, which is why it was the perfect marker. Three rows from the pavement, two bricks from the left. It told her that her old friend, Daniel Takei, had a dead drop waiting for her at the penultimate drinking fountain. Takei risking an old-fashioned dead drop had to mean something significant. She couldn't dwell on it there so she carried on as usual, challenging her PB all the way to the fountain.

Cassandra often stopped at this fountain, favouring it to having to carry a bottle. It also meant she could stop without suspicion and retrieve the hidden micro USB drive stuck under the rim. With two fingers, she slipped it under the strap of her watch.

It's now 20:00 and, after waiting all day with the USB in her pocket, through Op Underpin briefings, debriefings, intelligence reports, pixelated drone imagery, she is finally home in front of her laptop. Cassandra sits with her back to a blank wall in her bugged home, calculating the risks of what she's about to do. The USB is nested invisibly in her hand. On it, she hopes, is a clue—*any clue*.

From out of the corner of her eye, a black and white fuzz flashes into view and lands beside her.

"Oh hello, Figaro," she smiles at her purring cat as she scratches him behind his ear. He flops down in pleasure and paws her hand a little while she ruffles his slender furry tummy.

An old boy now, Cassandra's cat still has the incredible ability to lie in the most contorted positions next to her, or on top of her, for hours, without moving an inch while she trawls through data or compiles reports. With Figaro keeping her company, Cassandra inserts the USB into her laptop, and it immediately begins a programme that sits between what's actually on the screen and the bug recording everything the laptop does. It's not very sophisticated—it makes the bug think that she's reading the BBC News website—like sticking a photo of an empty corridor over the lens of a CCTV camera—but it'll buy her enough time—she hopes.

There are 33 files on the USB organised into two folders. In one folder, are the police report and witness statements from a hostage situation gone wrong in Washington DC, a video of it unfolding from outside the hospital where it happened, an article on the science of sonic booms, and some image files. The first images are of the crime scene following the hostage killing. There's a hell of a lot more damage than can be done by any kind of handheld gun. One picture summarises them all perfectly: a passage torn through the walls in the hospital, with the gunman in a pool of blood at the end of it. The next image in the series is the blast door from the 3/19 launch command capsule—blown off its hinges. At first, she thinks she must be missing something—but then she remembers asking Takei what could have done this. He's attempting to come through with the answer. She clicks open the next folder: technical specifications of HALO suits, experimental supersonic spy planes the SR-72 and X-43 (the latter apparently reaching Mach 9.6), but then sightings of Elvis, sasquatch, reports of alien abductions and a couple of other crackpot conspiracy theories. Either Takei has lost his mind or he's saying that there's no known technology to explain what happened in Montana, and that it's the same thing that happened at the hospital in DC.

At first, going back to the police report from the DC massacre reveals nothing new, but there's something wrong with the witness statements. They all refer to a young woman who arrived out of nowhere and vanished without a trace. But there's no statement from her. In the same folder, Takei's included Cpt Blake's statement taken after the nuclear launch. Clearly, Takei thinks there's a connection and then it's staring Cassandra in the face. When Blake told Cassandra he was *seeing double* after receiving his concussion, she didn't imagine he might actually have been staring at two women in the command capsule. *Was there a mystery woman in the launch capsule?* None of this is making any sense yet. Just another hole in the story—both literally and figuratively.

Connecting a mystery woman to 3/19 feels tenuous but Cassandra walks it through. There were no unaccounted footprints around the launch control building so anyone on foot would have had to have been inside already when the initial explosion happened. Or they covered their tracks when they left. It's not impossible to cover footprints or even tyretracks if the vehicle isn't too heavy. But the roadside security footage showed nothing and neither did radar. She's reminded of the virus on her own laptop, and that someone hacked the nuclear launch codes that day. Cameras and radar are fallible. In a HALO dive, the subject jumps from a plane at high altitude, picking up tremendous speed before opening their parachute at the lowest possible moment. The result is a very fast insertion of personnel while evading radar. But even if a HALO dive could explain a mystery woman's arrival and she hid out until she somehow blew the doors off the command capsule and gained access to Blake and Hanson, why? The launch order was sent, the officers would have followed their orders. Insurance, just in case either of the officers had doubts? The main building and external communication had already been cut for that. Why didn't either officer talk about this in their statements? And what the hell does any of this have to do with a hostage situation in DC? So, motivation isn't stacking up. *What about means?* Takei knows more than anyone about weapons technology and he's drawn a blank. There's only one other person Cassandra knows who might know something.

She and the man she needs to find are bound by a secret that saved their careers—maybe their lives. Maybe he'd help her again.

It was 1995 and she was on assignment at an R&D facility run by the MOD in darkest Wales. Among other things, she heard rumours that they were working on an experimental propulsion system.

Back then, she was MI5 and the youngest on a team of operatives tasked with safeguarding the facility from leaks. She saw and heard enough to figure out that some British scientists in Libya had something way beyond their understanding and that had the potential to destabilise the oil industry. Understandably, there was a race to put it under wraps and under control. She supposed it was some sort of advancement in renewable energy, and probably related to the propulsion system they were apparently working on at the facility. The MOD had recently seized everything and sent it to this facility in Wales. She remembers the arrival very clearly because it was the same night as a particularly scary haul of biohazard warnings, escorted by a HAZMAT team.

It was only two nights later that the shit hit the fan. She was watching through three-inch perspex as a virologist in full protective gear syringed the clear contents of a beaker into six vials in a rack. At first, she heard shouting down the corridor to her right and thought there'd been some sort of accident. The automated alarm followed and spread through the building around her. There have been a few occasions in Cassandra's life in which she's heard the sound of true terror of men and women facing death. Every time, it felt like a punch through the chest. Nothing, however, is more haunting than the three short bursts of machine gun fire that followed and the silence they cut out for each other.

She banged on the window but the virologist didn't hear her. She found the intercom button and shouted for him to *Go! They're coming!* That was easy for her to say. He was stuck—it would take five minutes to decontaminate and get out of his air locked chamber. As for her, the only cover was a knee-high stainless steel cabinet running along the wall behind her. She crouched and slid open one of its doors. Heavy footsteps ran up the corridor as she climbed awkwardly in with the stacks of manilla folders and empty glass vials and closed the door behind her.

She was unarmed and a novice against what she surmised was a group of heavily armed mercenaries. The facility's security team were clearly outmatched and easily put down and, now, whatever these men's employers wanted was open to them.

Inwardly, she shook with impotent rage. Outwardly, she lay deathly still, sandwiched between the sliding cabinet door and its other contents, holding her breath. At least three big men ran into the area and she listened to them wordlessly dial the security code and pass through the airlock into the chamber with the virologist. There was no sound of a struggle, just a single, controlled gunshot, a man shouting in pain and the men running off to the left. But it was only two sets of feet running; one of them was waiting behind for something. The drumbeat of shouting, screaming and gunfire continued, progressing through the building. Cassandra thought every single person in that building was going to die. Maybe there were others hiding. Maybe she could make it out alive if she just stayed very still. Maybe they were going to sweep back this way and pick up the guy they left behind. It was only a matter of time before they heard her breathing or she moved.

Cassandra was a fool to think she could do

anything against these men but she had to take a look. She drew open the door in front of her face just enough to see through. *Shit.* She froze. The man was facing her direction. She could see up to his waist only. Black boots, black combat trousers and the muzzle of an AK-47 offered no clues as to his identity. She couldn't risk more movement so she kept watching. Then, whatever he was doing, he turned his back on her. It was her only chance to do something and survive. Or die doing something very stupid.

She fully opened the door and crawled out, but as she left the cabinet, her shoe clinked against something glass and the enemy spun around. She pounced at him, stepping up his thigh and jumping on his back, wrapping her legs around his torso, using their joint momentum to take him to the ground. Exploiting the advantage of surprise, while she righted herself on his back and had him face-down, she removed the pistol from the holster at his hip. She tried to pin him with her knees but, with surprising strength, he managed to roll onto his side. She blocked a blow from his forearm to her neck and slammed the heel of her palm into his jaw. She was going to lock his free arm but she realised she'd already knocked him out cold.

Cassandra stumbled to her feet and dragged the unconscious pile of steroids and testosterone into the viral quarantine chamber.

Whatever was in there had been released when the mercenaries broke in anyway. As she was disarming him, there was a murmur behind her. The virologist was alive but bleeding badly from a gunshot wound just above his right kidney.

"Stop them," his hoarse voice was a whisper, "It--" he winced in pain, lying clutching his side as Cassandra took off her suit jacket and used it to stem the bleeding, "-- In the wrong hands --" he was fading in and out of consciousness, "but -- it does miracles -- it will save everyone. Just stop them,"

Whatever it was, it was her responsibility now. She had to go after them. But first she had to help the virologist. She lifted him to his feet but found he had no strength in his legs. With his arm around her shoulder, she dragged him to the airlock. She shot the internal security panel and, as they left the chamber, kicked the airlock closed behind her, trapping the mercenary as he began to stir. She left the pistol with the virologist and took the AK-47. "Watch him," she said.

The mercenaries' trail was littered with bullet holes, empty shell casings, blood and bodies. Cassandra knows that if she goes down the path of that memory, scrambling through the aftermath of that massacre, she might never get out. That's just what the survivor's guilt wants..

Sprinting, she burst out of a fire exit into the darkness of the night. She was in the carpark watching three men jump into the back of a black van. As it sped off, she was already at her Yamaha motorcycle with the machine gun strapped over her shoulder.

It was during the chase that followed that she and her quarry made it onto a public road where the van collided with the only other vehicle out that night.

The red Sierra flipped into a ditch and the black van careened off the unlit road and wrapped around a thick oak. Cassandra skidded to a halt, her bike threatening to fishtail out of control before she leapt from its saddle, running to the smoking van. The two mercs in the front of the van had been killed on impact. She lent over, killed the loudly running engine and pulled the key from the ignition, dropping it in the footwell. On the mangled dashboard, wedged against the tree was an open steel case, meant for the glass vials. Only one was intact. She grabbed it. Assuming there were survivors in the back of the van, she didn't have much time.

She swung open one of the back doors and quickly recoiled out of sight, around to the crumpled side of the wreck. She heard nothing from inside, so crept around the open door, leading with the AK-47. She peered around and, illuminated by the headlight of her bike, saw a mess of men, strewn around during the crash. The lumpy darkness of male bodies and their guns moved and groaned as they regained consciousness. She was outnumbered and outgunned. But they were blinded and hazy and she had enough rounds if she was fast enough. Time galloped on relentlessly but she couldn't just execute these men to save herself.

Sometimes she remembers that they shot first, and other times it was her, out of fear. The truth is, she dreads either version. Just one of the men got off a round before they were all riddled with her bullets and she was panting in the rain. Her breath misted up before her, creating a personal fogscreen between her and her deed. She was soaking wet with no idea when it started raining.

Through the pelting metallic rain, she heard a woman's panicked calls for help. *The red Sierra.* She ran back through the dark to the sound and slid into the ditch, scratching her hands and legs on snagging thorns. The upturned car was almost engulfed in earth and a great shrub, blotting out its lights. The woman's voice was urgent and hoarse.

"I'm coming!" shouted Cassandra. She wrenched open the slick driver-side door, "You're going to be okay,"

"No," the woman wailed, "No no

nononono," she was clutching her gut, "My baby,"

The steering wheel was jabbing into her belly. She was about Cassandra's age, even looked a little like her.

"My baby my baby my baby," and then she just sobbed.

She had to get back to the facility where she could use a phone. That far out in the countryside, it would be half an hour at least before an ambulance arrived; they'd need to cut her out of the car and airlift her. But maybe there was still a medic in the building.

"What's your name?" she asked, keeping the woman talking and conscious.

She groaned and winced before she could reply, painfully, "Aaliyah,"

She knew the woman was going to lose her baby if she didn't do something. Aaliyah was losing consciousness and Cassandra couldn't find the source of the bleeding in the dark, cramped vehicle. As she searched, she kept talking.

"Aaliyah," Cassandra said, "I'm going to get some things—I'll be back as soon as I can,"

She sprinted to her bike to get her field first aid kit and, when she returned, frantically trying to find the source of bleeding while the woman was still stuck in the car, she remembered the case with its biohazard warning and heard the virologist's words, *It does miracles.* As she felt the last remaining vial in her pocket, her mind raced. Then, suddenly, the woman screamed as the driver seat sprung back. Cassandra had lent on the seat's pitch lever. She was free. The two of them managed to remove her seatbelt and Cassandra dragged her out of the car.

She patched her up by the side of the road and decided she had to get her out of the freezing rain. She had no idea what internal injuries she may have suffered but she'd already moved her once and couldn't bring herself to leave her here while she went to call for help.

In the boot of the woman's car, she found the bungee cords she was looking for. With Cassandra's help, Aaliyah got onto the back of her bike and Casandra strapped the injured mother-to-be to herself for the race back to the blood-soaked facility and, by the Grace of God, salvation.

* * *

The plaster dust colours the water beige as it rinses out of Lucy's hair down her chest and arms. There isn't enough steam to hide in. She picks at the caked blood under her nails but can't get it all out. No matter what she does, she just seems to be making more of a mess. She feels like an idiot. She shakes her head and rubs her face, running her hands back over her ears and down her neck where she squeezes the flesh in an attempt to free some tension. She lets out an angry and fed up sigh and picks up the shampoo bottle. *You have no right to wallow -- or walk out alive.*

At that moment, the bathroom door clicks open. She almost slips in the bath, quickly grabbing the shower curtain for dear life, "Jesus Christ!"

Standing in the doorway, James looks simultaneously surprised and relieved, "Lucy!"

Seeing him standing in his boxers with his tousled hair, Lucy remembers that it's the middle of the night. *I can't keep doing this to him*. He steps forward and she would step back but he pushes aside the curtain and wraps his arms around her. Opening her mouth to chastise him, instead an involuntary sob escapes. She closes her mouth again and buries her face in his shoulder.

No more words pass between them until she lies curled up against him in bed, her head on his chest, his arm around her. It's James who breaks the silence.

"Do you want to talk about it?"

Lucy feels the strong, reliable beating of James' heart under her ear and the softness of the hair on his chest under her fingers. She wants to hang onto the moment for longer. When they are together, it's so much easier to clear her mind and simply *be*. But she worries about shutting him out for too long.

"I--," she begins, closing her eyes, "--I was

there in Washington, at the hospital, after that guy killed the hostages,"

James says nothing. He squeezes her shoulder slightly as if he doesn't know what to say or what else to do. She wants him to jump up and shout at her; ask her what the fuck she was thinking by not getting there sooner.

"I was too late," she admits, "I fucked up,"

He says nothing. Moments pass during which all she can do is replay the scene in her mind over and over, focusing on different details each time. Mostly, she imagines how things might have been different if she'd not hesitated to go and help.

"You couldn't save those people, but it's not your fault," he finally says, "I know you would have done everything possible,"

She barely hears him. He's being too nice—he doesn't get it. She wants to push him away, but she doesn't want him to go anywhere. She needs conflict, but can't bear to fight.

"I can't keep doing this," she says, thinking the ambiguity of it might be just enough to make him fight harder, feeling cruel the instant the sentence leaves her lips.

"Doing what?"

"I don't know. I'm sorry. It's not fair on you,"

"You're doing what you need to do," He's searching desperately for what to say, "I love you, and I think you're amazing,"

Warmer.

"You saved the world. Please stop beating yourself up all the time,"

Colder.

"I'll try," she rolls over to sleep, "I love you too,"

James kisses the back of her head and somehow, infuriatingly, falls immediately to sleep. People have told Lucy her whole life to stop doubting herself, that she can do whatever she wants when she puts her mind to it. She feels guilty for her own self-pity and tries to push it aside. Sleep doesn't come easily.

* * *

The primary-coloured madman cackles maniacally, throwing his head back and wailing at the sky. A frenzied orchestral string section underscores the terror as this parody of a toymaker waves his oversized controller at the schoolbus of terrified children. As they look on in horror, their fate hangs in the balance. A giant mechanical T-Rex rattles the bus in his steel jaws. His rampage has taken them high above the city, to the top of the Municipal Science Museum. By the command of the Toymaker, the mechanised menace threatens to drop the bus to the street below.

Now, the strings succumb to the gradual swelling of a deep brass section, heralding the arrival of our hero. The villain's horrified face is suddenly cast in a new harsh light, a dramatic contrast as the hero swoops in from above, red cape flapping. Lucy feels every note of music, every swinging fist and soaring triumph. He lands an almighty blow to the Robosaurus' flank and begins prizing open its mega mandible with his bare hands. Somehow, he tears off the jaw and catches the bus, stopping it from crashing to the ground.

While he places the bus down and checks that its young passengers are unharmed, the Toymaker makes a run for it. He clumsily scrambles only a few steps before he is apprehended by the hero, who crushes the oversized controller. As the hero takes flight with his captive, the school children climb off the bus and the crowd below cheer with jubilation.

Suddenly, confetti fills the air and the crowd applauds... Lucy. But as she carries the Toymaker, she realises her costume is nothing more than her coat tied around her neck like a makeshift cape. She feels ludicrous. *Will they see?* The dread and embarrassment are overwhelming. As she flies higher into the sky, the Toymaker wriggles and wriggles in her grip until she can't hold him any longer.

He's falling to his death and the pitiful,

hurt look on his face, his desperate, pleading eyes, fill her with shame. She can't catch him. Like a balloon, she floats uncontrollably up and up.

What she thought was confetti becomes smouldering ash and, as it falls on the people below, it burns their skin, turning their cheering into agonised screeching. Their fingers point accusingly at Lucy while the skin bubbles and blackens on their faces. The school children blindly running from the bus fall off the roof of the museum like a wave of lemmings.

Suddenly, gravity kicks in and Lucy falls towards the murderous, wailing mob as if being dragged down by their grabbing hands.

She wakes with a shout, soaked with sweat, the bed sheets tangled around her legs, in total darkness.

"It's okay," James says sleepily, stroking her head, "It was a bad dream,"

This can't go on. In this moment, James already asleep again, his hand still on her head, she stares at the ceiling and resolves to do something. Tomorrow, she's going to call David.

It was David who helped unlock her abilities and gave her the push she needed to not be afraid any more. He was there when she unlocked everything, when she flew for the first time. It all began with the attack at uni.

It was before Lucy knew she had these powers, she was in her third and final year at uni, doing a BA in History at Leeds. It was the wrong night out to take a shortcut home through the sparsely lit park. When she began to feel like someone was following her, she got out her phone to receive a pretend call. There was no harm in walking a little faster either. If she were walking along a road, she would have crossed to the other side. But there was nowhere to go but the single path she was on, cutting through the park. She picked up her pace. *Why did I come this way?* she thought. *I could have waited to leave with the others.* Then Lucy looked up ahead and saw four figures at the sides of the path. She told herself they had nothing to do with the guy behind her, but she'd still have to walk through them and feel their eyes on her and hear whatever disgusting comments might come out of their mouths at this time of night after however much drinking. Her heart-rate matched her footsteps as she put her head down as if walking into a strong wind.

She decided to speak, to make her fake phone call more real. She thought she'd say, "Hi, yeah I'm in the park too, see you in a minute," but she found that she couldn't raise more than a mumble.

It was like walking into a wolves' lair. As she passed between them, one of them put out his foot and tripped her, much to the amusement of the others. *What a fucking arsehole*, she thought.

She silently thanked the universe when she thought she was safely past them. Then suddenly: "Where you off to, babe?" came the voice, right up in her ear. Her heart jumped into her throat.

She kept the phone planted to her other ear, tried to ignore him and kept on going.

"Okay, see you in a minute," she said into her phone, "Just walking through the park,"

"Moody black bitch," another voice growled behind her.

"That's rude," grunted another.

Someone put his hand on her shoulder and spun her around. There they were, all five of them rounding on her. She ran but, before she'd taken five paces, an arm was around her throat. He stuck his sloppy, slathering tongue in her ear like some disgusting slug and breathed hot, wet breath over the side of her face. It stank of stale cider and cigarettes. He dragged her to the ground and pushed her face down in the dirt while he tried to kick her feet apart.

"Oh fuck," one of them gasped, "Mate, what fuck are you doing?"

She scrunched her eyes shut but she knew they surrounded her, leering down. In that moment, the taste of dirt in her mouth did something to her. It sucked her back in time to an age of innocence and uncovered a secret memory. She was no more than five, lying face down in the dirt. She'd just jumped off the roof of her house. In her frustration, she'd pounded her fists, breaking apart the earth in the garden until it suddenly swallowed her up. The newly uncovered memory unshackled something in her brain.

She'll rather forget what happened next. She was lucid and raging throughout. The exposed flesh and muffled screams and blood and cracking bones were not her own. But they were her doing.

In the end, Lucy found herself sitting on the ground surrounded by screaming boys. The slumped figures of the five thugs were bloody and torn and not one of them didn't cry for his mother. Their blood covered her knuckles and caked under her nails. If only she'd not taken a shortcut. If she'd walked home with a friend.

After that night, she was confused, scared, but mostly angry. She started getting into trouble. She was looking for it. It started with confronting guys trying to chat up her friends, and she'd become more and more mouthy to provoke a reaction, hoping one might resort to shoving her or making a fist. But she couldn't push enough to make it happen. Her friends would stop her or she'd stop herself. When she realised what she was doing, rather than quitting, she decided that night she'd head back out after her friends had all gone home. On her own, she marched out of the front door like she was wearing armour, feeling for the first time how powerful her body was, while hiding inside it. She went out into the dark alone, for every time she had a text to say, "Stay safe. Let me know when you're home," For every time she made a fake phone call passing dark alleys. Every time she'd feared looking over her shoulder, walked a little faster, crossed the road, taken a longer, better-lit route home. Every time she'd run the last bit to her front door and bundled inside and slammed it shut without looking behind her. Every time she had felt weak, in danger and like she had less of a right to be outside after dark.

Over the next few weeks, she broke up fights, started fights and beat up any sleaze creeping on a drunk girl who was just trying to get home. She targeted the worst clubs and pubs, but she never went back to that park. She would wear a hoodie and a scarf around her face so that, before long, rumours of a masked, indestructible vigilante were spreading online. That's what David said led him back to her, because he already knew her long before she could remember.

One morning, one of the girls announced that there was a letter for her on the table. This was the dining table sized area where post, handbags, scraps of food, hair ties and the fruit bowl lived in their shared student flat. It hadn't come far since it was an unstamped envelope, with *Lucy* handwritten across it. Receiving post that wasn't junk mail or a bill was an almost totally alien concept. She assumed it was an invitation to a party. She took it back to her room to read it. This was how David introduced himself and asked to meet her. The note said he wasn't police, that he was a scientist, he knew what was going on and needed to talk to her right away. He gave a time and a place at a cafe that wouldn't be full of other students.

Later that day, after she'd finally resolved to meet him, and they were walking with hot drinks in their hands, he told her a story about a meteorite, a secret research facility, a space virus that made host bacteria indestructible. It sounded completely made-up—it was like a 90s sci-fi action movie. Eventually, he got to her mum's crash. This was the part where he found her mum's flipped car in a ditch, her mum still inside, pregnant and barely conscious. He said there were broken vials of the virus around her, the C-416 he called it, and she'd breathed it all in before he got there. He called an ambulance and, when she regained consciousness in hospital, he was by her side.

Lucy's mum never spoke to her about the crash and Lucy had only picked up hints that her mum caught some sort of infection, which she always assumed was something to do with the birth or pregnancy. David said that after that he watched from a distance until Lucy's second birthday, when he finally decided that there had been *no observable consequences* of the virus. He didn't find out how wrong he'd been until nearly nineteen years later, reading online about someone who appeared to be just as invulnerable as the virus' host bacteria in the lab, making mincemeat of every sexual predator and thug in Leeds.

After that, she simply stopped fighting. If she was searching for meaning, he would help her find answers. And he did, for a while.

In his home laboratory in his garage, he showed her her own skin cells in a petri dish under a microscope. The glow from the computer and electron microscope display always gave him the air of a mad professor down there. He set up something like an old Van der Graaf generator on the table with the same petri dish, to show her how her cells work.

"Your cells are the most efficient power stations on the planet," the professor was said in wonder, "But energy in a closed system remains constant,"

He turned a black dial at the base of the generator and it began to hum with electric charge, "So energy isn't created or destroyed but moved or transformed,"

KR-ZAP! A bolt of blue lightning speared through the fizzing air between the petri dish and the great chrome ball atop the generator. It was this image that helped her figure out how to stop the nuclear missiles, when the instructions the woman at the launch base gave her had disintegrated.

Lucy realised, as the world rushed up to meet her and the first warhead, cold air roaring past her ears, desperate for breath, that the air around her hands was fizzing like in David's lab. She felt the same pins and needles in her palms and fingertips as she'd felt when she'd plunged them into fire, only much greater. She peeled her hands off the warhead and the air in between seemed to sparkle for a moment. Realising what it meant, she flew around to the front of the warhead and the thing pulled her hands in like magnets. Instantly, the fizzing and popping started again and the pins and needles shot up to her elbows. *Come on come on come on come on*, she thought to herself. Pain, nausea and desperation expelled a cry from her that she left in her wake. But she did it. She used her own body to absorb the potential energy stored within the warhead and neutralise it.

Tomorrow, if there's something wrong with her, David will figure it out. She's going to fly, she's going to bend steel bars and she's going to deflect bullets. Tomorrow, Lucy's going to be herself again.

*   *   *

Decades ago, seven-year-old Cassy paused for a moment by the back door of her dad's white Ford Escort. She could feel the tension pushing out from inside it. She didn't know what to fear more—his silence or his shouting—but she was certain she couldn't stand here staring at the handle.

Earlier that day, little Cassy had done something that now felt like it had altered the course of the rest of her life. Her *school career*, as the Headmaster called it, was forever tainted. She'd look back at it nearly forty years later and still feel a pang of injustice, and remorse.

The day had started with excitement and novelty, as Mrs Hyde brought out modelling clay. The room buzzed with the limitless possibilities such a thing presented. The buzzing carried with it the nervous glee of a classful of children sharing the knowledge that the noise-level was already pushing teacher's limits. Cassy was more nerves than glee and, when Mrs Hyde announced that they'd be making busts, Cassy shared Mrs Hyde's confusion as to why some of the boys found it so unbearably funny. Most notable among them was Matthew Wright. That boy had a constant menacing look, like he was always planning something evil. He liked to put mud down girls' jumpers when they weren't looking.

It was just Cassy's luck to be sitting at a table with him and one other boy, Freddie Archer.

Cassandra couldn't think of anyone famous who she wanted to sculpt so, instead, tried to recall her grandmother's face. While focusing hard on the disobedient clay between her fingers, she couldn't help seeing what Wright was doing. He'd made a grotesque face with dinner-plate ears and huge slug-lips. All the while, he was smirking, comparing it to someone behind Cassy. She stole a glance over her shoulder to see her friend, Doris, the only other black girl in her class. There were four black children in the entire school. When she turned back, Archer was poking a clay banana at the side of the golliwog's mouth and the pair had clearly never seen anything so funny in their lives. Doris had never done a thing to hurt anyone.

A burning bubbled up from the pit of Cassy's stomach, through her chest, across her shoulders and up her throat. She clumsily dived forward, snatched the model in her fist and threw it at Wright's face. She watched the tumbling ball of features soar over Wright's head and hurtle towards the classroom window. With a thud and a splinter, the glass cracked. The room was immediately and excruciatingly silent. Her heart stopped.

Cassy shot her eyes down into her sculpture, desperately willing everyone to carry on as before. It was too late.

"Bryce!" Mrs Hyde screeched like a siren.

Cassy heard the air, tables, chairs and all other matter part around the teacher's unstoppable path. Then, the icy burn of Mrs Hyde's hard fingers twisting Cassy's ear and yanking her forcibly out of her chair. Before she knew it, she was at the front of her class being interrogated. Her only chance was to explain what had happened and turn justice onto Wright and Archer.

"Just *what* do you think you were *doing*?" shouted Mrs Hyde.

Cassy steadied her shaking knees but she felt her cheeks prickling with emotion. Wright and Archer remained silent, glaring threateningly at her from their table at the back of the room. The rest of the class stared at her and just looked sort of shocked. She looked to Mrs Hyde as she spoke.

"Wright and Archer made an ugly golliwog and were making fun of me,"

"It wasn't you!" shouted Wright indignantly.

"*Enough*!" commanded Mrs Hyde. Then she turned to Cassy. "How *dare* you behave like that?"

The teacher was talking to Cassy, not Wright. "Look what you've done!" Mrs Hyde continued, pointing at the window. "Who's going to pay for that?" She didn't expect an answer. "Well, girl?" Maybe she did. Cassy couldn't keep up.

"I'm sorry, Miss," was all she managed.

It was as if the teacher hadn't even listened to what she'd said. Or she didn't care.

"Palms,"

Cassy accepted her punishment despite the muted furnace inside her. She wished she could explain but knew it was pointless. She'd lost.

The worst things about being caned were the injustice and humiliation. It hurt like hell but that was nothing compared to everyone looking at her and knowing how badly she'd screwed up and that she couldn't take it back. She imagined no-one would ever forget or stop talking about it.

She was given detention. There was talk of her parents having to pay for the window, at which point the reality of them finding out sunk in. Then the fear of how expensive windows are and the worry that they couldn't afford it, and not really knowing what that meant.

There were two things the headmaster said that stuck with her:

"I thought you were different," and, "I never want to hear about anything like this ever again,"

She spent the rest of the day in a daze, trying not to see the window.

Opening the backdoor of the car was like releasing an airlock. Wordlessly, she got in and waited for her dad to start. She waited as he drove and she silently watched the clock on the dashboard, unable to look directly at any part of him. For the entire 22 minute journey, he said nothing. He had to say something sooner or later but she realised he was waiting until they got home. She needed him to say something so she could gauge the situation. At the moment, it felt irredeemable. She felt irredeemable.

He got out of the car and she followed his bristling back into the house. As she closed the front door quietly behind her, he was already boiling the kettle and pulling a cup from the cupboard. When he turned around, his face was of disbelief and anger—searching for more than just the teabags. Before she could stop herself, she was compelled to offer him some words.

That one word, "Daddy," was like a pin to a balloon. He turned to look at her without moving a single part of his body except his eyes.

"How could you be so -- so foolish?"

"They --"

"It doesn't matter what they did,"

She couldn't believe this was coming from him—the man who she looked to to do the right thing.

"Cassy," he continued, "You need to know better,"

The kettle finished boiling but tea was no longer on his mind. He leaned on his fingertips on the kitchen counter, keeping his side to her, then stood up straight, turned to face her and planted his hands in his pockets. His white shirt was creased after a long day. She stayed rooted to the spot, the dining table between them.

"Look around you," he said. She darted her eyes around the room, uncertain. "I mean the outside world. You're too young to understand now but you need to hear this anyway," He took his hands out of his pockets and gestured to a chair. "Sit please,"

Sitting at this table, her father extolled to Cassy the truth of being Black in London in the '80s. It didn't matter how smart she was, how hard she tried at school, how well she behaved, she would always be looked on as lazy, angry and untrustworthy. He told her proving them wrong wasn't enough. They'd always be waiting and it would only take one slip-up. Sitting, listening to her dad, she realised the horrifying truth about the fire at New Cross that had only happened a few nights ago. She'd heard her brother talking about it late one night.

Her dad didn't finish indoctrinating her to the truth until her mum got home much later. At seven years old, it was like a door had been opened and she was taking a seat at the grown-ups table. When he was done with her, the three of them played poker that night.

Andrew, her elder brother, got home early. He was supposed to have been doing a shift at Mr Nelson's after school but something had happened. She could tell he was upset when he swung open the front door behind her back. He stormed in and the game was over. Before Cassy had a chance to turn around, he slung his school bag on the floor by the legs of the table and a couple of thick textbooks slid out of it.

"Andrew," their mum said, getting to her feet, concern on her face, "What's happened?"

"Pigs got me again," he spat back.

"Respect," admonished their dad, glaring firmly at Andrew, without standing.

He expected better language from his family and in his house.

"They searched you again?" asked their mum as she began fussing over his jacket and straightening him out.

"Yeah. *Again*," he looked at dad, venom in his eyes, "And you just play their game like a good boy,"

"Apologise to your mother," said dad, his blood boiling under his skin, "And go to your room,"

It was Cassy's bedtime too.

Not long after, Andrew sat on the edge of his bed in the room they shared while Cassy tried to sleep.

"This is bullshit," he said through the darkness. She didn't know if he was addressing her. "Someone's got to do something,"

During the long silence, she could feel his anger engulfing everything about her. She finally whispered, "About what?"

"Sus law. Everything. It's bullshit. Kenny and his boys are organising a meeting. *They're* taking action. I can't believe dad is so lame,"

It hurt Cassy to hear him talking like that about their dad but she was quickly distracted when she heard something from downstairs like muffled arguing.

"Sshhh," she hushed her older brother, straining to hear through her bed and the floor.

She thought she heard their mum saying *Oh my God.*

The next thing she remembers was sitting at the top of the stairs with her brother, secretly watching the TV over their parents' shoulders through the bannister, trying not to breathe.

It was the night Brixton burned. Looting, petrol bombs, bricks, bottles, fires, fighting. Forty-six cops injured, five seriously. The news didn't say how many Black people were hurt. They sat on the stairs in horror watching the whole thing. It was like war footage, but in their home country, on streets that looked so familiar. She couldn't understand why at the time but it terrified her. She had nightmares because of it. Andrew didn't go to the meeting. Neither she nor Andrew ever got in trouble again.

Now, sitting in a rental car, in another car park, the memory feels like ten lifetimes ago. She's trying to pull together threads that just won't meet, and everything Takei delivered raises more questions than answers. She rolls the story back to the beginning. It all started with the mental breakdown of Professor Terrence McAvoy in the early 2000s and his disappearance in Panama in 2009. She has no idea of the significance, if any, of Panama.

Cassandra closes her eyes and calls on the world map she has memorised. Shortly after Al-Nasser—McAvoy—went missing, Ali was beheaded in his own home. Next, in Munich, 2015, Engel Pfieffer aka Otto Fleischacker and McAvoy became some sort of pen pals. No matter how much time goes by, she still sees his exploded face on the floor of his kitchen. Op Turpentine was officially shut down but she kept tabs. MI6 stationed a man in the apartment and anonymous letters to Otto, probably from McAvoy, came every month, each another little light on the radar screen in her mind: from Buenos Aires, Tijuana, all over the US, then into

Europe, a winding snake stalking his way around the map. Then, without warning, the big one: Montana, 19th March this year, when the world nearly ended. The next day, 20th March, a letter from New York continues the unpredictable path putting McAvoy back on the other side of the Atlantic. He didn't take credit but it was his last letter in over nine months. Cassandra had wondered why he stopped—whether someone else got to him or if he got spooked and went deeper underground.

Then, in Washington DC, the first target on 3/19 a hospital becomes the scene of a brutal mass shooting. It was seemingly unconnected until Takei put together the holes, and the mystery woman.

She opens her eyes again. Still none of it makes any sense. To add to matters, on her phone is confirmation that McAvoy is still very much alive and active. After so much wondering, she has a scan of a new letter received today at Otto's address.

Dear friends,

You may believe that the world changed on 19th March but what really changed?

You can't hold off the change this time. My followers are many and invisible. They await my signal to bring about total obliteration and reset humanity. Since you will soon be at peace I ask that you spend what time you have left with love.

I do this with nothing but sadness for what we have become, and hope for the bright future I see for humanity.

Sincerely,
TM

After so much scrabbling in the dark, the directness of the threat actually comes as a relief. It's clearly addressed at the intelligence service. And this time he signed it: TM for Terrence McAvoy.

Aside from him finally confirming that he knows of Otto's death, there are two very salient points to the letter: 1) Some fresh hell is about to kick off and 2) McAvoy believes "they" thwarted his plans on 3/19. Whether it was inactive warheads or a secret satellite defence system was irrelevant—it was no act of God to him.

She pictures Papa reading the letter. In her mind, he quietly files it in a drawer and locks it away. What other hushed evidence, what trail of bodies is he amounting in the wake of his deluded crusade to control Terror? Ali, Otto, Zulu—are they on her or him? How many more are going to have to die while her people do nothing?

Before she picked up the rental car, she finally lost the intelligence operative who had the joyless task of tailing her. Her bag is packed, she'll soon be officially AWOL, and facing court-martial and jail-time when she's caught. She has just turned her back on three decades of service to hunt down McAvoy and stop him.

At 10:03, the passenger door swings open, evaporating her thoughts. The ex-MOD virologist has arrived.

"Hello, Professor O'Connor,"

CHAPTER 4

Meanwhile, across the city

Seeing Professor O'Connor is a dose of mortality, how much he has changed—aged—over the last two decades. Cassandra wonders if the slowness with which he gets into the passenger seat has anything to do with the bullet that tore into his gut.

When he looks at her and says her name, she remembers why she knew, even as they passed each other in the halls of that doomed facility in darkest Wales, that he is a good man. The calm warmth of his face makes her feel as though she is a sight for sore eyes. She feels guilty now for her secret shock at his grey hair and wizened face. *What else did I expect?*

"I wish we were meeting under better circumstances," she says.

"It's okay," he replies, "What can I help you

with?"

"I want to talk about what goes on in that place in Wales,"

He moves back in the passenger seat a little, his lips pursing almost imperceptibly, his brow furrowing, and he says nothing.

"I didn't have clearance for much then," she continues, "but people would talk to you. You were well on your way to being at the top of your game," It feels vulgar to flatter him. "All I heard at the time was that there was some experimental fuel and propulsion system; nothing of all the other work,"

"I think I know where you're going with this, Cassandra," he says, "But I'm not sure I can help," Cassandra sits back and stops talking. "The whole world is searching for the same answer," he says, "*What happened on 3/19?*"

It is strange to Cassandra that he says *the same answer* and not *the answer to the same question*. She wonders if it is a slip of the tongue or something else. Any subtle nuance in his language is a clue. She sits quietly. So does he. He is a man who has done his work in the world and has now withdrawn. *But is he at peace?*

"I do need to know what happened to the nukes, but there's something else first," she reveals, "and I have evidence it's all connected,"

He is unsurprised when she tells him the nukes weren't taken out by "satellite-mounted lasers" nor that no-one at NATO, the joint intelligence community nor any individual government appears to know what stopped them. He appears to know more than he is letting on. She tells him about the blast doors of the launch control capsule, and the wreckage at the MedStar hospital in D.C.

"Is there anyone from those days at the MoD that you trust, who would know about this stuff?" she asks.

He exhales, and looks out of the window at the carpark.

"After the raid," he says, "I had *trust* issues," His tone carries an awareness of the understated nature of his words. "I'm not on good terms with anyone from then," He looks to her with searching eyes. "In 2010, after sixteen years, I was diagnosed with PTSD, because of that night,"

"I had no idea,"

"No, of course. I've been getting help on-and-off since then. Now I run a peer-support group for people like us,"

She decides not to respond to this last part—if it helps his trust in her to believe she's wounded by the same events, so be it. He doesn't need to know about Munich.

"That's great, David," she says, hiding her disappointment.

"Why is it so important to you personally?" he asks.

"Okay, look," she says, "For more years than I care to remember, I've been tracking the individual who went on to perpetrate 3/19," There's no need to tell him how much it's cost her. "But he's still out there, and he's planning his next strike. We have no idea where he is, when he's planning to strike or how to stop him,"

"You know *what* he's planning?"

"If we don't stop him, it will spell the end of the world as we know it: The single greatest loss of life and stability in living memory," she decides to go for check-mate, with her best theory based on his letters and the information for which Ali gave his life: "He has *dozens* of weapons-grade, plutonium-infused bombs around the world, which he plans to detonate simultaneously," O'Connor's face slowly drops. "When the time comes, they will be strategically placed for maximum damage to the world's infrastructure—economies, political organisation, food sources, and life,"

The car is silent for 27 seconds as she watches the clock on the dash.

Finally, he asks, "What's the hospital in America got to do with it?"

"That's what I'm trying to find out. It seems to me that whatever is behind these *blast holes* or whatever they are, is the same, and my best chance at a lead. What is bursting through walls and nuclear blast doors and why? The hostage-taker at that hospital—he was at the far end of one of these things, with his gun twisted up like a pipe-cleaner. If that means some kind of new technology is out in the wild, then someone with that tech might be able to lead me to the seller, which in turn leads me to my man, if he used it at the launch base,"

"That's a lot of assumptions," replies the scientist.

"David, we have to stop this,"

"What if this technology doesn't lead you to your terrorist?"

"Then at least it might still do some good for the world in the right hands," The fact that O'Connor is still asking questions is a good sign. She prods once more: "We don't have much time. He could strike at any moment,"

O'Connor closes his eyes and bows his head. When he opens them again, he says, "We need to do this in my lab,"

For a man in retirement, Professor O'Connor's lab has an incredible array of equipment. It looks as though one of the labs at Edgewood has been airlifted and dropped into his house, with electron microscopes, centrifuges, refrigerators, computers, all blazing from the white striplights overhead. He must have one hell of an energy bill. But, for all the cold, clinical futurism, it smells like the grazed knees and TCP antiseptic of a school matron's office.

On the way over, O'Connor said nothing more than to offer directions. Now he sits at his wheely chair by a microscope. Despite her eagerness for him to get going, or perhaps because of it, Cassandra sits, taking the only other seat in the room—a folding plastic chair with a wipeable cushion.

"If I'm going to do this," he says, "I need a tea," and, with that, he gets up again, "Can I get you anything?"

"No. Thank you,"

"Don't touch anything,"

He leaves. He walks through a door into his house to make his cup of tea while Cassandra sits wondering what he could possibly be able to tell her. She stays exactly where she is until he returns with his drink and a plate of biscuits.

He sits in his chair with the steaming cup on a coaster on the desk to his side. He closes his eyes, and takes a deep and laboured breath. Anyone could see how much he is overcoming. Opening his eyes again, he speaks.

"You remember the civilian woman and her baby you saved that night," he isn't asking a question. "In the accident, she got mixed up with what those men stole. It was a top secret virus, called C-416. It's a long story; found in a desert on a meteorite, commandeered by the British Army, shipped to us at the MoD. That was what arrived a few nights before with the soldiers. When the vials smashed, she inhaled the airborne antigens of the virus. You thought it was an experimental fuel didn't you? That rumour was right in a way,"

"I don't follow,"

O'Connor gets up and walks a couple of steps and opens a stainless steel freezer cabinet, the size of a microwave.

"Right away, at the cellular level we were observing micro-instances of quantum levitation --" Before the icy mist clears, he removes something from the freezer. "-- which gave rise to a theory on frictionless travel, hence the stories of a fuel or propulsion system in that shipment,"

What he's holding looks like something from a butcher's shop, like a piece of tanned skin stretched taut on a wire rack. He places it on the desk while she watches in stupefied silence.

"This is a skin graft grown from that baby," The thing takes on a wholly more macabre light. His story jumps around so much, he's almost impossible to follow but she dares not interrupt the flow. Now he opens a drawer in the desk and removes a long lighter and hands it to Cassandra. "Please burn it," By now, she would play along just to help him get to the point. She proceeds to ignite the lighter under the skin. "You can throw almost anything at this sample and it will take the energy and either dissipate it harmlessly through its surroundings or send it back," No matter how close she holds it and waves the lighter around, Cassandra can see that the flame has absolutely no effect on the skin. "Do you notice how it even offers some protection to the frost that has formed on it from its time in the freezer?"

"So this is some sort of armour?" she asks in an attempt to catch up.

"No, not like that. This is the woman who saved the world,"

The information takes a moment to sink in.

"The baby? With the virus?"

"She won't forgive me for this," he says to himself and holds out his hand to retrieve the lighter. He begins packing away the freakish skin graft.

"You're telling me that baby, a woman now, is going around with invulnerable skin, punching holes in walls?"

"And catching nuclear missiles," he adds, "She can fly,"

There are times in life when reality seems to scramble, which is maybe what's happened to O'Connor's brain. This whole mad scientist routine is all a little too believable. He has spent the last twenty years locked away in his own garage, burning bits of leather on wire racks and fantasising about an omnipotent saviour to take away his troubles. This is a man who was, however, entirely cogent until they arrived at his house, but who is now talking about a flying woman. Perhaps he has chosen the baby for his fantasy because of the guilt he feels in not being able to save her.

"You think I'm mad,"

"You mean she flies some sort of jetpack or light aircraft?"

"No, like with a cape and tights,"

"David, I'm sorry. I shouldn't have bothered you. You've gone through so much," She goes to get up.

"Cassandra," he says firmly, "Why do you think those men slaughtered so many for those vials? Do you think I could have continued working for the MoD if I were insane? They funded my research; they bought all of this when I retired because they want me to keep going," She is still in her seat. Something compels her to stay. "You are more a part of this than you ever realised, Cassandra. You brought the baby and her mother to me. Together, we saved their lives,"

* * *

Only days ago, Professor McAvoy had his final in-person session with a patient before he must undertake his final leg. He delivered her such a well-rehearsed speech that now he remembers it perfectly.

"Let me take you on a journey," the

professor began, "To an eternity of wellness. Where your body and soul are perfectly contained and held in balance. The ebb and flow of nourishment, like the tide on the shore, sustains you. The beating of your mother's heart is all-encompassing. Her voice is carried down through her spine to you. The sounds of her digesting. Breathing. Laughing. Snoring. Humming. All surrounding you and all as they should be. This is all you have ever known.

"Gradually, the comforting darkness becomes a luminous theatre of deep, soft pinks, oranges and blues. The theatre walls will sometimes bear loud noises and sudden jolts from some world beyond but even these are acceptable in their way, for they are within the limits of your body's expectations. Millions of years of evolution have prepared you for every experience so far.

"This is the timeless equilibrium you knew in your mother's womb. And, at the time of birth, the explosion of light, the cacophony of sound, the bristle of cool dry air, the rush of oxygen to your lungs; these are all right too. The eruption of your own voice—your *scream*—as it pierces the air and all other noise, fits with your correct path. Your natural path from which you will soon be torn thread by thread.

"Newborn, you are swept away and put on a hard, lifeless scale for weighing, your prickling skin crying out for the warm softness of human contact. After all, your body knows how desperately vulnerable you are, that predators lurk in every shadow of the ancestral cave, as far removed as that is from the beeping, flashing, bustling maternity ward of a modern hospital.

"It's important to recognise that, at birth and for the first few weeks after, you are not fully conscious as we know it. You are aware but only your current state has reality, for you have no capacity for thought and no concept of past or future. This will develop in the coming weeks but do not misunderstand: time offers no consolation for what is to come.

"You are hurriedly scrubbed, wrapped in dry cloth and finally, if you are afforded this one mercy, placed on your mother, desperate to connect through your straightjacket, as if the tightness of the blanket offers anything like a human embrace. At least you hear her, smell her, feel her movement. Her voice, her breath, her heartbeat all offer sweet comfort and familiarity. As she begins to doze and the two of you ease into your shared rhythm, you are plucked off her and deposited in a hard, plastic box, an immeasurable, unseeable distance from her side. While she sleeps, you are left to suffer stillness for the first time in the eternity of your experience. Every moment of your life until now has swayed to the natural rhythm of your mother's body. Now, the world is motionless. It must be nauseating. Of course, you cry. And you cry and you cry. Helpless, you must be reunited with the rest of your whole world—your mother—and the safety she represents.

"With luck, you will be picked up and, with no sense of time, you just know you are in arms and all is well in that moment. As soon as your body calms, you are put back in your box, for a quiet baby surely has no needs.

"Your screams carry no hope because hope is built on an idea of the future that in turn relies on a concept of time. It is instinct that drives you to call out, every fibre of your being burning with unquenched need. Every time you wake, you wake in this unresponsive and infinite hell. Your casket has no movement, no warmth, no familiarity, no softness, no natural sound but your own desperation. No sense. No hope.

"After some months, your mother will begin to sleep train you, or in other words to torture you into conformity with an unnatural, incomprehensible schedule. You will scream until your lungs are an inferno, your skin yearns to the point of burning, your throat is sore and, eventually, you will weaken with exhaustion and be able to cry no more. In your muted torment, you open and close your fists, desperate to clasp onto something living. Rolling your head from side to side in search of a nurturing breast but finding nothing. Your only salvation is when exhaustion fully takes hold and you fall into fitful sleep. And then you awake again and repeat your whole personal hell. Eventually, your very nature is over-written by this experience and you learn that crying is futile. Your internal world is of no consequence to those around you with the power to soothe. Better to conserve your energy and not add more physical pain to your torture. Even when you begin to develop the idea of time passing, that there may be a future and a past, your short time alive stretches out your agonising minutes into a lifetime.

"By then, you know that life is unspeakably empty and that your needs are nothing. This is just the beginning of what our so-called civilisation inflicts on us and, when we dare to rebel, when we dare to reconnect to our own true voice, we are ignored or cast aside, called *sick* and prescribed drugs. This, my friend, is just the beginning."

The grey old professor paused, almost motionless, his hand on Patient M's hunched shoulder. They sat opposite each other in the semi-darkness, the room heavy with the sound of silent sobbing.

"So which is more sick, the society or the individual?"

As a student and a young man, Terrence

travelled to Central America to observe an almost uncontacted tribe that had been recorded by oil prospectors in the area. He had nothing they wanted, not supplies nor technology but they had accepted him temporarily for his medical skills. He was there to conduct an observation on a mother and her baby boy, from birth for as long as they would allow him. When he arrived, he found there were eight children ranging from newborn to sixteen and the pairing of mother to child was almost impossible since every mother seemed to be mother to the whole tribe. The familial structures became only clear to him and his *civilised* sensibilities when the families retired in the evenings to their individual homes of husbands and wives. They were a society content; only un-smiling when they were concentrating. They worked hard but wanted for nothing, and had seemingly no ambition beyond the simplicity of their lives.

For the first year, until Terrence's departure, the baby spent almost every waking moment in a sling on her back or front depending on what work she was doing. Even for feeding, she simply slipped the baby boy around in his sling to attach to her breast. The mother communicated with her baby by words and touch, massaging and stroking the baby boy's body. He would make satisfied gurgling noises as she did this, and he stretched and moved his arms and legs as she tickled his body. When he was held, comforted and nourished at his mother's breast, his whole body would relax and he would become limp, with a look of contentment on his face. At times such as this, the baby could introject his mother as an internal holding mother. In the baby's desire for the breast, his need to be given milk, and the resultant soothing and holding from his mother, the student could see clearly that the baby boy felt understood in both mind and body.

Tragically, the baby boy and his ilk were a dying breed. Civilised society today is so detached that infants' experience of this kind of connection is growing rare to the point of extinction. While some modern mothers may tend to her babies with the kind of reverie and attunement that that the young student saw in the jungle, none of that can survive the mother's abandonment when she returns to work after six months, before the infant's brain has fully developed the functional areas responsible for emotional regulation and "self-soothing", and the infant's learnt helplessness at the futility of crying out, his or her compliance, is mistaken for contentness. Or when the child is "sleep trained". Or their internal worlds are otherwise utterly disavowed because they are "only children" or it's time to "grow up".

Patient M, a girl when the Professor first met her, in her forties now, was the Professor's first shocking introduction to the impact of continued misattunement between mother and infant in modern society. He remembered thinking when he first saw M how friendly she looked with her bright red hair, wide eyes and smile.

Her early experiences, however, had formed the core belief that her emotions were unbearable to others and herself. M had not had the experience to develop the ability to take in a good feed and let her body collapse safely in the arms of a mother who is holding her in body and mind. Unlike the baby tribesmen, her early life experience of being deprived and ignored by her parents has dominated her experience of the world.

The desire to be received, understood, loved and accepted by another is profoundly powerful, but so too is the feeling of despair, of deep aloneness and of silencing our own needs, emotional states, our inner world, because we have not been met. While the therapist can learn to reach to the deepest part of his or her own personality to find empathic attunement to the physical and emotional experience of the patient, the emotional deprivation of generations has become a pandemic, too vast and wide-spread. It creates an ever worsening spiral of transgenerational trauma. There is only one way, in the Professor's mind, to break that cycle and end the suffering that engulfs the whole civilised world.

As a child, he remembers watching some Buddhist monks on a street in Paris. He was walking with his father when he saw them, to or from the hotel.

He dared not ask his father whether they might stand and watch the monks in whatever they were doing, which was beginning to draw a crowd, but he tried to shorten his pace to get a glimpse between the grown-up bodies, at little slices of the scene beyond: of deep red and yellow ochre robes, stooped figures and rather suddenly bright colours in wicker baskets.

"Come along, Terrence," says his father in a clipped tone.

Little Terrence double-steps, careful not to scuff his shoes on the pavement nor to kick his father's heels as he switches to his right side to see better.

That evening, over dinner at the hotel restaurant, where he remembers now that his mother is there, he plucks up the courage to speak.

"Father?" he asks and his father looks up at him with smiling eyes, "Who were those red and yellow men on the Champs-Élysées today?"

"Buddhist monks," His father has finished

his meal and is smoking his pipe. Terrence remembers the woody smell well. "They are practising focus,"

While this is by no means all he wants to know, it is a wondrous gem to which he will keep tight hold until tomorrow.

"Will they be there again tomorrow?"

"Yes, I expect so,"

They are there the next day and it seems to Terrence that his father slows down just fractionally as they pass—a gift to his learning son. This time, Terrence sees that they appear to be making a pattern on the wide pavement using coloured sand. He counts red, yellow, orange, green and blue filled baskets but he cannot see what it is they are actually making with their pattern. It fills him with excitement for what he might see the next day and soon, the mystery of the monks and their magical sand drawing outshines all else on the trip. It remains his only memory of that year of his life and his most important memory of Paris.

Day Five is Terrence's last day in Paris. He is determined to ask his father to see the sand picture but, to his fortune, his father has already thought of that and they are going out early specifically to see the monks. Terrence couldn't be happier or more in love with his father than he is now. He restrains his legs so that his excitement might not fizz over and cause them to carry him into a run ahead of his father's steps. His father waits at the back of the omnipresent crowd while Terrence politely squeezes through pressed trousers and skirts to the front.

There, he sees it for the first time and he feels as though he has stumbled deep down into it like an unwinding multicoloured rabbit hole into the centre of a warm, knowing universe. The portal is framed by many windows or doors repeated in a full circle, but no two the same. Around the banks, just inside of it, are blue or red flowers with no centre or separate petals but nonetheless, they are flowers. There are swirls too that look like they might come alive and pulse and wriggle in time to some secret shared rhythm. As he begins to feel lost in it again, the floral and geometric forms drawing him into the centre, it feels as though he has found something very important.

A school bell rings but he doesn't really listen. It feels unimportant, until the monks, who appear to have been standing around their work praying, begin wiping it out with brushes. Terrence's heart sinks as the monks brush the sand into the centre, mingling all the colours into one fine pile, stroke by stroke. The portal closes up and just as something is lost another is found inside himself. In the end, the monks collect the sand and begin offering pinches of it to the people in the crowd. It's gone but he can have a part of it.

Now, sitting on a bench along the broad French avenue, the Professor fingers the copper ring on his right hand and gently flips it open. It contains the murky mixture of sand from the monks' sacred mandala. He flips it closed and packs his journal into a water-tight ziplock, which in turn goes into his backpack, which itself goes into a plastic wrap, tied with string. Ahead may be his hardest journey to date. Tomorrow, at dawn, he will be on a beach, his feet in sand, staring down at a dinghy, no doubt with too many passengers and not enough life jackets. On his fake passport, he has travelled relatively unmolested through Europe, but there is only one way to make it back to England as a man hunted by the world he seeks to cure.

As healers, if we are committed to repair, to seeking understanding and attunement, we must bear the coming destruction as absolutely necessary for a dying world.

* * *

On the train, Lucy is haunted by another bad dream. It was so real, so loaded with emotion, it's another one that she can't be sure is not a memory.

In the dream she is very young—perhaps only three. She's with her dad in the garage. He's urging her on, saying, "Go on, Lucy. You can do it,"

The dream jumps ahead a little and she's holding something heavy and awkward over her head. It's cold, smooth and hard and, as she looks up, she realises, at three years old, she's lifting a freezer over her head.

Suddenly, there's a painful screeching and a slit of light burns into the garage as the door opens up from the outside. The last thing she sees are her mother's feet under the door before the freezer falls down on top of Lucy in a shower of frost and ice.

Her mum's voice penetrates her whole being, "You stupid man!"

"At least I want her to fulfil her potential!"

It twists Lucy's stomach like a wrench.

"Look what you've done! Was it worth it?"

Lucy's mum wanted so badly for her daughter to be normal. One school sports day, Lucy fell over in her race and, for a long time since, she thought that her mum looked pleased, like some sort of wicked witch, who'd fed her a poisoned apple. Her mum has always been anxious, a worrier, sometimes overprotective to the point of suffocation, but other times inexplicably cold and distant. That night, the night of the sports day, Lucy's parents had one of their blazing rows. All she remembers from that fight, like most of them, is the horrible, muffled sound of venomous, indecipherable voices through the floor, like ringing in her ears. But she could guess what it was about—her dad never wanted Lucy to be normal—he saw the word as beneath her. *Average is a dirty word,* he would say.

By now, Lucy has reached David's front door. She isn't sure whether the doorbell has worked but she doesn't want to risk ringing twice. She gives it a full three minutes of no response before awkwardly knocking. The frost on the ground and the mist in front of her nose are a reminder that it's probably pretty chilly today and her heavy coat and woolly hat aren't completely ludicrous. She's been wearing hats more often since 3/19. Finally there's movement on the other side of the frosted glass.

David opens the door and a gust of warmth greets her.

"Lucy," he smiles, stepping aside and welcoming her into his home, "It's good to see you,"

"You too," she smiles back.

Lucy steps off the quiet suburban street into David's home for the hundredth time and the papered walls seem to say *welcome back.* While she kicks off her boots, David is already in the kitchen making his cup of tea and her hot chocolate. She hangs up her coat, keeping her hat on, and pads down the carpeted hallway to the lounge where she drops herself on the old brown chesterfield and curls up.

"Did I say it's good to see you?" he says again.

He enters with a tray holding the steaming cups and a plate of Digestives. She smiles and thanks him as she takes her drink and three, then four biscuits.

"Sorry it's been so long --" she begins.

"Nine months,"

"Yeah. You got my message though?"

"Yes, thanks for letting me know you were still alive,"

She can't tell if he's just annoyed or angry. She doesn't know where to start. On the train over, she felt like she rehearsed every possible route of conversation but now that all just evaporates. She stares into the steaming chocolate and, after a while, begins in the simplest place.

"People aren't supposed to be able to do the things my body can do,"

She recalls the weeks of news coverage following 3/19. Every outlet said the warheads were never actually armed in the first place. This was followed by constant discussion of the defence protocol that kicked in the moment the inert warheads were launched. By now, every member of the public is a rocket scientist. Lucy knows the warheads were armed. She knows because she felt them turn her bones to jelly when she touched them. But the part about the defence protocol that would have brought them down safely were it not for her is too convincing. With that doubt comes the dread of what could have happened had she not been so lucky. She dropped a nuclear missile on Tokyo. She feels herself being pulled down to the waters of Tokyo Bay again.

Having sat quietly, as if reading her mind, David finally speaks.

"That bumf about lasers and inert warheads is rubbish you know," he says before taking a sip, "Typical government cover-up. If you couldn't do the things you can do, none of us would be here," his voice wavers, "Thousands of lives would have been lost, the whole planet would have been plunged into a nuclear winter,"

It doesn't make her feel any better.

"I'm afraid," She looks to David, then around the room and back to her mug, unable to fix on anything for long. "I don't have what it takes to be the person everyone expects me to be,"

"What do you mean?"

She continues, looking into her mug as if it holds the answers: "When your dad imagines you're some sort of prodigy, and you know deep down there's no way you can live up to his expectations, you self-sabotage to the point that you don't even know who you are anymore, because you just needed an excuse for not being the best, most beautiful, most intelligent, strongest one. All the while, there's a nagging fear that his love is contingent on you being someone you're not,"

She takes a deep breath and lets her shoulders drop. She removes her glasses and pinches the bridge of her nose. She's spent her entire life trying to be the perfect daughter for both of them.

David says nothing but, if she didn't know better, she could swear he just looked at his watch.

"Sometimes," she begins again, "I feel like it was all a dream and I can't really fly at all. I feel rooted to the ground like I can't move,"

David thoughtfully puts down his mug and stands.

"Let's go to the lab," he says.

On the way to what is actually his garage, David goes into lecture mode.

"Like proto-mitochondria in the earliest life, C-416 is fully assimilated into your cellular structure. Virtually the moment you were infected in-utero, the xeno-endosymbiont became an organelle. It wrote itself into your DNA. It isn't going anywhere. What we do know, however, as evidenced by the lack of manifestation until that moment of extreme duress at university, is that there is probably a psychosomatic component to the activation of your powers," None of this is reassuring. "Look," he pauses at the door from the hallway to the garage and turns to Lucy, "You have to realise that the most important thing is that you neutralised all those warheads that day. That you lasted so long and held off the effects of rapid decompression as you flew in and out of the Earth's mesosphere is testament to your personal strength and willpower,"

"I --"

"Lucy," he cuts in, "You have no reason to doubt yourself," He puts a hand on her shoulder and quickly removes it. "The world needs you to be confident—it needs you to take the right course. Now more than ever,"

"Why are you talking like this?"

He looks up from his feet to meet her eyes, his hand still on the door handle.

"There are some people here to meet you,"

No. Her world rumbles, knocking everything into an alien angle.

"What have you done?" she asks gravely.

"I wouldn't tell them who you are but -- you need to listen,"

She could run, for sure, but this isn't the man she's come to know over the last few years. Something must have really rattled him, must be really important for him to have betrayed her trust like this. But that doesn't stop it being a betrayal.

"Here," He reaches inside his cardigan and pulls out something white; the mask she made a lifetime ago. "I thought you might want this,"

It's an ugly thing. She'd had the idea to glue sections of a plastic Batman mask to the inside of a white lycra cowl to make her look authoritative and strong. The plastic scratches her cheeks, nose and brow but there is something powerful in the anonymity. Neither of them says anything as David opens the door into the garage.

Waiting for them, a pensive woman stands with her hands on her hips and a man sits very upright on the edge of David's desk. They both wear grey suits. Wearing the mask, Lucy feels ridiculous.

"Thank you for meeting us," the woman begins, reaching out her hand as if this were entirely normal.

With no real option, she shakes the woman's hand.

"I'm Cassandra Bryce and I work for the British Intelligence Service,"

The man stands and nods, a picture of neutrality, sizing her up maybe.

"This is my colleague, Daniel,"

Lucy says nothing yet. She wonders how good voice identification is in real life. She wonders whether they'll hold up something seemingly innocuous, like an ID card, and it'll take a photo of her retinas so they can find her next time she goes through airport security. She wonders what would happen to her life if these people knew who she really is.

For the second time this afternoon, someone reads her mind.

"We're not here to expose you or use you," says the woman.

"Nice mask by the way," says the man, as he passes the woman an iPad.

"We need your help,"

The woman unlocks the iPad and holds it out to Lucy. She doesn't take it—she's not wearing gloves—so the woman breaches the air between them and comes over to her side to show her the screen. It shows the kind of scene commonplace on evening news of the Middle East: charred rubble; twisted, exploded vehicles; the remains of people's lives. The woman swipes through the gallery as she talks.

"Iraq. Syria. Afghanistan,"

The images are increasingly hard to look at and finally the thing she was building up to starts: the wailing mothers, dead children, limbs, devastation. The woman senses Lucy's discomfort but she doesn't stop.

"Imagine this were every city in the world," The slideshow reveals a world map covered in red dots, "And imagine far greater devastation,"

Now it's the man's turn to speak:

"Hundreds of thousands dead. More mutilated. Millions sick," he says, "The world in collapse,"

While Lucy squints to count the dots, Agent Bryce slides her finger across the screen to reveal the black crater of the launch base in Montana. Lucy's heart jumps. She glances at the man, who hasn't moved and has his eyes firmly on her. David must have left at some point because it's just the three of them now. She wants to ask what all this is about.

"This was just the beginning," the woman says. She looks Lucy dead in the eyes. "You made sure he failed on 3/19, didn't you?" Lucy wonders the extent of what David's told them versus what they've figured out. "And then you became *The Hand of God*," she says as she swipes the iPad to show Lucy the hand indent, "This *is* your hand I understand,"

Unable to continue her awkward mutism any longer, Lucy finally asks them what they need.

She isn't convinced by her own attempt at an authoritative voice but neither of the agents bats an eyelid. Agent Bryce just exhales, and smiles with her eyes.

"You got yourself involved and put yourself at the centre of this," Bryce says, "And now we need you to end it,"

Lucy fears that they think she knows more than she really does or is more capable.

"How?" she asks.

"By being bait," the man quietly interjects.

"We've been tracking a global network of *dirty bombs*," says the woman, "– do you know what those are?" Lucy nods. "The network is composed of suicide bombers ready to simultaneously go out and blow the world back to the Dark Ages," Lucy is in way over her head. The woman goes on, "But something happened to change all that," There's that almost imperceptible, knowing smile in her eyes again, "You came along and created a new narrative—a symbol of hope and faith—something totally antithetical to this cult's belief-system. He's looking for symbols to destroy—and you are now the biggest one," she raises the iPad again to show the photo of the hand indent, "The *Hand of God* is bad for his messiah complex and he's looking for an opportunity to give them a sign—something big enough that they'll follow him to the end of the Earth. And, if they do, we have no idea how to catch them before it's too late,"

"What exactly do you want me to do?" she asks.

"Presumably, there's more to your costume than that mask," the man says. Lucy grits her teeth. This is ridiculous. But what wouldn't she do to save the world? The man takes a couple of steps closer. "He'll come for you and if, when the time comes, you don't do what's necessary and he wins..." he says, and his expression softens into something more imploring, "If you fail, the world will burn,"

"And if I do nothing," Lucy replies, forgetting her gruff alter ego, "the same thing happens,"

"*But*," says the man, "whatever happens, you must not make a martyr of him,"

There's a pause while the two of them watch to make sure she understands.

"So you'll do it?" the woman asks.

"I have to,"

* * *

Ashley's head is throbbing, her mouth is like a ball of cotton and a dull ache is slithering its way around her body. It's been like this since before she peeled open her eyes this morning and there's no sign of things getting any better. The good news is she's out. Despite everything, she managed to get herself out of bed without the allure of a joint or a drink and got herself to the computer store to clock in. This is a hell of a thing at this time of year. After a long day at work she came here. She looks around the chilly community hall at the half-dozen other losers, victims and societal rejects that always make up this sort of meeting. The room smells of gym mats and coffee breath.

She shifts her weight on the plastic chair and interlocks her fingers around her instant coffee a little tighter. Holding the novelty mug to her lips she puts up a vapour screen between her and the room.

The sad rambling of a guy called Ted breaks through.

"--it's just we talk about the difference between fantasy and reality, like how we gotta remember what's what and, well, what if, you know, there's all these signs that now even *healthy* folk are seeing," He pauses to assess the room but they mostly seem to agree. "Seems like things really do happen for a reason and maybe, after all, someone is looking out for us,"

His prematurely wizened face cracks a battered but daring smile.

"Thanks, Ted," picks up Jacob, the group's supervisor. He introduced himself earlier in a way that reassured Ashley she should keep her distance. She catches his eye and she tugs down her torn denim skirt. "Does anyone think Ted's observation could be an episode trigger?"

There's a lot of scratching, toe-tapping and hand-wringing until --

"Ashley, it's your first time meeting everyone. What do you think?"

Fuck you.

Despite herself, she has an answer ready.

"I think everyone's been saying the same

thing,"

Jacobs's eyes narrow.

"3/19 changed things," she tilts her head to Ted, "I don't know the guy but he doesn't look like he's communing with the pixies,"

If Ted's tripping into a psychotic episode, then so's Ashley and she just doesn't fucking deserve that right now.

After a moment, the chick with lupus speaks.

"I was sitting in the park the other day,"

There's a muffled snigger—an in-joke.

"After 9/11, I couldn't really look up at the sky. Every time I heard or saw a plane, I thought of those news pictures," She rubs her raw eyes as if clearing foggy glasses. "But after 3/19, I was rushing outside. I look up at the sky all the time. I was looking up the other day in the park and I was like -- it was hopeful. Most people don't really want to look up at the sky but I like it,"

There's a general murmuring of agreement and nodding. It's true—the hope part.

Part of her knows it's all bullshit but she can't help wondering about *The Hand of God*.

It all started with that nuke in Japan and the handprint—or what looked like a handprint. It looked like a handprint to a bunch of people anyway. Then there was that gay British pilot who went crazy and ended up a religious nut, going on talk-shows wearing one of those t-shirts and arguing with priests and science nerds. He swore he saw an angel. The British media said he was suffering from PTSD but Ashley's met enough war vets to know that ain't PTSD. Plus, she has history with the British government—good reason not to trust them. The really weird thing though was Beijing. They say the speed of the nuke tearing through the morning smog caused some sort of light display like the Aurora Borealis—or Aurora Australis being in the southern hemisphere. You'd have to be a moron to believe that one though.

After the meeting, she makes a quick exit, avoiding Jacob's gaze in particular. She bets that parasite's into some really kinky shit.

It must have been five years ago, leaving a place like this that she saw the professor for the last time in-person. She darted from the backdoor to her strategically parked car and jumped in, slamming the door behind her. There she sat for a moment, resting her head back, breathing and looking out the windshield. Hope is a weird and fleeting thing but something about the lit street had a magical air even then, before 3/19. She watched the vapour billow up from a manhole, following it until it mingled with the grey-orange clouds on the black sky. A looming face began to form before she rubbed her dry eyes and looked away to her mom's photo on the dash. She put two fingers to her lips and then --

"Hello, Ashley,"

She spun around, instinctively kicking away from her attacker, the steering wheel jamming into her back.

The faceless silhouette of a man was sitting calmly, erectly, in the back of her car.

"We're due a session, my dear," his British accent always carried a certain authority. As her panic subsided and she recognised the Professor, she became no less tense. "I'm sorry to frighten you but you left the door unlocked and it was awfully chilly outside," he explained, "Shall we go back to your apartment or would you like to talk here?"

Everything below her chest and above her knees was jello.

At her apartment, she fumbled the key in the lock.

She felt his breath on her.

She hugged a coffee.

He was somewhere behind her. She had her eyes closed while she leant back on her creaky couch.

"How are you feeling, Ashley?"

Groggy.

"You've been taking prescribed poison again,"

Help me.

"You need to help yourself,"

Help me. Please.

"Why have you strayed from the mission?"

I got rid of the drone.

"I did it for you," she said, "I wanted to show you. You don't need anyone else to fix the world,"

No, wait. That's not what happened. This was before he went away, long before 3/19. But 3/19 was her idea, *wasn't it?*

"You've gotten lost and confused, allowed others to distort your view," Was he moving around her apartment? "Do you not see that the world needs you?"

I don't know.

"I see that you haven't opened my package. I had it delivered to you especially but, if you don't want it, there are others who I visit,"

I want it.

She felt a weight with rounded sides being placed on her lap and opened her eyes. It was a small metal jar, like a medicine bottle. She could see liquid inside. She went to tear off the brown tape around the cap with what is left of her nails. *No*, that's not how it happened either, he'd mailed it to her. She'd been on her own when she opened it. He had given her some medicine then though, but something different.

His voice was in her ear, "Not yet," he said, "You are right: No-one real is left. Just as you said, it's just you, me and a few others. When it's time, this will be the only way to start again,"

Only the watchers are left.

Drink me, Alice.

The memory leaves her shaken, but she's stirred by some shouting to her side as she leaves the community centre.

"I said, *the fuck you looking at?*"

It was one of the guys from the group, having a go at a stiff who chose the wrong day to take a detour through this part of town.

"Shut up," she says, raising her voice just enough to be heard, "You complete dick,"

His head spins as if it will fly off, "*What?*"

"Just go home, dude," she mutters.

As she stands in the road between the community centre and her car, some of the others, including Ted, are gathering around the dick, turning him around, trying to reason with him and take him back inside.

"Thanks, ma'ame" says the stiff, "But I could have taken care of this myself,"

Sounds military, she thinks. And then he takes a step towards her, as the guy from the group is finally escorted inside. She knows the group is just beyond the threshold of the door behind her and Jacob will be on them any second to find out what's going on. And she needs to get away.

"Okay, whatever," is all she can think to say as she unlocks her car and opens the door. She knows she should go home now, but after what just happened she could really do with a drink, in a dark bar with some oppressively loud music. Or maybe it's that memory still haunting her and making her afraid to go home.

This establishment is dark, has oppressively loud music and has drinks. *Check.* She downs another shot at the bar and then sips her vodka coke. She lets the chemical scent of it gently burn the insides of her nostrils while she scans the bottles of all shapes and colours behind the bar. She doesn't like that there's no mirror behind the bottles so she can't see who's behind her or around her. Looking to her left, there's a guy standing at the bar, one person away from her, with a really stupid mustache. Like, who has a moustache? Especially a guy in what, his thirties? Her granddad probably has a moustache. *Oh shit.* It's the stiff from earlier.

She tries to turn but suddenly the bar has

become so crowded that the people piled behind her are blocking her way.

"Hi again," he says, right up in her ear, before backing away so she can see him fully, standing right next to her, expecting her to care.

"Oh, hi,"

"Can I buy you a drink? You know, for saving me today,"

"Sure," Never one to turn down a free drink.

"Oh, I didn't follow you here by the way, like I'm not a stalker. I live around here,"

"I didn't think that,"

She did.

"I'm Steve,"

He literally put out his hand to shake, like human customs are new to him.

But she shook back, tepidly, because that's what you do.

"Ashley,"

They chat a bit, standing at the bar, getting in the way. She's not really sure what they chat about, because she's listening but only enough to keep the conversation going, and she's getting a little tipsy. They've put away a lot but she can see that he's a little like her—he can keep up. The evening gets to a point where she can tell it only goes one of two ways. One: She calls it a night, gets in a cab and tries to be sensible. Two: She stays out and allows herself to have some fun.

She talks a good talk and she can put on a show when she has to, but she hasn't done this for longer than she cares to figure. *So why not tonight?*

They both stay out until he's leaning in and his hand is on her thigh while they're talking and she can feel that she wants it to go further. They go back to her place. There's no coffee.

The sex is sex. She doesn't connect to it. It makes her feel good and it gives her a release. Not a total release, although that happens eventually. She feels simultaneously fed by it and empty. She wishes it were different. She wishes so bad that she could just really feel what other people feel—connected, safe, loved, held, understood, accepted, received. At least that she could get out of her head and feel free. She wishes for a moment, when he's inside her, that it would never end and she could hold on forever. But no. When she's done, the idea of him staying over makes her skin crawl.

And now, while he's reluctantly looking for his shirt on the floor, he stops dead in his tracks. She thought she'd gotten rid of it.

* * *

At home, Lucy sits on the edge of the sofa, holding her mask, struggling to catch her breath. The mask has a hole in the back for a ponytail that no longer exists. Suddenly, sitting feels like the worst thing she could be doing and she jumps up, scraping her hands through her short hair. She tries and tries again to flatten it. She paces the kitchen. For some reason, she imagines her mother's accusing voice, *"What are you doing?"* The voice she heard whenever she was caught doing something she shouldn't—something that happened maybe three times in her compliant life. Those four words, however, or the shame they anticipated, had the power to freeze her in her tracks. Her spine would turn rigid like it had been shot with ice. There was never a battle between fight and flight for Lucy. Instead, she would freeze while her head spun with every possible outcome about to befall her, desperately trying to figure out a way to make everything okay. This time, she's been found out by much scarier people with much bigger consequences. But, like her mum, they say they're on her side.

She wonders now whether David was ever really her friend or just a scientist through and through, observing, recording, manipulating variables. He pushed her to fly, pushed her to test her limits and now, this.

When she looks in the mirror, she sees what she's always seen: a girl lost, torn between her head and the outside world.

She wrenches herself out of the mirror and forces herself to look at this moment and what's really just happened. She knows what she has to do and can't understand why it's so hard.

She used to watch so many superhero movies with her dad in which the hero would resist their destiny through the entire first act. She always found it ridiculous, and unbelievably frustrating, that someone wouldn't want to be a superhero. The reality isn't so simple now. It's not the threat to her life that worries her most but the threat she poses to everyone around her. She has no idea where to start. The world is going to either assume she's Wonder Woman and, therefore, perfectly infallible, or they're going to tear her down—or both. She thinks of the countless celebrities the UK media gloriously positions on a pedestal for the very purpose of later destroying them. The mob turns on them the moment they can expose something that doesn't fit the impossible image they have created. They'll be watching every single move she makes, waiting for a mistake. She's not sure she can handle the shame of being terrible. She could easily make any situation worse, because she simply doesn't know what she's doing and can't do everything people will expect her to be able to do. In real life, things don't conveniently fall into place. In her experience it tends to be the exact opposite; that if something can go wrong, it will. But this is exactly the kind of thinking that always gets her stuck. She looks away from the mirror again.

She knows she's at risk of going in circles. When she left David's house, she knew what she had to do—she has to stick to that now and remember that feeling. The world needs her. Fifteen people died at the MedStar hospital because she left it too late before deciding to go.

She's going to need more than this white mask she grips so tightly in her fist.

A few days later, the equipment and materials have all arrived. James thought the packages arriving were Christmas presents, legitimising her secrecy as she stowed them away under the bed and in the wardrobe. He's going to be disappointed.

The first thing she unboxes and sets up is a police scanner radio bought on eBay—*the superhero starter kit* she thinks to herself. The best place for it is in her bedside table, where she knows James would never go. When she opens the drawer, there's a clattering, scraping noise as something falls down the back of the table. She imagines the necklace he got her, with the compass, now wedged forever with dust and tangles of hair. Next in her deliveries, some cans of spray-paint: red and white. Holding one in each hand, she thinks about the importance of symbols, doubting her choice for the hundredth time. It wouldn't be good enough to dress in black and hide in the shadows. What she's creating needs to draw attention and needs to stand for something. After dismissing a bullseye again and again, she resigns herself to what feels instinctively right, if a little clichéd. She'll paint it later, when she can't put it off any longer. Next, she tries on the neoprene boots and gloves, which make her feel even clumsier than usual. What's next is the ultimate concession to symbolism. She pulls the broad, shallow box out from under the bed and tears it carefully open—the habit of someone always nagged by the thought that a purchase might need to be returned. The fabric is thinner than she'd expected and there's enough for spares but it's a nice red, for a cape. She refolds it carefully and places it back in the box, nestled in tissue paper. She takes a deep breath.

Costumes are always easier in movies. The stars also have bodies sculpted to be shown off under skin-tight, paper-thin material. Despite herself, however, when she finally takes it out of the packaging, Lucy feels a little buzz of child-like excitement. She kicks off her clothes and hops around trying to get into the wetsuit. It just has to look the part, and not accentuate her lumps and bumps. She struggles to negotiate the thing up over herself and pulls her arms into the sleeves. *Why the hell is this so difficult to put on?* After zipping it up, she stands in front of the mirror and pulls on her mask. She'll need to re-colour the whole suit but it looks—surprisingly—okay. She turns to the side, sucking in her stomach and standing straight. She went for the thinnest neoprene wetsuit she could find—hoping it won't actually look like a wetsuit when it all comes together. For a moment, she thinks this is actually going to work. She almost doesn't want to take it off.

An hour and a half and a paint-fume-induced wheezing-fit later, Lucy stands in her red and white costume, cape bunched at her shoulders, bold red crest from her sternum to her navel. She's not sure the symbol really looks much like a phoenix but it'll mean something to her and a symbol of any kind is still a symbol. She clenches her fists in an attempt at looking heroic and, closing her eyes just for a moment, allows herself to float gently off the floor. She opens her eyes to stare at a woman she has somehow known her whole life while everything in the world has changed around her.

The front door clicks open. *Shit*. Lucy comes crashing to the ground. Her head spinning, she catches sight of the bedside clock. It's 1:25am —James just got home from his shift. In a panic, as she tries to pull off her boots, she ends up spinning midair like a catherine wheel, trying to avoid falling into the wardrobe.

She is still desperately trying to conceal her heavy breathing under the bed-covers when

James steps into the bedroom, looking shattered and world-weary. No use pretending to be asleep now, she's forgotten the bedside lamp on.

"What are you doing up?" he asks, thoughtlessly untying the drawstring of his jogging bottoms.

"Oh, I thought I'd wait for you," She surprises herself with her quick-thinking. Her heart is pounding.

She props herself up in the golden luminance of the lamp as James' eyes take her in. In her rush to get undressed and into bed, she hadn't time to put on a nightie—the bed covers slip down a little to the rise and fall of her breasts. Seeing her, the hunger in his eyes dims everything else around him as he takes off his sweatshirt, his body cast in bronze by the lamplight. He steps towards the bed. Lucy's breath catches as their eyes meet.

He wants to take control. He wants to take his time. As he moves over her, he pins her wrists to the mattress and she feels the tension from her whole body release. Her nipples harden under the soft bedsheet as her back arches. He kisses her neck gently at first, before becoming rougher. She loves his power. As his lips trace a path down her neck, her collar bone, to her chest, he runs his hands down her wrists, her arms and pulls down the covers. She can feel how much he's enjoying her body as he runs his hand up the inside of her thigh and keeps going. Her legs wrap around him as he takes her nipple into his mouth, holding her other breast in his strong grip, and a swelling current runs through her, connecting his body to hers as her hips push up on his torso. He has her completely under his power, her mind clearing of all but this moment and its anticipation. He moves to look at her, their eyes drawing them deeper together. He takes her mouth with his, gently biting her bottom lip and kissing her again. She can feel how ready he is for her, rubbing through his boxers and the lace of her underwear. Neither of them can take it any longer—she pushes down his waistband and he pulls aside her thin lace.

* * *

Sweat trickles down Jill's spine, pooling at her lower back. Her arms tremble, forcing herself away from the floor for the ninety-seventh time. Nearly there. Her elbows threaten to buckle and it feels like something is going to snap. A drop of sweat dangles from her nose.

"Come on!" she barely gasps to herself.

Ninety-eight.

Nine months earlier, not long after her encounter with the Black lady from the OSI, her brother's friend Bill at the Sheriff's Department texted her. He said he had something for her.

"You said '*anything unusual*', right?" Bill caveated in the bar they arranged for the meeting.

Jill felt like her time was being wasted—his story didn't seem unusual at all. What was worse, she was in a dive bar with one of her brother's dodgy friends.

He had to lean in close to compete with the terrible '90s rock and the glare from the neon lights behind the bar. But it turned out that the story he had for her was her first genuine clue. A guy's credit card had been stolen in that very bar—that was the uninteresting part. Mysterious girl, a little dangerous looking, the kind of thing that excites gray middle-aged types, a bottle of vodka and *bam*: wallet emptied. But then the card was used to buy some very interesting items, like chemical fertiliser—the ingredient of choice for homemade bomb-makers —nitroglycerin, swimming pool filters, industrial levels of sodium carbonate, and a top-end radio-controlled drone.

"So where was it all delivered?" Jill urged.

"A derelict residence," he said, "A doss-house,"

"What did you find there?"

"Nothing," He took another swing of room-temperature beer from the bottle, "FBI turns up—takes it all off our hands,"

She waited until daylight to take a look at the residence for herself. She'd never been anywhere like it. The windows were all boarded up. Outside, what was once the lawn was covered in broken glass, garbage, cigarette butts, bottles and cans. A crumpled mattress was propped against the wall, stained brown, yellow and black, what was left of its stuffing weeping from a tear like a stuck pig. The door was a graffitied and stickered board, angled in the frame. She thought about knocking.

"Fuck off!"

She nearly wet herself. Directly above her, a man was poking his head out of a hole in a boarded window. He looked freshly dug up. Composing herself as best she could, she called up politely:

"I'm looking for a friend of mine,"

"Sure you are," he spat back, "Now fuck off!"

She didn't need telling again. She was lucky he didn't launch something at her as she hurried off the premises. She needed another way.

The convenience store across the road provided her second clue. The clerk told her about every one of the doss-house's occupants. They didn't always make his life the most pleasant but it was the one Jill met who was the real problem. The shop owner called him Crag Face. It fit. A couple of weeks previously, someone new had turned up: A young, raven woman in a beat-up old Ford began parking a couple houses down.

She'd wait for a delivery van to drop off a handful of parcels and then jump out of her car to sign for them. It went on for three days as packages arrived there. When asked, the clerk told her the girl doing the pick-ups was white, slim with black hair.

"What was the delivery company?" she asked.

"Various different ones, ma'am. UPS was one? Amazon?"

Outside the store, Jill thought over what she had to do. She wasn't by nature a liar or a scammer. She paced a little as she found UPS's customer services number on her phone. She just had to give them a call and pretend a package was meant for her. As her thumb hovered over the call button and she struggled to imagine herself behaving so out of character, like an actor playing herself, she called upon the memory and the pain of kneeling at the edge of the still burning launch base. And Danny.

She pressed call.

"Hello, I had a parcel delivered but it hasn't come and the tracker says someone signed for it but I don't have it and I need it," She's never been great with people but she tries hard. "It's really important. Can you tell me who signed for it please?"

"No problem, ma'am," the help desk employee intoned professionally, "Can I get the parcel or tracking reference number from you please?"

Damn. Anyone else could have talked the operator around.

The following week, she had a call with her boss—indefinite leave while the official investigation continued. He wouldn't confirm whether she or Flt Cpt Blake were still suspects but she was *advised* not to leave the state. As long as they were suspects, the Air Force and OSI clearly had no idea who was really behind 3/19, and presumably hadn't been debriefed by the FBI. This all suited her just fine though—it left her to make plans. Then the OSI turned up unannounced again—yet another agent—and effectively ordered her to wind her neck in, as if they knew she was running her own investigation.

One-hundred. A couple more jabs and uppercuts on the sparring dummy, milkshake, large breakfast, unravel handwraps, undress, shower.

She began searching for raven-haired girls at AA meetings. When she made no tangible progress towards snaring her quarry, she went to bed and fantasised about what justice would feel like. And she tried not to think about Danny anymore. It was easier to dream of vengeance. As more time passed with still no clues, she built on her fantasies, adding details, filling gaps, until they were plans. She moved out of her brother's place into a rental. Her plans needed her to be strong and, over time, she acquired a pull-up bar, kickboxing dummy, loose weights and a crash-mat. It was never about catharsis; it just kept the fire hot. She moved from AA meetings to NA. Then she was asking questions at rehab clinics, which led her to backstreet pharmacies. *Nothing.* Maybe it was fruitless because the people she spoke to at these places had some duty to protect their clientele. They had no idea who was really lurking in their midst. But Jill did, and she'd find her. The possibility that some pick-pocketing bar-fly could have been the mastermind of 3/19 never crossed her mind. But she was part of it.

As soon as Jill's plans were fully formed, they stopped being satisfying and she found herself fantasising again, only the fantasies were more visceral every time. Fantasies became plans again and her imagination stepped up a gear, over and over. She needed it that way to feel like it did justice to Danny and her colleagues. It was too hard to think about him—but it was always easy to think about killing his murderers. The days clustered into weeks and weeks fell into months.

Tonight, on her run, she finally found her. She was passing an NA meeting place and there it was—a beat-up, rusty old Ford in the alley behind the hall. There must be thousands of Fords in Helena but she knew this was it. The sight of the vehicle quickened something in her chest. Its owner stole the card that bought the materials for the bomb that destroyed the launch control building—and would lead Jill to her vengeance.

On the opposite side of the street from the hall, she paused to look at her watch: 20:16. She reckoned she still had time before the meeting ended so she jogged over towards the vehicle. She had a slim-jim at home, something she found online that car thieves slide down between the window and door to unlock it. One of her plans had been to lie in wait in the back of the car and surprise the bitch—force her to tell her who dropped that bomb and then, for Danny, just like in all her plans, she'd beat the thief to a bloody pulp and track down the murderer. As she got near the car though, she knew she couldn't do anything out in the open, even at night. She kept on walking, past the car. She knew what she had to do. She would wait there and finally see her face, get some pictures, then she'd give her brother's friend Bill a call and maybe he'd run the Ford's plates for her, get an address. She was pretty sure the FBI telling the local cops to back off would keep the thief safe from arrest. So she found a wall to lean against to look casual and removed her phone from the pouch on her arm.

As she waited, she got cold. She wondered if this was the right plan, worried that the girl might disappear after tonight, that this might be her only chance to catch her if she can't convince Bill to help. She ran through the alternative in her head. If she could have gotten her motorbike, and her tools, she could have followed the car and ended it that night. Assuming the meeting was going to finish at 20:30 at the earliest, she might have had time to run home and get her bag and bike.

She imagined her feet pounding the asphalt; she was probably a six minute run from home—she checked her phone: it was 20:20 already so she'd be home at 20:26. Even if she somehow managed to get in, grab her bag from under the bed, metal clattering inside it, sling her leather jacket on and run back outside for her bike, she wasn't sure she could get back outside, unchain her bike, and speed back here by 20:30. She remembered that the last time she went out on her bike, the lock had jammed and she'd nearly broken the key trying to open it. After nine months, she was so close to nailing this psycho that the thought of her bike-lock was infuriating.

Time passed and 20:30 came and went. She hopped from one foot to the other to keep warm. Her legs were starting to freeze in her running tights. She could have gone for her bike after all. She watched and waited and, at 20:34, a black-haired, black-clad waif strutted out of a back exit. She looked more like a celebrity leaving a nightclub than Jihadi Jane.

Jill watched the girl cross the street and then too quickly whipped up her phone to start recording. *To hell with subtlety*. The girl got into her car and drove away into the night. Jill tried to convince herself that she had enough, at least for now: the girl's face and the licence plate. She called Bill. There was no answer so she left him a voicemail: "It's Jill Hanson. Please call me as soon as you get this. It's important,"

Now, stepping out of the hot shower, Jill catches herself in the mirror. She looks into her own eyes, searching for someone she recognises. She's in there somewhere—she'll return when this business is over with. But now it's time to go find Bill.

When she's semi-dressed, she finds herself in front of the mirror in her bedroom, staring at the sinews and hard muscles of this new body, coiling tightly like steel cables throughout her arms and legs, her stomach like a sheet of armour plates. She's still staring, counting on this woman machine in front of her to do the task no matter what is thrown at her, when she calls the Sheriff's Department. She's told that Bill isn't on shift tonight but, when she turns from the mirror and tells the officer on the other end that she's

Jill, Tom Hanson's sister: "Oh, hey Jill. Yeah, if you really want Bill, he's prolly at Jesters down on North Rodney Street,"

On the approach to the two-storey gray concrete building, there's not much to give it away until you can hear the music. As she gets around to the corner entrance, there are a couple of neon signs for whiskeys on the wall and a sign above the door: The Jesters Bar Package Goods. It's the same bar she met Bill before. Inside, it's deceptively small, loud, dark and windowless. And it's busy tonight

It's only around ten-thirty but the queue at the bar is three-deep. *Where are you, Bill?* She walks around, checking out the players around the pool tables, then the electronic darts boards. There's no band playing on the stage but multicoloured disco lights illuminate the walls and the people standing around drinking and socialising. She's never understood why people would come to somewhere like this to meet—shouting over the music into each others' faces. No sign of Bill anywhere yet but he could be in the restroom, or jammed in amongst the throngs at the bar trying to get served.

Scanning the front row at the bar—those most likely to move off first—she sees another girl with jet black hair, but a head taller than Jihadi Jane, and ignores her and keeps looking for Bill. She thinks maybe she can see Bill's balding head at the bar and, stepping closer, Jill has to navigate her way through elbows, and varying degrees of cooperative strangers. The closer she gets to the bar, the less happy the clientele are about giving her space to get through. It's slow going and before she gets to the queue itself, she sees it's not Bill. When it's beginning to feel like Bill really isn't here, she turns around to go outside for some fresh air and her heart almost stops.

Between people's shoulders, she sees *the girl* heading for the door—Jihadi Jane—raven-hair, skinny and clad in almost as much leather as Jill. She almost didn't see her because, behind her she appears to have a boyfriend in-tow. It was her at the bar—she must have been standing on the foot rail as she leant over the bar. There are a dozen people between Jill and the girl now. She has no plan for this. But she's not letting her go again. The girl's companion follows the petite creature closely as she weaves through the parting male bodies towards the door.

"Jill!" she hears the nearby shout, muffled under the din of the bar, "Jill, hi!" It's Bill. She doesn't know what to say, he's now standing right in front of her and she's trying to see over his shoulder and get past him.

"Bill, I've got to go," she says as he clumsily steps around her, "Sorry,"

"I just saw your missed call," he lies.

"Sorry, not now,"

When she gets outside, the couple are getting into a cab. Thank God she hasn't lost them she thinks. While she's mounting her bike and getting on her helmet, they drive off, but she sees where they go, down North Rodney Street.

With her foot slammed on the bike's accelerator, she catches up to the cab just as she would have lost it around a turn. She keeps her distance and tries to keep herself together, to regulate her heart rate, which thuds almost painfully against her ribcage, held tightly by her padded biker jacket. She soon catches her breath as she eases into tracking her quarry once again.

Eventually, the cab signals to pull up outside an apartment block and Jill stops at the same time, a block back from them. This isn't like hunting elk with her dad anymore—she can't wait for her prize to re-emerge; she has to be able to follow her into the building so she needs to see exactly how they get in. Realising her mistake, she starts up the motor and rides over to the other side of the street, parking with the cab between her and the apartments. Staying on the bike by the curb, she watches the pair of them exit the cab—the girl gets out on the roadside so Jill can see her face again; she looks cold and calculating. The guy she's with is still a faceless mystery. Jill wonders whether he's another chump the girl's screwing over or something more meaningful. They stumble up the steps together and, as the cab drives off, the girl unlocks the door invisibly and they go inside, the guy so close behind her, they seem conjoined.

Now she has another choice: Either she finds a way inside while they're both in there or she waits to see if one leaves before the other. She hasn't accounted for a boyfriend in her plans. But now she knows where she lives. She could wait here and see if the boyfriend leaves. Sitting on her bike by the sidewalk in the dark might draw attention but she hopes most people are fast asleep by now. She decides she'll wait an hour and come back better prepared for the boyfriend in the morning.

Two hours later, it's about one in the morning and she hasn't left. She's been pacing for about the last hour but it's getting seriously cold, even with her base layer and bike leather. Her ass is frozen and the couple are still inside. She doesn't know what else she expected—she just hasn't been able to leave yet. Struggling to stay awake, she crosses the street to investigate the outside of the apartment block, not looking for anything in particular. At the door, she finds a dial pad to buzz the individual apartments and what looks like an electronic fob panel, probably used to open the front door.

Out of nowhere, a siren bleeps and the blue light cast on the door almost gives her a heart attack. The squad car slows to a crawl as she turns towards it.

"Excuse me, sir," says the officer through the open window, "Do you live in this building? Oh, excuse me, ma'ame, I couldn't see you there,"

Think fast.

"Jill?!" calls a confused voice from the other side of the car.

The car stops and Tom's head pops up from the other side as he gets out and starts making his way towards her.

"What are you doing here? We got an anonymous complaint about a biker..."

CHAPTER 5

The hand that rules the world

Lucy knew it was another dream from the start. She could watch through her own eyes and kid herself that she had some level of control but it was a dream nonetheless. She stood resplendent in her costume, surrounded by high-tech equipment, screens and dials. It sounded like the bridge of the Enterprise in Star Trek—all beeps and whistles. It was a superhero's secret hideout, her secret hideout, inside Big Ben's clock tower of all places. She struggled to remember the proper name for it as if it was incredibly important—Elizabeth Tower maybe. The giant clock face smoothly and silently glided open on its hinges, out into star-filled space. She realised she was controlling it with a key fob like a garage door. She had a mission to complete and it was out there. Suddenly, she was flying over an ocean towards a beautiful tropical island but, as she got near, robotic sentries the size of small cars rose out of the water and flew towards her, lasers and bullets firing, hitting her skin, feeling like someone pinching her. She felt a swelling sense of injustice—why were they picking on her? She swung her fists at them and kicked her feet, smashing them to pieces until they stopped coming for her. As she arrived over the island, laser cannons popped up from behind boulders but she decided to keep flying as they pinched her skin with their shots. Eventually, she stopped at a vast metal door on the side of a mountain. She landed on the soft ground and began punching the door. It felt like trying to punch underwater, but suddenly the door raised up and opened to pure, pitch blackness. A cave. The pit of her stomach twisted as she desperately tried to open her eyes and wake up. It felt like something was coming out of the darkness towards her —something monstrous and huge. She heard herself say, "You must have known you couldn't hide from me, you fiend!"

Finally, she managed to wrench her eyes open with a moan that became a muffled scream in her pillow, attempting to secure her place in the waking world.

She lay, propped up on an elbow, in the semi-darkness of her and James' bedroom, lit by the dim glow of charging phones, and the streetlight outside their window.

She ran the dream through her mind in a

bid not to forget any detail but she could already feel it slipping away, leaving just a few images and a deep feeling of dread. She knew she couldn't go back to sleep but she also couldn't face the mundane stream of social media awaiting her on her phone. She had to get out of there.

James stirred in the bed beside her. *Don't wake.* She slipped carefully out from under the covers, not letting her feet touch the floor, and hovered across the carpet to the wardrobe. Her heart raced, pumping adrenaline through every vein as she opened the wardrobe door with a creak. She remembered something: She hovers back over to her bedside table and lifted it away from the wall. The compass necklace was right there.

Moments later, she was in the kitchen hurriedly trying to get into her costume. Desperately hoping James stayed asleep, it felt like she could get caught at any moment. When she was dressed, she floated through the blue darkness to the hallway mirror. In a twisted sort of farewell to her own face, she pulled down her mask, its rigid, heroic angles transforming her.

Since before she could read, Lucy's dad fed her on superhero movies and Saturday morning cartoons; X-Men, Spider-Man, Justice League. When she was old enough, he gave her, with great expectation on his face, her first graphic novel: Trinity by Matt Wagner. It was a sort of Golden Age throw-back, a retrospective blueprint of the idea of Superman, Batman and Wonder Woman (the comic book fan's holy *trinity*), as if it was saying, *This is how it should be*. She still has it, with all her other comics and graphic novels accumulated throughout her childhood and teenage years, mostly at Christmas and birthdays, in boxes in a cupboard, unable to read them, unable to let them go. Back then, the connection with her dad made Lucy feel special, perhaps partly because her sister never got any of it. Charlotte could make fun of her all she wanted while Lucy dreamed of soaring above the clouds and the simplicity of good versus evil. Her first memory of flying wasn't really flying at all but Charlotte was there, to mock her.

She was going as fast as she could, as fast as her little legs could take her, determined and jumping. Little Lucy was running around the playground at primary school, all mown lawn and hard tarmac. Her hooded coat, hanging off her head and flapping behind her, a makeshift cape. One fist tucked close to her chest, the other jutting out in front of her, she soared around the playground, running and jumping, running and jumping. If she could just jump enough, it really almost but not quite felt like flying. It took a lot of concentration to fly and she didn't always remember to look where she was going. Run-jump, run-jump. *Bump*. Little Lucy collided with the worst possible person: her big sister, Charlotte. Charlotte was in Year 5 at the time and she didn't like Lucy one bit.

"Who are you pretending to be?" demanded Charlotte, towering over her sister frighteningly. Lucy just wanted to carry on playing but now that was ruined. Charlotte would just be mean.

"I'm not pretending!" she said back, not quite as loudly and fiercely as she'd wanted.

"Yes you are!" Charlotte was not going to let Lucy go easily, "You're not a superhero! You don't have superpowers!"

Lucy could feel her cheeks prickling and her eyes getting watery but she mustn't cry in front of everybody. Charlotte's friends were all standing around by then, annoyed at the interruption. Lucy put her hands on her hips and puffed out her chest, "You've just not seen them,"

"Stop pretending!" Charlotte shouted. Lucy must have been really annoying.

But it wasn't long before Lucy "grew out" of it. In the end, her mum's palpable lack of understanding, interest or approval of boys' superheroes was all it needed. It's with a pang of guilt that Lucy remembers sitting with her dad watching cartoons, only to go on to reject it all. She wonders what he'll make of her now.

Lucy folds away the compass on the inside of her right glove. She has found her way to Thailand, where, hundreds of metres below, the land has been swamped by the worst monsoon since 2011. Entire villages have been destroyed —there's no telling yet of the toll on human life —but perhaps she can help get people to safety. The water is diseased and full of dangers and many families are shut off from support. Below her is an endless brown, murky lake, peppered with corrugated metal sheets like stepping stones to nowhere. They are the roofs of people's homes. There's no-one she can help here.

She pushes herself to race to the next submerged village but, just as she's about to take a deep breath and take off towards the horizon, movement grabs her attention: a billowing tarpaulin on one of the roofs. Something about the movement seems unnatural—and she's right. There are people taking shelter under there. Lucy wishes she had a plan and wonders what's wrong with herself. Luckily, tangled in a gnarled tree, she spots a small truck with a wooden trailer. That will have to do. Rather than hang in the sky formulating her next steps, she pushes herself on, wrenching the trailer from the truck with her hands. She continues to run through possible plans, as she flies the trailer towards the roof.

As she approaches, some of the people under the makeshift tent see her and get to their feet. If she's going to do this right, she needs to focus and get out of her head.

With the trailer raised above her head and her cape flapping behind her, she takes a breath and steadies her voice.

"I'm here to save you," she says, "Get in,"

With two families already on the precarious roof, she awkwardly flies downwards feet-first into the water until it's up to her neck and, holding the trailer over her head, the survivors can step onto it. Even pressing her cheek against the bottom of the trailer, the warm, thick water sloshes around her chin. *I'm here to save you?* She rolls her eyes behind closed lids.

"It's okay," she calls, trying to encourage them to move. She hears them talking to each other, probably arguing about who's going to tell the dumb westerner that they'd rather wait for the Red Cross. Slowly, however, they begin to move, and she feels the weight of the trailer shifting. She can't check if they're all on so she waits an unnecessary amount of time after there's no more movement above her head.

"Okay?" she shouts, assuming some words must be understood if shouted loudly enough.

Thankfully, someone shouts back, "Okay!"

If she'd prepared, she would have figured out where to take her passengers. There wouldn't be any safe, high ground that wasn't already desperately over-crowded. She imagines starving and sick people fighting for somewhere to take shelter. Maybe she'll have to take them far out of the country to find somewhere unaffected by floods, marooning them somewhere new. She flies up and up to get a better view of things again and turns slowly around. There must be somewhere safe. Halfway around her turn, the people above her begin shouting and she sees a stretch of long white shapes on the horizon. She begins flying towards it but it becomes no clearer until they're almost on top of it.

Before them is a complex of dozens of white tents on the muddy ground—a UN relief centre. The crowds below are jumping up and down, shouting and pointing at her. She can't tell if they're happy to see her but she supposes it doesn't matter. She now sees doctors, volunteers and locals shuttling food and supplies around the temporary settlement, all stopping in their tracks to see a woman in a spray-painted wetsuit flying in the air, carrying a trailer of people.

A clearing in the crowd appears beneath her as she lands and clumsily sets down the trailer, and a cheer erupts from the crowd. As she helps people out of the trailer, they each, individually embrace her for a very short moment of thanks. Her fears about her powers disappearing seem a million miles away as she realises the applause is for her.

She looks around for something she can do here but all she sees are faces looking back at her and she realises she's too disruptive. These are the first people in the world to see her in her costume. But now she knows about this place, she can bring more survivors. There are a lot of them. She works through the night and into the next day, helping people who've already done whatever they can to protect themselves and their families from the rising water. Some are very unwell and in a state of exhaustion when she finds them. Others have managed to take food or clean water with them but their supplies weren't enough to last more than a day or two.

Another day has passed since she left England. She hopes James finds the note she left him and understands.

Dear James,

In Washington, I didn't act when I could have. Being afraid of making things worse is no excuse for not to try to help. I feel like, my whole life, I've been ~~thinking~~ over-thinking and never doing. Now, I think it's time to get out of my head and do something. I promise I'll explain one day. Please don't worry—I'll be safe. Back by Monday.
I love you,
Lucy

* * *

Ashley's skin crawls as reality takes another turn. It's become impossible to distinguish reality from fantasy, or nightmare, and it's petrifying. It's so difficult to feel grounded that it's like seeing everything upside-down. Sitting up in bed, she strains every compliant mental capacity to understand what she sees on her laptop screen.

At first, she thought she was just clicking onto the latest viral video to flood the internet. It would be some movie studio's marketing campaign or a hoax from a nerd with too much time on their hands. It began as a pixelated cell phone video, shot in the desert somewhere—it was supposed to be the Middle East, judging by what the men were wearing. You couldn't see any of their faces. The focus of the video was a round hole in the ground. As the image became less blurred and grainy, Ashley could see something was in the hole, poking out of it like a termite mound, but it was bluish black. She fumbled for the button to unmute the laptop's speaker and turned up the volume. The talking and shouting was made indecipherable by the rushing wind on the cell phone's mic. Nothing she could understand. One of the men bent over and picked up a baseball-sized rock from the ground. As he raised the rock above his head, all other sounds were torn through by the woman screaming, pleading for her life, praying, before her voice was whipped away again by the wind. It was a woman in the hole. The man launched the rock at her. He stood just a few feet from the rim. Ashley's stomach clenched. She couldn't look as the rock hit. She kept her eyes on the man, somewhere in his centre—she didn't want to look at his face either—but she couldn't stop the video. It felt like someone's fist was around her own heart. All the men were then holding rocks. They were all throwing them.

Suddenly, the camera swung to the desert floor and as if one of the rocks had hit the cameraman. Maybe that was the payoff—one of the evil bastards getting hit by a misthrown rock. But then he pulled the camera back to the scene and what Ashley saw made her feel simultaneously conned and relieved. Standing over the hole, with a foot planted on each side of it, was a woman wearing a superhero costume—just not any superhero Ashley recognised.

What happened on screen next was a shaky blur—which always makes CGI more cost-effective. The superhero moved quickly, grabbing the men two at a time and flying them to a van, throwing them into the back of it. It was a nice touch when at the end she came for the cameraman and you got a good look at her.

That wasn't CGI. From her eyes and the part of her face that wasn't masked, you could see that she was beautiful. Her eyes were something like fool's gold. Her skin was dark and smooth, striking against the white of her costume. Then the cameraman was thrown in the back of the van too and the superhero slammed the doors. Everything went black and that was the end of the video. If only that were the end of the story.

Below the video was the thumbnail of a CNN news report titled, *Flying Woman Real?*

"It was in this spot in front of this women's refuge in Kabul," regaled the composed reporter, "that history may have been made," She continued, "Multiple eye-witness reports confirm a story ripped right from the pages of a comic book,"

Behind the reporter, in front of the refuge was the filthy once-white van from the previous video. Ashley checked the publisher of this video —CNN's official account.

Ashley's skin itches. Everything everyone's told her her entire life tells her she's sick and that none of this makes sense because she's confused and doesn't know what's real. But then she hears a familiar male voice—her Professor—and he tells her she's not sick. Society's sick. It's getting harder and harder to put a meaningful sentence together in her head. She needs something. One of the

Professor's weed pills? The vodka in her bedside drawer?

Ashley has now watched every version of the video, read everything there is. Apparently the Taliban had sentenced the woman to death by stoning for adultery. The men had received the welcome they deserved at the women's refuge and the victim, who it turned out was a doctor, had insisted on taking herself to hospital and was now under police guard.

Again, Ashley comes back to the same sight, now freeze-framed on her laptop and etched into her memory: the heroine's face. As she searches, she finds herself drawn into this face in front of her; being lifted up in the woman's arms and held to her as she soars. Staring further, underneath the stern, matriarchal mask, Ashley senses a warmth and compassion. It's too much to bear. She unpauses the video and the woman is released from that moment of tenderness, to surge across the screen like a banshee. There is a darkness there too, something raw and black; like a bottomless well. But at least that Ashley understands.

When the video finishes again, a hush falls on Ashley's whole apartment. She sits cross-legged on her bed, in quiet contemplation. A tiny flutter, like the flap of a single butterfly wing, ignites inside her. She wants to crush it in her fist—hope is a dangerous thing—but a little bell chimes in her head, nudging her attention to her bedside table and the little medicine bottle inside it—the reset switch for the world.

She scrubs her skin under the scalding shower but, when she looks down, she still sees it. Sickening black tendrils slither, tug and coil their way from between her toes. Up over her ankles. Around her calves. Threateningly and quiveringly across her thighs. She picks up her razor but can't shave her legs while they're there. She's afraid they'll trap her hand and pull her down, crushing and contorting her. The bodysnatchers aren't real, she tells herself. She squeezes her eyes shut but that only accelerates things. The constricting darkness has already crept up the back of her neck and has its slimy grip around the base of her brain.

What started this morning as the usual voice refusing to relent has descended into a waking nightmare. Ashley needs to get out before it's too late. She can already feel the energy sapping from her legs. The shower is thirteen and a half paces from the safe-zone.

"Fuck off!" she screams once more as if it will listen this time.

Useless dirty cunt, it calls her.

She cautiously gets out of the shower and dries. A few minutes before getting in, she was on her laptop. She thinks. The digital clock, next to the bottle and the small lamp that lights the room, tells her it's 07:47 Dec 1. The effort of stringing together a coherent timeline of the day is nauseating. The flying woman. Her handprint. The Hand of God? Are they the same thing? Is this woman God? Is she a witch? This is what she was trying to work out.

Whatever she is, she stopped the reset, kept the world as it is, kept the slimy black tentacles of depression alive, evil people in control. Or is she healing the world like everyone else says? There's dirt under her nails. It's wriggling.

"Get out," she says to the voice she dares not name.

You forgot the thing, it replies.

That's it. The Professor said she needs to wait until his signal, but she can't wait any longer.

That night, with that guy from the bar: Steve. As he was leaving, he stopped dead in his tracks. She remembers now.

"What's this?" he asked. *Fuck. It's the end of the fucking road. That's what it is.* "Is this a drone?" *He's a fucking government spy, you moron!*

"Um, I don't know -- didn't I tell you to get out?! You creep! What the fuck are you doing here? I'm drunk and you took advantage of me! Get out!"

See what a fucking idiot you are? Who would

want to fuck you? Other than to teach you a lesson? Get rid of the fucking drone. Or don't. See what they do to you.

She pulls on some jeans, a t-shirt and some boots. She finds a rubber band and scrapes her wet hair into a ponytail. She made the "thing" using the fluid in the Professor's metal jar, a bicycle brake lever, the wires from inside the wall and the parts from a cordless fogger. The whole thing went into a backpack, the busy end pointing out the top. She's got the bag on now, as she zips her puffer jacket over the top of it.

You'll take it off because you're a useless shit and a coward.

She wants to tell the voice to shut up but it's beginning to scare her. There's a thick, industrial-looking chain on the floor, with a huge padlock. She doesn't know how she got it. There's no key. It wraps around her body and through the bag's shoulder straps three times before she locks it tight in place and puts her jacket back on over it.

"See. It's on,"

Perhaps accepting that it's the end, its grip on her loosens a little—enough that she can make her bed and tidy her room before she goes. When she's done, she switches on her laptop, loads up her CamGurlz profile and begins the pre-recording she created for her final night on earth. She thinks whichever FBI agent's on shift tonight is in for a treat. It's time to go to the window. She has a long way to travel and they could still catch up to her and stop her at any point. The floorboard creaks. Behind her, the laptop chimes sycophantically as tokens she'll never use begin dropping into her account. The thought sends chills up her spine and the black thing around her spasms with brief ecstasy. She can tell it's thinking about choking her.

When she opens the window, she can't understand why the snow isn't cold. Finally, she unravels a long rope, ties one end to a bed leg, dangles the other end out of the window and makes her final departure from her apartment without the slightest sense of ceremony. Disgust is what repels her down the side of the building away from her room.

A few moments later, she's in her car. The plan was that she'd complete the drive to New York City in three days, sleeping in the car to avoid detection. But this is a race against time.

* * *

In the rearview mirror, the pair of fog lights burn damply through the thickening grey snowstorm all around the car as Cassandra drives herself and Takei perilously on. She hopes she's left enough food for the cat.

There's a motorcyclist with a death wish

ahead, whose rear light Cassandra uses as her guide through the blizzard. She suspects the dull Christmas lights twinkling in the snowy ether on either side keep them all on the road. The car with the fog lights has been behind them for seven minutes. In the mirror, she watches the faint indicator finally foreshadow the car's departure before it turns off what's left of the road. It's 07:27 on 1st December and Cassandra and Takei have been AWOL for three days. They're racing against two clocks now: the Doomsday Clock and the Papa Clock.

The moment Cassandra went AWOL, she was in trouble. When she arrived at Heathrow with Takei, they were both dead meat. But they got through. Or they were allowed through. It's only a matter of time before Papa starts looking for her and passing through an airport is like leaving a lit flare. It'll be obvious Cassandra's re-opened Op Turpentine and trying to snare McAvoy. They arrived at Heathrow, went through security and checked in separately and she and Takei sat away from each other on the plane. It was the same for their transfer at Salt Lake City. In fact, over the fifteen hour journey, they didn't acknowledge each other at all until he picked her up outside Helena Airport, Montana. This was all so he could continue the mission in case she was arrested at any stage. Luck, or some other machination, kept them out of jail this time.

The reality of what will happen to the world, how many people will die, how many will have their lives torn apart by global economic and environmental collapse, is too vast and impersonal to comprehend, like a disaster movie that just doesn't connect. Instead, it's the thought of Papa's old desk full of McAvoy's letters that drives her on. That's what reminds her she can and *has to* be more than be an observer.

The comfort, however, of being an observer was that there's no need to think about things too deeply, like the incomprehensible miracle of a young woman with superpowers who stopped the end of the world on 3/19.

Cassandra drives herself and Takei through the worst snowstorm to hit Montana in a decade, down what she supposes is another road of anonymous flats. If Hanson could hide her meeting the flying girl on 3/19, she could easily be hiding something else—something that might lead them to the *how* or *who* of the launch base attack, and narrow the net around McAvoy. They'll find out soon enough.

Her phone breaks the silence.

"Ben?" she answers, knowing only he has the number for this burner.

"Hi, I don't have long so just listen," he says, "The phone number you used for your OSI alias just got a voicemail, I'm going to forward it to you now, and then I can't talk to you again,"

Within seconds, her phone lights up with a voice note. It begins with a man clearing his throat and then speaking in an American accent, in an intentionally deepened voice: "I have just discovered the identity and location of the 3/19 bomber. Her name is Ashley and you'll find the drone she used to drop the bomb on the launch control base in her apartment..." As he gives the address, Daniel taps it into the car's sat nav. They're close.

"Why would someone call the OSI and not the FBI or the police?" Daniel asks.

"It's Blake," she replies, "Let's go check it out,"

Suddenly, Takei springs forward, peering through the windscreen and shouts, "Hanson!"

"What?"

"Three P, twenty-two, ninety-four B," he reads from up ahead, "It's her bike,"

"What the hell?"

He's right. They're stopped at a red light, close enough to the biker with a death wish to see the licence plate through the snow. The traffic light turns green. The rider turns right, the same way the sat nav is telling them to go to the suspect's address. Cassandra follows without hesitation. Hanson, or the person riding her bike, is wearing thick, weather-proofs and helmet and a long, camo rucksack. It looks exactly like a tactical rifle case. The display in the car's dash reads 17°F, about -8°C.

"Do you think hunting season is still on?" asks Takei.

"I don't think anyone's going hunting Elk in this,"

As they continue their steady pursuit, it becomes obvious they're going to the same place. Cassandra remembers the rifle above the fireplace at the brother's house and how it held Hanson's attention. The woman was planning something even then.

She keeps their distance and, after eight minutes without suspecting a tail, Hanson cuts across the road and stops her bike on the left. This is the street. Christmas lights adorn every fifth house, throwing faint neons over Hanson and her bike. Cassandra drives past and keeps an eye on her in the rearview, ensuring she doesn't fade into the storm. She dismounts but doesn't chain up the bike. It looks like Hanson is waiting for the car to be out of sight so Cassandra indicates and takes the first left.

Cassandra and Takei exchange glances before exiting the car. Of the many things said in that look, she's sure one is a mutual wish they had weapons. They quickly put on their heavy coats and hats, the icy breeze biting anything left exposed, and run to the corner of the block, snow and frozen lawn crunching beneath their feet. Cassandra takes point and peers around the cold concrete. Hanson left her bike in the unlit area between two streetlights and is keeping her head down, walking fast. She's hung her helmet on her bike but it looks like she's wearing a balaclava, and she's still carrying the tactical bag. Now, she looks over her shoulder, pivots away from the road and skips up the steps to one of the blocks. Cassandra holds herself and Takei behind cover and watches the woman enter the building.

"Go!" she half whispers, half shouts over the wind.

The pair run down the street, desperately trying not to slip on the gritted pavement, snow pelting them in the face. She imagines herself watching from one of the surrounding buildings, listening through an earpiece.

Before they reach the steps, Cassandra sees the security panel at the front door. *Shit.* They'll need to dial a code to release the door.

"I need something from the car," says Takei without missing a beat. Cassandra hands him the keys and he runs off. He returns with an ice-scraper and a determined look. "Excuse me," he says as he steps up to the door and reaches toward the electromagnetic lock at the top of the frame. He proceeds to forcefully wedge the ice-scraper between the two parts of the magnet and, with surprising strength, breaks the connection and releases the door.

It's dark inside—no windows. There's no automatic light in the hallway but, like a silent whirlpool, a skylight pours down the centre of the stairwell. Suddenly another light comes on, two floors up—it seems some of the sensors are working—and now they know where Hanson is. Takei stays by the front door as Cassandra skirts to the bottom of the stairwell. They can hear the heavy, slightly shuffling footsteps of someone carrying a load up the tiled steps. Takei joins her to look up the partially silhouetted stairwell. The sudden image of Fleischacker sends shivers down her spine. The icy wind outside blows through his pulverised skull in her mind, whistling a ghostly note through what's left of his teeth. They have to get to Hanson before she enters the flat—Ashley's flat. She's already at the top of the building now and they're all the way down here. *Anything to stop her going in there.*

"Jill?" she calls, attempting a friendly shout. The feet above scuffle to a halt. "Jill," Cassandra repeats. She can feel Takei's wide, questioning eyes but she continues, "Don't do it, Jill."

Even as the words leave her mouth, her racing mind finds the way in. She hasn't stopped to think about what Jill Hanson is obviously doing here. Hanson's distraction when they first met, Cassandra's instinct that Hanson had some sort of mission of her own, her focus on the gun, survivor's guilt. It's dawning on her that Hanson is on a revenge mission. But Cassandra and Takei need Ashley more than Hanson needs her revenge. Cassandra's words are met with silence, which means she's caught Hanson's attention.

"There's a bigger picture," she calls up.

Cassandra and Takei have begun scaling the steps. She doesn't know if Hanson has had time to take out whatever is in that bag and all she and Takei have are their wits.

"Who are you?" echoes Hanson's disembodied voice.

"Come down and we'll talk," she calls before realising her mistake. She changes tack to appeal to Hanson's sense of justice instead. "We need your help,"

Suddenly, a sound from below pulls on Cassandra's already strained senses. The door to the building just opened unheard, but the storm bellowed in before it was shut. It's on an automatic lock so the only way it opens is someone dialling the code. Nobody moves, except whoever is in the lobby. After a pause, she hears heavy, clomping footsteps across the tiled lobby floor—shaking off the snow across the shared space is both inconsiderate and dangerous. Now, he or she loudly rummages in their pocket as if looking for their key. He even clears his throat and coughs a little for good measure before finally getting his door open and exiting the scene into a ground-floor apartment, apparently going home at 07:49.

From the location of her voice, Hanson must have noticed that the two agents are now more than halfway up. Cassandra turns to look at Takei behind her. She slowly raises her empty hands above her head for him to copy. They continue their slow ascent like this. They hear the quick but drawn-out unzipping of the bag. Takei's grasping hand just scrapes Cassandra's coat as, without thinking, she breaks into a sprint.

She reaches the top and skids on the tiles, clasping the bannister as Hanson, at the other end of the landing, stands up, holding a rifle. Hanson spins to face her, gun pointed at Cassandra's gut.

She freezes, her heart beating against beads of ice on her chest.

"Why are you following me?" demands Hanson.

In the corner of her eye, Takei comes around to Cassandra's side, still showing his empty palms. As she tries not to fixate on the weapon, she focuses on her own breath, every second of which feels like victory snatched from the jaws of death.

She needs to say something. She has to be unfazed. She keeps her hands where they are; one on the bannister, the other by her side. Hanson doesn't seek power, respect or fear. She needs someone who understands her desire for justice, but who also knows a better way.

As Cassandra pulls her eyes off the weapon up to Hanson's face, Hanson unexpectedly softens by half a degree.

"Agent Christchurch?" mutters Hanson.

The name washes her with momentary relief, but she still needs that rifle pointed elsewhere. No-one moves or says a word. Cassandra analyses, partly to distract herself from the idea of Hanson's finger on that trigger, and the bullet glaring at her from the darkness inside that barrel.

It's not the same rifle that she saw at the brother's house. This is finished with camouflage and a matte black barrel. Hanson has already zipped up the bag, probably intending to take it into the apartment with her. It's rigid as if containing a long box. Hanson is sweating, but more likely from heat than nerves—her breath is steady and her eyes are fixed on Cassandra. Hanson has removed her balaclava but is still barely recognisable. Above all, her eyes have changed, like rough-hewn diamonds chipped out of a rock-face through long, hard toil. The open layers of winter gear and biker leathers remind Cassandra of the bomb disposers in Iraq.

"I found her," speaks Hanson in a quiet monotone, her eyes unwavering, "The woman who bombed launch control,"

"Then we can help each other,"

Cassandra reminds herself that this has nothing to do with ISIS—Al-Nasser isn't even real. This is about vulnerable psychiatric patients, like Fleischacker, abused and manipulated by a twisted and evil man. *How did the missileers find her? And what is Hanson's plan?* A high-power hunting rifle isn't going to be much use in close-quarters so, if the bomber really is in that flat, she probably isn't planning on firing it. The box in the bag suggests something else, worse than death, at least to begin with. Whatever happens, Hanson entering that flat won't end well.

Cassandra stays exactly where she is. She needs Hanson to come to her. She continues, "We know who she's working for but we can't find him,"

"She's going to tell me," Hanson replies.

"What if she doesn't know?" Hanson's jaw and forearms loosen a little. If she's going to get Hanson to come over, Cassandra needs to dangle a carrot. "Look, we can't talk like this here --" Suddenly, she's cut off by a sound from the flat.

Everyone's attention is now on the other side of that door. It was something tapping—and now a creak. *It could be pipes*. Hanson's chest visibly puffs up as she holds her breath. Cassandra doesn't doubt that Hanson could bust through that door. "If you go in there, we're going to have to try to stop you," Cassandra takes a step now, "And we're totally unarmed," Some dark corner of Hanson's soul might relish being mown down in the crescendo of her vengeance, but Cassandra bets she doesn't want to kill two unarmed colleagues. "Help us get them all,"

There's little more she can say. Before long, she realises she's counting her own heart beats. She gets to twelve before she shakes herself out of it. Finally catching her breath, she feels how much she is holding onto the bannister for dear life.

"Fuck," Hanson mutters.

Finally, Hanson takes her eyes off Cassandra and looks to the ground, fixing her gaze at some point on the tiles. In a quick, precise movement, Hanson swings the rifle up away from Cassandra and Takei. She places a fist on the door, as if she's about to punch through it, but then lets her hand drop.

She spins on her heel away from them, kneels, unzips the bag, returns the rifle, and re-zips it. Cassandra can't see what's in the bag.

Hanson lobs the words like a grenade as she strides down the landing towards them: "This better be good," Bag over her shoulder, she walks between the two of them, creating a space they didn't know was there.

As they turn to follow, Takei comes alive, "We've got a car. We'll talk there," he offers. The pair hang back a second and he asks Cassandra quietly, "You trust her?"

She barely questions it.

"She came up totally clean and she's not with McAvoy" she mutters, "But she is hiding something,"

In the seven minutes it's been unoccupied, the temperature inside the car has dropped to only marginally warmer than outside, which is still 17°F. The machine weakly dribbles warm air while they sit in the vapour clouds of their own breath. Takei is in the back with Hanson; Cassandra sits across the driver's seat.

“So who you're British Intelligence?” supposes Hanson.

“Yes,” answers Cassandra.

“Why are you following me?”

“We're not. But we had to find you,”

“Am I bugged?”

“Your cell phone is, yes.”

“Huh,” Hanson thinks for a moment, probably remembering calls she's had, messages, pictures she's sent. As it happens, she has nothing to worry about. “What do you want with me?”

Now Cassandra has a decision to make.

“First, tell us how you found the bomber,”

Eleven minutes later, Hanson has told them everything. And Cassandra is increasingly concerned about what the FBI has been doing, or not doing, on this case for the last nine months. It sounds like Hanson secretly used her brother, Tom the police officer's, licence plate scanner and laptop last night, although she didn't admit to that explicitly. Hanson is worried about the FBI too.

The young woman Hanson found is the same young woman Blake gave them in his voicemail. Cassandra, however, is yet to see any evidence she's their bomber.

“And the door code?” asks Takei.

“I didn't need it,” she says, "I buzzed a neighbour and said I had a delivery,"

Cassandra motions to the clunky bag on the seat between her two passengers.

"What's in the bag, Jill?"

Hanson instinctively places her hand on it. She's biting the inside of her cheek. It appears Jill Hanson isn't completely lost beneath her new hardened exterior. She looks at each of the agents and finally reaches over to open it up. Takei plucks up the rifle, checks the safety and empties the chamber. Then he looks pensively at the large cardboard box in the bag. Hanson was planning on playing a delivery driver to bring Kindle to the door. Cassandra has a vision of Pandora's Box as Hanson opens it up. The hard metal objects reveal themselves in the dull light in the back of the car. No wonder Hanson hesitated, and it's a good thing she did—it means she hasn't been completely lost to the darkness.

Inside is an assortment of heavy metal tools: a wrench, a claw hammer, a screwdriver, a hacksaw. But also a tape measure and a spirit level. Hanson has emptied an entire tool box. Cassandra thinks the truth may be that Hanson was simultaneously burying the tools of torture out of sight and creating more of a burden for herself to carry. This is the same shame that caused her hesitation to open the bag. Someone this conflicted may be more of a liability but right now the pros outweigh the cons.

In contrast to the top layer, what lies beneath is premeditated. She's packed cable ties, pliers, duct tape, a car battery, jump leads and a hessian sack.

No-one says a word about it.

The hint of something Cassandra saw in Hanson nine months ago has been honed and made lethal, but she's not a monster. She appears to be forcing herself to look in the box, like she really can't bear the sight.

Now, there's just one final obstacle ahead of Cassandra making her decision.

"Tell us about the woman who appeared in the command capsule on 3/19,"

Hanson blinks. She takes a deep, uncomfortable breath, crosses her arms over her stomach and then uncrosses them. She zips up the bag.

Finally, she says, "I didn't know if she was real,"

"When you met her?"

"No. Then she was as real to me as you are now. But, the next day. And over the last nine months," she pauses, "How could she be? How could all that have happened?"

"Tell us what you remember. Please,"

Hanson's eyes find a spot in the distance and fix. She's transporting herself back there.

"The capsule was shaking like we were under direct attack. We'd just launched the entire arsenal of ten Minuteman III intercontinentals across the globe," Her breathing intensifies. It sounds like her mouth is drying out. There's a risk now that she becomes too overwhelmed and the details of her story are buried by emotional and physiological feedback. "Everything was red. The sirens were piercing. Flt Cp Blake was on the ground. There was an explosion—from the blast door,"

"Her?"

Cassandra speaks to try to keep Hanson with one foot in the present. Hanson looks into Cassandra's eyes.

"I don't know how she got there. I turned around and she was just there, right next to me. Her clothes were burnt and covered in soot. A t-shirt and jeans like she'd just walked in off civvy street. Average height, slim build. Black I think. Curly hair in a ponytail,"

"What did she do?"

Hanson looks away again, finding that same spot in the distance through the snow, into the storm.

"She asked me how to stop the missiles. But once the launch is triggered, you can't stop them. She said she could get to them. But that's impossible. By then, the missiles would have been approaching four miles a second. She made me draw a diagram of how to disarm the warhead," Her eyes shift up and to the right, digging deeper into her recollection. "I don't remember her leaving,"

That's enough.

"You asked if we found you via your bugged cell. We didn't," Hanson's eyes narrow and come back to Cassandra. "My colleague and I no-longer have access to those resources since we started working independently. Unfortunately, we believe there's a cover-up in play and it'll lead to the next attack. We're the ones who are working to prevent that,"

"So what's your plan?" she asks.

Good question. Hanson's night has now taken a couple of pretty significant gear changes. Another personality might have bugged out at this point—perhaps even the Jill Hanson from nine months ago—but not this woman.

Working with Hanson, Cassandra and Takei could put Kindle and her flat under twenty-four-hour surveillance. But there's no evidence the communication with McAvoy is two-way. They could be wasting their time, the world's time.

"There's one man at the top of all this," she begins, "He's pulling Kindle's strings and countless others'. But she might know something,"

There's a good chance Kindle knows nothing and there's an equal chance she has nail guns and a boiling kettle waiting for them.

"Then why did you stop me?" Hanson asks.

"Mr Takei and I had a colleague—the best of the best—who was murdered entering one of these places," Hanson's plan wasn't terrible, but, unlike Hanson, Cassandra knows what to look for in an interrogation. Hanson doesn't know about Munich; her plan didn't account for the possibility of boobytraps or weapons. She knows nothing about the state of Kindle's mental health. Cassandra has to assume there will be both boobytraps and weapons and she can't assume Kindle will be in there on her own. She needs a different plan. She needs Kindle to let her look around. Then she needs to figure out how to convince Kindle to answer her questions, preferably without maiming Cassandra. It dawns on her that she might have just found a better use for the flying girl. "So here's the plan,"

CHAPTER 6

One false move

"Idiot," Steve reflexively and quietly chastises himself as he fumbles the key into the ignition. He's leaving for the pokey town he grew up in, forced to take leave before it expires—the leave; not his town. He can think of many places he'd rather be—a yacht in the Bahamas would be nice—but he has a duty to his father. Leaving well before sunrise, in the darkness of this relentless blizzard, he hopes he doesn't encounter any other vehicles on the road.

Getting up early has never been a problem. It's getting to sleep that's the issue, made all the more worse since that day in March.

The final jab at him, to really test whether he was some kind of raghead sympathiser was when, a couple of days after the most brutal and repetitive debriefing he'd ever had, Steve was called upon by a black woman from the OSI. She asked all the same questions he'd already gone through, testing the consistency of his responses, making sure he wasn't making anything up. He wondered whether Hanson had set him up to deflect attention from the fact that she'd pulled her sidearm on her superior. That was the real crime here (obviously not including the terrorist strike itself). Unlike him, she accepted her leave straight away, which should have given her enough time to get her head straight and reflect upon her actions. Steve didn't look her up after they were both reassigned. Maybe she'd been discharged.

All the pressure and doubt though—he had to admit to himself that it got to him. He started to privately wonder whether this was what he wanted to be doing with his life. When sleep finally came, he dreamt of being in the backseat of a speeding car, only no-one was in the driving seat and he was trying to drive it from the back. The steering wheel was erratic and the brake pedal always just out of reach, the car getting faster and faster. Sometimes in the dream, Samantha was next to him in the back, sometimes in the front passenger seat, sometimes he was utterly on his own. He always woke up as the car was crashing.

And then, last night, sleep evading him again, he went to a bar. On the way, he'd taken a different route than usual, past a community centre where he knew they did AA meetings and support groups for mental health. He'd heard about it in relation to his mom. He has no idea why he went that way that night but there was a bit of a commotion outside the place and he was pretty much attacked by some psycho coming out of there. And that's how he met the girl. He felt instantly connected to this fucking girl. If he starts now, he knows he won't be able to stop thinking about why he was drawn to her—it's not a road he wants to go down. He's never done anything like that before and vows he never will again.

But, for whatever reason, maybe he was meant to meet her, and to find the drone. He was getting his kit back on when he saw it, lying there, under his shirt. A large, radio-controlled drone, like the one that the bomber would have to have used at the launch base, rigged with extra wires and a claw on its underside that looked like it was made from Mechano. He panicked. He didn't know what to do. He'd just fucked the bomber. He grabbed his shirt and got out of there as fast as he could.

He was three blocks away before he realised he didn't know where he was and needed a cab to get home. The next morning, he found OSI Agent Christchurch's calling card to tell her everything, when he realised they would never believe it was a coincidence. If they already suspected an inside job and then he just happened to stumble onto the 3/19 drone, they'd think he was just trying to deflect guilt from himself. They say serial killers do the same thing when they pretend to be innocent members of the public, just helping the police in any way they can with their investigation. But, as this was going through his mind, the call went through to voicemail.

The key finally finds its home in the ignition. The wipers turn on and smear a giant bird shit across the windshield.

The drive is long and tiring, and the blizzard doesn't let up until he's well clear of Montana. He tries to remember how long it's been since he last made the trip. Since his parents' divorce, he spends any available Thanksgiving and Christmas with his mom—it's the right thing to do. This year, his leave is in December so it'll be Christmas with mom but, since his dad's stroke, Steve's heard a nagging voice telling him he ought to check in on him more often. He hopes he's not going to regret it this time. It's quite the detour from mom's place.

Finally, the procession of white picket fences heralds his homecoming, no sign of any inclement weather out here. There's an odd atmosphere too—there always has been—it's as if nothing ever changes—every day is the same as the last—no one dies—no-one gets out—except him—and Samantha. He drives past a mother packing three or four kids into the back of one of those ridiculous people carriers outside her dishevelled house; toys on the lawn and everything. She looks like she could have gone to his school. Surely she feels the failure of getting stuck here her whole life—and her kids will probably do exactly the same, pumping out kids of their own until the whole town is populated by little clones. She probably lives next door to her mother. He shudders at the thought, knowing—hoping—he's meant for more.

It occurs to him that he's going to need some supplies if he's going to get through this with his sanity so he makes a left and pulls into the town's one gas station.

A TV dinner for one that looks like it's been decomposing in this lukewarm fridge for as long as the guy at checkout, and a bottle of bourbon—for dad.

"Any gas?"

"No, sir,"

There's a little stand of mints—the extra strong kind Steve likes—so he slides a pack onto the checkout alongside the bourbon. And then he throws them back in the stand.

"Never mind,"

His drive to the home takes him past the old family house. His dad, the strongest man on earth, still plans on getting out of the care home and returning here—not out of sentimentality—but because no-one's taking what he worked so hard for. Steve's key slides smoothly into the lock. He's the only one who's been here since the stroke, to pick up some things for him—despite his protesting—and then every time he's visited since.

It's strange how a house feels when no-one's been there in a long time—like walking around the inside of a photograph. Everything is exactly as he left it, as if it were just last night. Except one thing that catches his eye: a photo frame face-down on the mantel above the stove. He doesn't remember putting it that way. It's him and his dad in front of the old car, loaded with camping gear and fishing rods —must have been fourteen at the time. It was their one and only father-son trip and he's always held on to the idea of that. He thinks he must have knocked over the picture on his way out last time. His uncle took the photo in the morning before they set off —he was the photographer of the family. Father and son both had such expectations of catching something.

"You can catch us breakfast, Steve," his dad said jovially the first morning, clambering out of the tent. Steve wanted to make him proud.

Sat gently swaying in the water, gazing out at the view together, Steve felt a silent connection between them and smiled. They were two men, with mutual respect for each other, spending time together not out of parental duty but because they were on a level and enjoyed each other's company. It was a bond and an understanding that surpassed other relationships. They were father and son. It didn't matter that they came back to shore empty-handed. His father strode from the boat to moor up and instructed Steve to steer the rest of the way into the bank. But Steve had never been on a boat before. He bumped the shore by his dad's feet, unsettling the ground.

"Jesus, Stephen!" his dad snapped.

His heart nearly burst on the way to the pit of his stomach. The day was ruined. He'd fucked up. Such an idiot. His knees shook while he desperately tried to do it properly but his dad, like an ox, took over, pulling Steve and the boat back in. Just like that, Steve was a little boy again. He'd blown it.

Thankfully, his dad had forgotten about it by the evening, but it put a sour taste in the air for Steve. Everything else would have been perfect, if only he'd been paying enough attention and used his common sense. He stupidly could have knocked his dad into the water—he was lucky his dad was so solid.

He looks away from the photo to his black leather shoes. Time to go.

At the convalescent home, Steve rounds the door to his dad's room. He's lying on his bed watching daytime television when he looks up, half at Steve, half at the dead space somewhere between them. There was a time when his dad would have snarled something derogatory about the kind of crap he now watches avidly.

"Hello," he says, "Come 'ere,"

"Hi, Dad,"

"I'd get up," he straightens himself out a little but not enough, "but I'm really tired,"

Steve takes the hard chair by the side of the bed and places the grocery bag with the bourbon on the floor.

"Still haven't shaved off that fluff?" says Steve's mustachioed father, "Makes you look like a queer,"

"You're the only one who thinks that, dad," returns Steve—the best he can come up with.

"Speaking of which, have you got that dyke fired yet?"

He's referring to Hanson. Steve hasn't told his dad that Hanson had pulled her gun on him, but he didn't need to say much for all the blame to be fully laid at her door. Dad couldn't consider for a moment that Steve could have done anything wrong. When he'd told his dad that his subordinate was a woman, that was it, not only was she a lesbian but also probably some sort of anarchist feminazi. His time as County Sheriff meant he was never wrong about a person's character and Steve should pay heed. Never work with women. Women in the workplace have something to prove and are intimidated by strong, successful men like Steve. Their emotions have no place in the Air Force, that's for sure. It was like listening to a ninety-year-old, not a fifty-something. It's a shame but Steve knows he'll never change him, and his dad's own father is worse. Still, it's exhausting.

"Hey, Dad," intervenes Steve, "Watching anything good at the moment?"

When it's time to leave, Steve stands up, shakes his father by the hand, pats him on the back and takes the bag of bourbon with him. It's for his own good.

On the road, driving back to the old house, something catches his eye. There never used to be a travel agent in this town. Visions of a better life. A better week at least. His stomach wakes him from his reverie and he thinks of the lukewarm plastic meal waiting for him. He takes a left and pulls into the lot of the fried chicken place.

Inside, he's got his eye on a family bargain bucket when the codger in front in the queue turns and Steve recognises him.

"Mr. Stanton!"

"Um, hello,"

Don't be ridiculous, Steve. He's not going to remember you.

"It's Steve Blake," he says hopefully, "You taught me sixth-grade social studies,"

"Erm," Mr. Stanton clearly has no idea who Steve is but wants to be kind. "Steve Blake?" Maybe the penny did just drop. "Oh yes, of course. How are you? Have you been in town long?"

"Arrived today," Steve replies, relieved, "Visiting my dad,"

"Staying for Christmas?"

"I --" Steve notices that the kid at the counter is waiting to take his order. "I'll see. I might go see my mom up state,"

"Well, have a Merry Christmas," says Mr. Stanton, waving as he approaches the exit with his two bags of hot chicken.

Steve has never been very memorable. He'd kind of loved that teacher though. While he ponders how many kids a teacher is supposed to remember, he's interrupted.

"Say," Mr. Stanton says, turning back around, "Didn't you grow up and join the Air Force?"

The joy of recognition is met almost immediately with the fear that he might know *exactly* who he is. The last thing he needs is talk of 3/19.

“Oh yeah,” he says, attempting to look non-committal, rubbing the back of his neck and looking to the side, “I’m a Captain, sir,”

Looking like a man with an idea, Stanton says, “That’s right. We’d love for you to come and talk to the kids at school. An old boy who made it in the world—it would really motivate them,”

Of course, when Stanton leaves, Steve realises schools are on vacation until next year. It wouldn’t be anything special anyhow, probably a bunch of disinterested soon-to-be drop-out baby-machines. Besides, he’d be too busy.

When he finally pulls up outside the house again, the full bottle of bourbon in the passenger seat topples onto his leg. He remembers Samantha’s hand on his leg and how her breath smelled the last time he saw her.

Steve shouldn’t be here.

* * *

The hot studio lights prickle Anthony Spitelli’s cheeks. He can pilot an F-15 fighter jet at Mach 2.5 but can’t stop being ejected from this conversation, interrupted again before he could begin. He needs to find a way back into it if he is going to make his point.

“-- No and I don't think she's necessarily

anti-Muslim either," continues one of the other guests. Anthony Spitelli already met her on another TV debate earlier this week. She's a Muslim and a human rights campaigner. Her name is A'dab Ateş. She speaks quickly and fluently, leaving little air for Anthony. "And, like any sane person, I don't believe in stoning in the 21st Century, but she needs to tread very carefully when it comes to enforcing her own views on others. Or at least, we need to be wary of her doing so,"

She talks about Her as if She is just a person. That's what needs to change. If --

"But she's also reportedly rescued dozens of flood victims, put out a factory fire and perhaps even stopped the runaway train at Waterloo last month," interjects the host.

He turns to Anthony, invitingly. *Thank you.*

"Yes," Anthony begins. He chooses his words carefully since he knows that one wrong word and he could come across as a religious lunatic. "We need to understand that She is so much more than a person. The fact She doesn't see the world like we do is a good thing. When I saw her after she dispensed with a nuclear missile like it was nothing to her, I felt it, like many others like me; how She represents a new beginning—a new chapter in mankind's relationship with God,"

“Most people see her more as a superhero than an angel, don’t they?” challenges the host.

“Truth, Justice and The American Way,” smirks the other guest, a man who resigned as Foreign Secretary about a decade ago, attempting relevance now, “But I would be interested to know *exactly whose side* she's on. Wouldn’t it be *great* to have a chat with her? But, *yes*, I agree with you, A’dab, we *do* need to be *wary*. Everything she does could have *wide-reaching* political and economic implications. For instance, *some* groups *are* claiming she's on some sort of *Crusade*,”

“Time will tell,” the presenter muses superficially, “That’s all we have time for but thank you for joining us, and thank you to all three of my guests today,” He turns his chair directly to one of the huge TV cameras. “In the meantime, if you have an opinion on the *Superwoman*, we want to hear from you. You can join in the conversation on social media and follow us for updates as the story develops,”

Anthony’s lost again. *A new chapter in mankind’s relationship with God*. Anthony’s relationship with God was dead when his parents found out he’s gay. When what the Church considers a most sickening and shameful sin was exposed, and his degenerate soul was condemned to an eternity of damnation, it was his mother, not God, that found it in her heart to accept him. His mother was the only one who didn’t threaten fire and brimstone. But now, God has sent an angel to save Anthony's life and change the world. God chose him to be the first to see His angel for a reason. He just has to figure out why.

* * *

Cassandra ends the call but keeps the phone in hand. It's 07:59 MST on 1st December. O'Connor promised he'd try to contact the girl and relay Cassandra's request. She's used to waiting but that doesn't mean she has to enjoy it.

Before going to check out Kindle's car with Hanson, Takei moved theirs around to the front of the apartment building to better see through the worsening visibility. Now, still in the car, she watches the building while she waits for O'Connor to confirm the girl's attendance. She may be calling in the cavalry but she's not entirely stepping back. She'll be in there with her. Takei will wait with Hanson in the building's entrance in case anything goes wrong.

Without their combined body-heat, the temperature in the car is dropping and snow is starting to pile up on the windscreen. Through the fog of her condensing breath, the snow on the windscreen and the snowglobe outside, she picks out two shadows coming her way. It's Takei and Hanson. They're running.

To her surprise, Takei comes around and

opens her door.

"Car's gone," he says, "She escaped out her window,"

Takei will be looking for approval to search her flat but she won't give it.

So much for the flying girl.

"You two stay here and warm up,"

She's already getting out of the car, facing the cold slap of the wind, and Takei knows he can't dissuade her. Cassandra needs Takei to stay with Hanson, who hangs back, her face obscured. Ordinarily, she'd let her go; tell her to get some sleep, forget about what happened tonight, forget about the two MI6 agents she just met, and go back to being a law-abiding citizen. But she and Takei are out here on their own and on the run. She needs a team.

Looking across the road at the building, the absence of a Beta team ready to drop in looms in the distance of another world, along with a proper plan and an authorised operation.

When she reaches the back of the building, she sees what the others saw. The light by the window of Kindle's flat is still on, burning through the snowfall like a lighthouse, calling weary seamen to the rope dangling from her open window five stories up. Frost isn't settling on the still-warm rope—she was here only moments ago and they missed her. The suspect has left no footprints, probably dragging something behind her to sweep the snow.

Cassandra heads back to the front of the building. She misses the crackle of an earpiece she isn't wearing, feels the rub of a Walther PPK she isn't wearing. Instead, the barbaric monkey wrench inside her coat pulls down on her left side. There's a reason she's here, she reminds herself. McAvoy has to be stopped, and maybe they can still catch up to Kindle.

The door to the building is propped open by a bundle of post she didn't see Takei leave there. Inside, there's no shaft of light down the stairwell—no doubt the roof is capped by impenetrable snow now. She begins the climb, waiting with her heart in her throat for the security lights to flare upon her approach. She unsheathes the wrench too. By the second step, her heart is pounding as if she were scaling a mountain. Janice, the work therapist, warned her this might happen. No matter how much of a fool Zulu was, Cassandra blames herself for everything that happened in Munich. With her teeth, she removes the thick glove of her free hand and places her palm on the cold, hard bannister. It becomes her connection to the present, away from exploded heads, brain splatter and splintered skull. She draws her attention to her breathing and notices how it feels to draw in the air through her nostrils, down into her lungs. And back out again. She notices the feeling of the bannister in one hand and the weight of the heavy-duty wrench in the other—a practical tool to keep her alive if necessary. It's enough to keep her going and, already, she can breathe more freely. This isn't Munich.

When the security light does flicker on as she scales the first floor, it's reassuring.

The lock on Kindle's door is easily picked but the door doesn't budge. There must be auxiliary locks secured from the inside. The monkey wrench would be no match for the heavy fire door. Time for Plan B. She rings the buzzer for Kindle's nextdoor neighbour—a single white caucasian male in his early thirties—and explains that there's been a report of a gas leak and she needs to check all the appliances on this floor. When she's in the neighbour's apartment she makes a beeline for the back room, which turns out to be his bathroom. The resident stands concerned behind her as she throws up the sash window and the storm bellows in. With her head outside, she can see Kindle's window about five feet away, the rope emerging from a pile of snow forming on the sill, which brightly reflects the ceiling light inside. If she misses the ledge, there's still the rope—which by now is brittle and icy.

"What are you doing?!" shouts the male behind her.

She ignores him as she clambers awkwardly out of the window. Climbing through, she clings onto the frame with her gloved fingertips and, as she gets outside, presses herself tightly to the side of the building, grounding her feet firmly on the slippery ledge. Cautiously standing, she feels the difference between looking up five stories and looking down. The wind and snow bite at her face. The ground is nowhere in sight and, for all she can see through the snowstorm, she could be at the summit of Mt Everest. Standing upright on the ledge, back to the wall, she shuffles to the edge, the storm now a cracking bullwhip from every side.

For a moment, staring at Kindle's ledge, she feels the threat of her feet encased in ice, frozen to the spot. It's only a threat. For Ali, for Otto, for the crew at the launch base, she throws herself over the bottomless precipice to the other six-inch window ledge. She doesn't close her eyes once, even as her front foot skids on Kindle's ledge and her back knee smashes into the side of it. Her whole body is bent forwards, with every muscle stretching for the rope as her foot slides off the ledge and everything else follows. She gets her gloved hands around the rope but, as she feared, it's slippery as Hell and she keeps going, rope sliding through her gloves as if it were air. She grips with all her might and her body slams backwards into the side of the building.

When she looks up, she's only slid down one story. Under her feet, she feels a ledge and lets it take her weight.

Her knees and elbows are shaking and her right knee feels like it's bleeding heavily despite the cold. Her hands are hot with rope-burn. But she is now pulling herself towards Kindle's flat.

Cassandra finds herself in Kindle's bedroom. The first thing she sees is the open laptop on the bed, but she needs to process the whole room—she can't afford to miss anything. Immediately, something else jumps into her peripheral vision at floor-level. A frame-like structure with four propeller blades: a large, radio-controlled drone. She keeps scanning, floor to ceiling and back. A bicycle frame. A messy desk, a waste paper bin containing a tied and full plastic bag. A hole in the wall.

When she’s as confident as she can be, she starts towards the laptop but stumbles as her smashed knee buckles. She limps the rest of the way. She swivels the laptop to see the screen and isn't sure at first what she's seeing. A raven-haired girl in her underwear on a bed with fairy lights entwined around its frame. The girl appears to be typing and then looking at something to the side of the camera like she's interacting with something or someone. Elsewhere on the screen are messages and usernames, a little coin icon and a counter. She realises the room, the bed; it's here where she is now. This must be Kindle. The bed has been made since this video was taken, with the hospital-folded corners of someone who's worked in healthcare, hospitality, or served in the armed forces. But the time on the screen is now, 0803, as if the video is live. She presses the Esc key but nothing happens. Whatever she presses, nothing happens.

She needs something else.

After the laptop and the drone, the next thing she'd observed was a bicycle frame. It has no back wheel and, most disturbingly, one of the brake levers has been removed. Cassandra knows now that Kindle has a DIY dead-man's trigger, which means they need to find her *fast*.

There's a double wardrobe, a small chest of drawers and a bedside unit with two drawers. Clothes are neatly folded on top of the laundry basket. There's a desk with three computer monitors, two computer towers under it and various computer kit Cassandra can't identify: anonymous black boxes with coloured lights and tangled leads. Other than the equipment, the desk is tidy but, by the desk is a waste paper bin containing a bulging plastic bag, tied in a knot, its semi-transparency revealing fizzy drinks cans, junk food cartons, a vodka bottle. She feels an inexplicable protectiveness to preserve the delicate veil this room represents. But she needs to find this woman.

The top drawer of the bedside table is full of life: tissues, tangled jewellery, aspirin, sleeping pills, another empty bottle of vodka, old parking tickets, vibrator, broken earphones, receipts, some loose change, bank notes. The bottom drawer contains only one thing. She lifts out the beautiful old wooden box covered in stickers. The wrench lands a shattering blow and Cassandra begins sifting. Inside are Kindle's passport, which Cassandra pockets, and stacks of letters. *Bingo.* She scoops up the laptop and letters ready to get the Hell out of there.

CHAPTER 7

The Doomsday Clock

Lucy hasn't slept in three days. Every time she considers going home or stopping to rest her feet on the ground, her mission compels her on. Agent Takei's words ring in her ears: He'll come for you... If you fail, the world will burn.

Her fear of stopping isn't just about those words but, whatever is going on for her, there are more important things to deal with now. She must go on looking for things to do and she must keep on the mask.

Then why am I here? She floats in the darkness of the night sky above the dirty yellow glow of London. She rubs her eyes. She struggles to recall the journey here but days are running into each other and now the last thing she remembers is a tower-block fire in Warsaw.

Perhaps she should just rest her eyes for a moment—on her own pillow.

She should be so lucky.

She finds their flat after orienting her position against the London Eye. As she flies towards it, she begins to imagine that James has shut the bedroom window, but it's always been open when she's needed it. She pulls herself through the frame as if swimming through a reef and allows her eyes to adjust to the gloom. The bed is empty. The bedside clock reads 22:04. The soft, well-worn bed draws her in with its downy, imaginary tendrils but James' absence nags.

He's in the kitchen scrolling on his phone with a blank expression on his face, wearing the bottom half of the pyjamas she got him last Christmas. His "*Hi*" sounds so normal, like they saw each other for lunch earlier and she's just got home from work. It's not like this is the first time they've seen each other in days and she's been nearly killed four times. *Does he still even care? Should he?*

"Do you want to go to Dan and Emma's for New Year?" he asks.

Seriously? She's standing here in a superhero costume, covered in oil and grease, worn and scraped. Holding her mask in her fist, her hair's a mess, she's wearing no make-up and she looks like shit. He's acting like... No, she's not going to do this right now.

"I'm going to bed," she manages to say.

"Oh, yeah, alright. Night,"

I'm going to kill him.

"Look, I don't really feel like thinking about New Year right now," then she draws first blood, "But you can go,"

He makes a point of closing all the apps and locking his screen—she wonders when she learnt to recognise the thumb movements—but he still can't look at her. Still struggling with feelings.

"I'm worried about you," he says. *Why's he making this difficult?* A fight would be so much easier. "This feels like the first time I've seen you in weeks," he continues, "Every spare moment, you're out in your costume," Now she can't go to bed, but she still can't tell him what's going on. She can't burden him with her reality; the knowledge that everything could be about to end at any moment. He turns and looks at her where she stands, by the door between the kitchen and hallway. "It's like you're looking for something. What else happened at the Professor's?" He puts his phone in his pocket.

"Look, I'm *fine*," she mutters, "Honestly,"

He looks perplexed and a little sceptical but concedes, "Okay, I'm coming to bed too,"

Her guilt can't compete with the soft pillow perfectly forming around her head as she sinks into bed. She could barely open her eyes if she tried. She suspects James will be awake next to her for a while longer but she knows she'll be asleep in seconds.

"I don't believe you," he says.

She wishes they could have this conversation in the morning instead.

"What?" she groggily mumbles through the pillow without moving.

"There's something wrong. At first, you not wanting to talk about it was fine..." he trails off.

She fights the urge for silence and forms the minimum number of words: "But it's not now?"

In the quiet that follows, Lucy wonders if he's still awake. As if with great effort, he finally says, "I feel like I'm losing you,"

And with that, Lucy is awake. This could be more serious than she thought. Yet again, she's reminded of how little she looks outside of her own drama. The sudden fear of losing James shocks a lump into her throat that threatens to obstruct anything she can say. She sits up and looks at him in the darkness, finding a furrowed brow and teary eyes.

"You aren't losing me—I love you with all my heart," Putting her arms around his neck, she says all she can and means it, "I'm sorry,"

"Why can't you let me in?" he asks.

"I will—I just—Not yet. It wouldn't be fair,"

In the morning, she doesn't remember falling asleep. She knows nothing was really resolved but, hopefully, they'll both feel a little bit better.

She goes to work in the morning. The commute is the perfect reminder of how lonely London is. Millions of people crammed in together in silence, no eye contact, no talking—just constant automated messages from the train, recorded one after another by a woman locked in a recording studio reading from a script.

It doesn't take much acting to appear to be unwell at work. The more of her colleagues tell her that she should still be resting, the better. *Very nasty bug, wouldn't want to spread it.*

Someone even said to her, *Stop being a hero.*

If going to work and spreading the flu virus is heroism, at least she knows where she's been going wrong. *Thanks, Geoff.* In her head, she gives him a sarcastic double thumbs-up.

The next day, she emails in sick again.

* * *

"I hear the whispers in the air," said Patient R, "In the wind—it's talking to me again,"

"And what is it saying to you?"

"The same as before," he said and looked away from the webcam for a moment, distracted, "Calling me. The sunlight is beaming into my room through the window today, and it's telling me to hope,"

"Hope can be good," answered the Professor, attempting to reach his patient through the void of the internet.

"It's telling me to hope because the world is getting better," The Professor listens, as another of his followers wobbles on the tracks he has laid for them, threatening to derail. "Do you know what I mean? I know it sounds crazy but I feel the hand of God, like He stopped the nukes as if to say, '*I got this*',"

It was another difficult session in the aftermath of 3/19, made all the more so by the necessity to conduct them all from hotels, motels and hostels. The contents were symptomatic of a greater emerging problem for him and his mission. Despite this, however, and the Herculean challenge it presented, it galvanised the Professor's resolve.

Months later, he stares in the mirror at a man he doesn't recognise, in someone else's home. The lines on this face are deeper, like cuts. His skin has become more like parchment over time too. There are now permanent dark shadows around his eyes and at his temples. He is being ravaged by this cancer. Long gone are the days when he could imagine a future looking like a retired movie star. The idea, and that young idealist who had it, are so far from reality that he can't help but smile. *How far we all are from reality*, he concedes.

Turning from the mirror, he walks down the overly-decorated hallway to the drawing room. His refuge within his temporary accommodation, the room is filled with books from floor to ceiling, all chosen by him. In the centre of the room is a solitary wingback armchair in oxblood leather. To the side of that, a small, circular, French-polished table presenting a glass of water. Before he sits, he removes his notebook and pencil from the inside pocket of his jacket and his spectacles from the breast pocket.

It all begins with the ancient, unspeakable loss mankind has inflicted upon itself for the sake of what we call progress. Our ancestors reach out to us through the ages, in what Jungians call the cultural unconscious, trying in vain to illuminate the truth through myth, stories and dreams. One such truth is this loss, most famously represented by the eviction from Eden with its lesson that, for knowledge, we sacrificed a paradise of meaning, connectedness and personal truth. We're left simply with the hint that something is missing. Most get no further in their search for meaning than noticing that simple clue. Life never feels complete, our hearts never feel full and we are never content for long. The further we *progress*, the further we fall from our truth and the more invisible it becomes.

The proliferation of consumerism; the obligation to have it all and sacrifice nothing except to serve ambition; the destruction of the Mother sacrificed at the altar of *progress*; the consequent disavowal of the power of early-life interactions on the development of the Self; all these things and more are the milestones on the road to mankind's spiritual atrophy. Despite millenia of being social creatures with deep and powerful interconnectedness, we are learning to avoid at all cost the vulnerability of needing one another. As a result, it is now estimated that one in ten five to sixteen year-olds is suffering from a mental health problem. The number increases with each generation as the inextirpable cycle continues. It is already at crisis-point.

He has seen and heard too much suffering in his life. The child who witnesses boxing matches between her parents, cradling her baby brother, who grows up to birth multiple offspring of her own each from physically or emotionally abusive fathers as she blindly struggles to repair her past and, in doing so, repeats it. Or her brother, who is so determined not to become his violent father yet so afraid of his own anger that he not only becomes an emotionally abusive adult but turns his internalised loathing onto his own body. Some can be saved and some save themselves, but the vast majority are locked into this psychological confinement, unequipped with any self-reflective thinking that isn't guilt and shame in disguise, armed only by their early relational experiences. Their life is a *gaol* filled with the many trap-doors and boobytraps of their dysfunctional emotional regulation.

Professor McAvoy's great curse, and responsibility, stems from the knowledge that we live in a world so defended against its own guilt for this damage, so rejecting of the responsibility to change, that the only course for correction is apocalyptic.

A faint knock at the door draws Professor McAvoy into the present moment.

"Excuse me, Professor," the woman begins, "but you asked me to tell you as soon as the new writing materials arrived,"

She is the widowed Mrs. Wimberly and a study in a kind of individual intervention unattainable at any meaningful scale in the populus. If it were attainable, there would be no need for the Professor's plans.

When they met, she was in crisis herself. He remembers hearing her voice for the first time on the car radio. He had been driving somewhere and the host of the programme had been drivelling on about the foremost matter to the world at that point: *Do you put your chocolate in the fridge or the cupboard?* Incredibly, functioning human beings were texting in with their strong opinions on the matter. It went on for some minutes, during which time the Professor remembers saying aloud to the radio, "If reality is so unbearable, please just have a labotomy. And put everyone else out of our misery,"

He changed the station, landing on a channel broadcasting an interview with a famous children's author of whom he'd never heard.

"-- around that time you went to Sierra Leone?"

"Yes. It was there that I adopted my daughter," said the author, "I named her Wednesday because that was the day I acquired her,"

"She was just a baby, wasn't she?" directed the interviewer rhetorically, "How was it trying to start up an investment business while looking after a baby?"

"Well," smiled the author, "Yes, it was tough. But we just had to get on with it. One night, we decided enough was enough and we just let her scream and didn't go to her,"

"Oh, gosh, yes," sympathised the interviewer, "I think we've all been there,"

"That baby screamed and screamed and screamed. For hours. Until eventually, she just collapsed, exhausted and fell asleep," she said triumphantly.

Her brain flooded with cortisol, her throat raw and her cheeks burning with the lesson that no-one comes, thought the Professor.

Now look. Carol Wimberley is a woman transformed. While Wednesday is at school, Carol stays here for her own special education. For simplicity, the Professor has taken lodging with them both. Mrs Wimberley listens to her daughter and knows that her needs are important even when she does not understand them. She cooks, she cleans, she sings, she soothes, and she pursues her own interests. All this makes her happy and has given her daughter a mother. A society that encourages its constituents that they can and should have it all is a society that forgets the need for all people to serve, both inwardly and outwardly, to be truly satisfied. To serve and be served, to dominate and be dominated, to love and be loved—as in the teachings of the Zen philosophy, fulfilment comes from harmony, which is balance in all directions.

"Please leave them by the door, Carol," he instructs, "Thank you,"

As she bends, her white silk blouse stretches, providing a hint of the rope harnesses she wears beneath. *A balance in all directions.* He feels his old body responding. He sees that she places a newspaper on top of the brown cardboard box of stationery. Before he can open his mouth, she is gone. Mrs. Wimberley knows full-well that the Professor has removed himself from the world of current affairs.

He returns to his notebook and to the last word he wrote: *apocalyptic*. He doesn't like the word. He feels his father instructing him to tear the page out and start again, as he did so many times when he was a boy, practising letters to obscure aunts he would never meet. Nevertheless, his great plan should soon come to fruition, if only he can finally overcome the shift in his patients that he first noticed with Patient R. In his online meetings with them, he has seen how they have each taken recent events and projected onto them their own meaning.

The common thread, however, is that the events of 19th March have been distorted into fable. The apocryphal *hand of God*, demigods, superheroes and saviours permeate the collective unconscious once more, rooted in the aforementioned deep sense of loss and need for the return to an earlier, more soulful existence. The population misinterprets the purpose of these myths and finds misguided hope that the toxic status quo will be maintained. At this pivotal moment in human history, the Professor must navigate the emergent paradigm on the behalf of his apostles. Professor McAvoy must become like a lighthouse now.

Ashley Kindle, Patient K per his journal,

has shown him that what she and the others need is firm action to remind them of their reality and the role they must play. The risk is greatest now, while each of them is in possession of their deadly little packages, painstakingly syphoned from the single source he obtained for them. Any one of them could be discovered and caught, at which point the defences with which McAvoy would be battling would be doubled. Borders closed, national lockdowns, world-leaders in hiding. If his apostles remain strong and strike as one, across the globe, the world won't know what has hit it.

There was a rumour that ISIS had obtained weapons-grade plutonium. The truth, however, was that they had something far more devastating. It wasn't until the Professor witnessed ISIS conducting its one and only human trial that he saw for himself.

The subject was an outwardly fit and healthy young man, in his early thirties. A miniscule trace of the airborne antigen was released into his sealed chamber, which also contained enough food to keep him well-fed for a month and a tap for running water. An exhaust pipe took the air of the chamber through a filter to the open desert above. Al-Nasser and several other high-ranking members observed through a plexiglass window. For the first several days, there was no evidence that anything was amiss with the gentleman. After seven days, a retractable wall was withdrawn to join the chamber to another, in which there was a second, uninfected inmate. On Day Nine, Inmate 1 began coughing. On Day Ten, the first pus-filled lesions appeared on his hands and neck. By Day Eleven he was clearly dying and, on Day Twelve, his life was over. Inmate 2 was dead by Day Nineteen. As promised, the virus appeared to have been transmitted while the first inmate was asymptomatic. It was the perfect silent killer.

As this thought finds its way to the tip of his pen, Mrs Wimberley's newspaper tugs at the periphery of his awareness.

When he reaches the door, he must support himself on the frame to catch his breath, staring intensely at the unmoving paper while the room spins around it. He waits to no avail for his vision to clarify and, knowing that if he stoops to collect the paper, the rush of blood will send him tumbling, he slides down the door-frame, cursing.

Had he not removed himself last year from *the news*, he might not feel so utterly disoriented as he reaches forward. Normally, global change does not come overnight. There is usually a gradual procession during which the road is paved for something like the Trump presidency or the rises and falls of Fascism. Whether or not one observes them fully at the time, in hindsight all the predictors tend to be apparent. What the Professor finds on the front page of the newspaper, however, defies every established convention.

It is as though, aware of the threat posed by the Professor and his apostles, the incumbent cultural unconscious has manifested an immune response. The front page of the newspaper heralds the arrival of a figure who is the very antithesis of the Mother the world so sorely needs. Superficially, she appears to be the 'omnipotent rescuer', whose empathic concern for the abused and helpless is felt all the more powerfully due to what has been projected onto her. Powerful and ambitious, she is the very personification of the Witch archetype, representing the primordial feminine concern with herself. So awesome is the Witch archetype's hunger that she absorbs others' life-force and turns it into her own power to use as she pleases. This flying woman is a symbol that reinforces the lie that one can live life with no limits and no self-sacrifice. There is no wax between her wings to be melted by flying too close to the Sun.

A lesser man would attribute this synchronous moment to fate, but the symbolism is too obvious to the Professor. He now knows what he must do to set his apostles on course.

* * *

Steve finds himself staring. His eyes have followed the contrail of a passenger jet that thundered overhead but now he just stares blankly at the sky out of the window of the old folks home. He doesn't bother to shake himself from the daydream—he allows himself to sink back into the vision of intercontinental ballistic missiles pummelling into the horizon. The resulting thick mushroom clouds blot out the sun and the world burns silently in his head.

"Have you been watching that one with Ted Danson and the blonde girl in the afterlife?" his father asks in an attempt at conversation.

"No," Steve breaks away from the window to look at the yellowy man.

"It's not bad," he pauses for a second's thought, "She kinda looks like your prom queen did,"

Steve's back prickles. *Why the fuck would he even go there?* Steve's dad isn't such an idiot that he doesn't realise how cruel it is to talk about Samantha like that. Or maybe he is that emotionally retarded. He imagines punching the old man but the thought of his fist connecting with his spongy nose makes him sick. Deep down he knows he doesn't have the balls to do it.

"Go on," his dad goads, self-pityingly. He's

seen something in Steve's eyes. "Hit me then,"

Steve looks around for a bottle and sees nothing. His dad isn't drunk, this is just the way he is now. Technically, Red Brick is a convalescent home.

"Dad, I'm not going to hit you, just don't talk about her,"

He feels the concussion wave and the airbag slapping his chest and face all over again. Clenching his jaw and squinting away the unwelcome memory, he looks at his fallen saviour, this old bastard, sitting in front of him. It makes him want to cry. Thank God for the care nurse that arrives to check his dad's blood pressure.

By the time he gets back to the house, he's exhausted. He imagines Samantha making him a cup of hot coffee at the counter. Instead, he uncaps the nearly empty bottle of bourbon left by the armchair and pours himself a glass, and then another, swallowing hard on his resentment. Before long the bottle is empty and Steve is scanning the sky through the window, cracking open a can of beer. A truck rumbles past along the road and he's transported back to the launch command capsule, the lights going out and the world flipping upside down. Oblivion is just a key-turn away. Or a pull-tab.

A sickening acid feeling is rising up in his

belly just as his recollection reaches the moment he ran face-first into the blast-door, trying to save his own skin. He wonders again whether Hanson ratted on him and his superiors are holding his cowardice as some sort of ammunition. Maybe they just don't want to make a bad PR situation any worse by exposing one of their own. One way or another though, it's only a matter of time before he's outed. He breaks through the intrusive drama playing out in his head with another pull-tab. The second can always tastes less bad.

The tab clapping into the top of the full can, accompanied by its frothy fizz, is a sound familiar to Steve's childhood—a childhood spent in this house. He realises that he hasn't given it any time since he's been here and gets up to walk around a little. Only a few steps into his tour, he pauses at the cellar door. He doesn't think about it—he just walks over, takes the key from on top of the doorframe, unlocks it and steps into the darkness. Since that day in the command capsule, he hasn't managed to lie in a bath for feeling closed in, let alone climb down into a cellar. *How many beers did I have?* Finding the cord hanging to his side, he switches the light on and descends the wooden steps.

He used to hide down here where it now smells of damp concrete and lighter fluid. The air is stale and still, gripping him firmly as he passes through. It's crazy how memory works, he thinks, as he remembers descending those steps hundreds of times but doesn't remember ever leaving.

The cellar is walled on three sides by mostly bare, floor to ceiling shelves holding only odd paint cans, clothes pegs, light bulbs, a roll of string—just random junk. The walls are thick concrete and there's at least a foot of concrete overhead and sturdy beams and pillars supporting the structure throughout. He takes a gulp from the can in his hand and finishes it, slurping through his teeth. There's something else about the cellar, he notices: it's utterly, utterly silent. No road noise, no refrigerator humming, no neighbour's radio. Just the sound of his own breath.

CHAPTER 8

Time's up

The 1 Train jingles with cheery families. Carl's never been to New York before. He's never been so far East in all his life. They're heading to his new mom's sister's apartment somewhere. Carl's new parents are called Chris and Christy. In three weeks, it'll be Chris and Christy on Christmas Day.

Maybe it's the season but here people actually talk to each other on public transport. It's not the New York he heard about. They're making eye-contact and everything. He looks around at so many groups of tourists wearing heavy-looking backpacks and trying to control wheelie suitcases that keep threatening to either topple or roll away. They're mostly other families. Having been excluded from having one his whole life, he feels like he's finally been let into the special club—the biggest club in the world. It's fucking great.

Out of nowhere, a baby starts screaming and threatens to puncture right through the happy moment. He hates the sound of babies crying and immediately starts looking for the source of the noise. No-one else seems to care —least of all Chris and Christy, who are talking about the meatloaf of '98 or something.

The train stops and a bunch of people clear out. Thankfully, the crying stops too. As the crowd shuffles and reconfigures, space is made by the doors and someone catches his eye. She's like some sort of albino goth chick but she's an absolute babe. Okay, that's probably an over-statement but she's definitely the hottest girl in the train car. She's much older than him, probably like 20 or something. He wonders whether she's been there the whole time or she just got on. He does his best to keep looking without looking so long that she'll look back. He has to look away a couple of times. She has nice long ashy hair, creamy smooth skin and incredible eyes visible over a cheap medical face mask. He can't see her tits through her big coat but she's totally got thigh-gap and he can imagine her ass looks great the other side of her tight jeans. Speaking of tight jeans, he remembers he better not let his head get too carried away.

He notices a cool tattoo on the back of her hand. It's this really intricate rose and he realises he's seen it before—like in a lot of detail and this isn't the sort of tat you pick out of a catalogue. He's seen that hand doing some awesome stuff. Although she looks totally different, it's definitely her. He can see it in her eyes now. His heart thuds a single big thud: It's Piper from CamGurlz.

Sometimes, in some sweaty excitement, he'd send her a message. Always something he'd cringe at afterwards and it was always pointless —she wouldn't do anything on camera unless you paid for a private session, which someone always did. She'd just say, *Going private,* and vanish while some other guy spunked cash at her. He always felt like he just missed out, while the temptation to log into Chris' PayPal taunted him. The most he ever got was an accidental nip slip.

And now, here she is and he's the one feeling exposed. He is weirdly ashamed to see her in real life. Thank God she couldn't possibly know who he is. *But what if she can tell?* He quickly averts his eyes and stares at the door to her side.

She's hot though. As time ticks by and the subway rumbles on, he wonders about saying something. Just something smart and cool. He looks at her again and sees something in her hand. It's pretty weird because it looks like a bicycle brake lever. Actually, that's more than weird. He remembers a movie that had a suicide bomber with something like that. She doesn't look like a suicide bomber. *But what if she is?* He doesn't want to make a big scene if he's wrong but it's not one of those things you're supposed to keep quiet. He checks the map above his head; it's six stops until they get off.

He can't help his imagination. The bomb would obliterate everyone in the carriage in a fireball. It would blow a hole in the side of the carriage, derail the train and cause the whole thing to crunch up like a soda can. Anyone who wasn't engulfed in flame, burning alive, would be smashed around and crushed. Black smoke would fill the subway and there would be dead bodies everywhere, trapped underground. It was a case of being incinerated, crushed or suffocated. Or all three.

He turns to Christy, who's sitting on his left, and tries to interrupt her conversation with Chris.

"Hey. Um. Can we get off?" he asks quietly. No-one hears him. "Can we get off please?" he asks a little louder.

"Why, honey?" asks Christy, "Whatever's wrong?"

"I just really think we should get off now," he tries to say quietly and calmly, while desperately honestly enough to get through to her.

"Well--" she begins, obviously not sure what to say. Chris is paying attention now too.

He can't tell them, that'd be stupid. But she

could be about to blow up the whole train. *Fuck*. He doesn't want to die. But maybe he's just being a dumb kid.

"I -- Can we get off? *Please*?" is all he can manage. It comes out a little louder than he'd expected.

Other people start looking. A lady standing a little away in the aisle turns her worried head to investigate. The guy with her is looking too.

"Everything okay here?" the guy asks.

While Chris and Christy shuffle and make friendly noises like they're on the case and everything's fine, Carl feels the guy follow his gaze to Piper255. Her hand is now pulled up in her sleeve. She's begun looking not so great—like she's uncomfortable; sweaty, scratching her head, staring at the floor. This isn't good. His heart beats loudly in his chest and in his head, pushing inside his ears with every thud.

He remembers how, after 3/19, everyone seemed to talk about how fragile the world is and how precious life is. He thought that feeling would last forever—that it had changed his life, changed him, given him a new perspective. Now he realises he didn't learn his lesson at all. It only took days for him to go back to wasting his time, jerking off to CamGurlz. He hadn't really done anything with his life except keep himself distracted, even after meeting Chris and Christy. There is so much he wants to do.

The train stops. It had been slowly grinding into whichever station they'd reached without Carl noticing until now. The doors open and Piper's eyes bolt. Then, like a Dementor, her wispy black form vanishes through the nearest door.

He stares deeply at where she had been standing and takes a breath.

* * *

After all this time, the woman from 3/19 is real. Somehow, Jill had buried the thought of this mystery woman in the prairie outside that escape hatch. The only way she knew how to move on was to dedicate herself to a mission, focusing her mind and body on it until there was nothing else. And then these two dirty British agents arrive, dig everything up and throw her off the trail. So far their collusion has only brought them full-circle, hunting the bomber again after she already had her in her sights. But maybe she can use them to get to the man supposedly responsible and put an end to all this.

She spent nine months with the threat of her sanity crumbling. Nine months of guilt for getting out of launch control alive; the shame of being used by terrorists; the horror of what befell

Danny and the rest of them while she was a hundred feet below. If only the Brits really knew who they have with them, who she really is.

There was a time when Danny was the only person alive who really knew who she was, but now, she fears he wouldn't even recognise her.

One weekend, they'd gone camping together, not far from base, but she'd somehow let him convince her to do it after she'd told him about her camping trips with her dad.

They lay on hard roll mats on the dusty earth, breathing in the sweet smoke of their campfire, which she knew would hang to her hair for as long as she could hold off before washing it out, and stared up at the stars together. They'd spent the day laughing and fooling around. Danny had brought a tent and stupidly forgot the poles. After a moment of tension, where even Danny thought maybe he'd royally messed up, she couldn't help herself, something surprising happened: she laughed. Forgetting the poles was just the sort of thing Danny would do. She wasn't even tempted to lecture him on paying attention or taking the wild seriously. They spent the next hour and half stripping twigs and branches to use as poles instead, only to eventually realise it was better to string the thing up between a big rock and a tree and be done with it. She realised that, for all his goofy jokes and dumbass behaviour, even in the midst of the absurdity of a couple of Air Force officers failing at putting up a tent, Danny never made her feel shame.

Lying there, as the campfire dwindled and the stars and moon shone down on them, he said, half to the sky, half to her:

"You are so much more than you let people see," and he turned his face towards hers, "You know?"

"What are you talking about, Danny?"

"Well, look, you are great at your job, but there's a whole other side to you. This suits you out here, Ranger Jill,"

"That's Flight Lieutenant Ranger Jill to you, sir,"

"You can call me, Yogi Bear if you like,"

At this, she pretended to puke.

Her phone buzzes in her jeans pocket. Tom's caller ID displays a photo of him and the girls, taken when they were babies. Jill should be with them, not here, half-way across the country. But she can't let go; she can't let Danny's murderer go. If she answers, Tom would try to talk her out of it. Or worse, she'd lose her nerve.

"I'm sorry," she whispers to the breeze as she declines the call.

The taste of old coffee cloys in her mouth as she rediscovers it. The deserted, snowy street where she stands is barely a street. It's a smelly gap between buildings with a road running down it. The whole of New York smells like garbage left in the rain. The big city carries a constant droning sound like it's running on one huge diesel generator. She was sick of it after the first hour.

Caught here in this concrete maze, there's nothing to blend into—no people, no cover. Instead, Jill turns on a heel and abandons her post at the entrance to the King's College. She'll walk to the next corner and, before reaching it, one-eighty and head back. Keeping moving is her way of appearing natural in a city where no-one stands still, on a street where there are no people.

Agent Bryce had figured the bomber would be avoiding airports but she insisted they do the same—that they couldn't risk themselves being caught. So it was a road race. The letter in the box clearly stated her designated target: The New York Stock Exchange. Based on the miles, they'd figured the murderer was planning on arriving today or tomorrow. Their advantage was that they could drive in shifts and only stop for supplies and lavatory breaks.

Yesterday, Jill and Agent Bryce reccied the area around the Stock Exchange and identified observation points while Agent Takei arranged handguns and radios. Jill has the corner of New Street and Exchange Place, south of the Exchange. Takei's covering the exit from Wall Street subway station, to the west. Bryce is at the exit from

Broad Street Station outside the front of the Stock Exchange.

It's only December 3rd but Christmas has arrived in NYC. She's haunted by yesterday's crowds of shoppers and tourists bustling along a taut line between seasonal cheer and explosive stress. Walking among them, the flashing lights draped around windows and the tempo of the twinkly music drove her heart to beat faster; simultaneously magical and threatening. Like an obsessive lover. Today's crowds will no doubt be building already but not here in no-man's-land.

She didn't want to fall in love, which was fine because she didn't think she could. Danny had acted like it was the same for him but he wasn't winning any Oscars. When it happened, they were a year into their four-year nuclear tour. On a nuclear tour, everyone knows what they have to do. Everything was fixed up, everyone learnt the manual and their checklists were drilled to perfection. The room for human error was tiny. While not on alert tour, which was most of the time, the crews sat in pairs at mocked-up control stations, in a large hangar, day in day out, fighting reruns of virtual nuclear wars. Perfection.

For Jill, the PowerPoint-fuelled hour-long pre-deployment briefings were a highlight. After all, the key to winning any war was preparation.

Danny sat across from her in the briefings but that was as much as he registered in her mind. He was blond, gentle-looking and looked too young to shave. So she was a little surprised when the only other female on the base, Flt Cpt Jacoby, raised an eyebrow one morning and said:

"Wish me luck, Hanson, I'm going down with Danny Daley,"

Other women in the Air Force thought it was acceptable to drop rank and talk female-to-female like this all the time. Jacoby had been paired with Danny for an alert tour.

"Pardon?" Jill had responded.

"Look at him," Jacoby replied, motioning across the briefing room as the teams were dismissed. Her eyes flared as she spoke, "Face of an angel. Body of a god,"

Jill didn't see it. She was partnered with Flt Cpt Blake and would think nothing more of Danny until months later.

In training for the alert tour, they were told that the main enemy was boredom. For twenty-four hours, a Missile Combat Crew Commander and Deputy Missile Combat Crew Commander would be secured in the command capsule, ready to receive an Emergency-Action Message, monitoring missile status and remaining vigilant. The reality was that, a hundred feet underground, most pairs would cosy up in their slippers and snuggies and exchange tall-tales, binge movies and play cards, while standing by for nuclear war. It was a different world to topside. It put Jill on edge.

On her first alert tour with Blake, she woke from her sleep shift still wearing her flight suit and resumed her duties in the capsule. Blake gave her the creeps. She could see his little moustache twitch when he saw her, and his salacious, disappointed eyes took her in, in all her stiff, regulation uniform. To her relief, he never mentioned the navy blue snuggie and slippers that remained in his kit bag.

Later, it turned out Jacoby had gone down with more than she bargained for—a bug. It was serious enough that it went on until the two-person teams were shuffled to cover her absence. Jill was paired with Danny for the next alert tour.

When he saw her in her flight suit in the capsule, he laughed so hard he sprayed cookie crumbs all over his grey sweatpants. He laughed like a child, as if the mess wasn't a significant threat to the control instruments' functioning and, therefore, national security. Choking, he apologised and explained that it was nervous laughter. He said he felt like he'd turned up to school in his "underoos". As he brushed the crumbs from his crotch he asked if she minded.

The command capsule never felt smaller than when she was in it with Danny. It felt like they were sitting on top of each other. You learn a lot about a person over an alert tour but, later camping, Danny had told Jill she was like a closed book that first time.

He asked if she minded music—she allowed it, as long as it was quiet. His tinny speaker sat on the control panel and played Bob Marley. She survived the twenty-four hours through sheer determination.

Their second alert tour, it was Stevie Wonder. Danny sat there like an idiot, drumming his fingers and bopping his head. Jill monitored the status of the missiles and quizzed herself on the contents of the protocol manual. But, when it was his turn to check the systems, the music was turned down and his face took on an expression of stony severity, uplit by the rainbow of colours from the digital read-outs. It was a wonder to her that he could be such a playful, happy idiot one moment and this unshakeable professional the next. But only for as long as he needed to be.

Despite the processed air constantly pumped into the capsule and sucked back out, the smell of chocolate chip cookies persisted. It was like it was in his hair, the pores of his skin. She imagined he showered with it. The phrase, "man-child", occurred to her and she thought about offering him a glass of milk, as if he needed looking after.

On their third tour, Danny presented her

with a gift. It was a sage green hoodie, to match the flight suit she was still wearing.

"It's your color," he joked.

A long moment after she put it on, she looked at his navy sweater and said, almost too quietly, "Blue and green should never be seen,"

She instantly regretted it, realising it could sound like a come-on when it was the opposite. And a lesser man might have made a big deal of Flt Lt Hanson cracking a joke. Instead, his eyes narrowed and his schoolboy smile emerged, before he whipped off his navy blue sweater to reveal a white t-shirt.

It was on this tour he told her his life story and the messy relationship he'd just gotten out of. Out of politeness or something else, she told him a little about her childhood and how she still liked to go hunting with her dad. When he told her he grew up in San Francisco, he somehow made a little more sense to her. He was not like the other guys she knew in Montana. And it was in those moments of opening up that she thinks they became each other's "what if". Not that either of them realised at the time.

Later that night, when the tour was taking its toll and her mouth was half-full of microwaved nachos, she heard him mumble something:

"You look like an angel," he'd said.

She assumed he was mocking her so she

took his slipper and threw it at his head. She knows now he wasn't, and she wishes she could go back to that moment.

It was the last alert tour they'd have together. Jacoby was back on her feet by the time they got out.

The following day, Jill avoided Danny at the morning briefing and at the mess hall. But for some reason she missed his energy and his childish tastes.

A few days later, his tray clattered down next to hers at breakfast and, even in that environment, she smelled the cookies on him. *Where does he keep them?* But, as she felt the warmth of it, she realised she'd missed that too.

After a *hello*, they sat and ate in the noisy canteen without talking. Neither felt the need. As they both walked out, he began the words that sealed their fate.

Her earpiece crackles, catapulting her into the present day. The cardboard coffee cup has gone cold in her hands. Her mind is drawn to something colder—the handgun in her jacket. She's about to readjust the earpiece when a man's voice breaks through.

"I have eyes on target," It's Agent Takei. Hanson's mind fills with the smell of hot smoke and burning. She throws the coffee cup and runs. "She looks no more than nineteen," he says, as if she's already dead. "Cops are arriving and clearing the area,"

*   *   *

Gradually, the haze lifts from in front of Ashley's eyes. It feels like tentacles receding to the depths. Against it, a message of absolute certainty and urgency clambers to her out of the corners of her mind: *Don't let go. Whatever you do, don't let go.* Panic threatens to take her under, squeezing its coils around her throat, but she reminds herself she can breathe—with one big breath, and then another. *I am Ashley Kindle.*

She's never been here before but she knows it for what it is. The smell of pollution, the noise of traffic and people, the concrete and steel skyscrapers, the unmistakable yellow cabs. Despite the still, cold air on her ears, she's hot—it feels like her whole body is steaming.

She's never blacked out like this before. It feels like she hasn't washed in a couple of days. Putting her hand in her pocket, she feels her car keys.

There's only one reason she would drive to New York.

She desperately hopes it's not too late, but there's a thick, heavy chain around her body and a sharp pain in her hand. Raising it into sight, she sees the bike lever. She has been squeezing it so long, it feels like she's grasping a burning coal, with hands made of ice.

Something rises from the pit of her stomach, into her lungs and bursts out of her throat as a scream:

"HELP ME!"

When she was little...

Ashley used to like watching butterflies. In the garden. In the fields. Behind the house. She used to catch grasshoppers there.

One morning, she went to her mother to bring her lemonade. She remembers it was summer because the sky was clear blue and the air was hot and dry. Her mother was sitting at the kitchen table, talking on the phone. The curly cord stretched past her neck back to the wall by the calendar. Mommy loved the phone. She also loved her projects—in front of her, the table was covered in cuttings from fashion magazines. The ice clinked and the lemonade fizzed happily as Ashley put the glass carefully down away from the bits of paper. Her mommy smiled and winked at her.

She went into the garden to find Daddy. He was squatting by the flower bed so as not to put his knees in the dirt. He didn't like using the gardening gloves Aunty Pauline got him so he took the lemonade with his one clean hand.

Even though his other hand was mucky he always managed to keep dirt from under his fingernails —something Ashley wasn't so good at. She got dirty all the time and it was the only time he really ever scolded her. She made sure she always washed her hands as best she could with the lavender hand soap but he never noticed. He loved the lemonade and gulped it all down in one go. Then he let out the biggest, most satisfied sigh. This made Ashley so happy. Next on her mission were her two brothers. Bringing them cold lemonade on a hot day would earn her at least a day of no teasing she thought. Most importantly though, they'd be happy. She smiled broadly as she went about, almost dancing to the sound of the clinking ice.

* * *

The target has reached the Stock Exchange, activated a dead man's trigger and is screaming for her life. It all happened too quickly. The moment the target cleared the corner to come in front of the statue of Washington and Federal Hall, she appeared to mentally collapse in on herself, and screamed with all her might for help. She'd bleached her black hair, and was wearing a face mask like so many do at this time of year now, making her harder to spot and allowing her to get this far before Takei clocked her. There were hundreds of people but, immediately, Cassandra was being pushed back by an NYPD officer, before the police were even setting up a perimeter. Then they began arriving in marked and unmarked cars and on foot, clearing the whole area and creating a perimeter. It was a masterclass in anti-terror tactics. Hundreds of civilians one moment, gone the next. But it was too quick, like they knew. SWAT will be here in moments. They're waving people still inside buildings to get back now.

This is bad. Cassandra needs Kindle to get to McAvoy. As she's pushed back down Broad St, along with dozens of others, Cassandra can still see Ashley Kindle in the far distance, standing quivering in an open red quilted jacket, worn over an industrial chain. Even from this distance, she can see her cheeks are as red as the coat and slick with tears. Behind Cassandra, more police officers are hurriedly establishing a perimeter with metal crowd control barriers that were already waiting on corners.

She can't see Takei or Hanson, who would be behind barriers at either end of Wall Street. Hanson remains characteristically quiet on the earpiece.

The cops aren't talking to Kindle. *Why aren't they talking to her?*

"Takei, why aren't they talking to her?"

"They're talking with their guns," he

replies.

Kindle is running out of time.

"She's our way to McAvoy," she says mostly to herself. Out of nowhere, a police officer runs towards Cassandra, barking at her to get behind the barrier, as if she's not moving along with the others. She realises that Kindle only has as long as it takes for the police to create a large enough perimeter. "British Intelligence. I'm here to help," she tells him.

"Help by hauling your ass to the next block," he orders.

She stops in her tracks, even as he roughly grabs the shoulder of her coat to force her back. She loosens her shoulder and twists her body around him until they've switched places. He's about to drag her to the floor when she breaks his grip and steps back. He pauses for half a breath and looks at her. Then he gets on his radio.

"Got someone here says she's British Intelligence and wants to help,"

A disembodied voice hisses its reply, "Put her on,"

"She's here," he says as Cassandra steps closer.

"What have you got?" asks the radio.

"Let me talk to her," she says calmly, "In person,"

"Absolutely no way, ma'ame," is the answer, "Swinson, get her out of here,"

"No, wait!" she pleads, "Her name is Ashley Kindle. She's from Helena, Montana, and she's my asset,"

"Your asset is about to blow herself up in front of all these cops and holiday shoppers,"

"I'll be able to find out where she's placed the other bombs," she bluffs with a half-truth.

She can hear the cogs turning.

"No deal. You talk through a loudspeaker,"

Her mind is abuzz, imagining possible dialogue and what may or may not work. She's seen a couple of negotiations with suicide bombers in her time. Neither were successful. For someone in that situation to open negotiations is a severe betrayal. This is different. It's more like talking down a jumper—and one who's asked for help.

Cassandra decides to stall.

The officer detaches his radio from his lapel for her to hold. She speaks into the mic and her voice is relayed to a loudspeaker she can see being held by the man in charge, standing behind a patrol car, surrounded by armed police, about thirty metres away.

The first words she chooses will determine the course of the next few minutes and the lives of everyone here. In most situations like this, it's useful to offer the subject a sense of control by delivering dialogue that enables them to say "no", and removing the pronoun "I" from your speech.

Normally.

Ashley is terrified, she wants help, she may be confused and, therefore, having a sense of too much power may be overwhelming. She needs to be contained. On the other hand, it might help to remind her she has choices, that McAvoy isn't here and she needn't fear him. Most importantly, Cassandra needs to calm the situation, which she will do by listening.

"Ashley," the name screeches and reverbs along the system. Cassandra hopes the removal of Ashley's anonymity will lead to better decisions on all sides. "We're going to get you out of this. You just have to hold on a little longer. Can you nod for me if you can do that?"

Cassandra can see that Ashley is confused, looking for the source of the voice, which clearly isn't the man with the loudspeaker, and probably worrying about how they know her name. Perhaps this wasn't the best move given Kindle's paranoia. It's time for the next move.

She turns away from the radio to address her earpiece's mic, "Now, Sentinel,"

* * *

There's a world in which Lucy, still reeling from the ambush in David's garage, woke up the next morning, kissed James goodbye and went to work. She would have ignored David's voicemail too; let her secret, girlish sense of betrayal turn her away from her responsibility. She longs for the simplicity of sitting at the breakfast table on Christmas Day in three weeks time, her only worry the self-help book she got her mum: an ill-conceived time-bomb in her weekend bag.

She didn't ignore David's voicemail. And she's skipped out on work again. Thousands of miles across the ocean, she crouches on a roof watching the NYPD cordoning off the area around a panicked suicide bomber. This woman is one of the network of dirty bombs set to bring the world to its knees. It must be in the woman's backpack. Something black and cylindrical is poking out of the top of the bag.

Lucy stands on the edge of a roof with a rooftop terrace garden over her shoulders. Down on the ground, somewhere around here is the famous Fearless Girl statue. She's close enough to hear the sounds of the street and, even without her glasses, she can see the epaulettes on the police officers' shoulders.

She hears Agent Bryce's electronically enhanced voice echoing up from the street, talking to the bomber. Now, through the earpiece pressed into her ear by her cowl, Bryce gives her the signal. Lucy steps to the edge of the roof. The cape and cowl make her someone else, or allow her to be. With all its regality and strength, she can feel like she's acting a role. Still, with the wind whipping her cape out in front of her where it flaps wildly, the height makes her nervous.

Maybe it's the natural human instinct for self-preservation, but jumping off a building is harder than she thought it would be. The wind rushes around her and whistles through the cowl into her ears, threatening to take her feet out from under her. Her heart races as she does her best to focus on where she needs to be on the ground, right in front of the suicide bomber, and tries to ignore all the other people and noises and lights crowding into her peripheral vision. Holding her breath, she jumps over the edge.

It's a short fall. She lands on her feet, squarely in front of the bomber. She looks younger than Lucy, with the face of a child but eyes that have been through too much; pale blue and full of tears.

Lucy spots which hand has the trigger and quickly clamps it with her own. The girl is shaking all over, begging through the snot and tears.

"Please --" she whimpers.

With the trigger depressed, the immediate danger is over.

"I'm here to get you out of this," Lucy replies.

* * *

The street in which Jill stands stinks of piss and throngs of spectators are jostling against her at the metal barrier where they watch what unfolds. The target has turned around and Kindle is at her *six*. SWAT and NYPD have formed a perimeter but are focused entirely on the target; they don't seem to care what goes on beyond it.

Being denied the chance to look Danny's murderer in the face again and hold her to account leaves an acrid taste. The Brits want to take Kindle in for questioning, and Jill did let them convince her. But it's getting harder to agree with their point of view, especially seeing Kindle in the flesh once more. Jill's body surges with adrenaline at the thought of this drugged-up, psychopathic narcissist walking around and doing as she pleases. And then there's the fact that, if they take her in and she helps them find the big boss, she'll strike a deal. Then there'll be no way Kindle will get what she deserves; what the Air Force deserves of her, what Danny deserves. What Jill needs. Unless Jill takes matters into her own hands.

Ashley Kindle murdered the entire launch base to ensure no-one could raise the alarm on 3/19. Jill imagines her dropping the bomb on the base before heading home to shoot up and let the world be fucked by nuclear war. She destroyed what hope Jill had of true love and happiness.

She is remorseless, twisted and evil. And here she stands, on her way to kill again, asking for mercy.

Jill barely notices her own hand on the pistol in her jacket. She convinced Agent Bryce that, as a team, all three of them need a firearm. There was a part of her that harboured a secret ulterior motive, but now it feels like that part was right all along. Maybe now she needs to park her professionalism and instead do what's right. Calmly, she removes her earpiece and drops it on the floor, immediately lost amongst many feet.

It feels as though her whole life has sharpened into the arrowhead of this moment—to the point that the decision no longer feels like it's hers to make. Her hands and gun are like one thing at the end of her arms, not entirely her, not entirely other. The trigger is pulling on her finger. The pistol is tucked in so neatly to her body that it could be an extension of her guts as it points at the bomber's head. The hairs on the back of her neck stand up like they always have, since she was a kid, contemplating the mortality of the quarry at the other end of her barrel. Only this isn't an elk.

* * *

Cassandra watches from within the ranks of the NYPD and their stupefied silence. Her heart is drumming a steady but powerful beat. Her underarms are slick. She hears the order to *Hold fire* and the reminder: *She's still on a deadman's trigger*. It's working.

"She's taking it off," a voice to her left murmurs in disbelief. It's the cop whose radio she used.

Sentinel is opening the girl's red puffa jacket. She snaps open one of the links of the industrial chain with her thumb, like it is nothing more than paper. Her heavy red cape hangs taut from her shoulders to her calves. The chain doesn't fall but hangs at the bomber's flanks. Sentinel pulls it through the bomber's bag straps like a thick, coiled snake before dropping it to the ground at arm's length. Cassandra half expects the chain to rear up and strike.

Kindle looks ready to collapse. Cassandra worries that the girl is too far gone to save—too far gone to be of help in their hunt for McAvoy. Sentinel appears to be focusing on the trigger first. That's good. Even partly obscured by Sentinel, it's clear Kindle isn't kidding and among the seasoned cowboys around Cassandra, there's an audible intake of breath. The girl's torso is a mesh of wires, a tangled briar of colours, twisting through the coat sleeve to the trigger in her hand. Sentinel has to remove the bomb without breaking any wires or accidently detonating the explosives. *This was a mistake.*

Suddenly, the bang harpoons Cassandra's

heart. Instinctively, her knees buckle and she drops to cover, finding the dozen cops around her doing the same. Screams rise from the spectating crowds. Her back is against the wheel of a squad car, her heart like a freight train but, when she realises she felt no blast, she begins surveying the area and finds it's completely undamaged.

Into the echoey silence, the order is screamed to “HOLD FIRE!”

Cassandra’s gaze turns to Kindle and Sentinel. Kindle is limp in Sentinel’s arms. Her head is lolled over one shoulder. Her face is missing.

“Hold fire!” the order is again shouted amongst the ranks.

Cassandra scans desperately for the shooter. Behind the dead young girl, NYPD officers crouch in firing position, weapons drawn. Thirty metres behind them, at the metal barrier, two dozen on-lookers are timidly getting to their feet. The shooter is amongst them, standing, pistol tucked in at her stomach, still pointing at the bomber, finger on the trigger: a vengeful, love-sick fool with a gun.

Hanson sees Cassandra and runs.

"Ma’ame," comes a man's voice from behind, “You need to stay where you are,”

She turns steadily, every Black bone in her body telling her *don't even think a threatening thought*. There are four FBI agents, two in uniform; and the most senior is the one addressing her. He looks like every day is a hangover.

"British Intelligence, you said?" he continues.

The next few seconds will define everything. The FBI being here means one thing —they've known all along. They've been watching Kindle since she stole the wallet and they called off Helena PD. That also means they were probably watching when Cassandra, Takei and Hanson met at her flat. And, since they didn't arrest anyone, they were also hoping Kindle would lead them to someone. But, tracking the 3/19 hack to Kindle doesn't mean they know the identity of the man behind all this—whether that be Ibrahim Al Nasser or Terrence McAvoy.

They'll each have at least one firearm, maybe a taser. There are at least twenty NYPD officers in the area now.

"Am I under arrest?"

"British spy. US soil. Interfering with a US federal investigation," the boss replies, weighed down by the events that just unfolded, "Do you want to be?"

She lets a man search her. He removes her revolver and her earpiece. They escort her to a black van manned by a pensive driver. She's asked to get into the back with the other four men.

* * *

Through the numbness, somewhere below it, a trembling scream rises up in Lucy's body but fails to break through the silence. The unbearable weight of the girl in her arms takes all her strength not to crumble to her knees. She can't tear her eyes away from the dark red hole in the centre of the girl's face where her nose and lip should be. Blood is streaked out across her rosy cheeks and continues to flow in and out of her mouth where her top teeth are missing. She was alive just seconds ago.

Lucy's chin is hot and wet. She can taste the girl's blood too.

She thought everything was under control. She closes her eyes and turns her head away, feeling the bomb's desperation to explode through the girl's chest. *Move.*

Opening her eyes, she forces her attention on the impossible mess of wires. There must be a way to break down the problem. She needs to see the whole thing.

The smell of blood sticks to the inside of her nose. While still holding the trigger in one hand, she gets down on her knees and lays the girl on her back. She takes a deep breath and leans in with her mouth. She can feel the girl's body heat on her face as she grips the coat between her teeth and begins to tear with the other hand. She has to keep forcing the fabric but, eventually, she tears all the way down the length of the sleeve with the wire. She's close enough to see the serial codes on some of the strands of wire. When she kneels back, it looks more obviously like the wires are one continuous length wrapped around and around her body.

To unravel it, she's going to have to unwind it around the body, at every pass risking accidentally reducing the pressure on the trigger.

The quiet sound of an electric motor grabs her attention as it grows louder and louder. It's coming from behind her. Turning, she sees it's a small, six-wheeled robot with a large mechanical arm. A male voice on the megaphone tells her, "Tape the trigger,"

The mechanical arm drops some black electrical tape on the ground within reach.

As she unravels the wires, with the trigger taped down, the girl's body slowly slumps to the ground.

She looks cold without her wire wrap.

Lucy stands, and wipes the tears from her eyes and the blood from her chin. The bomb could still be on a timer. Holding the bag and the bundle of wire, she gradually floats up into the air above the horror.

When she is so high that she can see the whole of Manhattan, she keeps on going. When the sky grows dark and she can no longer breathe, and her face feels frozen, she notices whatever is in the bag has expanded. She needs to get rid of it before it's too late, pirouette and launch the bomb into the abyss. But something happens.

With her fingers still wrapped tightly around the trigger, the bag explodes. But there's no fireball. It tears open in an expanding cloud of freezing air, sending large pieces of hard plastic in all directions, revealing the innards of whatever machine was contained within. She doesn't understand.

When she returns to the city, the bomb disposal robot is turning over the girl's body, looking for more. Agent Bryce is nowhere to be seen.

* * *

Chemical and biological weapons. The worst kind of suffering. Daniel's stomach turns to think of what has been done and what will be done with them. These are not the weapons of an honourable fight.

He runs from Sentinel to the police line.

"Stay back!" he shouts, "Don't approach the body!" M4 Carbines, SIG Sauers and Glocks spin in his direction. "You're still in danger,"

He works on the knowledge that if you make a big enough fuss—but not so big you're shot—you might get to meet the boss.

"I have critical information about that body," he tells him, "It's a matter of national security. But," he says, "I need asylum,"

"What're you talking about national security?"

"Please, this is very important, sir. But I need guaranteed asylum for my colleague and myself first,"

"I can't grant you asylum,"

"Then you better make a phone call, quickly,"

The boss looks like Robert de Niro circa *Heat*, with a FBI jacket and baseball cap. "Alright," he says, eyes narrowing, "who are you?"

"My colleague and I are British Intelligence operatives, seeking asylum from the political persecution of our country's government, in exchange for extremely urgent information essential to avoid massive loss of life on US soil and beyond,"

"You what?" he says dumbfounded, "You want to defect?" Daniel doesn't reply, as he desperately hopes no-one goes near the body. "Alright, HOLD POSITIONS!" the boss yells and fishes out a phone from his jacket.

Daniel doesn't mind waiting as long as no-one goes near that body without full CBRN protective suits.

After a while, De Niro comes back and

says, “Okay, what is it that’s so flaming dangerous about that body even though there’s no bomb?”

“Do we have asylum?”

“Look, you can’t just be granted asylum but, if your info checks out, you and your colleague—wherever he is—will be granted protection and given all the paperwork to start the process,”

“*She*. And I believe she’s already in a van with some of your colleagues,”

He gets back on the phone.

“It’s done,” he says when he returns.

“Good. Thank you. My name is Daniel Takei. It’s a pleasure to meet you,”

When Daniel and his new friend, who it turns out is called Vincent, arrive at the FBI’s NYC Field Office in the Jacob k. Javits Federal Building, Daniel is searched and x-rayed. Once through security, Vincent takes him to a small meeting room on the ground floor. There’s a small grey table in the centre of the small room, with three plastic chairs. On the table is a jug of water with three paper cups. In the hallway, Vincent has a brief exchange with someone else and is dismissed.

“Good luck, Daniel,” he says through the crack in the door as the new guy steps inside and closes it. Back at Wall Street, Vincent listened carefully and ensured no-one approached the body until a hazmat team arrived. He saved countless lives.

"You'll need to sign this please before we begin," says the new guy, handing Daniel a slab of papers, "Your compatriot has already signed,"

It's time for the contingency protocol. The man sits down, taking an unusually long time tucking himself in under the table, until the edge of the table is right up against his tie, and then shuffling in further still, as if oblivious to Danel watching him. He moves the closest cup away to the left side of the table. He doesn't invite Daniel to sit down but he holds a ballpoint up in the air and looks at him.

"So what does British Intelligence have to do with an attempted domestic attack by a young, mentally unhinged, immigrant woman?" He says it as though every word is an indictment.

"I could ask you the same thing about the FBI,"

"Your friend is being far more cooperative, Mr --" he glances at the papers in front of him as though he doesn't already know, "-- Tay-key,"

He'd grimace if he weren't so used to it. "We're here because we want to help. We know Ashley Kindle wasn't a lone individual, and with her gone we've all lost a key witness—the link to the rest of the network," The interviewer doesn't bat an eyelid but Daniel is about to through in a few more chips: “Agent Bryce and I have two extremely valuable components to bring to the table should you wish to work together to save the world,”

“Go on,”

“Firstly, the flying woman is our asset,” For the first time, the man with no name seems to be listening. “Secondly, while they may think they’re being subtle, it’s common knowledge that the CIA has been agitating for a regime change at MI6. We can make that happen without anyone besides Agent Bryce and me getting our hands dirty,”

There's a half-second pause while the man with no name computes the offer, after which he switches the conversation back to the beginning; "What were you doing at Wall Street today?"

"We were waiting for Ashley Kindle," he says before partially revealing his hand, "When Sentinel made herself known to Agent Bryce and me, it was obvious her involvement in 3/19 had been covered up. But we didn't know why. When Agent Bryce raised it with her boss, he grounded her. It didn't fill us with confidence that the threat had truly been neutralised. We went to Montana looking for the missilers to find out what else was missing from the reports,"

"You didn't just drop it, like you were told?"

"The people behind 3/19 are still at large. We might not get so lucky next time they try to wipe out the planet. So, yes, Agent Bryce took it upon herself to track them down and asked for my help. When we--"

"Do your people know you're here?"

"Yes, although we came without authorisation," he says, so that now this man knows they're facing court martial back home, "When we intercepted Hanson, she revealed that she had been investigating the 3/19 bomber and was convinced she'd found her. She was en route to her apartment,"

"And that was whom?"

"Ashley Kindle. When we got to the apartment, Kindle didn't answer the door. Fearing for public safety, Agent Bryce entered the apartment. Kindle was gone but there was a letter indicating that she was probably going to Wall Street."

"Quite the story. Did you know she had a bomb?"

"No,"

"Yet Agent Bryce feared for public safety?"

"We felt that apprehending the 3/19 bomber was a matter of public safety, yes,"

"At no point did you think to speak to us?"

"We still don't know who's involved in the conspiracy,"

"Conspiracy?"

"Covering up Sentinel and who-knows-what-else surrounding 3/19, like how the hell it was allowed to happen,"

"Yet here you are now, offering your help,"

"It's a calculated risk,"

"Yet a few days ago, you didn't trust anyone. You endangered countless lives by not calling it in," the investigator exclaims, with faux outrage, "You think we would be complicit, that we would knowingly allow her to carry out her attack?"

"The letters in her apartment made it clear she was part of a network. We were concerned that you'd shoot our only lead. We took a calculated risk to save countless more lives,"

"We'll see about that," he says coldly, "Let's go back to the *flying woman*,"

That was a misstep from Daniel. He'd been goaded into a defensive attack. Taking a breath, he begins on the latest track set out by the investigator, "Our code-name for her is *Sentinel*. We called her to Wall Street when Kindle made herself known. She is the reason the human race wasn't wiped out on 3/19—you probably know that already,"

"And you think we need your help? You think that will exonerate you?"

"Will your actions exonerate you—and the rest of the US intelligence community—when you bring down the man you've been hunting?"

"Who are we hunting?"

He's signed the paperwork, he's got his promise of protection. So why does he hesitate?

He casts his mind back to dark streets in Helena, in the comfort of the warm car, before the events at Kindle's apartment.

"If the mission is compromised," Cassandra said, checking the rearview mirror again, "We buy immunity from the Americans,"

They may not have been so quick to go against everything they'd ever upheld had they not been on the run from their own country. They both knew it already but Cassandra was now making their pact spoken. If they were extradited and court-martialled back in the UK, the op and any chance of stopping McAvoy would be over.

To make this work, they would have to convince the Americans that it was more worth their while to grant protection and hide the British agents from British eyes than to trade them. In the world of international espionage, that's easier said than done.

"As long as the Americans believe our bosses know we're here, they'll think twice before killing us, but what do we offer them?" he asked.

"Everything," she said, "Except the McAvoy / Al Nasser connection. Yes, the Americans would love to cry foul and remove Papa for burying it, but suppose they already know McAvoy and Al Nasser are the same person; then they've held off from Papa for another reason. Meaning they might have something to lose from exposing that truth,"

"Or they're just biding their time,"

"True. Maybe until they've nailed McAvoy themselves. Either way, if we're going to stay alive, we need leverage on Papa. Let's be frank," she said, checking the rear view mirror, "Papa's known since we set foot at Heathrow. And it's Papa I'm worried about. Who knows what he'd do to cover up his culpability in this op,"

"Okay, so if he knows that we know, and he can't get his hands on us if we're under protection here, he'll want us to come willingly back home,"

"Right. Because if we choose to defect, it's game over for him,"

"So we promise the Americans we can topple Papa, and we let them protect us," he said, not quite convinced, "What can we offer him to convince him not to kill us anyway?"

"The flying girl," she said.

"Who are you hunting?" Takei echoes the question, "There's always someone pulling the strings," This room with the FBI investigator is much less comfortable and much less nice-smelling than that rental car in Montana and he has every intention of getting out. "Having an asset like Sentinel, an asset who is completely indestructible and indescribably strong, who can be anywhere in the world, wherever you need her, in an instant? Just think of all the times a suspect has just slipped the net, been one step ahead. Not any more. Not with Sentinel on the team,"

* * *

Steve couldn't say how long he's been here. The buzzer at the door rang at some point, travelling along the walls and through the floor until it was a barely audible, dull fussing sound intruding at the door of the back of his mind. At first, he guessed it was probably Mormons or Girl Guides. A couple of stupid stereotypes. *Then who would come calling here?* The whole town knows his dad is at the home and no-one, other than Mr Stanton, would remember Steve. His chest gets a little tighter and he pauses sweeping, propping the broom against a shelf of soup tins, above the tinned meats and fish, and below the tinned beans.

His back is on fire, owing to years of accumulated dust and detritus that needed sweeping. He heard somewhere that dust is mainly human skin. He imagines a rat scuttling past his feet. *Scurrying around in tunnels* is how his dad thought of Steve's duty at the launch command capsule. The idea makes Steve feel claustrophobic. He wonders again how long he's been down here.

Time to go outside. There's still a bare shelf that needs filling, above where the two-way radio is going, and he should see his dad today.

The steps up to the cellar door creak threateningly as he climbs. Steve hates horror movies.

Without the armchair, the house feels even less like home, but the shelter needed seating. An armchair for one is fine. It's left a dark square on the rug, like a shadow beneath an invisible obelisk. A commercial airliner growls overhead but, looking out the window to see it, the bright winter sky burns his eyes. On the powerline outside are three crows pecking viciously at something. To his disgust, he realises it's a fourth crow; dead but still standing. He didn't know they do that.

Nothing of note happens on the drive to the grocery store. *Nothing of note* could be the name of this town. But then another, more fitting image crosses his mind: *Here lies Flt Cpt Steven Reginald Blake. Nothing of note.* And another: *The driver of the vehicle was not found to be under the influence. Fit to drive. Nothing of note.* And: *Cause of death: Nothing of note.*

At the store, Steve has chosen his cart badly. One of the front wheels keeps getting stuck diagonally and jamming the whole thing to a halt. He's too far through the doors to do anything about it now and he's already filled the cart with multipacks of canned vegetables, fruits and more fish. He's looking at some powdered meal supplements (just add water) when he hears a familiar male voice down the aisle. He can't quite figure out who it belongs to but he feels deep down that it's not a voice he wants to hear. Staring intently at the ingredients on the side of the tub he holds, Steve considers whether he can complete his supply run at a later date. *That's hardly being prepared is it?* His internal critic is beginning to sound more and more like his father —in both senses. He hurriedly throws a couple of tubs of powder into the cart and moves on in the opposite direction to the voice. He doesn't know why he recognises the voice but the last thing he wants is to have to talk to someone he's got nothing more in common with than a shared schooling.

Finally at the checkout, Steve is handing over his card when he looks past the attendant right at the owner of the voice, paying at another checkout aisle. Steve knows exactly who he is.

Without warning, the world crashes down in Steve's head. He feels like he's sinking into the floor. He shoots his eyes down and hopes he hasn't been spotted. No matter what happens now, he can't look up. When the payment has gone through, he takes his card and marches toward the exit with his defective cart, chin tucked in, eyes fixed on the floor ahead.

Heavy footsteps accelerate behind.

"Blake?!" the accusation roars.

Pretend like you haven't heard.

Steve gets outside but Samantha's brother is already virtually on top of him. Spinning him around by the shoulder.

"You murdered my sister, you son of bitch!" Mike spits. Steve can't make a sound. "What the fuck are you doing here?" everything Mike says is a snarl, "I said I'd kill you if I ever saw you again,"

"Hey!" hollers an old codger across the parking lot.

It's just the distraction Steve needs to break free. Just in time for Mike's wife or girlfriend or whatever to arrive. Behind his back, something she says to Mike is enough to hold him off and to allow Steve to get to his car. Through the prickling, hot skin all over his face, he feins normalcy, innocence. As stays intent on unloading the cart into the trunk, he resists the urge to jump in the car and speed off. He's never unloaded groceries quicker. His knees and arms are shaking with adrenaline. Maybe he could go back and stand up for himself, but Mike hasn't done anything wrong.

When Steve gets into the car, his stomach launches itself out of his throat. He doesn't stop throwing up until there's nothing left to give.

It was 2004: Senior Year. Steve had been in love with Samantha since they were kids.

Samantha barely knew his name.

Years before that, when he was much younger, his mom figured over breakfast one morning that he had a crush. As well as feeling utterly exposed, he was too embarrassed to discourage her when she got carried away with the idea of *Stevey* having a girlfriend. To his mom and all her friends, this mystery girl became Steve's secret girlfriend. The truth was, he sat in class every day for six years, staring at the back of her head, fantasising, trying to glimpse just one of her dimples or her pale blue eyes. If only she turned her face, he might have been able to catch her attention. Of course, he tried to get her to notice him but she was always hanging out with the popular crowd and always had a boyfriend. He never had a chance to ask her out. Maybe there was safety and comfort in knowing that he'd never ask—his imagination was enough. Once, she smiled at one of his jokes and said he was funny—his grin nearly stretched off his face. Moments like that confirmed that his imagination wasn't enough after all—he had to ask her one day. One day, Steve would get his chance.

In the run-up to Senior Prom, Samantha had an apparently blazing row with her serial cheater of a boyfriend, who'd evidently fooled around with her best friend. Steve couldn't have been happier when she dumped him. Obviously, he was sad for Samantha but she'd soon forget that asshole. He just hoped her brother, Mike, didn't put the guy in hospital. Then her ex would get her sympathy and she'd start visiting the hospital and she'd see him as vulnerable and damaged, and he'd say he's screwed up and he'd try harder and, that would be it, they'd be back together. Steve had to make his move. She'd need a date for Prom and all the usual boyfriend-material would be taken.

The first challenge would be getting her on her own to ask her. He knew the bus she used to get home after school so he'd wait at the stop and ask her there. He considered waiting at the stop the other end of her journey, when he could guarantee she'd be on her own, but there was a good chance she'd think it was creepy rather than romantic. He couldn't risk it. This way, she'd only have two girl friends with her when she arrived to wait for the bus and Steve thought they were friendly enough. Not the 'megabitches' that comprised a major part of her group.

He gave it three days after her break-up. He had to give her time to recover and he didn't want to just be a rebound, but he didn't want to leave it any longer and he was already worried someone else was going to beat him to it. So, three days after the break-up, Steve was waiting at Samantha's bus-stop when he saw her coming with her two friends, Cheryl and Darcy or something. They came and stood right next to him. It was getting awkward—he hadn't said anything yet and the longer he left it, the weirder it would be.

"Hi," he mumbled and smiled, half at Samantha, half at the asphalt between their feet. She didn't hear him. He'd tried to start a conversation while the girls were still chattering. He waited for a lull. There needed to be one before the bus arrived. Oh, Jesus, they'd realise he doesn't get this bus. *What am I doing here?* "How, you doin'?" he asked. He tried to be cool as she looked at him, realising he was talking to her, but he didn't know what to say next. "I heard about you and Leon,"

"Oh, hey," she replied with a faded smile. *That bastard.*

"So I wanted to ask you if you'd wanna maybe go to the Prom with me?" He surprised even himself. It was like he wasn't in control of what he was saying. He just came out with it. Right there.

"Oh," she chuckled, his heart sank, "You?" she said in disbelief. What had he done? There was no way to backtrack now.

"No of course not -- I mean -- Obviously..."

"Sorry, I just -- that's really sweet -- you're really sweet -- but I don't really know you?"

It was all making sense until she said that last bit.

"Yeah, you do," he defended himself, "We've gone to school together for..."

"The bus is here," Cheryl intervened.

"Sorry!" called Samantha as she stepped onto the bus. Steve's head reeled while he watched the bus fill with passengers. *What's she sorry about? Why can't she go with me?* Then he realised: she must be back with Leon. It was too late when he then realised he'd missed his own bus home.

After that, things got even more awkward and the days until Prom dragged out unbearably. When the night finally came, the corsage he bought went in the trash and he went with his friends. Turned out, none of them had dates. It was probably the least memorable night of his life until Leon showed up with some new girl no-one had ever seen before. He saw it all playing out from a distance, to the sound of *Hey Ya!* by OutKast. The couple arrived while Samantha was —dateless—by the drinks table with a selection of her friends. The whole lot of them stormed over to Leon and the girl and the row ensued. Who knows what was said but Samantha pushed him a few times and her friends were pretty verbally vicious to his date. Security actually asked Leon and the girl to leave since she wasn't a student at the school.

The night was nearly over by the time the drama had cooled—or at least it felt that way. Steve found himself standing by the drinks table where Samantha had been, trying to make sense of it all, while his friends around him talked about something else. It was this moment that he decided to have something a little stronger than was on offer. He headed to the bathroom and, when he got into a stall, took his dad's hip flask out of the inside of his jacket. He didn't know why he'd taken it and filled it with bourbon in the first place but now it had a purpose. He'd have enough to give him a little courage but not so much that he couldn't still drive home. He saw his dad do it all the time and his dad was Sheriff. Then he went looking for Samantha.

He found her directly outside the girls' room, on the phone to a taxi company. She still looked beautiful, even with black mascara hastily wiped off her red cheeks and tears in her eyes. His heart began racing out of nowhere. She wasn't just beautiful, she was absolutely smoking. He didn't even wait for her to get off the phone, just for her to stop talking for a second.

He leant against the wall, his shoulder scrunching up a junior's project pinned to the corkboard. He tried not to care.

"Let me drive you home?" he asked casually.

She looked up at him, having not noticed him before and took the phone down from her ear. Steve couldn't believe what was happening but she smiled, nodded and sniffed.

She held onto his arm as he escorted her to his car. She didn't say anything until he opened the door for her and she said, "You're a really sweet guy, Steve," Her breath smelled of bourbon, just like his probably did. It was warm and sugary and close.

He did his best to suppress his goofy grin, which persisted until he was set in the driving seat. He fumbled the key a little but, thankfully, she was looking out the window at the time, staring at something unknown to him.

"Seatbelt," he politely insisted and then watched as she pulled it across her chest and clicked it into place. Her dress was purple and simple, accessorised with a thin silver necklace of diamonds and a matching bracelet. He noticed she wasn't wearing pantyhose. He quickly inserted the key and started the engine, feeling a little woozy, he cleared his throat and swallowed. Then he remembered the breath mints rustling around with the hip flask in his jacket. He had two mints and then offered the pack to Samantha, who took one with another smile and popped it in her mouth.

They hadn't been driving long when they got onto a badly-lit backroad. There was something wordless passing between them the whole way. She was breathing heavily and occasionally shifting in her seat, rearranging her dress around her thighs, running her hands through her long brown hair. His mind was buzzing with potential when something leapt out in front of them. Steve swerved to miss it but over-steered and lost control. He tried to pull the car back and it spun around and suddenly everything lit up right in front of them and there was a feeling of weightlessness and then Samantha screaming.

When he woke, Samantha had a tree branch sticking through her chest. It pinned her to the seat. Her head was flopped forwards.

The cops didn't even breathalyse him. His dad was the Sheriff.

The stench of Steve's own vomit still stings his nostrils and the acid burns the back of his throat. He's driven right to the spot where it happened. The tree's grown.

* * *

Anger. Pity. Disgust. Sorrow. The Professor is not immune to these energies, but considers this a strength, particularly when they may be harnessed to propel oneself toward a positive objective. He hunches over the granite breakfast bar and writes the same letter for the eighth time. Of late, the boundary between the fiction he creates for his followers and his own beliefs is becoming increasingly permeable and, as such, a source of growing disquiet in his mind.

Mid-sentence, he places the pen neatly at the side of the unfinished scripture, which sits elevated atop the remaining blank sheets. He closes his eyes, leans back, cups his hands on his lap, takes a breath and lets himself plunge into the depths. The Professor's unconscious envelopes his consciousness as an ocean takes on a drop of water.

Ashley Kindle, the woman who would become his Patient K, was a beautiful tragedy: Hans Christian Anderson's Little Mermaid. She knew not the folly of her dreams and what they would cost her: her compulsion to leave the Professor's side meant self-annihilation for naught. If she had stayed the course, through her sacrifice she would have been part of the transmogrification of the collective and personal unconscious, returning herself and the rest of humanity to the essential path: The Return to Eden.

Instead, she was shot in the back of the head and had her face blown off.

"Fuck," he mutters to himself.

The heavy and carnal scent of marijuana and sweat fills his nostrils and travels down his body. He loved her.

In his early work with her, she would repeatedly tell him that he was not what she wanted, that he was useless and couldn't possibly know what to do with her. During these sessions, Terrence felt her attacks as if they were an attempt to drain him of his faculties, to evoke in him apprehension about his ability to withstand her. With her constant interruptions, stopping him before he could complete a single sentence in her company, she challenged his very capacity for thought. It would be some time before they would develop a plausible way of being in a therapeutic dyad.

"*Until you make the unconscious conscious, it will direct your life and you will call it fate.*" he said to her.

In the countertransference, he understood her experience of being silenced and angry, and identified with her unconscious projection into him, feeling powerless and at her mercy, even frightened that at any time she may become too aggressive or worse he would retaliate. His aim during this phase was to withstand the attacks and contain them, demonstrating that he could survive, holding a position from which he could start to think about what the attacks meant.

He recognised himself taking up a hateful position and wanting to abandon her, like the mother that left her to her father's abuse. In the presence of another, K felt violently unwanted, frightened and abandoned. This fear of abandonment is equivalent to that of dying, falling apart at the pain that is present in the experience of being left alone. In early infancy, the baby lacks the inner resources to bear such emotional experiences and turns to self-protection. Dissociation becomes a primitive protection to which the individual frequently resorts. These non-thinking, dissociative defences can cause injury to the capacity to feel as well as splitting off parts of the self. Terrence knew, however, that his task was still to stay patiently with the disconnectedness and annihilation and gradually make sense of it, always cognisant that underneath lay the great fear of nothingness.

Terrence also recognised in himself the emergence of a deep sense of shame. For the child, shame first arises when his or her excitement is met by disapproval, dislike or rejection by the parent. He believed this deep shame was the legacy of K's early relational trauma and childhood abuse. The Professor had to silently acknowledge what K could not bear, and stay with her until she could stand it. Being with the patient through the countertransference involved being able to work with his identification with the suffering of the victim, but also the sense of himself as an abuser in the patient's eyes. She would put him in the position of abuser again and again and he would hate her; desire to abandon her, to ravish her, or both.

He took solace, however, knowing that what would solidify and make intractable re-traumatization in the analytic dyad was not the enactment itself but if he failed to acknowledge it. It was his confession to himself and the exploration of the source of the feeling of his shame that enabled the Professor to become more fully conscious of the countertransference and to use it responsibly.

The Professor comes coughing and spluttering back into the moment and opens his eyes to the dimly lit kitchen. Here, the smell of fresh fruit and bread clashes with the metallic. Occasionally, the pipes in the walls sound like the whining and beeping of a hospital ward. He must finish the final line before signing off and beginning the ninth copy of the letter.

Watch for my sign. Soon, we will end this nightmare together for the world to be reborn as paradise.

If he had sent this letter just a few days ago, perhaps he could have preserved K's life until she was ready. Without her, the world must count on the remaining number to settle it.

CHAPTER 9

You'll never be one of us

There's a wolf in the darkness at the end of Steve's bed. Long black hair, black shiny nose, black eyes, and black gums surround razor-sharp fangs. It smells like vinegar. Steve is frozen solid. If he moves, the wolf will pounce. It doesn't move either. Its bright, beady yellow eyes bore into him like it wants to rip him apart and eat his skin. Steve's throat and chest tighten.

As his eyes come into focus, the wolf fades away into the shadows and he reluctantly accepts that it was never really there. *Bad dream,* he thinks.

Pouring himself a glass of water at the kitchen sink, the stench of stale booze from the drain irritates his nose, drawing from him an involuntary grimace. Drinking was his old man's problem, not his. The old man who drank his way to a stroke and getting put into a home. The old man so full of bile that he liked to hang Steve's biggest fuck-up over his head and keep him hostage to it. And the way he talks about Samantha, because he's become such a self-pitying wreck that he actually wants Steve to beat that red spongy face of his to a pulp. *Do it.*

The thought repulses him. *You could kill the old fuck in his sleep.* He squeezes his eyes shut as if it'll help shut out his own thoughts. He often hears his dad's cynical comments. Things he's said or would say if he were there, usually over Steve's shoulder telling him why someone's an idiot.

He goes back to his bedroom to get dressed for the busy day ahead. Upon entering the room, he notices the bed sheets are wet with piss. *The wolf got you good.* That's more like it.

* * *

When the Hacker Bomber of 3/19 left the reservation, she created a serious issue. And what followed would do little for damage control. But, right now, CIA intelligence operative Wally Soufan can't think about that, or how the FBI let her get across seven states and waltz right onto Wall Street. His focus is the one batch of letters that could actually save the world.

"O-eight-hundred hours," Soufan reports

into his radio, "The Hostess and Junior are leaving the nest,"

There's no-one to answer. His reports are monitored by a CIA radio operative—a condition of a joint covert op on British soil. They'll be recorded and submitted with the day's report.

Across the road from Wally Soufan's parked sadan, Carol Wimberley and her daughter are walking out the front door of the house that is currently sheltering the world's most wanted man. Terrence McAvoy is a psychopath of the highest order and totally beyond anything with which they could threaten him. He could be thrown into Guantanamo Bay for the rest of his life and not give them the locations of the viral bombs. If they were to pick him up, they have no idea where and when his cult will detonate, how many there are and what other resources they have. But the Agency does know that McAvoy is the most dangerous man alive. They created him after all. And they know how he communicates with his cult. So now all they can do is watch him and let him lead them to their quarry.

The lady, Wimberley, is taking her daughter to school, just like she does every weekday. They'll be tailed wherever they go now until the girl is at school and the mother is home again. One of Soufan's colleagues will watch the school until the girl leaves. Eventually, the mother will be caught posting the package of letters or passing them to a third party, probably a courier, for further distribution.

If they can get hold of them, they'll have the locations of McAvoy's deadly cult army and stop the virus.

* * *

Agent Takei was the only one to meet Lucy at the emergency rendezvous point after what happened to Ashley Kindle. After Lucy's fumbling attempts to figure out what to do with the "bomb" wasted so much time. Enough time that Jill did what she did. She can't believe it was Jill who killed her. Jill Hanson, who gave her the instructions to disarm a nuclear missile all those months ago.

She'd been flying over land for a couple of minutes when she slowed. She'd followed the thick, choking trails of the missiles' exhaust fumes halfway across the world. From her vantage half a mile up, she could finally see the end of the trail. She squinted into the distance, half-blind, her glasses somewhere behind her in the North Atlantic, the wind swirling around her ears.

When her sight landed on what was left of the launch base, she felt sick in her throat. Engulfed in flames, belching and spewing black tarry smoke, half the building had been flattened while the other half was in ruins. She took a deep breath and propelled herself fists-first down through the air, toward her only hope of stopping the madness that was unfolding. In less than a second she was crouching in the rubble at the centre of the inferno, eyes streaming and lungs desperate for air. Through the smoke and embers, she might have seen a bloody charred hand, fragments of burnt cloth. She had no idea how many bodies surrounded her nor if any were still alive. She had to press on. Wiping her eyes with the back of her hand, she blinked away the stinging for just long enough to see what looked through the distorted air and tears like lift doors. Lucy took the gamble and sprang from the ground. Tearing through the doors as if they were paper, she pivoted and flew straight down the shaft. Before she could see what she was doing, she had burst through the roof of the lift. The smoke above cut out any daylight but there was no time to wait for her eyes to adjust. Allowing her feet to touch the ground for a moment, Lucy blindly groped forwards, her fingers finding a hulking steel door like a bank vault. *Breathe*, she told herself.

There was no time to think. No time to second-guess herself. With one determined shoulder-barge, the vault door buckled and artificial light sliced in from the other side. The metal rods that secured the door, each as thick as a man's arm, ploughed through the frame as the whole structure flew off its over-sized hinges. Almost as quickly as it was revealed, the light went out and everything turned red. In front of her was a junction. To her left was another door, to her right, past the mess she'd made and through an open blast door, was a small room and a woman. Under the emergency lights, the red woman was motionless, staring back at Lucy with frowning analytical eyes. The woman, she would later come to know as Jill Hanson. In one heartbeat, Lucy touched down in the small room with the her.

"How do I stop them?" Lucy demanded urgently.

"Who? Who's done this?"

"Not *who*. How do I stop the missiles?"

"You can't -- It's too late -- Is word out? Are people getting to safety?"

Lucy's eyes darted down at her watch. *We don't have time for this,* she thought, and some guy had appeared barking orders. "I can catch them. Just tell me how to disarm them,"

"You..." the word hung there for a second, uncomprehendingly. Then the woman, Jill, spun around to a console behind her.

She began frantically scrawling something with a pencil and clipboard. Lucy squinted over the woman's hunched shoulder to see.

"Here," As she spoke, she scribbled lines and arrows, "You need to open here, separate this whole section from here but, whatever you do, don't touch these or let this touch that,"

The man was getting more persistent, "Let's go!" he shouted.

Throwing them into the Sun would have been too simple, Lucy thought. The woman straightened herself out and tore off the paper. Lucy shoved it deep into her jeans pocket.

"Thank you,"

She was about to take off when the man got in her way, clumsily hopped out of the small room, ran straight into the demolished blast door and knocked himself out. Looking back on it now, Lucy realises Jill was pinching her own arm as if trying to wake from a bad dream.

It doesn't make any sense that this was the same woman who had killed this other young woman in cold blood. But Jill ran. And Agent Bryce was dealing with the FBI. That left her and Takei. She stayed in the air away from him as she told him what she'd seen. It turned out this was the right thing to do as she became aware that the explosion had sprayed her with something that was now defrosting on her costume.

"This changes everything," he said.

After a pause while his mind worked on something, he asked if she had somewhere she could go and isolate for a couple of weeks.

He wanted to get away to deal with other things but Lucy insisted he explain it to her. He said something had never sat right about the idea of dirty bombs. There's no precedent for an effective dirty bomb and McAvoy would need hundreds if he meant to instigate a global catastrophe. He said he and Agent Bryce, whom he called Cassandra, had reluctantly agreed not to assume McAvoy's plan would be logical. But the idea of a biological weapon made so much more deadly sense.

Assuming the worst, each of McAvoy's followers would go into a crowded area —his letters had hinted at locations of strategic importance for economy, politics or supply chains. They would release a virus or other contaminant, infecting a critical mass of individuals to spread it before protective measures such as quarantining or the wide-scale distribution of a vaccine. Uncontrolled, infection rates would be exponential, especially if transmission can occur during the pre-symptomatic phase. The release of a single dose, let alone multiple sites simultaneously, could easily become a global pandemic. If his plan is to decimate the population of the planet, perhaps, said Agent Takei, they should stop assuming he can't do it and start preparing for the worst.

Takei told her she should behave as though

she had been infected, to shut away and not see anyone for at least a couple of weeks. He and Bryce were going to have to disappear for a while for other reasons.

When she got back to London, she made three phone calls. First, she called David. She told him what had happened and what Agent Takei had said and he told her how they were going to handle this. Before going to meet David for quarantining and tests. Second, she called her dad, just so she could pretend everything was normal for a few minutes. Of course, he knows it's her on the news, and she quietly listens to his excitement and pride and tells him about what she's been up to in the way daughters talk to their fathers. Finally, she called James. She told him everything that had happened in New York, but not about McAvoy or his plan, so James thinks Ashley Kindle was a one-off. It was so good to finally talk, to finally offload something, even if it wasn't the whole truth. He tried to ask loads of questions but she cut him off and tried to reassure him: after all, David is a specialist in viruses.

She entered David's house through the kitchen window, meaning she could land unseen in his garden and giving her the shortest route to the internal door to his garage laboratory. He was waiting for her inside, wearing a bright green inflatable hazmat suit. She'd never thought about it before but it's unbelievable that this highly dangerous biology lab exists in total secrecy in the middle of a suburban residential area. The doors were air-tight, the ventilation system was filtered and UV-treated, but still. *Who knows what he keeps in there?* Well, now she knows: *her*.

“And how are you feeling now? Any symptoms yet?”

“I feel drained and thirsty,” she said, “And like I could cry every five minutes,”

“Okay,” he motioned to a folded pile on the floor by the door behind him, “There are some clean clothes here. Please don’t go near them until you've washed your hair and body using the antibacterial gel in that bottle on the side,"

He asked her to tell him everything again, especially about the bomber’s backpack.

“It looked kind of like a leaf-blower, blowing out steam,”

“Any colour?”

“No, just like when you breathe out on a cold day,”

"Droplets stay in the air a little while but fall to surfaces reasonably quickly," he said, "So if it were droplet-based, she would have wanted to spray it in people’s faces. I don’t think she could’ve gotten very far doing that. That it was rigged with a trigger suggests she was going to keep it in the bag and have it disperse into the air directly above wherever she was standing. This all sounds like an aerosol to me. She was probably supposed to go and stand in a busy, enclosed space so, by the time anyone managed to stop it, the air would be full of the pathogen and lots of people would be inhaling and exhaling it. Did she have a mask of any sort?"

"No,"

"So she was either on a slow and painful suicide mission or she was immune. We need the body,"

"I think the FBI have it,"

He took her costume away in a sealed drum for testing. Every time he left the room, he slid a special secondary door across the internal door to his house that created a tiny air-lock just deep enough for a person to stand and hose himself down with disinfectant. A little motor whirred as it pumped the air. She could hear him squirting more disinfectant all along the corridor, in the kitchen and around the window.

The first night, sleeping on a camp bed on the garage floor, feeling unsatisfied and a little gross after a microwave lasagne for dinner, she dreamt about dying.

It began with no maniacal laughter, no soliloquising villain, no sound at all except the CHUG-CHANG CHUG-CHANG CHUG-CHANG of a slowly approaching scrap metal grinder and the WUD-WUD-WUD-WUD of the conveyor belt drawing Lucy towards it. She was pinned to the belt by an unknown force along with shards of metal junk all being carried relentlessly to the end.

She desperately looked around the dull grey factory for a way out. In the far distance, the machinery spat out rows of robots that each immediately began some sort of work.

Packed tightly in a section to the side of the grinder, cordoned in by metal railings were people she recognised: the two MI6 agents, David, James, Charlotte, her cousins, Grangran and many more.

Suddenly the machine sped up and the conveyor belt began moving so fast it was as though it was pulling her by her feet towards the grinder. She tried to call out to her friends and family for help but there was no sound. They didn't look up at her at all, they were looking at clipboards or conferring about some secret. No matter how hard she strained her every fibre to scream, she couldn't make more than a hoarse whisper, drowned out by the machinery.

She doesn't remember any more of the dream but her muted helplessness and the impenetrable indifference of everyone else hung around her neck most of the next morning. It was like a talisman made to ward off the greater evil, the more existential dread she was facing. She doesn't dream about the dead girl, of McAvoy or of viruses.

In all, it was two weeks, quarantined in David's lab on her own. Two weeks off work, away from home, away from James and going insane. On the second day, David brought down a laptop and every day thereafter she watched trash on Netflix and video-called James. It was the most time she'd spent with James in weeks, maybe months. And it was really good, until it hurt.

David would talk to her too of course, via video call from a room in his house. Every day, he told her how many more days of isolation she needed and it changed at least three times as he decided something new about the virus. He also told her about the tests he was running on the particles he'd removed from her costume. He brought her food and drink, soapy water in a washing up bowl and towels. Every time, disinfecting before he left. She began to feel disgusting.

Her quarantine ended and David gave her the all-clear to go home a week before Christmas. She was lucky.

"In its frozen form in near space, the pathogen stuck to your costume. As it defrosted back down on terra firma, it remained in droplet form on your clothes until you got here," David told her.

This was his way of telling her she didn't inhale anything. She hasn't had so much as a sniffle, or more of a headache than normal. But, even as she left, he kept his distance as he waved her off. Habit, she hopes.

It's now Christmas Eve and it's her youngest cousin—Beatrice's—birthday. James has convinced her to go and they're both now on the Tube to Grangran's. Today is how Lucy celebrates Christmas with her mum's side of the family, since her mum has distanced herself from them. Her mum prefers Christmases with Lucy, James and Charlotte and says she'll see the family over the period between now and New Year. On the day itself, Lucy and James will either be with her mum, her dad or James' family, getting in visits to everyone else whenever they can on the days leading up to and following the day itself.

Lucy's mind is cast to long, sleepy drives when she was a child, Chris Rea on the car radio, staring out of the window, imagining herself flying beside the road, speeding past electricity pylons, streetlights, signposts. One time, they drove into London, which her dad hated. In his words, you'd have to be an idiot to drive into

London. The tension in the car was something to which she and Charlotte had become accustomed, but it was so powerful it's a wonder anyone could breathe.

Her dad asked her about school in his way of asking without asking.

"She'll get straight As and A*s, won't you, Lucy?"

In truth, her mock exams had given her As, Bs and a C. She must have been thirteen or fourteen. It was always said that Charlotte got "all As and A*s" but, in hindsight, Lucy is sure she'd heard at one point that there was a C in there too. This is the power of believing the myths her dad creates for his family.

"Yeah, probably," she answered.

Suddenly, the car jerks. Everyone is pulled to one side and the flying Lucy outside the car is forgotten.

"Shit!" shouts her dad, "That *bloody idiot* made me miss the turn,"

Within moments, they were irredeemably lost in some alien town with narrow roads and graffiti. Her mum kept telling her dad to stop and ask for directions. Eventually, she threatened to get out of the car herself. By the second time she shouted at him to stop the fucking car, he just drove faster and told her that if she wanted to leave she can *fuck off* and he'll look after the girls. Lucy couldn't understand what that had to do with being lost.

The Tube announces their stop and it's a short walk in the drizzle to Grangran's. The door to the building holds a world of familiarity that seeps from its grains, with its old-fashioned thick, dark wood and its rippled glass window, the metal buzzer with time-worn buttons for each of the flats. It fills her with a sense of family; of Christmases and birthday parties past, crammed onto long trestle tables Grandad used to borrow for the day and put together under paper tablecloths.

Lucy gets the sense Grangran doesn't like to do the big Christmases anymore, but they carry on, instigated by her aunts, despite the bitter sweetness, and every year they are something less. He used to hang the ceiling with paper chains and edge every flat surface with a different colour of tinsel. He would spend what seemed like the entire morning skewering cheese and pineapple on cocktail sticks. Lucy wonders what it's like where Charlotte is and makes a mental note to message her later.

James stands behind her on the narrow steps. It's still quite new to James, and a world away from his white middle class family in Sussex. For him, being surrounded by the chaos of her family must be like being an astronaut on an alien planet. Lucy can relate.

At least two of her cousins, Beatrice and Shelley will be in the kitchen sitting around the table with Grangran, or making cups of tea, helping themselves to something or helping Grangran out. They visit every day as they live in Flat 1 on the ground floor with Auntie Doris and Uncle Jack. Grangran lives in Flat 3 on the second floor. Her other cousins, Elizabeth, Jade and Gabriel, and Auntie Jude and Uncle Edward live only a few Tube stops away and are here almost as often, probably daily. She buzzes 3, the door clicks and they step in.

When they reach the door to Grangran's flat, she has to knock and wait for one of her cousins to come and open it. It's Beatrice. She greets them with her warm, energetic smile, a hug and a kiss on the cheek.

"Happy birthday!" Say Lucy and James in chorus.

"Thank you!" Beatrice answers in a very Tobagonian accent, before spinning on a heel and leading them into the main room.

Unlike Lucy's mum, both her aunts inherited the accent and way with words, which her cousins sometimes use too. Lucy, on the other hand, is *broughtupsy* because her mum and dad lived in the sticks and she went to a nice school full of white kids. Her cousins think it's endearing to call her *posh*.

As they enter, Shelley has Grangran in

stitches with a story. Both of them are bent over crying with laughter, sitting at the table.

Shelley wails, impersonating someone, and really hamming up the patois, "She says, '*Ay yah yie! He's been gettin' into all kin'a t'ing!*'"

Beatrice jumps into the tale to add her own embellishments, while going to a cupboard to get mugs—she was making coffee when Lucy and James rang and Beatrice picks up where she left off. While it's so good to be back, Lucy hasn't missed the utter confusion in which she spends 60% of her time here. Now she has James though, even more bewildered than she is, to whom she is like a half-qualified interpreter.

Grangran looks up and immediately gets to her feet, with her huge open smile and open arms, and a ubiquitous tissue between her thumb and palm.

"Lucy!" She squeezes Lucy with her unnatural strength and plants a powerful kiss on her cheek. "How are you?"

"I'm good, thanks, Grangran. You?"

"Oh I'm okay. Hello, James, it's nice to see you. Come 'ere," She accosts him with love too.

Before anyone's had time to catch their breath, Gabriel and Elizabeth arrive behind Lucy and James and they're shuffled forward into the room for more hellos with everyone. From here on, the rest of the family spontaneously arrive in spits and spurts, leaving only Lucy's mum out, in her two-bed terraced house near Dunstable.

"Allyuh get yer bamsees down now," commands Grangran.

And everyone, from seventeen-year-old Beatrice to fifty-something Uncle Jack, sits within moments, at the table, on the sofa, and Lucy and James perch on the armchair together.

"Who wants what?" asks Elizabeth, and Beatrice and Auntie Doris get up to help with the incoming drinks orders.

"You look well, dear," leans in Auntie Jude, "Are you feeling better?"

"Yeah, thanks," Lucy has now missed so much work, so many family video calls, so much life, she has lost track of what illness she has lied about when, "It was pretty awful but I'm better now,"

"The new haircut suits you," Jude says of the mess of hair that has slowly replaced Lucy's baldness from nine months ago, "You look like *a sassy young t'ing*',"

Christmas loses its magic when you have the weight of the world on your shoulders. And it becomes bitter sweet when it could be the last. In the ensuing hour, Lucy and *"poor James"* are told they're too quiet, too polite, shouldn't listen to certain bad influences from cheeky cousins and their tall tales (despite barely being able to follow them anyway), and that they must think everyone's mad. It's everything they're told every time they visit. It's exhausting, and she knows it'll never change, but maybe she'd miss it, even though she's clock-watching.

Afterwards, as they walk to the Underground, James remarks, "It's amazing. They really have no idea who you are. They think you're a totally different person," He isn't talking about her powers, which only he and Professor O'Connor know about. Her family just don't *see* her for anything other than their image of her, which hasn't changed since she was five. It's the same for all of them but she and Charlotte are the only ones who seem to mind.

In the home county where Lucy grew up, her mum was the only Black woman most kids ever saw. Her parents, Lucy's grandparents, were part of the post-war Windrush Generation, acting on a sense of duty, and the promise of new lives and prosperity. Her mum has spent her life walking with the dreams of a generation of immigrants packed onto her slight shoulders, believing she has never been good enough.

With a Tobagonian mum and Irish dad, Lucy has been *othered* her whole life. Too White to be Black, too Black to be White. When it's intentional, when it's from Black people or White people, there's always the assumption—subtle or not—that she belongs to another group, *the other side*.

Unusually for an Irishman of his generation, their dad doesn't have any brothers or sisters. Lucy and Charlotte's knowledge of his parents doesn't extend much further than that they live in a little village outside Cork. Their dad's Irish accent is barely perceptible.

When Grangran and Grandad arrived in the late 1950s, rather than the dream they'd been sold, they were faced with a country declaring "No Irish, No Blacks, No dogs". Through sheer grit, despite the hate, the riots and the exclusion, Grangran eventually became a sporting champion, and not just the first female member of her golf club but the first Black member too.

Lucy used to think Grangran was the only person in the world who understood her, and that she would never judge her, but Lucy still never felt it was right to try to describe her experience to someone who'd gone through that. She never found the words to describe what it means to not have the kind of relationship with her, any of her aunts, uncles or cousins as they have with each other, for her and Charlotte to be the "*posh cousins*". They all live in different parts of London, but they might as well be in the Caribbean for how close she feels to them. When her cousins call her Grangran, it has a different quality;

like they own it and Lucy and Charlotte merely adopted it. It's the one thing that holds Lucy and Charlotte together—their shared experiences of their parents and *the family*.

"You get used to it," she replies.

* * *

Steve is in the bunker watching the news. His mouth tastes of stale beer and his wet moustache irritates the corners of his mouth, which it has done since he stopped trimming it. He cracks open a fresh can.

Yesterday he and his dad had a mini pre-Christmas at Red Brick convalescent home. The place is already a gaudy homage to crepe paper, tinsel and Brenda Lee, but it was something. His dad asked him where he was at Thanksgiving, and told him that's the real holiday, and Steve told him again that he was working and that, no, he wasn't on nuclear alert tour anymore, that he'd been taken off tour nine months ago. He didn't tell him he is drinking every day and has been for months. At least, unlike his dad, he knows when to stop.

He took him Chinese takeout food. Steve's dad didn't bother with his fortune cookie. But Steve did and he wishes he didn't. Instead of a fortune, it contained a bad joke. He started reading it aloud, *"What lies at the bottom of the sea shivering?"* When he saw the answer, he tried to brush over it. He said it quickly before scrunching it up and shoving it in his pocket. "These are getting worse," he said. He noticed a bin right there but the joke and its punchline remained awkwardly in his pocket, scratching his leg. *A nervous wreck.*

He'd offered to take his dad out for the day, back to the old house, but the old man had insisted he didn't want a fuss. He had a lot of excuses not to leave for a man so determined to get out of there one day.

He got his dad a Lee Child book. His dad got him a $50 voucher.

"Wish your mom a happy Christmas from me," his dad said as Steve finally left.

He still had time to work on the basement before the drive to Mom's for Christmas Day, and that's where he is now, in the basement, sitting in the armchair, drinking beer, watching the *flying woman* on the news. It's all the media can think of calling her.

Unexpectedly, Steve's moustache drips onto his shirt. He looks down and freezes at the sight of it: a red splash the size of a quarter on his white t-shirt. The nosebleed rockets him straight back into the command capsule. His nose is throbbing and his shoulder is screaming, but it’s not how he remembers it. He's in the wrong place: still sitting at the console, turning the key. Hanson's sidearm is at the side of his head ready to blow his brains out. His whole torso is so tight it's like he's at the bottom of the ocean, but everything is bathed in red and stinks of vinegar.

He feels he has to get out of the bunker but finds that he can't move. He's stuck to his chair. It's like he's simultaneously here in front of the TV with a can of beer, and back in the capsule being suffocated by the noise and pressure. His face feels like he's been hit by a two-by-four. He wants to throw up. He tries to stand and the rooms start to spin, sending him back to his ass in the chair. He can barely breathe. He's stuck here for what feels like five minutes or more, unable to pick himself up or shake himself out of it.

When he closes his eyes, he feels women's faces standing over him. He tries to slow down and begins taking big, heaving breaths that come out as moans. He figures he's hyperventilating. *It's a panic attack. Pussy.* So he keeps trying, with more big, long breaths, which eventually, finally, slow things down and bring him back into the room, with such great relief at the gradual slowing of his heart that he can’t stop the tear that rolls down his cheek.

A long time later, he takes another deep breath through his blood-encrusted nose and wipes his eyes. According to his mom, he used to get nosebleeds all the time as a very young kid. He used to get them when the weather was hot, so he's told. They were never small bleeds—always enough to soak a fistful of tissues. The last time he had one, he was six or seven, maybe eight, and it's the only one he actually remembers. His uncle was living with them at the time. He can't remember why or for how long but it felt like a pretty fixed arrangement.

He needs a change of scene and manages to get up and walk to the bottom of the steps to the shelter. Here, he feels it necessary to pull the cord even though he knows this one has no use—the cord for the lights is at the top of the steps.

But it turns out this cord does do something: the room is plunged into red darkness.

The red light has something to do with his uncle staying with them when he was a kid. Now, of course, he knows what a dark room is. Back then, it must have been creepy, but exciting too—like when a submarine was under attack and the captain declared red alert. But that's where the memory ends, there's no more to it.

As Steve stands at the foot of the stairs to the bunker that used to be his uncle's dark room, he slowly turns, to aid his recollection. Now he remembers, there were trestle tables against the wall with broad, shallow trays of liquid, black and white photos pegged to strings zig-zagging across the ceiling, and the overpowering smell—the smell of vinegar. *What were they doing in the pictures?*

Steve pulls the cord to shut it out and starts up the stairs. Behind him, he hears the words,

"You. Shouldn't. Be. Here,"

* * *

Back at Wall St, there had been a couple of seconds of creeping panic before Jill realised what had happened. The knowledge didn't do anything to calm the adrenaline surging through her veins but it gave her focus. She hadn't pulled the trigger. Someone else had shot Kindle.

It was obvious it wasn't any of the cops around the perimeter in front of Jill, but Kindle had been shot from behind, where Jill was standing in the crowd. She just caught Bryce's eye before turning to look up and there, three stories up, a muzzle was hastily withdrawn into a window. She ran.

As she got towards the entrance of the building, she saw a man standing there, but he saw her first, and her weapon. His eyes popped.

"I have one of them," he said into his earpiece, without moving from his position, but reaching into his jacket.

She ran again.

"Freeze!" he growled behind her, but he didn't shout. That was important. "FBI!"

She ran faster. She couldn't help it. She just knew she had to get out of there. Her feet pounded the asphalt down a street she didn't know, running through scaffolding and billowing tarpaulin, until she saw people. She arrived at a church and turned and kept on going. The street became more dense with bodies the further she ran into the safety of the crowd. Warmly wrapped pre-Christmas shoppers and tourists ambled, oblivious to the danger just a few blocks away. Jill wove her way through them the best she could, her pursuer somewhere behind her and gaining despite the thickening crowds.

"She's got a gun!" a woman screamed just a foot from her ear and all of a sudden chaos struck like she'd just kicked the top off a termite nest. No-one knew which way to turn because no-one knew where the danger was.

"Everybody get down on the ground!" he shouted now. Her hunter was back on her. "FBI!"

Some people got down but most people kept running, on the sidewalk, into the road between yellow cabs stuck in traffic, between the smoke of steaming manhole covers, eventually getting to the ground through a kind of stumbling and tripping to their hands and knees, before lying on their bellies in the cold. Jill stood perfectly still.

"Drop the weapon!" he barked behind her.

She did as she was told, letting it clatter to the ground at arm's length. She didn't know what to say, whether she should say anything. She just did as she was told.

"Keep your hands where I can see them and turn around!" he shouted, "Slowly,"

He wasn't moving from his position, about 45ft away. She turned to face him and saw his glock in his two hands pointed at her face. He wore a baseball cap and bomber jacket but there was no FBI insignia on him. Death felt closer than it had ever felt 100ft below ground.

"I've dropped the weapon. I've turned around and my hands are where you can see them. I'm complying with everything I'm told,"

It wasn't right and she knew it. They'd just executed Kindle and were going to do the same to her. Where were all the cops now? *Shit*, she thought. She couldn't call Sentinel without her earpiece. She was on her own.

She didn't really think about what she did next.

"Hands above your head! Now get on the ground! Lie down! Face down!"

She slowly got to her knees first, with her hands above her head and then she bent forward and lowered herself down with her arms, slower still, feeling the movement in her triceps, as she got into the familiar position of a push-up.

"Put your arms out!"

She did. Then, as she lay prone, like a toppled crucifix, he approached. All that training. For nothing. When he was just a few paces away, she could smell woody tobacco wafting from him —like he rolled his own cigarettes.

"Don't look at me!" he shouted angrily.

And then he jammed his knee into her spine and she felt her ribs grind on the sidewalk and the air compress out of her lungs. When she turned her face to the side to breathe, he shoved the muzzle of his glock into her cheek and ordered her to lower her hand.

He knew he couldn't reach it to cuff her without leaning over, giving her his centre of gravity. This was her chance she realised. To the eyes of an observer, she was no longer a threat to him, she'd been disarmed, she'd complied with everything else and she was pinned to the ground.

"Give me your hand!" he ordered.

She didn't move. There was a brief moment when she could feel his weight on her shifting, as if figuring out what to do next was playing out through his body. Then he must have gone for her hand because he leant over too far. His weight was on her far side for just a split second when she spun under him. His gun went off inches from her face as her left arm, the arm he'd been reaching for, that she'd swung up and under her body, came around. She swiped at the wrist holding the weapon, driving the barrel towards the sky as he rolled over her, off balance. He'd managed to grab her left sleeve just as she spun and she used that to pull him round, and then she was on top of him, using every ounce of her strength in that one arm to smash his hand into the ground and release the gun. But that wasn't going to end the tussle. Holding his right wrist in both her hands, she flung her legs around his arm and chest, with his arm, still holding the gun, running up her torso. She counted on him not daring to shoot for fear of hitting a bystander. She raised her pelvis, locking his arm and causing him to finally drop the weapon. She kept leaning back, pressing his out-stretched arm against her body. She knew that this was the only way to end it and get away. His wailing and the crunch and pop of his arm breaking were sickening. She took his gun—there was no way she could find hers—and she ran again.

She was lucky every cop in Manhattan seemed to be at Wall Street. She was lucky that he'd not had back-up and that no civvy took it upon themselves to be a hero.

Now, she sits on a train to a bus station where they might already be looking for her, and prays for more luck. Not that she deserves it.

As the ringing in her ears finally subsides, she realises she's deaf on one side—the same side of her face that stings and burns from the gunshot.

Kindle is dead, along with any hope Jill had of justice, or revenge, and getting to those who called the shots. All Jill has achieved is to break an FBI officer's arm—a guy doing his job, following his orders, who may never work again. She asks herself how bad an injury like that is.

Anyone looking now would think she's staring out of the window. But she isn't. What would they see to look at her? So hard and guarded, rigid, poised, ready to fight. What has she become? She stares into her own reflection, oblivious of anything the other side of the glass, yet feeling everyone else present in the carriage. She can hear one of the doors between carriages, sliding open and closed because of a faulty sensor.

It takes too long to find someone she recognises in the glass—she finds it in her eyes, the same eyes she's stared into every day of her life, since she was a child trying to make out what others might think of her, wondering whether her soul was as much a mystery as the doe's caught in the hunter's crosshairs. If the eyes are the window to the soul, they're her only hope of finding hers again. *Will Agent Bryce see goodness when she looks into my eyes? Or will she see a murderer who raised a gun to the back of that crazy woman's head?*

Her heart turns to a knot in her chest as she relives the look in Agent Bryce's eyes—she wonders whether she would still have run if she'd recognised the look at the time. That look was one of horror, of complete and utter disappointment, of shame. Jill had convinced Bryce she was one of the team, that she could trust her, even give her a sidearm. It now also dawns on her that she's broken the conditions of her leave by being outside the state of Montana. She's betrayed Bryce and Takei, she's betrayed the Air Force, and she's failed Danny. All these things are worse than being a wanted fugitive.

She has to clear her name. Not just for herself, but for him. And for Tom, for the girls. For her parents. For everyone that ever gave a shit. To do that, her luck needs to last, at least until she can figure out a plan.

* * *

Christmas Day. At Mom's. Steve feels himself the most sober he's been in weeks. Someone has to keep it together and it's not going to be her. She doesn't drink, that's not the problem, she doesn't need it. He takes a deep breath and resolves to have a nice time, pushing her comment to the back of his mind, where it reverberates, quietly buzzing:

"You're not eating enough," she said.

It's a standard motherly nag but it grinds because it's the same sort of thing she says Every. Single. Time he sees her. *You look like you've lost weight* etcetera. If it were true every time she saw him, he'd have vanished by now, which would be a lot easier.

"I don't think so, Mom," he replies, "I'm eating just fine,"

The food smells good at least. His plate is overflowing with a huge portion but he knows that no matter how many servings he gets through, she'll push him to eat more. Then it'll be telling him to drink water. *Don't you get a headache? I get a terrible headache if I ever drink even a glass of wine*, and so on. He remembers when he was a kid, she'd always ask him if he wanted a sandwich and even if he said *no*, she would bring one anyway. When he'd grown up, he mentioned it to her, asking why she always still brought him food if he said he wasn't hungry. He felt ignored. She said, "If you said you weren't hungry, I would just make you less,"

Mom's not a stellar cook so Christmas dinner is not a spectacular affair and, having spent the cooking time fretting about what could go wrong, she spends the meal apologising for the burnt potatoes (they're only crispy at the edges), the under-cooked veg and the dry turkey (it is a little dry actually).

Steve can feel himself getting mildly

agitated, and is self-aware enough to realise that she's generally not a good influence on him. While at first, it can feel good to be reunited with her, he soon feels his stress levels rising to the point at which he can't wait to leave. Problem is, he tends to forget about that when arranging visits and he's now faced with five days and four nights from December 23rd to December 27th. The clock across the kitchen on the opposite wall ticks loudly. He straightens out the gold and red seasonal napkin on his lap.

Looking at her, you'd be forgiven for thinking everything is totally fine. She clings onto a kind of wilted beauty, over the years looking increasingly like the photo of her own mother on the little table by the TV. He doesn't remember his mom's mom but he does remember his dad always dismissed her side of the family as a bunch of *mad women.* It made it easier for his dad to cope with her rejection of him but, judging by how his mom is now, he might not have been far wrong.

His mom left his dad when Steve was a teenager. His dad used drink to cope, which, after years of it, eventually led to his stroke. Then his mom had a nervous breakdown, a *psychotic break.* She'd always had mood swings—like she would run hot and cold at home—and the occasional weird idea but, after leaving dad, she just started to go completely fucking nuts. Like, downhill fast. Eventually she was checked into a hospital for people with serious mental problems. She's in her own place now but she has someone come to visit her every couple of weeks to check she's looking after herself properly and taking her meds.

He considers asking her about her side of the family, but he can't bear the idea that dad might be right. He's interrupted as he struggles to think of a conversation topic.

"How's work?" she asks.

"It's fine, thanks. I'm thinking of transferring into something different,"

"What's wrong with looking after bombs?"

"Mom, they're missiles. I don't just look after them. I'm a Flight Captain--"

"-- But you don't fly a plane,"

"No. When I'm on nuclear alert tour, I have quite a lot of responsibility—more than if I were just flying a plane,"

"Oh,"

It's futile. She thinks he's just playing with toys at work. She has no idea how hard he's worked, how highly skilled he is, how senior and important he is. He wishes he had a simpler job, like a Judge or Surgeon, so she'd get it.

"Come on, Mom," he says, "Let's pull our crackers,"

Later, when they're doing the dishes, he

has drunk enough and been worn down enough, but he still can't make himself ask the question.

"*Mom*," he imagines himself saying, drying the plate she just handed him, still covered in suds (why not rinse it first?), "*Before you got ill and had to go to hospital, were there any signs that you noticed that maybe something wasn't right?*"

But he doesn't ask. And he knows it's because he's too afraid. Instead, he says: "I wonder what movies are on TV tonight. There's always something at Christmas,"

* * *

Lucy flies through shifting shades of lavender and lilac skies, chasing the sun after it has already sunk below the horizon, willing its return, to reverse its setting. In the void between Christmas and New Year, after days searching for *she doesn't know what,* she no longer knows where she is in the world. She has skimmed the endless sea, soared through the salty Sarahan sky, combed her fingers through the leafy canopies of jungles. And she has scoured relentless concrete and halogen cities, over and over. Just to be seen. Just to see.

As she looks down now, upon a twilight-lit city, she realises that somehow she has returned again, to London. Is it James, she wonders, who brings her back time and again? Or is it something else? It's strange to think, as she compels herself across the world, as she wonders and searches, that she's anchored to a place. It's like there's an invisible string tugging on her heart.

She isn't sure exactly where she is in London but it's always the Thames that gives the city away. She can see she's South of the river, maybe Croydon or Peckham. She's probably only 300m high as a red van catches her eye. She doesn't know why it's caught her attention. She's never seen one like it before; a bit like a transit van but too shiny, not like the bashed-up white vans you normally see. It's not driving especially fast but it brakes suddenly and screeches to a halt outside a small block of flats. A man gets out either side and one walks around and opens the van's back doors. The other man is hidden from view now, having gone up the steps to the front of the block where there's a stack of empty pizza boxes nearly as tall as him. A third man gets out of the back, helping a small woman or girl who's struggling to clamber out. Something feels weirdly familiar, a sort of slightly sicky feeling in Lucy's stomach that she can't ignore. The three men have shaved heads and are wearing matching black Adidas track suits and white trainers. She finds herself now only about twenty metres above them.

One of the men, the one who'd opened the

back of the van, the short one, looks up and sees Lucy.

“Shit,” she hears him say.

The other man follows his gaze and the third, the driver, who’d been waiting by the front door, emerges from his nook by the pizza boxes —she notices he has a cross tattooed on his neck. They say something between them and the one with the girl resumes marching her onto the pavement towards the building.

In the time it takes for her heart to beat once, Lucy's feet slam into the ground between the Third Man, the girl, and the building. The pavement crunches beneath her boots—because she misjudged the landing entirely. As she steadies herself, her cape flapping to her calves, Third Man pauses and the girl looks at Lucy through bleary eyes, her body like a wooden puppet propped on the man beside her. She looks about eleven. She’s still wearing her school uniform.

“Sent home from school,” Third Man says through a yellow smile, “Not feeling well." His mouth is framed by purple lips and stubble.

What has brought Lucy here? By what infinitely impossible fluke has she arrived at this moment for this girl?

Lucy isn’t sure whether to smile at the girl or to show the truth of her fear for her. “Are you okay?” Lucy asks her.

There's an odd moment while no-one knows what to do next.

"She'll be fine," says Neck Tattoo from Lucy's right, ushering Third Man to carry on. "Can I help you?" he asks Lucy.

Short Man, who'd been the one to open the back of the van, comes up behind Third Man and the young girl. He looks anxious, his eyes shifting from Lucy to Neck Tattoo, to the back of the girl's head. Lucy has no idea what to do; does she really have any clue what's going on here? Can she just accuse these men of something unspeakable? One thing's for certain: the girl needs help. Feeling as though she can't leave room for negotiation, Lucy says as clearly as she can:

"I'm going to take her to a doctor,"

"Okay," Third Man says to her surprise, "Thank you," and he smiles again, visibly relieved. Because he's genuinely concerned about the girl or because, if Lucy takes her, he and his mates can run?

Neck Tattoo and Short Man don't seem to like the idea though. Wordlessly and unanimously, the decision is made; Third Man lets go of the girl and she falls to the floor like her strings have been cut. Short Man and Third Man spin and run for the van. Neck Tattoo disappears into the block of flats. Lucy instinctively dives for the girl and scoops her up. She can't take her anywhere high or out of sight so she flies her twenty metres down the road and rests her in a doorway.

"Wait here. You'll be okay," she insists.

Third Man swings open the driver side door and grabs something, turning back to Lucy with it in his hands. The bullets feel like so many cajoling fingers as they tear into her suit and flatten against her skin. She sees the panic in his whole body as he tries to scramble into the driver seat next to Short Man. Swooping around to the front of the van, Lucy raises both fists in the air and brings them crashing down on the bonnet, crumpling the entire front of the van. The two men scream in agony so she knows it worked —she's crushed their legs inside and they aren't going anywhere.

She strides around to the driver-side window, smashes her fist through the window and plucks the little machine gun out Third Man's hands. The warmth of the gunbarrel in her fist is almost soothing. She squeezes it and flicks her wrist, taking its own energy to use against it, leaving it frosty, twisted and useless. The whites of his eyes, tremble with conviction and fear. It makes him look like an angry little boy.

She turns to the girl, realising that she doesn't have much time for what she has to do next. The young blonde-haired girl is sitting up now, rubbing her face, mumbling something.

"My phone," Lucy just about hears her say,

"I want to call my mum,"

"Okay," says Lucy as she scoops her up again, "but first, let's make sure you're okay,"

Lucy already spotted a hospital earlier and it doesn't take them long to get there. On the way, she finds out the girl is called Sasha. The last thing she remembered was those men calling her over to their van to ask for directions.

Lucy doesn't stay at the hospital. When she returns to the van outside the small block of flats, Short Man, still trapped with Third Man, has managed to get a mobile phone and is shakily trying to tap something into it. *Good*, she thinks, *let them all come*.

She walks up the steps to the door through which Neck Tattoo disappeared earlier. She feels each step beneath her boots as if there's a part of her trying to keep her rooted.

With one hand flatly against the white plastic door, she pushes it inwards, the whole thing bending, buckling and crashing inside. At that same moment as light pours past her into the darkening street outside, and the sound of police sirens claws its way through the night air towards the building, she sees in front of her in the hallway a paralysed figure holding a black holdall—it's Neck Tattoo trying to run for the door before she burst through. Behind him are at least eight other men, filling the space back to the door at the opposite end.

"Fuck!" shouts Neck Tattoo in panic. He tries to turn around, but in the bustle, he's blocked by his friends.

Faced with all of these men, Lucy's worst fears for Sasha unfurl in her mind and she feels them crawling under her skin. *How many girls are in this place?*

Lucy begins walking down the hallway. As she reaches Neck Tattoo, something shifts and the human traffic jam somehow finds space to part, but not for her, for a mountain of a man thundering towards her. His huge shirtless body is covered in tattoos. He takes up almost the entire hallway as he comes for her, others pressing against the walls to let him pass. He pauses for half a second, sizing up Lucy with a snarl, before thrusting his wrecking ball of a fist towards her gut.

She catches his fist—it's so big she can hardly curl her fingers around it—and she crushes it. Whatever drugs he's on, he doesn't scream, he only grits his teeth, but it has to hurt. Now she puts her other hand on his chest and launches him back through the others like they're bowling pins.

Fire rushes through her veins and drives her on. Marching her way through the hallway. She doesn't fight, she just walks, an unstoppable force. Like a train through rain drops, she powers unswayed through bodies to get to the stairs she now sees through the door at the end. One after the other, several at a time, a seemingly endless torrent of these raindrops gathering and streaming over her remorseless body passing through. It becomes nauseating but she must go on. As one of the men topples off her and she walks over him, there's a sickening crack.

Finally reaching the top of the stairs, she sees that every door on this floor has a padlock on the outside. She already knows what's on the other side, in those rooms. But nothing slows her down now. As she breaks off the first lock, the police and ambulances screech to the building and, as she opens the first door, she hears the cacophony of shouts, "Armed police!" and the screams of her victims breaks through.

In all, there were twelve girls and one boy in that house, two in each room, except the boy who was on his own. Their ages ranged from around Sasha's age to early twenties—Lucy's age. None of them spoke. Later, Lucy travels in the back of one of the ambulances full of the children. The police had wanted her to go with them but frankly they knew they couldn't stop her. Later still, she stands vigil at the hospital, in the ward area of the Accident and Emergency department; standing still for the first time in so long that it's dizzying. Police guard the passages away from the ward. Even so, she can't bring herself to leave despite not serving any purpose, as doctors and nurses rush around her between the blue paper curtains that envelop the beds. She wants to escape the memory of what happened today but, as much as she longs for one, there isn't a moment when she can feels she can go. Even if she could get away, she doesn't feel like she has anywhere to go to, and something feels unfinished.

The suit her whole life has been leading up to wearing is now so claustrophobic. Half of the white paint of her costume has long worn off, exposing streaks and patches of the black underneath. On top of the mud, silt and sand from the last few days, she notices fresh splashes of blood. She wonders where the men she beat and trampled have been taken, if they're in the same hospital somewhere else, if she killed any. She re-hears the crunch as one of them hit the floor. She re-feels a nuclear warhead crumpling in her fingers, perilously close to detonating. Her stomach twists and she forces herself to focus on one of the blue curtains in front of her, the child invisible behind it. The same blue paper curtains as in the hospital in Washington, when her need to over-think and over-complicate, her fear of the unknown and the uncontrollable, let those people die.

So what does she do now? In the aftermath, with the consequences of rushing in?

This world tour of Lucy's, rushing all over the globe, looking for things to do: she can justify it as all part of the plan—making herself as much of a target as possible for McAvoy—but she can't kid herself any longer. If she doesn't make peace with her fears and self-doubt she will never control anything, least of all her own destiny. She'll be a pawn in other people's plans her whole life, until checkmate.

"Make your move," Grangran would say when they played chess, "The game is out here, not in your head,"

Grangran is legendary at chess, golf and fish pie. When Lucy would try to play golf with Grangran, she tried to help her clear her mind. She'd say, "No amount of thinking is going to hit that ball,"

Lucy was meant to be an intelligent, academic thinker—not very physical or coordinated—so she decided she preferred chess to any other sport. Chess is totally cerebral—or so she thought, because Grangran the chess master always tried to convince her that chess requires her intuition too. Lucy didn't get what intuition was, and was sure she didn't have it. She's still sure she doesn't now.

"Thinking will only get you so far," Grangran said, "Intuition is your mind working in the background. It's putting things together, noticing things you can't see or *think*... When your intuition tells you something, listen," she said calmly as she plucked up Lucy's queen once, "It doesn't always speak and, when it does, sometimes it's a whisper, so listen hard,"

When she was older, probably thirteen—upset about something—paralysed as she is now in this hospital—not knowing what to do next, she remembers Grangran shattering her teenage angst-ridden silence: "You lost,"

She remembers the words as clearly as if Grangran were speaking to her right now. They sounded uncharacteristically cruel. She remembers at first thinking Grangran was telling her she'd lost at something she didn't know she was even playing, some secret game only Grangran knew about, but then the words began to turn in her young teenage head, *"Are you lost?"*

"What?" Lucy asked.

"You don't know where to go,"

"No, I'm just thinking,"

"You sound angry," the bluntness of Grangran's reply shouldn't have taken her by surprise.

The lines on Grangran's face framed deep, beechwood eyes and round cheeks that looked like they should always be smiling, even though they were not. *Why did Grangran look so sad that day?* Her eyes were deep wells of sorrow. As Lucy buried herself in her jumper, stretched over her knees, Grangran's sing-song voice became almost the whole memory.

In the hospital ward now, Lucy's mask suddenly feels wrong and unnecessary, offensive.

In the memory, Lucy looked at her Grangran's beautiful face and wondered silently whether Grangran saw Lucy's mother's features and curly hair; or whether she saw a White girl, her father's daughter.

Grangran asked, "What makes you happy?"

It struck Lucy, as it still does now, as a strange question. Although it should have been simple, when she thinks about it, she realises she doesn't have an answer, even now. The version of herself she'd conjured in her fantasies would have put her hands on her hips and said something like, *Seeing justice being served*, but she never learnt the honest answer to this simple question. It has always felt like a perverse thing to answer; like she hasn't earnt the right to think about herself in this way. Right now even more so; with what she's seen today, and with the fate of the world in the balance, what she wants, what makes her happy, is irrelevant.

"I don't know,"

"You don't know?" Grangran asked, "What do you worry about?"

"Making a mistake,"

“Ah," she said, as if all Lucy's previous answers had led to this. "But mistakes are inevitable," she said, "You can’t get *unlost* without them. You can’t find your path,"

Easier said than done.

When you have the power Lucy has, mistakes destroy lives. And she doubts "finding her path" is what is going to save the world from destruction, but back then, as a torn-up thirteen year-old kid, something compelled her in that rare moment. Trusting Grangran more than anyone, she turned to her and their eyes met. She asked, full of the angst of youth, “How do you find your path?”

The pools of Grangran’s eyes pulled Lucy in and narrowed.

“You start walking,” she said simply.

But I can’t leave here, Lucy thinks to herself now in the hospital.

Grangran continued, “What do you think will happen if you don’t do what’s expected of you?”

Lucy buried her face in her jumper. Her parents were unpredictable in different ways and she never knew which version of either she was about to see. Her mum could be encouraging, interested and creative, but she could also be cold, cut-off, unsympathetic. Not only did her dad have two very different demeanours but he could switch like a light without any indication that a change had happened until he said something. His enjoyment or tolerance of something could vanish without warning, resulting in a sudden and blunt cutting down. Her mum's anxiety and her dad's judgement were the two most powerful forces in the house.

Lucy couldn't answer the question at the time. She couldn't see what she did as conforming because even her thoughts conformed. She just felt lucky that she was how her parents wanted. Now she sees, if she wasn't exactly as they wanted, it wouldn't have been tolerated. What that would have meant though, she doesn't know—she just feels the guilt and shame that surrounded it.

Her dad has mellowed but he is still opinionated to the point of disgust. Naturally, when she was a kid, his convictions had her trapped. Sharing in his views was a matter of emotional survival that meant she couldn't hold her own thought for even a moment. Soon she learnt that it was safest to become a cynic and a critic like him. Despite this protecting her views from scrutiny, her behaviour, intelligence and performance still had to meet his high expectations. This wasn't because he was ever cruel to her. On the contrary, it was even worse—

he put her on a pedestal. He stopped her living, as much as her mum did.

While her judgemental father put her on an impossible pedestal, her anxious mother was primed to collapse at any moment. Her mum worries so much about every little thing that, in her fifties, she has reached the point of virtual paralysis. Back then, she was both impossibly fragile and frighteningly hard, like a pecking bird. David believes it was her mum's anxiety that led to Lucy unconsciously suppressing her abilities.

Is it all connected? Is she so afraid of moving, of making her own decisions, because the fear of getting it wrong has been so ingrained in her? Is this why there's no middle-ground between being paralysed by over-thinking and rushing in like she did today? Is that where her non-existent intuition should be? She knows if she is going to stop McAvoy, she has to find the strength to take control and move in the right direction, but is she brave enough to misstep, and can she afford to?

She makes a mental note to visit Grangran and thank her—for never making her feel like she'd be judged.

She reaches across her body and pulls her cape off at each shoulder. Affording it only a short moment in her hands, she drops it in a hospital bin for contaminated waste.

CHAPTER 10

You will rue the day...

It's New Year's Eve. Tiny snowflakes flutter gently and catch on her eyelashes as Lucy glides silently over London. The last smudge of burnt orange fades from the sky, the sun already below the horizon, and lilac ink seeps across the clouds. The falling snowflakes, that were like golden butterflies in the last rays of sun, become almost invisible now and seem to gather in the lights of the tallest towers and the streetlights further below as they flicker to life. In the new darkness, the flakes take on the look of falling ash over the Big Smoke.

She loosely follows the serpentine course of the Thames, east towards Vauxhall. It is always so black and so bottomless at night.

She's made a nightly flight over London since, by some miracle, she found Sasha and the other children. But, something like that won't happen again. In the real world, there's no Bat-Signal, no sudden bank alarm as masked robbers laden with money bags make a getaway. No super-hearing alerts her to the pleas of a little girl whose cat is stuck in a tree. Even the police scanner is proving useless: the police basically do their job without her. So what is she doing? It's been over a month since Wall Street; Christmas came and went. She's beginning to think MI6's plan isn't going to work. She should pay them a visit; walk straight into their weird glass and concrete office. It's just up ahead on the riverbank. She won't of course; she's had the same thought every day for the last week.

Following her *world tour*, patrolling the capital and being as visible as possible is still her only move, while McAvoy's side of the board remains completely invisible. As a result, her "face" is plastered everywhere she turns. At work, every news channel on the screens around the office is looking for its angle. She tells herself it doesn't matter what people say as long as it's about her and McAvoy is listening. But that isn't true. It matters. The pundits range from cultists, like Anthony Spitelli, to haters with the power to make even Lucy fear herself.

"We don't need another White saviour" some say. If only they knew. She's always felt so inarticulate when it comes to her place. Is she another privileged, self-appointing saviour,

positioning others as impotent, reducing the complexities of their experiences to her own heroic deeds? Who is she to get involved? Does it matter? The dragging feeling in her heart shifts to the pit of her stomach, pulling her down to the waters and reminding her of Tokyo.

She'll pass Waterloo Station soon. When she does, she'll see the giant banner someone has spread over the roof saying: *THANK YOU.* She can still hear the screeching brakes and screaming crowds of the runaway train. Her skin prickles as she remembers the broken glass under her feet. Not long after she returned from her world tour, after too many close calls with blades, she invested in some armoured biker leather. Still painted red and white, still the same mask, and the symbol on her chest, but the cape stayed in that bin at the hospital, probably incinerated with the contaminated waste by now. She hopes it's a little more sensible than a wetsuit. There's something else that's changed. Through the gap at the back of her cowl, her hair, that she's let grow out over the last few months, feels like her for the first time. There isn't much in her life that has ever felt that way, so it feels good.

A moment after she passes the MI6 building on her right, she sees something that stops her in her tracks. Her eyes fix on it and she flies onward to check what she's seeing. On a tower block facing the river, on a high corner balcony, a man sits on the ledge, outside the railing. Lit from behind, he has a wiry cruciform silhouette. As she gets closer, he raises his arms at his sides like he is expecting to take off on the wind.

She does her best not to startle him; approaching slowly and to the side, she comes down into his view. In the dark, his face dimly up-lit by the street below, his hollow cheeks are exaggerated by sharp shadow, the temples on his bald head are sunken. His dress shirt and trousers hang loosely off him like a scarecrow. He must be freezing. He doesn't acknowledge her even in the slightest, his eyes virtually dead and his whole body now motionless except the wind fussing with his shirt.

"Excuse me," she says, "Are you okay?" *What a stupid thing to ask,* she thinks. He doesn't hear her. She has a chance to try again. "It's cold out tonight,"

"What?" he replies, as if emerging from a trance.

She comes further around to his side so they share the view.

"I mean, it's a beautiful view but it's very cold," she says, with no knowledge of what cold means.

The man looks down to the black river below, his arms still outstretched like wings.

"Do you know what I'm doing here?" he

asks, suddenly more alive, and perplexed by this silly girl talking about the weather.

"It looks like you're planning to jump,"

"Right. I don't need help, thank you."

"I'm sorry I didn't offer it,"

She doesn't know why she said what now sounds so cruel. But who is she to stop him if he wants to end his life? Isn't it his right?

At this, he turns his head and looks at her. She meets his bewildered gaze.

"You mean if I were to jump, you wouldn't try to stop me?"

"I'd want to," she replies, "But what would be the point if you don't want to live?"

She surprises herself. He drops his arms a little but he doesn't take his eyes off her. She looks back to the view across the Thames. The gathering black clouds are lit dirty-yellow by the city.

"Oh," he says, "So you are here to watch?"

"No," *Am I being cruel?*

"Well, I really think it's time you disappear,"

The old man awkwardly and painfully climbs to his feet on the narrow ledge, using the railing for support. Lucy thinks he may fall whether he wants to or not. He straightens his flapping shirt, sticks out his arms and his chin.

"What if you change your mind on the way down?"

"I'm absolutely certain. This world is not worth being a part of,"

Now that they're talking, she thinks maybe she can help after all.

"I know it may feel that way now," she tries, "but there's so much good in the world too,"

"You have no idea do you?" he sneers.

"Maybe. But I believe there's always a way," she offers, somewhere between pleadingly and apologetically.

"What does that even mean?" he asks bitterly.

She draws conviction from her mask and her anonymity, the icon she is meant to be, and everything that has happened over the last ten months.

"There's always a way. No matter how bad things get and no matter how much you think you can't go on,"

"This isn't about whether I can go on. This is about whether I want to live in a world like this. And the answer is *no*. This is my way. We could all do well to leave this cancerous world behind. But unlike you," he begins again, "I am going to do something to really make the world a better place,"

"By killing yourself?"

His eyes are full of rage, maybe even victory. She's seen these eyes before, on a different face, one full of hair; a younger, fuller face. His glare penetrates her skull as his old face emerges at the centre of her world. Everything else falls apart around it.

"Not just myself," he says. For a moment, she can't speak. She can only watch as he opens his right hand to show a little black cylinder with a button at the top, and she knows he has a bomb. It's McAvoy. "You know who I am? Good. I know I look a little different" he explains. Now, motioning the trigger, he asks, "Do you know what this is?"

"You sick--" she cuts off from her rage and panic, "Where is it?"

Waving vaguely at his head, he says, "Well, the cancer is in the blood now, my lungs, my brain --" He trails off, seemingly bored by his own game. The whole time, his expression is like stone. He's not pleased with what he's doing, yet neither is he angry. She feels like a misbehaving child in front of a disappointed teacher.

"The bomb," Lucy responds as firmly as she can.

McAvoy waves the trigger in his hand. "Come," he says as he lifts his leg over the railing, "Slowly," Now's Lucy's chance: She could grab the trigger while the old man climbs back onto the balcony. But he could just as easily press the button. No, she needs a clear path to pounce forward and grab his wrist: She can crush the bone before he can do anything. But if the bomb is also on a timer -- "I want you to see this," he says, "but not so much that I won't push this trigger if you don't come now," he says.

She needs to get to the bomb. The lights on the balcony are lit but, through the floor-to-ceiling windows, the apartment beyond is pitch black. She flies over the railing and steps onto the balcony where he is waiting for her. He walks ahead and opens the door to the apartment. She follows a few paces behind. She waits for him to find the lightswitch and turn it on before she enters and, when she does, he turns to show her the trigger again. Holding it at eye-level, just a few feet away, she is struck by a millisecond of doubt, and just as she realises what it really is, the pepper spray squirts in her eyes. She has no words, no point of reference for this pain but something tells her this is what fire should feel like. As she instinctively raises her hands and turns her face, squeezing her eyes shut, she barely notices the sharp scratch on her neck.

She screams in pain and anger, "*What are you doing?!*"

He can't possibly think he can beat her with pepper spray. She leaves the ground to get back and create some space until she can see again, trying to blink the burning liquid away. But as her toes leave the floor, she starts to feel light-headed, like she's tumbling back into a swimming pool, about to drown. She needs to sit but there's no ground. She can barely open her eyes, as she turns and makes for the door, but everything is going dark.

* * *

Wally Soufan hates penguins. Not that he knew until he finds himself staring down at a pile of them, staring sycophantically back at him with their little seasonal greeting.

As expected, the FBI used the secondary explosive they planted with the drone to justify executing Ashley Kindle, but killing her did not progress the mission, nor particularly help the wider political situation. On the one hand, she was the opponent's chess piece, removed from the board without arousing suspicion or concern. Pawn takes pawn. But, she was allowed across seven states and into Manhattan with a bomb—the public don't need to know that it contained a virus. *Alhamdulillah* for the flying woman.

Recently, the FBI has become so thinly stretched and under-resourced that something bad was inevitable. Perhaps not their first mistake was putting only one operative on Kindle's street. Wally heard they'd blamed the blizzard for her escape, but they didn't even know her car was missing until the following day when the next agent arrived to take over the shift. They knew immediately that, if she'd made a covert getaway, she meant business but, since they already knew about the letters, they knew where she was going. They put operatives at the airport and every train station, bus station, service station and gas station on all the main routes from Helena, Montana to NYC. And at Wall Street, Broad St and Fulton St subway stations. But for all their intelligence and strategy, they couldn't spot a woman who'd bleached her hair and donned a face mask, until she was standing in front of them screaming for her life.

Executing her was their last-ditch effort to elevate them from complicit morons to public saviours—and it could still work. To do this, a mechanised bomb disposal unit was brought in to "find" a secondary explosive on the body. Publicly, they take the credit for identifying the threat and eliminating it. Privately, heads are going to roll. Even before all this, to say the FBI needed a win would have been a serious understatement. Some say the FBI is in its death throes. Wally can only hope.

In the aftermath of 9/11, the Bureau was in crisis. Sloppy procedures and petty inter-agency conflict were being exposed on an almost weekly basis, with the finger pointed squarely at the FBI and CIA for letting 9/11 happen.

Then, President George W Bush dropped them a lifeline. He was savvier than he was given credit and he knew the intelligence community was how he was going to win his fight for the hearts and minds of the people. He said, "Every nation, in every region, now has a decision to make. Either you are with us, or you are with the terrorists." And so, it wasn't *ragheads* in body bags that would win his intangible War on Terror, it was stories.

From the moment he uttered those words, the cogs were in motion. The Bureau had a way to talk up the threat because, suddenly, there was the fear of a sleeper cell in every city. And they had an enormous amount of work to do, which would need an immense budget. Applications to join the FBI and CIA were at an all-time high. In scouring the land, the Bureau's efforts were seen as valiant, tireless and widespread.

That was partly true—they were tireless and widespread. Following 9/11, the FBI became the biggest recruiter of terrorists in the United States. Sure, it started as an experiment but it soon became so easy and so scalable that the Bureau could barely pump the breaks.

The method went like this: 1) Make up a terrorist plot, 2) find someone to sign up to it, 3) arrest them. It was child's-play. Someone, always brown, always identifiably "other", would pop their head up in some way, usually by simply being dumb and desperate enough. The Bureau would surround that person with false friends to lure them in. Perhaps they were broke and on the verge of losing their home—in fact, it almost always involved money and never involved religious ideology.

That's all it took. No-one had to do anything except agree to the plan. For over twenty years, there was a near one hundred percent conviction rate for these "foiled terrorist plots". All the prosecution would need ask the jury was, "Is it better to send them to jail or let them roam the street?"

The "terrorists" in all these convictions were currently spending the rest of their lives in jail. Soufan is personally aware of around three-hundred cases over the last twenty years. That's more than one a month, serving twenty to thirty years each.

Not that it's any consolation to said convicts, but eventually, the FBI overstepped their mark: They tried to impeach President Donald Trump. Mysteriously, after a twenty-year run, the media started to shine the spotlight on what the FBI was doing, starting with *The Liberty City Seven*.

So, it wasn't the threat of a catastrophic terrorist attack on US soil that got the FBI and CIA working together, it was the threat of another term with Trump. It would take the two agencies working together to pull off a sting so big their value couldn't be denied.

To make the FBI and CIA both heroes again, they created *Picasso Al-Nasser*. By the time Soufan knew what was happening, he was already part of it.

It was no longer enough to find a pleb or a desperate imbecile. And the mark couldn't just put his name to a plan. It took months of planning to find someone with the drive and intelligence to infiltrate the upper ranks of ISIS, but with the naivety to be malleable.

Unfortunately, someone got it wrong. Terrence McAvoy, by then known as Ibrahim Mohammed "Picasso" Al-Nasser, was Number Three on the world's most wanted list when he disappeared. No-one had any idea how he did it. But they knew it was him behind 3/19. Heads were going to roll and the FBI and CIA were on the verge of drawing battle lines again. With the stakes higher than ever before, and to avoid an inter-agency civil war, they agreed to work together to find him and put him away.

The Bureau scored the first point, finding McAvoy's accomplice in Helena, Montana: Ashley Kindle aka The Hacker Bomber. When they searched her apartment and found the letters, however, they found a much bigger problem. McAvoy had somehow amassed a global network of such accomplices with dirty bombs derived from the stolen plutonium. Or so they thought, as it has just turned out there was no plutonium but something far worse. They realised he had been playing them since the very moment they recruited him, if not before, and now they had to dismantle the network they'd armed with the perfect killer virus.

The Bureau watched Kindle, adding up the evidence: the drone, the letters; but the CIA still needed to find the locations of the virus spreaders. They knew Kindle had no intelligence for them but they couldn't let the supergirl take her from them at Wall Street. If Kindle led any other group to McAvoy, the game was up. So she was executed.

Now Wally has to phone his boss to explain why their months-long, million-dollar operation has so far yielded no more than some Christmas thank you cards to the friends and family of Carol Wimberley.

* * *

“Who are you pretending to be?”

Lucy feels herself waking into an on-going conversation. The words echo around her head. She feels compelled to answer, even while her mind and body grope motionlessly in the haze for some clue.

"I'm not pretending,"

She finds herself in total darkness waiting

for her eyes to adjust. The man with whom she's speaking is just a few feet in front of her but she can't see him. She's sitting in a hard chair—and she doesn't think she could get up out of it if she wanted to. Even her costume feels heavy. And she doesn't like his question.

"Yes you are," he insists.

His tone is so much like Charlotte's when they were kids that she could almost believe she's sitting there next to him. *You've just not seen them*, she remembers saying in the playground.

Now, like a picture suddenly coming into focus, Lucy remembers.

"Where's the virus?" she demands as she gets to her feet.

She can't understand how it's so dark she can't see her own hands in front of her face, and no sooner is she standing than her legs start to give in and she is powerless to stop herself slumping back into the chair. She realises upon landing that it's a wheelchair with hard rubber armrests and a stiff leather seat. But it doesn't move. *What have you done to me, McAvoy?*

"Virus?" he repeats, like a snake amused by the mouse in its tightening coils.

“Where's the virus?” she repeats, or at least she thinks she does—it sounds like a mumble.

"Perhaps you need some more time to reflect,"

She can feel herself drifting off.

"Are you ready to talk?" He asks from a distance.

"Where's the virus?"

Silence again.

She's awoken in torment. An excruciating barrage of whistling, beeping, screeching and hooting. It's as if each layer of noise has its own physical form of violence: hammering, drilling or burning their way into her eardrums, and expanding inside her skull.

"LET ME SLEEP!" Her own voice barely registers under the cacophony.

“How are you feeling?” he asks when the noise finally stops.

* * *

It was going to be Wall Street that did it. Papa’s refusal to acknowledge that McAvoy and Al-Nasser are the same person and his refusal to implement a meaningful hunt for either had nearly unleashed a deadly, uncontrollable virus on the world, with one of the world’s most important financial districts at its epicentre. Not to mention that they could have arrested the pair behind 3/19 long ago. All Cassandra was going to have to do was, via her FBI handler, convince the UK Foreign Secretary to investigate the conclusion of Op Turpentine, including the unredacted *Turpentine letters*. She was sure it wasn't going to be easy for them—not without Papa finding out about an investigation into his business, under his own nose. But there were only a couple of conclusions to draw regarding him: it was either gross misconduct or gross negligence, and either way, even the current UK government's Foreign Secretary couldn't ignore Papa's culpability. So when they offer him early retirement on a full pension, that would have been something Papa couldn't refuse. By the time her handler would allow her to speak directly with the UK Foreign Secretary, she would already have written down everything she knows, from Munich to now—the final nail in Papa's coffin, and absolution for Cassandra and Takei. She was sure US Intelligence already had a new, more amicable *Papa* lined up to take his place. The outgoing Papa would bellow and bristle while he was neutered. He'd probably try to take down others with him —Cassandra for certain—but Cassandra still had Sentinel and, as far as British Intelligence was concerned, that's a trump card.

For her, removing Papa was going to be the easy part. The most conscionable. The first part of the deal, however, was giving them the miraculous young woman she's come to call Sentinel. They clearly suspected that toppling Papa would wipe Cassandra's slate and buy her freedom to return home, which they couldn't allow, not with what she knows. Cassandra's unique selling point to the US, however, was Sentinel, and they couldn't lose that. So it was Sentinel first, then Papa.

It was a hard pill to swallow, but it was Cassandra's best option for getting Op Turpentine back in action and stopping the unstoppable virus. In order to accept Sentinel as an asset, they needed a means of contact, leverage and a first meeting. In that order. She handed over the phone number for Professor David O'Connor—whom she said was Sentinel's handler—along with the location of a USB stick Takei had planted at the last petrol station they'd stopped at on the way to Manhattan. He would corroborate its existence too. On the stick were ID documents and files for the twenty-three year-old Black British woman, her mother and father, siblings, grandparents, cousins, aunts and uncles.

"You think the IDs of her and her family are enough?" her handler questioned, "The threat of *outing* her identity?"

"Nothing so risky. We can deport her whole family back to the Caribbean with no prospects and no life,"

"How?"

"We have form,"

The UK government's *Hostile Environment* policy was initiated in 2012. The legislation resulted in the Windrush Scandal, which saw hundreds of Caribbean immigrants and their descendants, many of whom had never set foot outside of the UK, detained, deported and denied legal rights. Sentinel's family could easily be swept into the long backlog of unresolved cases. It was good enough for Cassandra's interviewer.

From the moment she handed over O'Connor's phone number, the clock had begun ticking, and the FBI had politely bundled her from their building in Manhattan into a car to a safehouse. All this time, she had no contact with Daniel Takei. She realised, without surprise, that the FBI feared the integrity of their New York City headquarters and felt the need to hold them elsewhere.

The car arrived at Pittsburgh. By then, the FBI would have retrieved the USB and called O'Connor to set up the meeting. He knew to accept and play along but not to do anything. The question was how long it would be before they started getting impatient and threatening him, and whether he could take it, before the rest of Cassandra and Takei's plan paid off.

A built-up place like Pittsburgh is not the ideal location for a defensive safehouse, which meant either they were using it as an observation point and the meeting with Sentinel was nearby or they were stopping off on the way to somewhere else—she hoped not Guantanamo. Either way, she wouldn't be there long.

The car stopped on a tree-lined street of tall, tightly packed rows of red-brick townhouses. The weather was wet and the trees were bare. There was a smell of rain in the air. There were five concrete steps up to the front door. She was escorted by the driver of the car and his partner, both wearing earpieces. Both white caucasian men in their early thirties. Friendly enough but serious about their jobs. And so they should be. As soon as they got to the top of the steps, one behind her, one in front, the door was opened from the inside. Another white caucasian man in his mid-thirties; bigger than the other two and wearing a black bomber jacket over, by process of elimination, a holstered glock under his armpit. Also wearing an earpiece. Down the narrow hallway, past a closed door on the right, was what looked like a kitchen, with—from what she could see through the empty door frame—a table and chairs, with a hand of playing cards face-down on the table. That was at least two men waiting here for her plus her two escorts, so far. She was taken upstairs by the driver while the other man walked with the bouncer towards the kitchen. The driver was calmer now and even welcoming.

He jogged gently up the stairs ahead of her and turned at the top, smiling tentatively and motioning for her to go ahead past the bathroom into a bedroom.

"Sorry, we don't really have time for

the tour, ma'ame," he said, "But you won't go wanting. There's the kitchen downstairs, but Marco and Pip will get you whatever you need. Rest room here—toothbrush and shower and so on. Bed in there. I'll be back later with a change of clothes for you,"

They really were in a hurry, but so was she. The bedroom was at the back of the house. Those at the front would be used as observation points. That meant Daniel wasn't at the safehouse. Two spies in one house would have made for a difficult night of babysitting. If she were in charge, she would have placed them in separate towns—or states ideally—so that, should they decide they were better off not defecting and escaped, they'd spend long enough trying to find each other that the FBI or police would have time to catch up with them, or that they could catch one as bait for the other.

She had to get to the Red Roof Inn Parsippany, off the I-80 to Manhattan—the secondary Emergency Rendezvous Point she'd agreed with Takei. She was counting on him escaping his safehouse the same way she was going to escape her's, by exploiting its natural weaknesses. There are certain requirements of safehouses, particularly those in built-up areas used as offensive positions for covert operations. They were more about visibility and access than custody: the ability to observe approach, easy escape routes, convenient hiding places and access to transportation.

When the driver left her, she knew one of the others would be up shortly to check on her, and they would continue regular checks thereafter. She closed the door to the bedroom and went to the window at the far end. To her delight, the window had the key in its lock. When she heard the front door open and close and heard the car driving away, she unlocked and opened the window as wide as it would go. She looked down to the small, shabby yard outside and was hit by the gusting wind from outside Ashley Kindle's window just days earlier. Her knee throbbed. The exterior windowsill was slick with recent rain. The distance between her and the ground below appeared to stretch to infinity. But that wasn't her plan; heart pumping hard, she turned towards the bed at the other end of the room, dropped down to the floor and slid under it. Then she heard the heavy footsteps coming up the stairs.

He didn't knock. From under the bed, she could watch as the door opened, and see first his legs step inside. She could tell he was built like a mountain. It took him less than a second to realise she'd gone. "Oh shit," he called gruffly, as he ran to the window. "She's gone!"

As fast as she could, she kicked herself out from under the bed and ran for him while his back was turned. She had to finish this before his friends followed. But he turned just as she was getting to him. With no way she could go toe-to-toe with his weight, she spun around the back of him and reached up to throw her arm around his thick neck. She didn't have a chance to complete the lock with her other arm before he was throwing her over his shoulder. She countered by hopping over his sweeping tree trunk of a leg and turning in front of him. As she came around his body, with her free right arm, she unclipped and removed his glock from under his armpit. With him still twisting her captured wrist in the meaty clamp of his fist, she jammed the magazine into the vulnerable tendons on the underside of his wrist, momentarily weakening his grip enough to jerk free. Skipping back, she kept the raised pistol between them and took off the safety.

"Don't move," she ordered. She had hoped to get around behind him but it was too late.

From behind her barked another voice, "FREEZE!"

The doorman had been the one other man in the house and he was now in this doorway, pointing a gun at her.

"Back-up will be here soon," he said, "You're not leaving,"

She most definitely was leaving.

"Actually," she said coolly, "You're going to put your gun down or I'm going to blow beefcake's face off," The guy hesitated for a second as he tried to figure out whether she had it in her. She gently began squeezing the trigger. "Look, I've had a very bad day and I'm on my way to stop the extinction of human life, so I really wouldn't test me if I were you,"

Less than a day later, at 20:07, Cassandra was sitting on the creaky bed in the little room at the Red Roof Inn, holding the old phone at the bedside table. The receptionist was telling her that her husband, *Mr Smith*, had arrived. It was in that little room that the two professionals phoned AliasAnon for one last favour—a direct line to the UK Foreign Secretary.

And it is now more than a month later, Christmas spent in a motel pulling a cracker over twin beds, New Year watching the fireworks on a different motel room's TV. After staying ahead of the FBI for just long enough to get to the covert chartered jet to bring them home, Agents Bryce and Takei sit across from the new *Papa* behind his glass desk, in his glass office. A white caucasian male in his fifties.

"Let me begin by welcoming you both back to British shores," he says, "Your commitment to the ethics and the principles of this organisation have more than earned you both your full pardon. The Foreign Secretary and I are extremely proud and grateful, and are confident that you will continue to serve Queen and country, but also to collaborate within the *global* intelligence community to apprehend Terrence McAvoy and neutralise this threat,"

"Thank you, sir," chorus Cassandra and Daniel.

"I have officially reassigned you both to Op Mantis," he looks between them, seeing their understandable confusion, "It was time to open a new ledger on this one. Op Turpentine is finished. It's Mantis now. Both your previous assignments —Op Underpin and Op Spindle—are taken care of,"

"Thank you, sir," they repeated.

"Agent Bryce, you are to take over the operation from Agent Knox. He has already been briefed and has the handover ready,"

"Thank you, sir," she nods, "Our priority now has to be securing a vaccine. Kindle's body --"

"Agreed, Bryce," he says quickly, "But there's something else," She feels motion behind them and turns in her chair. When she sees who's walking in, she stands. Takei follows suit. "Mantis is a joint op," Papa says behind her.

In front of her are a man she recognises and a man she doesn't. The former, a stooping figure that straightens up as he enters the room, strange to see above ground and out of uniform.

"I believe you know Lieutenant General

Hilton,"

She stares.

"And this is Mr Jones," he says, still sitting behind his desk, "Hilton is with the CIA. Jones is MI5. They've been watching McAvoy for some time,"

She had no idea Hilton is CIA. Her mind rushes: *Was his role at the joint intelligence committee in Virginia a cover? What was he really doing there?* But most importantly, *They've been watching McAvoy?*

"You're not going to run away again are you?" asks Hilton.

* * *

She feels dirty. Her thighs and backside are damp and itchy from sitting in a puddle of her own pee. It's cold.

"You are filthy," a gruff voice barks from the shadows, his contempt palpable.

Her mouth is dry and stuck, but she manages to speak.

"Where am I?"

He ignores her. *I feel drunk*. The room spins and everything feels heavy.

"My name is Ibrahim Muhammad Al-Nasser," he growls like a king of lions, "It is a name feared throughout the world by *infidels* and *unbelievers*," he pauses and when he speaks again his voice has moved across the empty black space, "Some call me *Picasso Al-Nasser*,"

In the pauses, she listens to the clinking of light metal objects. Her heart, the only part of her body with any strength, pumps frenetically, near explosion. Everything else is limp and woozy. It's pitch-black. She has no idea where she is nor why she can't move. Her underwear sticks uncomfortably to her but her arms lack the strength to do anything about it. Her costume is gone but she can tell she's still wearing the leggings and t-shirt she wore underneath the armoured leather. She remembers now what's happening.

"McAvoy!" she shouts into the darkness.

He ignores her again.

"Do you know why they call me *Picasso*?" Again, the sound of metal, laid out on a hard surface. "You will find out, imposter. Soon. We have all the time in the world, you and I,"

McAvoy has left her with a monster. Suddenly, he pulls a rough bag over her head and snatches it taut at the base of her skull. She can't move and for a moment she thinks she can't breathe. Her head is pulled back by something tied around it. When she breathes, the bag sucks into her mouth and sticks there when she breathes out. She tries to close her mouth but can't.

While she's still learning to breathe

through the cloth, a torrent of cold water falls down on her face from the darkness. It fills her nose and throat. She chokes and tries to bring herself forward but is completely paralysed. She tries to turn her head away but a strap around it pins her in place. The water stops but she still can't breathe and when she desperately gasps for air, she sucks in the water from the dripping wet cloth and chokes again. Air is all she needs. Air is life. Her whole world has become her mouth and nose, sucking in water instead of the air she so needs. She manages half a breath when suddenly, another downpour of water hits her like a tidal wave and she begins to panic as she drowns. It's all so quick. When the water stops, her throat begins to close, the inside of her head is on fire. All she can think of is that he is going to kill her. She is going to drown the next time the water comes.

"*What's your name?!*" he demands.

Before she can even think about the question, the water comes again and she is drowning. Her body useless and weak, her lungs filling with water as consciousness slips away, her mind screaming while her body convulses lamely.

"*What's your name?!*" he demands again from the abyss.

Anything to make him stop. *Just say a name.* It takes all her strength: "Sarah!"

"Wrong!" he shouts with such force

in her ear, bringing her from the edge of unconsciousness.

Another barrage of water and all Lucy can think about is air, and saying whatever she can to get some. *How can he know my name?*

"*What's your name?!*"

Her mind flails to stop herself choking and spluttering before he begins again, "Lucy!"

"Wrong!" This time his voice is behind her, ready with the next deadly flood of water.

When it comes, consciousness slips through her fingers.

* * *

By the time Lucy overcomes the eighth warhead, her hands won't stop shaking, her head is pounding and her mouth tastes of vomit. It's the middle of the night above what must be New Delhi and that niggling doubt she knows all too well is creeping in. She tries to focus through streaming eyes on the hot orange glow of the Indian metropolis less than a mile below. This moment's hesitation is the worst thing she could do. *What am I doing?* Almost her entire life has been spent outside the moment, always from one project to the next. Always something new that needs to be done, another book that needs to be read, another friend that needs to be supported. When something becomes routine, she needs something more. Anything to keep her from stopping. Now, the thought that follows her into the solitude of the vortex is that those billion people might be a hell of a lot safer if she'd stayed home rather than pretending to be a superhero. At the other end of her short burst of flight, now countless miles above the earth, she pirouettes, her joints screaming, and jettisons the missile out into space. Then she zooms back into the safety of the atmosphere.

Floating in the darkness between layers of cloud, trying to catch her breath, Lucy just needs to sit down. It's a totally disembodying experience not knowing which way is up or down. If she stops flying for a second, gravity would quickly tell her which way is down, but she's too afraid to stop in case she can't start again. She wheezes on the thin air for a moment longer and her hair brushes her ears, telling her she is the right way up. *But which way to go now?*

East again. *But which way is that?* Back at the launch base, she had made a choice. She couldn't chase all the missiles so she put the two that went west out of her mind as best she could and went on. *Running out of time*. But surely those two kept going west. Lucy looks for her watch but it's missing. Based on the cities targeted so far, if the warheads were going West from Montana, at least one of them must have been headed for China. Lucy puts the fingers of her right hand to her chest looking for something else she knows isn't there. James once bought her an ornate silver compass on a delicate necklace. It was his way of saying, "I'm okay with this," even though he worried terribly about her. He got it inscribed with *Never lose your way*. It's currently sitting somewhere on her dressing table at home, with an impossible knot in the chain. There's no way she can find the two remaining missiles.

Paralyzed by uncertainty, she runs both hands through her tangled and sweaty hair feeling brittle, burnt ends crinkle uncomfortably under her fingers. As her hair tumbles back around her ears, she realises her ponytail has been burnt off entirely. She watches her breath freeze in the darkness and wipes frozen tears from her cheeks. *I should never have been here in the first place*. With no choice but to keep moving, Lucy swoops downward through a thin layer of concrete-grey cloud. As the cloud soaks her clothes through, reality does the same to her mind. She knows that, after a certain point, it was blind luck that got her this far, circumnavigating the globe, trying to keep going in the same general direction, following smoke trails, seeing tiny glints of metal hundreds of miles in the distance. She never should have wasted precious minutes finding the launch site. What's worse, each time she quantum propels herself from one country to the next, it's like closing her eyes on the motorway, slamming her foot down on the accelerator and hoping she can judge it all right. Sooner or later, she was bound to drop the ball.

Once below the cloud, she turns on her back and closes her eyes, feeling despair washing into her. She has to fight it. Lucy tells herself this isn't her; that she doesn't wallow or feel sorry for herself. Lucy works bloody hard and gets shit done. *But what can I do?* She was given these abilities, she's up here now and there's no-one else who can stop the apocalypse but her. But she has no idea where or how far the next one might be. No, Lucy's smart; she should be smart enough to work out which way is China.

The Indian subcontinent has a pretty recognisable coastline but, in the middle of the night, shrouded above and below by cloud, she can't figure out if she's even above India any more. She needs the sky.

With the beginnings of a plan, Lucy scans the horizon, finding a cloudless patch not too far away. Within seconds, she's below a starry sky and sees the beautiful, almost-full moon to her right. And now there's the North Star. That's it. Filling her lungs with air and her heart with one final wish that there's still time, Lucy launches herself forwards, keeping the white glow of the moon on her right, just as it had been when she flew from London to Berlin to Moscow. If she keeps the moon on her right and slightly behind her, she must be going northeast. The moon urges her on from the other side of the waterfall of light and darkness that envelops her in the vortex.

Ahead, the blackness turns to the darkest navy blue and then mauve. She is approaching dawn but she sees no missile on the horizon and she desperately needs to take another breath. Slowing until air can reach her, she drinks it in and looks down on the thick grey mass of Beijing smog below. A vapour trail hangs perilously above, pointing down to a small puncture in the smog. Shooting down through the hole, she chases the missile to the other side of the pollution, grabs hold of it about a few hundred metres from the ground and keeps going. *Shit.* They are hurtling towards a squat rectangular building in the middle of a vast concrete square. Lucy goes through the motions and moves her body in front of the warhead but the roof of the building rushes up to them and she instinctively kicks her feet out to cushion the impact.

In that instant, Lucy's world turns white and she feels the missile actually moving through her as if she has lost her solid presence. *No.* But she still feels the thing in her hands as the two of them float in this formless white space. As colour gradually ebbs back into the world, Lucy finds herself hovering above Tiananmen Square. Somehow, she absorbed the missile's inertia and stopped it dead in its tracks without detonating it. Looking down at her hands and arms, sickly pale with tinges of green. She feels slick with sweat and her sodden t-shirt clings to her.

In a daze, Lucy glides up with the missile towards the dense smog cloud. Suddenly, the smooth shell of the missile slips from her fingers. Panic kickstarts her heart and she's able to shake away the fuzziness in her head to quickly catch it again. Tucking it under her arm, she accelerates through the smog, out of the atmosphere and throws Number Nine into space. Dizzy and nauseous, she finds the moon again, places it on her right and heads east to Tokyo, the next logical target. But the missiles would have reached Tokyo before Beijing.

Faster, faster, faster. But it's not enough; Lucy doesn't feel fast enough. She has to let go of everything, let go of thought, let go of physical form, let go of life and become nothing. Allow herself to be carried by the singular will to be where she needs to be. The mental strain drives an anguished scream through gritted teeth. It feels as though she's tearing through the world while she's bombarded with images of shattering glass and steel and the dying screams of millions of extinguished lives. The vortex around her grows until it becomes a space in which she could move around; a cockpit of an invisible jet.

Lucy watches a star-spangled Greek

goddess leaping from the cockpit into the dusty pink of the nearing sunrise. She is beautiful, powerful and sexy. Everything as a child she dreamed to be, but is not. Her voluminous black curls crash and tumble like waves on a smooth shore as she snares a missile with her golden lasso. The goddess rangles the missile into submission and casts it into space where it glides silently into inky oblivion.

She gasps for her life. Falling out of her delirium and slowing her flight to catch some air and stop her head from spinning, Lucy finds herself surrounded by skyscrapers. Hundreds of people below are running in panic but they are not looking at her. The military and police are trying to evacuate them from the missile screaming through the dawn towards them.

She wakes herself up vomiting water and stomach acid, her head free from its bonds.

"Your name is *worm*,"

She's back in the room with that monster. Her nostrils burn with the smell of her own bile on the cloth bag over her head. Everything hurts. As he begins strapping down her head again, and she tries to fight, she sees herself from above, drowning in Tokyo Bay.

This time, as he tortures her and brings her to the brink of death, he doesn't bother to ask the question.

"*Worm!*" she screams desperately through the water and cloth, "Worm! My name is worm!"

He barely pauses as he picks up the next bucket of water.

"I don't believe you,"

What does that mean? Another hit with the water. She can't think. Air is everything and she has none of it.

Who are you pretending to be? Maybe Charlotte was right—where are her "super powers" now?

As if scissors just cut through her reality, her torturer releases her head and removes the bag. Her neck burns so much, she has to grit her teeth to raise it and, when she has lifted her head, the room spins and she vomits water again.

"Now that you have had your bath," he snarls genially, "we may begin... Worms do not pant!" he snaps. "Worms do not whimper!"

What did I do wrong?!

Without warning, his hot breath suddenly trickles down her neck. If only she could move. He places a sharp cold blade on her cheek, just below her eye, and slowly, sickeningly pulls it across her face to her lip. She screams with agony as she feels her face splitting. She retches but there's nothing to give.

"It is pathetic that you think you are a person,"

My name is Lucy Sequoia Hazel, you sick fuck.

In an explosion of warm light, two legs appear in front of her. It's the first time her eyes have seen anything since she arrived here and it stings. When she is able to open her eyes again, she begins to recognise them as her own outstretched legs, a lamp illuminating them from above. Her feet are propped immobile on a wooden board resting on something in the shadows. The man's thin hand emerges from the shadows and touches her with just one finger, tracing along her exposed foot from her ankle to her toe joint, examining her. Her instinct is to retreat from his repulsive caress. But she can't, and he has let her breathe, for now. He does this five times, once for each toe. He moves to her other foot and does the same.

"You could move if you want to," he says, and she doesn't like what he implies. "You stink," he says.

He pauses his caress while he says this, retracting his hand back into the shadows. *What's he thinking about?*

"I don't need another bath!" *Please. Not the water.* Lucy feels ashamed of how pathetic she sounds, pleading with this evil monster. He ignores her plea anyway.

She hears him moving around to her side,

he scratches her arm with something and, when his hand re-emerges from the shadows by her feet, it's holding a hacksaw.

"These little feet," he says, "Do you think you, a worm, have feet? No, worms do not have feet,"

He takes the saw to her ankle and grates its serrated edge along her flesh. The sound is sickening, like cardboard. Before she can scream, she passes out.

* * *

The siren blares outside the growling car as they speed behind the fire engine. Cassandra, Takei, Hilton and Jones' view through the unmarked car's dash-cam is beamed to the large screen in an operation room at MI6 HQ in Vauxhall. They stand transfixed as the pursuit roars ahead of them. Cassandra's heart is in her throat. Not so long ago, what they are doing in this room would have been out of the question.

Papa enters the room behind them, followed silently by an assistant carrying a cardboard tray of disposable coffee cups from Pret. Cassandra hears the whistling kettle in Otto Fleishacker's flat. Her palms are clammy despite the chill in the room.

Less than an hour ago, following their introduction in Papa's office, the four of them took a room along the corridor to *get acquainted*. Jones stood quietly in a grey suit, clearly a field operative who'd climbed the ranks, trained so well to blend into the wallpaper that he struggles to be seen, until he speaks. Takei appeared to be thinking about something else. And then there was Hanson, the American spy.

"How long?!" she demanded, no attempt to hide her anger. "How long have you been watching him? While Ashley Kindle died? While he armed his followers with his virus? How long?"

Deep down, if she really looked, she might have noticed that what was *really* upsetting her, more than her wasted hunt for McAvoy, was Hilton's deception, or rather, that she had failed to spot it. As a spy, she is used to being surrounded by other spies, but she spent a lifetime honing her ability to understand people and their intentions, to be an expert judge of character. As a black girl growing up in London in the '80s, it was a matter of survival. She realised, however, that she at least got Hilton's character right; his behaviour had not changed, he'd just been running double-time as a CIA operative in the military. When she looked deeper still, she realised it was Hanson that really shook her. Although the FBI had publicly taken credit for gunning down Kindle and eliminating the threat, Cassandra had seen Hanson. The FBI were taking credit to save face, because they'd let Kindle get across the US with a deadly virus and because Hanson, her real murderer, had presumably gotten away.

"Three months," he said, appearing prepared for backlash, "Since he turned up in Callais looking for passage to England,"

Hilton explained that a CIA asset, probably a human trafficker, reported a person of interest had been sent his way. It was safe to conclude that he had traversed Europe once he'd made it out of the Middle East, most likely by way of Turkey. This was in November. Instead of arresting him, the CIA let McAvoy cross the English Channel. That was the point in the story at which Jones spoke and drew all eyes to him. He was insistent that Cassandra and Takei knew that MI5 took control once McAvoy reached British soil and followed McAvoy to a residence in the South East of England. Hilton was keen it be known that the CIA called MI5 to tell them McAvoy was coming and that he was their suspect, in their operation. Either way, MI5 had been watching ever since, and sharing intelligence with the CIA. Hilton explained all about the letters Kindle had received before McAvoy reappeared and how they concluded that McAvoy was talking to a vast network of followers in the same way. He explained about Carole Wimberley, and how McAvoy himself hadn't emerged from the house since he first entered. Finally, he accepted that no letters had been sent in the three months they'd been watching the house.

So, yes, while Kindle died, the CIA and MI5 were watching McAvoy and, because of Papa's arrogance and defensiveness, MI6 were none the wiser. Both the CIA and MI5 knew Papa couldn't be trusted yet instead of doing something about it, they cut him and, in doing so, the whole of MI6 out of the picture.

"What's to say he'll send any more letters?" she asked "You think that's the only way he and his followers have been talking?"

"Why not?" defended Hilton.

"A diabolical network of penpals?" jibed Takei.

"You're right," said Cassandra.

"What?" exclaimed Hilton.

"I mean he's right that it sounds ridiculous. The answer's in the timeline," she said, thinking aloud, "Muhammed Al-Nasser disappeared in 2014. What was McAvoy doing for the years until 3/19 last year?"

"Travelling around Europe recruiting more followers?" answered Jones, partially.

"Probably, but what about Kindle? And the other postmarks in North and South America?"

"Well if he arrived via South America on a fake passport, he could have gotten in illegally through the border with Mexico," said Hilton.

"Okay, but you don't just meet someone

once, recruit them to your apocalyptic cause and then keep them on board with nicely written letters. Motivation goes cold. Would letters keep them warm over so many years?"

"There's something else," said Takei thoughtfully, "Why would he go to all the trouble of recruiting an army to distribute his virus if he himself could travel? There would be nothing stopping him from spreading it himself,"

"For that matter, why couldn't he just save some cash and mail the virus around the world?" asked Hilton to the air.

"Well, viruses aren't like Antrax," explained Takei, "What if it needed to be transported in a liquid suspension and vaporised for airborne transmission?"

There was a pause while the four of them tried to figure out what this all meant. Cassandra was first to speak.

"So he was in hiding. He was in hiding so he couldn't travel. The last time he left the UK before he boarded a one-way flight to Syria was in 2011 for a weekend in the South of France. So I don't think he did his recruitment before he joined ISIS in 2012,"

"And he couldn't possibly recruit his followers with letters," said Jones.

"Online?" asked Hilton.

"We're monitoring the internet and phone traffic at the Wimberley house," said Jones, "And there's been nothing,"

Although this was standard procedure for up-close surveillance, the realisation sent her heart thudding, "When was the last time you actually confirmed he was still there?"

"What, you think he tunnelled his way out?" retorted Hilton.

"You let both Kindle and I escape out of back windows, Hilton," she said.

"That was the FBI," Hilton grumbled.

"There's really no time to argue about this," she said, "No letters. No suspicious internet traffic. He's not there. And Carol Wimberley is our new key witness,"

"We don't know that," Jones implored.

"We'll go incognito," she said, "Worst case scenario: he's there and gets spooked, but he still needs to enact his plan sooner or later,"

"Okay, what are our options?" asked Takei.

After a moment's thought, Jones said, "Okay, let's go down the gas leak route," and he pulled out his phone, "I'll get us a fire engine,"

"Not very original," she said, "but it'll do,"

Now, the fire engine comes to a halt and the car, their eyes and ears, screeches in behind it. The assistant, now sitting at the computer to the side of the big screen, flicks the view to one of the field operatives' bodycams as he gets out of the vehicle. To make it authentic, the fire fighters, who are the real deal, and the police officers, who are disguised MI5 and SO-13 anti-terrorism, begin knocking on the doors of the houses and ordering the occupants to file onto the street to be stewarded to a safe distance. They tell them there's been a serious gas leak and they have to evacuate the area immediately. During this time, it begins to rain, the familiar sound of the sizzling spray and the patter of drops on the officer's body armour surround them. They watch now as the bodycam approaches a house, following a fireman.

"This is it," says Jones.

She exhales slowly as the fireman steps to the side just enough to give the camera a clear line of sight as the front door opens from the inside. The pit of her chest tightens and burns.

The woman who opens the door is white, in her mid-fifties, mousy blonde-grey hair, a silk blouse. Carol Wimberley. She looks like a panicked mannequin.

The fireman's voice can be heard through his back: "Madame, there's a major gas leak on this street and we need to evacuate the entire house immediately," he states clearly and firmly, "I need you and everyone out now please. Is there anybody else inside?"

The woman's voice can't be heard but there's a half-beat when her head turns fractionally over her shoulder, almost imperceptible.

"Yes," she says. She goes away into the guts of the house and returns with her daughter. She shakes her head now. "No one else," she says and they step outside into the cold rain.

The fireman says something only partly audible about needing to check inside. The officer with the bodycam goes into the house.

Cassandra quickly leans in and slams her finger onto the computer's keyboard, connecting the mic. "Don't forget to check for boobtraps," she appeals.

Suddenly, her pocket vibrates on her thigh and her phone rings. It's the virologist, Professor O'Connor.

She picks up wordlessly. Not taking her eyes off the monitor.

"Hello?" It's David O'Connor's voice.

"David,"

"Oh my God! You're alive!" he exclaims.

"Of course I'm alive. What's going on?"

"Cassandra, I've been trying to get through to you for days," he says, clearly exasperated.

"I've been away—I've only just gotten my phone back,"

"I thought they'd gotten to you. I didn't know who to trust. I couldn't very well leave a message,"

"David, slow down. Breathe,"

"Okay. Two days ago, I got a call from the

boyfriend of our mutual superhero friend," he says, "To tell me she's missing,"

"Shit,"

The room looks at Cassandra.

"I convinced him not to report it—said that if he did her identity would be blown and her family would be in danger—that I know someone who could find her so hold tight—I made him a promise, Cassandra. The poor boy's going out of his mind. What's going on?"

If Sentinel is missing, there's a high probability McAvoy has her.

If he has her, we've lost.

* * *

The Professor's study of interrogation and brainwashing began before his sojourn to the Middle East but it was there that he perfected the technique. At first, he was an observer, the student of the incumbent interrogators as they performed their work on the unfortunate members of the local population to have fallen foul of their own neighbours' accusations. Their grandfathers had been trained by the KGB, their fathers had been trained by the CIA and now, they, third generation torturers represented leaders in their field, if that is not too perverse a term.

ISIS was embroiled in a Soviet-style witch-hunt, with its inevitable path to collapse from within and without clearly prescribed countless times throughout history. However, the lack of self-reflection and the superiority of unconscious machinations over conscious rationality always ensure history's repetition.

As Ibrahim, the Professor exploited suspicion and vanity in pursuit of his necessary evil, climbing the terrorist ranks over the bodies of his bosses. It was a simple matter to dismantle his comrades with the right word here and there, whether in his proficient Arabic or his mother English. ISIS was surprisingly cosmopolitan. A lesser man may have, under the intoxication of anonymity, would have diverged from his ethical path, but he never, even as Ibrahim, abandoned the hippocratic oath. The psychological duress caused by his work within ISIS were deeply saddening side-effects in his treatment of the fundamentalist condition. During his time with ISIS, he brainwashed dozens to the point of catatonia, and single-handedly made a greater contribution to the descent of ISIS than any NATO allied country.

When he was a younger man, it would have been no trouble to sling the flying girl's body over his shoulder and do with her as necessary. In this old, sickly body, dragging her limp figure nearly finished him off. He sat wheezing on the floor after finally very awkwardly hoisting her up into the wheelchair. His repose was short-lived, however, since he had work to do before the anaesthetic wore off.

He had already rolled the chair onto a decorator's plastic sheeting to protect the grouting from any accidental bodily fluids. He abhorred violence and hoped there would be no blood, but he knew there would be vomit from the waterboarding and she may urinate herself under paralysis. A mop and several towels had, therefore, been on standby behind the breakfast bar.

It had been more years than he cared to remember since his medical training but he had practised on himself until he was ready to establish his subject's IV. He prepared two infusion bags: one for the anaesthetic and the other for the last of a Russian psychoactive serum code-named SP-117, which he had obtained in Afghanistan. This *truth serum* is tasteless, odourless and has the convenient effect of the recipient having no recollection of their time under its influence.

The Professor pauses scrawling in his notebook to look up from the breakfast bar down the hallway, to the zone of the apartment in which *Lucy Sequoia Hazel* resides. She dreams fitfully in the other room. Her wet, clinging clothes set his mind to wondering whether it is possible for her to catch a cold. It's too late to ask, since the truth serum is expended, as eventually will be the anaesthetic.

If she dies, she becomes a martyr, a near-infallible symbol, an even more powerful force around which misguided hope will rally. The only true way to defeat the Witch is to bring about her alchemical transmutation into the Mother, to have her join his mission and disavow the toxic status quo.

Her inhuman strength and virtual invulnerability complicates matters. It was good fortune that he observed on news footage her vulnerability to laceration and, therefore, puncture. He has realised that, while her body appears to absorb energy directed at it, a sharp blade or needle passes through her flesh just like the rest of us. When he takes her off the IV, he needs her to believe she is powerless to escape. To that end, when she awakens, still under bodily paralysis, she will see two "bloody" bandaged stumps in front of her.

He turns to his uneaten bowl of soup and the plate of soft bread. For a moment, he isn't certain whether he used the same butter knife that he previously froze and drew harmlessly over his subject's face in another part of his ruse. He is tired.

Tomorrow night, he must turn off the

lights again and begin *Step Two*. Having used Picasso Al-Nasser to break down the subject's connection to reality, her concept of *Self*, and any knowledge that she can easily escape once the last of the medication has worn off, the Professor must now return to embark on a journey with the two most prevalent and motivational emotions: *Guilt* and *Shame*. As he knows from years of experience, this will enable progression to the subject's self-betrayal. When her identity is metaphorically drowning, she will denounce herself, her loved ones but crucially, the traumatising belief system she and the rest of the world uphold.

When she denounces the status quo, he will give her the opportunity for redemption, step-by-step, before ultimately granting her rebirth as his angel of purifying holy light. No longer will she stymie his catalysation of the new world. She will transform from a seductive symbol of the perpetually wounding old world into a call-to-arms for his disciples. A beacon like he once was for them. He will "heal" her body, he will give her back her miraculous powers and her costume. That is when she will fulfil her purpose. If he fails, his followers may be lost forever, along with the rest of the world, in the delusion the establishment has created for them, and that this flying girl has fortified.

But before that, he must say his final

farewell to Ibrahim Muhammad Al-Nasser.

Persona. From the Greek *to sound through*, for the masks worn by the performers of Ancient Greek theatre. These masks not only allowed the actors to play many different characters but for the audience to both see and, through their resonance, hear their performance from the distance at the back of the ampitheatre. The masks themselves were not created to withstand the ages but their image, their stories and their impact remain today. *It is time to lay down this mask*, he thinks privately in his bedroom, as he lights some white sage in a quiet ritual of cleansing and transition, and closes his eyes. Sleep never comes easy but tonight it will perhaps be a little less tormented.

* * *

In her dream, Lucy is a pine, standing on a hill. When the wind comes, it blows hard and she bends and creaks, her thousands of needles wavering. The sky darkens and darkens and the wind becomes stronger until she is filled with fear. Her roots go deep underground and there she realises they meet with others. Above ground, she is not alone but one of many pines all over the hill becoming a forest, all swaying under the barrage of the wind, clattering as their pine cones find the fertile soil.

In another dream, she is wading through water along a dimly lit corridor entering rooms on the left—also full of water—to see a person in each before moving to the next room. Some of the rooms have masks outside for her to put on before she enters. In others, she is handed the mask by the person inside, who insists she puts it on before they acknowledge her. The first room is her school P.E. teacher. In another room, she meets her dad; in another, her mum. Even Grangran is there, and she wants to play chess with her. She begins to pay attention to the masks she's putting on, layer after layer, finding it harder to breathe. Pulling them all off together, discarding them in the black water, their collective hollow eyes long for her, fatally wounded by the rejection, as they float away. Anthony Spitelli, the pilot she nearly killed on 3/19, is in one room, looking at her in ecstatic adulation, as he tries to force on her a carved marble head. A white friend occupies another room and insists she wears a murky black mask. A black friend in another room insists she wears a white silk mask. The water has been rising and time is running out. Soon she will have to swim but, for now, the water sloshes around her waist. She opens a door and the room is completely filled by a huge, writhing worm. It coils to fill every space, no beginning or end visible. It must be six feet thick. She turns to look back down the path she has come and the water is gone. The masks are hanging by string from the ceiling. As they twist and turn in the air, showing their different sides, they form an image that, if she just moves to the right place, will reveal itself. All together, the masks form an incomplete picture of Lucy's own face. The view becomes her bathroom mirror, where the missing parts of her face are fogged up from the shower she just had. She reaches out her hand and wipes away the condensation.

* * *

With insufficient evidence to charge Carol Wimberley, she remains in police custody under the Terrorism Act. Her daughter, Wednesday, has been taken into care to ensure she has no contact with McAvoy. If he wants Carol and Wednesday, maybe he'll make himself known. Neither MI5 nor SO-13 found anything to lead them to McAvoy or his followers. The family computer was clean enough and the fantasy of finding a list of addresses anywhere quickly evaporated.

Now in the MI6 *sweatshop*, it's just as Cassandra remembers it: the stale air hangs with dogged determination and the safely grey room is illuminated by striplights, row after row of desks are laden with computer monitors, and dozens of analysts tasked with unravelling codes, intercepting threats and finding lost things. The vast room stretches almost the entire footprint of the riverside building and has been open-plan since 2001, when, suddenly, the pressure to work collaboratively mounted exponentially.

She stands behind a young woman who is sitting at one such desk, Josie Border. Josie has been assigned to her team of seven, for risk management and scenario planning. She sits at a computer monitor adjacent to Ben's, working on a spreadsheet of numbers.

"What are you doing?" Cassandra asks.

"Um," she says, turning, "I'm modelling population extinction under best- to worst-case vaccine roll-outs, within most likely pandemic spread, Ma'am,"

She finds it helps every so often to remind herself and the team why they're doing what they're doing. Cassandra thought she needed Kindle's body, but of course it's being held by the FBI. Ordinarily, since she and her partner reneged on their deal with the US and smuggled themselves back to the UK, she wouldn't expect to see it any time soon. Takei is attempting to make light of the situation—and failing—but he's right about one thing: thanks to them, British-American relations are pretty much the worst they've been for about two-hundred and fifty years. But now they're working with Hilton—again—so that's something. Hilton tells them the Americans are sequencing Kindle's blood cells, looking for antibodies that might provide a clue about the virus or its possible vaccine, assuming there is one and she took it before she was murdered.

The image of the girl's pulped face is added to Otto's whistling skull in Cassandra's mind. Every night, when she's exhausted her mental photoreel of clues, she asks herself how she could have gotten Hanson so wrong. And she blames herself for Ashley Kindle's death. That one she can't put on Papa. The old Papa nor the new one.

Along from Ben's empty chair is Alexander. Alexander heads up the financial investigation team.

"What do you have, Alex?"

"So we've been looking into McAvoy's bank accounts again, looking at his private clients and patients but nothing interesting so far,"

She turns to Tim, next along from Alexander and in charge of what's affectionately nicknamed *cavity search.*

"Tim, how are you getting on with the hospital records?"

His team's been scouring all available records from mental hospitals where they know McAvoy worked and those in the cities postmarked on his letters.

"We're doing what we can," he replies, "But it's taking time and bodies—we're finding a lot of places don't have fully electronic records,"

"Prioritise those that do," she orders, "Just start building the list of patients he discharged,"

At this stage, every conversation feels like a Hail Mary; like she's just keeping herself and everyone else busy. And she doesn't feel lucky.

She's had enough.

"This isn't going to work," she says to Takei when she finds him by the microwave in the sweatroom kitchen, "We don't have time to trawl through a decade's worth of hospital records, and then what? Go door-knocking to all his old patients in HAZMAT suits? How long before they start hearing about it and releasing the virus? We need McAvoy. We need him to call them off,"

"You've been through this with Hilton and Jones," he replies, picking up a bowl of porridge, "McAvoy is beyond threats, we have to catch him out, let him lead us to his followers. What we're doing *here* is the back-up plan,"

"And what if he doesn't slip up? Isn't he in the final stage of his plan now that he has Sentinel?" she pauses for breath and rubs her face awake, "And if one of his followers can go rogue and get herself all the way to Wall Street, how do we know the virus isn't already out there somewhere, spreading right now? This invisible enemy could already have won and we wouldn't even know it --" she trails off.

* * *

Lucy's drowning and swallowing water, in huge gulps. At first she thinks she's being tortured again but this is worse. She's underwater. It's pitch black and she's sinking, tied around her chest to the wheelchair. Panic.

She kicks her legs and thrashes her whole body. The rope breaks with ease. *Up. Go up.* In an instant, she finds herself falling again, but this time through the air. Beautiful, cool, life-giving air, and thudding onto the ground where it's muddy and shingly. She rolls onto her back to catch her breath and immediately vomits viscous Thames river water. At any moment, he's going to take her back. He'll taunt her, tease freedom just to flaunt his control and teach her a lesson.

"Please, enough!" she calls out lamely, through a throat that feels torn up with razor blades.

She can't bear to be free any longer, knowing it won't last. But it does. She waits and waits and he doesn't return.

She's thinking about getting up and finding her way back to him when exhaustion starts to take hold. She couldn't stand anyway—he took her feet, when he was trying to take her name, trying to take everything about her and turn her into something else.

When she wakes again, it's still dark and he hasn't come for her yet.

She hopes with whatever hope she has left that she hasn't given that bastard what he wanted. She renounced everything for him, but deep inside, she has held onto herself.

The city's lights illuminate above but they don't reach down here on the inky shore of the river. Her dizzy mind swells, threatening to overflow with terror, disgust, shame, desperation, but most importantly, with the feeling that the danger is not over. It swells up inside her and bursts as a primal scream, both a laugh and a cry.

She wakes again, being rolled onto her side by figures crouching over her, asking her questions.

"Hello, love," the man says loudly, "Can you hear me?"

They're running their hands over her body in quick, purposeful movements as if searching. Still weak, she begins to look around. They're wearing bright yellow and green—paramedics. *Thank God.*

"Shallow pulse" says the woman holding her wrist, "Can you tell me your name, love?"

Worm.

"L-Lucy,"

"Okay, Lucy, are you in pain anywhere?"

"Can you sit up for me, sweetie?"

She manages an affirmative groan but, when it comes to it, she's less able than she thought.

"V four. Puncture marks in left arm,"

"And right,"

"BP 66 over 90,"

"Can you tell us what you've taken, Lucy?"

Lucy shakes her head. She's beginning to shake all over. They're now shining a torch in her eyes.

"E three,"

"Can you raise your arm for me, love?"

"I'm going to give you a little pinch on your finger,"

Ouch.

"M five. GCS twelve,"

"Okay, Lucy, you can lie back down, now. We're going to lift you into our ambulance now, okay?"

"You just lie back. Can you tell me your last name, Lucy?"

The journey is fast, as she lies on the stretcher for more checks. The inside of the ambulance is cast in blue light and Lucy notices for the first time that it's morning outside, in the city. *Daylight.* One of the paramedics—the man—stays with her while the other drives. She thinks he's the nicest man she's ever met. She thinks she could cry. As it goes on, and the haze sharpens into a hangover, she's compelled to talk.

"What's your name?" she asks.

"I'm Matthew," he says with a smile, "Can you remember at all what happened last night?"

Her heart rate spikes.

"No," she lies, and shakes her head for too long.

"Okay," he says with care.

When she looks down for the first time, she jumps out of her motionless body. Down there, at the ends of her legs, she sees a cruel joke: two feet.

"Are you okay, Lucy? What is it?"

"My feet!" she cries in a panic,"He took my feet!"

She begins to weep and can feel the way Matthew's looking at her now, differently. Her body is shaking again, uncontrollably.

"It's okay, Lucy, I'm here," he says with his hand on hers, "It's alright,"

"He cut off my feet," she says through the tears.

At the hospital, she's wheeled through double doors, and along corridors until she's parked in a room and lifted onto a bed. After Matthew says goodbye, a female nurse asks her if she's able to change herself out of her wet clothes and into the hospital gown she has for her, but she doesn't leave her. Lucy catches a glimpse through the curtains of the police waiting outside for her. Her legs won't work so she changes clothes sitting on the edge of the bed. Her filthy clothes are taken away in a bag. In that dark place where he kept her, he made her wash with a cold soapy sponge, sometimes warm if she'd been good.

"Can I have a shower?" she asks.

"We just need to wait for a few things, but," she gives her a smile, "I'll get you some wipes and other bits,"

Slowly, she feels herself cascading out of delirium into the hospital room, into her body, and her mind is still there. Just. While the nurse is gone, two police officers come through the blue paper curtains. A man and a woman. The woman asks about who she's been with, what drugs she's taken, how she got to the Embankment, had anyone forced her. When she tries not to tell them her name, the male officer tells her this could be a criminal matter so she'd be best to co-operate. It's incredible how quickly the atmosphere changes from caring for a victim to roughing up a criminal, as if this is somehow her fault. Her mind turns to James and for the first time she can remember in a long time, she misses him desperately. She wants him to know she's alive and okay and she wants to be with him, but there's no way of contacting him, not without blowing everything. The nurse returns with the "wipes and bits" and the police give Lucy a break, for now.

Afterwards, Lucy feels clean and dry for the first time in weeks. It's like a new body and it's wrapped tightly in crisp hospital sheets. Pressed down at the bottom of the bed, attached to her legs: *Feet*. Her feet.

Her inward smile of relief is short-lived. There's a commotion on the other side of her curtained sanctuary. The energy of the ward has changed. There's a subtle increased tension and steady but purposeful rush outside. She hears a familiar but unexpected voice, telling the officers to stand down. They anxiously concede and stomp away, but not so far that Lucy can't hear them getting on their radio to their boss. The curtain slides open and in steps someone wearing a white full body protective suit, like the kind in CSI shows, and a black gas mask.

"Sentinel?" she says in the familiar but echoey voice, Agent Bryce's face now clearly visible through the plastic visor. She's carrying a clear plastic bag with a jumble of things inside. Lucy forgets any mask she's ever worn herself.

"What's happening?" she asks, terror threatening at the edges of her heart.

"It's her," she says to an invisible other; an earpiece Lucy guesses. Then, to Lucy she says, "It's a precaution. Now, where is he?"

Lucy's mind spins. She feels weak, her stomach is empty, her mouth tastes of metal. The possibility of infection threatens again. She's done her part—she's found McAvoy.

"You can't go after him," she says.

"That was never the plan, Lucy,"

She knows my name.

Bryce steps closer and takes something out of the bag—a smaller one about the size of a sandwich bag. "You've drawn him out and now he will lead us to his followers—we just have to watch,"

"But there isn't time for that now,"

"What is it, Lucy? Has he released it?"

If Lucy tells Bryce where he is, she'll be sending her and others to their death for sure. Out of the sandwich bag, Bryce produces a little white stick, like a long cotton bud, and a narrow strip of paper.

"It has to be me," she says, "I have to go,"

"No way. You're in no fit state," Bryce inspects Lucy's drip, "And this hospital is going into lockdown as we speak,"

Lucy doesn't know whether she can face him either. For all she knows, he could have let her out, having done something to her, turned her into his weapon. Perhaps that's what Agent Bryce is afraid of too. McAvoy knows how to hurt Lucy, maybe he knows everything about her. But she can't let anyone else go.

Searching for strength, she tells herself he never really broke her. Somehow, she always held onto her one single truth: that she is not what others make her. In some ways, her entire life had been preparing her for that.

She was always the other. Telling James you get used to it was an understatement. From her dad, with his comic book hero expectations. To her mum, who held her back at every turn. To her white peers who treat her black and her black peers who treat her white.

She is not all one or the other. Not all her dad nor all mum. Not all passive nor all active. She is a thinker and doer. This was no different: this bastard breaking her body and trying to break her mind, telling her she's a worm and that she is powerless, trying to force another identity on her. She has strength and she can use it. She has her own history and growth behind her and the infinite possibilities of the future ahead of her. And she can catch a nuclear missile with her bare hands.

The guilt she felt when discarding the masks in her dream was a message too, she's certain. Perhaps it meant to tell her that she is none of these things people say she is, yet they each have something she can understand and use. Even the worm with its message of humility. She can own whatever part of it feels right. Make it hers if she wants it. Take away his power.

"What is that for?" She asks Agent Bryce of the stick in her hand.

"It's a field testing kit," she says raising the paper and stick, "It'll tell us whether you've been infected,"

Scraping the stick around her tonsils makes her gag and her eyes water. Bryce wipes the swab on the paper, which she replaces into the clear ziplock bag and seals it in.

"Thirty minutes," she says, "For the result,"

“It doesn’t matter. I can do it. I know what I have to do,” She could now see another gas mask in the plastic bag Bryce brought in. Bryce doesn’t look convinced. Her eyes narrow on the other side of the plastic visor.

"You've done your part, Lucy. You can stand down now. Thank you,"

She wretches a little, as she draws out the shockingly long needle from the back of her hand. Pulling out canulars is not as easy or painless as in movies.

Seeing her own body intact is one thing but feeling like it really belongs to her after the experience he put her through, is something else. McAvoy tore her to pieces. In there with him, she had no concept of time or reality, just one endless nightmare. In there with him, reality was what he made it.

She hasn’t used her legs in weeks, but it all starts with the first move. She sits up and puts one foot on the floor and then the other. She feels the hard, smooth floor under the soft soles of her feet. Feels how her toes grip as she leans forward and applies more pressure. The muscles in her thighs harden in anticipation. One move and then the next, with the next few planned out. Beyond that, she will have to see what unfolds, knowing she always has options, and each step reveals more. *Move your pawn and you still have fifteen other pieces.*

She knows McAvoy knows her weakness, but she also knows that he cannot control her with his illusions any more.

"My whole life, people have told me who I am; what I am and am not capable of," she says firmly, "I'm the only one who knows,"

She doesn't bother trying to stand on her feet—she knows her muscles have wasted, strapped to that wheelchair. She floats, inches off the hospital floor, making her seem taller than she is.

"You can't leave," commands Bryce, "Not until the test result,"

"What about that?" She indicates the black rubber gas mask in Bryce's bag.

"The respirators only filter what you breathe in, not what you breathe out,"

"Well there's only one place I'm going—McAvoy's flat,"

Bryce *must* know there's no time to lose.

"At least tell me where so the area can be quarantined," Bryce concedes.

"It's a block of flats on the East bank of the Thames, halfway between Vauxhall Bridge and Lambeth Bridge," she hopes he's still there but expects he's long gone by now.

"I had changed my mind when I saw you," Bryce says as she pulls the gas mask from the bag and hands it to Lucy, "It's a military respirator. Put it on and breathe normally," Next she removes the main bulk of the bag—another white suit like hers, a couple of foot coverings and some latex gloves. "It's not biker leather but it'll protect your skin, hair and clothes from contagions. And you'll need this," she gives her a mobile phone. It isn't the last thing in the bag but it's the last thing for Lucy. "There's only one number stored on there. Call it when you get there and tell them who you are,"

CHAPTER 11

The final chapter

The unnatural anguish of splintering wood and smashing glass in the night shook the Professor violently from his deep sleep and propelled him upright, as if a pair of firm hands on his shoulders. His heart pounding in his chest made the sick old man dizzy. The Professor's first thought was that he had been found and it was all over. He feared all was lost and as he sat paralysed, trying to think what to do, he had a vision of armed men in black storming the homes of every one of his followers. After the last pieces of glass tinkled to the floor, however, silence descended on the cold, clinical flat, followed by the crescendoing bellow of wind and the gentle clattering of blinds in its thrall.

The girl. This was his next thought: that she had escaped. In the darkness, he extricated himself from the still unfamiliar bed and crept as best he could to his open bedroom door. Peering around the frame, down the hallway to the girl's chamber, his adjusting eyes revealed her escape.

"Fuck,"

Searching was not worth the amount of energy it would have taken him in his infirm state to get along the hallway. With mere weeks to live now, if he is lucky, he staggered back to his nightstand, coughing involuntarily and began to get dressed.

Now, he sits on yet another unfamiliar bed, in his dimly-lit and odorous final refuge, before he must gather himself for the ultimate step. He lights the metaphorical fuse with the tap of a finger on his phone's screen. The Witch's escape has accelerated the plan but only by a week. With just a week more, he would have had her. The full process of breaking her down and building her back up again would have been complete and he would have sent her forth into the world, to stand atop Mt Olympus and urinate on what has become of mankind. He would have transformed the creature who threatened to be his mission's undoing into his most beautiful and archetypal symbol to catalyse his apostles.

The Professor is, however, meticulous and his contingency plan may still suffice. When it has finished uploading, he again watches the video, the fuse that will trigger his apostles.

It took several attempts until her words were no longer a banshee's wail and were as audible and enunciated as necessary. In the video, the Witch's face in her mask looms close and almost maniacal as she utters her denouement:

"The whole world is fucked," she says, spitting quiet condemnation, "It's time to tear it down and start again,"

Magically, the group message introduces his apostles to each other for the first time. He ponders at the experience for them, who have had only promises of each other's existence, finally having confirmation of their faith, and the power now compelling them to act at the time and date he has instructed.

Now, he must rest again, for tomorrow is the day that marks the beginning of the end for many, but the dawn of a new era for the fateful few. He will need as much energy as he can muster to fulfil his personal part in judgement day, by striking at the heart of this country's status quo, and one of the most recognisable symbols of the establishment.

* * *

James' voice is like the first drops of rain in the desert.

"It's me," Lucy croaks, her throat closing up.

"Oh my God, Lucy," It sounds like he's getting up and moving around. "Where are you? Are you okay?" She can't speak. "Lucy?"

As her eyes well, she manages a single shaky word, "Yeah," and then she closes her eyes and swallows back tears, "I'm okay,"

"Where are you? Do I need to come and get you?"

"No, I'm okay. I have to do something before I come home,"

"Can you talk?" He asks, "What's happened to you? Where have you been?"

She can't think back to the terror she has endured or she won't be able to speak. She has to keep going forwards, flying over the Thames—at least for now, until she's done what she needs to do. And, finally, she will rest. James must have been going out of his mind with worry. She could have been dead in a ditch for all he knew.

"I was--" How does she explain? "Someone got me. But I'm okay now. I promise. I'll explain everything when I see you," she can't keep everything from him any longer. *I promise*.

She can already see the stretch of the Albert Embankment where she met McAvoy.

She thinks she hears James sobbing on the other end of the phone.

"I love you," he says.

"I love you too,"

"Please come home,"

"I will. But I can't until it's safe,"

"When?"

"Really soon. I promise,"

As they hang up, she sees the balcony and puts on the gas mask she's been holding in her other hand. The glass building reflects the winter sun, glaring golden and blue through the mask's visor. She approaches fast, squinting. She hears the gasps and shouts from the few people below, and the honking of car horns. The wind whips at the paper-like protective suit.

Strangely, there's no familiarity to the shattered glass doors and debris on the balcony; they spark no recollection of escape, even as she gets close enough to touch them. At the last moment, she slows. The thought of him in there, lurking in the darkness makes her skin shiver from the inside out. Below her feet, the tiny cubes of broken glass, like gravel, cover the balcony floor. She cautiously floats into the flat.

The balcony doors lead to an open kitchen and living area. Inside, the low sun casts long shadows; so many dark corners this creates for him to hide. Yet she feels strangely separate to the place. This is not the same place she escaped. It is light, despite the shadows; a modern luxury apartment with a Thames view.

She remembers Agent Bryce's phone in her hand again and starts recording video, funnelling the world inside his flat through the little rectangular screen. The pipes at the back of the freezer make a sudden cracking noise and the fridge begins to hum. This little sign of life makes her heartbeat just a bit harder. The sound of her breathing in the mask intensifies. The place darkens and outside it begins to rain, the noise competing with her breathing, water bouncing on the broken glass on the balcony.

She fights the feeling that someone is here and could walk in at any moment. There's fruit in the stainless steel bowl on the breakfast bar. It tells her he was living here with her, between stints of torture, while she sat somewhere in a puddle, drugged to oblivion, crying for it to end. It was done in a room off the hallway. A door lies broken in half that way.

Looking back at the balcony, she sees two IV stands lying prone in the rain. They must have been dragged out behind her and snagged on something. The memory makes her arms ache.

She searches the flat, leaving the kitchen and living area to come back to last. First is the bathroom. His toothbrush is there—it doesn't look new. There's toothpaste scum in the sink. She can't bring herself to touch the scrunched towel on the rail but it's clearly been used. She has to get over her repulsion, turn it off, so she can properly search—urgently. Thousands, or millions, of lives are depending on her tracking him down. The cabinet over the sink contains no clues—toothpaste, a comb, men's shaving things. On the back of the bathroom door is a white bathrobe with M.C.W. embroidered in navy blue on the chest.

The next room along the hallway is where it happened. When she looks at the broken door, she doesn't remember but she feels it splintering into her shoulder. Floating over the door, staring into the room via the gas mask and the phone, she feels no connection, no feeling except dread. Her experience of this place was in total darkness. Now, with light bouncing in from the hallway, it looks like a seedy film set. It's as if she expects to find a part of herself in here. There's something large, black and ominous in one corner, which she can't look at. Every centimetre of wall and ceiling is covered with tiles of sound-proofing foam. The ceramic tiled floor is covered in clear plastic sheeting, taped down. There's a mop and bucket in one corner. The bed is made with plain white sheets and untouched. One corner of plastic sheeting on the floor has been peeled up but it looks like he gave up on trying to remove the whole thing.

The wardrobe is empty, bar some wire hangers. She half-expected to find her costume hanging there. In another corner is the thing she's been avoiding since entering the room—a black sheet strewn chaotically over a large cardboard box with something sticking out of the top.

What she finds when she pulls away the sheet should make her feel better, but instead makes her stomach turn. Sticking out of the top of the cardboard box are two plastic legs, wearing her leggings, the ones she wore under her costume. Where the feet should be, there are two stumps wrapped in bloody bandages. Her feet —the mannequin's feet—are in the bottom of the box with a hacksaw.

She wonders whether she's floating six inches off the floor to preserve the crime scene or because she is afraid to use her feet. *Keep going.*

The door to the second bedroom—his bedroom—is wide open. Inside, the bed is unmade, the sheets in a twisted mess half on the floor. The draught from outside picks up and blows past her into the room. He was sleeping here while she sat slumped in that chair just the other side of the wall. The wardrobe in this room is full of clothes. The drawer in his bedside table is empty. Just a lamp on it.

Back in the kitchen, the cupboards contain nothing suspicious; she pulls everything out onto the floor, empties the fridge and freezer. It's just someone's flat, a normal lived-in place wrapped around that torture chamber down the hall.

There's no device or bomb. It would have been so easy if there were a big nuclear bomb sitting here like in a comic. A bio-weapon could be as small as a deodorant—and look like anything for all she knows. Maybe it's already in the air, or the virus is laying invisibly in wait on an innocuous surface. She adjusts one of the mask's chafing straps at the back of her head and turns to leave.

She wants to go home. She ends the recording on the phone. But, as she looks down to put away the phone, forgetting the suit doesn't have pockets, she notices something on the floor between the breakfast bar and the fridge. It's a small scrap of paper, miraculously visible amongst the pasta and tins that crashed around it when she emptied the cupboards. She picks it up and holds it in front of her gas mask, squinting at the scribbled hand-writing:

Car park: C0159

James' old flat had a similar code for the underground car park. Still holding the paper, she turns to look outside, contemplating how far McAvoy could have gotten by now. No-one drives in London so the only reason for a car is to get out of the city. Or else to move something too big to carry. Or maybe it's just his way of not being seen. But what was it Agent Bryce said in David's garage? He's targeting major cities around the world. If that's true, no matter how far he gets, he's going to want to return to London.

The garage is small but it's full of expensive-looking cars, so shiny they look like they're never driven. He isn't in any of them. There's CCTV in every corner, every pillar and by every door, so that'll help Agent Bryce and her team.

Back at the flat, she floats out over the balcony into the cool but close air. The city skyline is gloomy and wet, clouds still rolling in from the West, blotting out the low sparkling sun. Straight ahead, past the balcony, past Lambeth Bridge, on the other side of the river, is Westminster Palace and the Houses of Parliament.

She calls the number on the phone.

"Verification code please," answers the female voice.

Agent Bryce didn't give her a code. But she did give her a codename.

"Uh, Sentinel?" Her own voice sounds almost robotic inside the gas mask.

"One moment please," The moment is short and, when the voice is back, Lucy's caught pulling the mask off her face, flying high into a cleansing downpour. "Please repeat,"

"Sentinel?"

"That code isn't recognised,"

The line goes dead.

She calls again.

"Verification code please,"

"Look. Agent Bryce gave me this number. I'm the flying woman. My codename is Sentinel and I'm at Terrence McAvoy's secret hideaway in the centre of London,"

"One moment please,"

The moment is long. More than three minutes go by before the operator returns.

"Who is this?"

It's a man this time.

"I'm Sentinel, the flying woman, I think I know how you can find Terrence McAvoy,"

"Okay, tell me everything,"

She explains that she thinks they should be looking for a car that left Peninsula Heights flats in Vauxhall within the last twenty-four hours. She tells them to find the flat with the smashed balcony and that he has a biological weapon, that he may have already released something into the flat. When she's done, the man on the phone tells her to keep the phone on and gives her a new number to call. He says it'll go straight to Miss Bryce now.

Above ground, she's thinking about her next move when the phone rings. It's Agent Bryce.

"Sentinel?"

"It's me," Lucy replies, "I'm at Terrence's flat. I just spoke to one of your workmates. Terrence isn't here but I think he has a car,"

"Yes, I know. Thank you. I thought you'd want to know that your test showed up negative —you don't have the virus. But, if you've been in his flat again, it could be on your suit. You have to wait there until one of my teams arrives so they can contain any possible contamination,"

The gnawing dread that had been threatening at the edges of her mind shows its face, like a monstrous insect. It doesn't go away now as it takes on the meaning of this place. It was one thing to methodically work through room by room, object by object, but it's another to have to kill time here, where she was trapped and tortured.

"Sentinel? Do you understand? It's imperative that you don't go anywhere, and don't take the respirator off until you're given the all clear,"

"I get it," she replies, "Thanks. I'll be here," She feels that the conversation ends here—Bryce has more important things to do, and Lucy begins her way back down to the balcony—but then, "Wait—Agent Bryce? How are you going to stop him?" The secret agent might easily brush her off with an enigmatic response. But she doesn't.

"It's like you said—things have changed now. We can't afford to wait for him to expose the network. We have to bring him in, and work with the risk that he doesn't talk,"

"But he won't talk," says Lucy, "He's -- he's barely human," she remembers fragments of his raging speeches, his venomous hatred for what has happened to everyone in the world, "All he cares about is wiping the slate clean with humanity,"

The pause is only a second.

"He cares about his followers. Ashley Kindle was immune—her blood contains the antibodies,"

She waits on the balcony, or rather floating a few inches above the balcony, watching the London rain soak the skyline and gush from the balcony above this one, like she's the other side of a waterfall. Slowly, she allows gravity to take hold, for her feet to become grounded on the gritty surface of broken glass, shuffling it away so she can feel the tiled balcony floor under her feet through the flimsy plastic foot coverings. She decides to leave.

She flies up and out from the balcony. She pulls off the gas mask and throws it through the broken glass doors. Then, under the pelting of rain, she carefully unzips and removes the protective suit, turning it inside out and tying it into a ball before discarding it in the same way. Finally, she removes the gloves, careful not to touch them on the outside either, before chucking them in with the rest of the stuff. Her soon wet hospital gown clings to her in the wind and rain but she finally feels free.

She takes to the sky now, straight up. Despite her longing, she can't fly straight home in the middle of the day, but she finds comfort in a familiar process. Step 1 is to find one of her rooftop landing spots on the horizon. Step 2, she holds her breath and propels herself fast enough to be invisible. Step 3, she slams on the brakes at the last second so she doesn't destroy the roof of the building. Step 4, she finds her secret bag of spare clothes, gets dressed, jumps to the ground behind the building and walks home in the rain.

Walking down Commercial Road on her own two feet gives her the kind of rush she used to feel when flying. But when the crowds start to thicken, she quickens her pace, hoping this isn't a mistake and that the suit and mask ensured she hasn't become a spreader.

She can't remember the last time she arrived home like this—the normal way—through the door, scaling the steps to their flat and stepping over the junk mail on the mat. It's warm inside and the bulb in the hallway gives a comforting golden light. But something's missing too; it's quiet.

"Lucy!" James calls, rushing out of the kitchen down the hallway. His usually stoic face looks like it's breaking. But then he stops, staring at her like he's afraid of her as she raises her hand in warning. "What's happened?" he asks.

Standing there, in a kind of standoff with the man she loves, Lucy does her best to explain everything. From meeting Agents Bryce and

Takei in David's lab, to McAvoy and her world tour, trying to become his target, to the woman at Wall Street with the bomb that turned out to be something else, about airborne biological weapons, and she forces herself to remember meeting the old man on the balcony—McAvoy himself—who drugged her, tortured her and tried to brainwash her, before she escaped.

She expects a long moment of silence while it all sinks in.

Instead, she watches as James' medical professionalism kicks in. He rubs his face, waking himself up and wiping away tears and says, "Right, I'll get the shower on. I'll chuck you a bin bag and you can get undressed there,"

The whole time she's in the shower, she knows James is out there, just a few metres away, sitting on the edge of their bed, waiting to see her again like she's waiting to see him. McAvoy recedes temporarily behind the image of James.

As she dries off, she calls to him, finding it easier to talk from another room.

"J, I'm going to stop him,"

His reply comes through the open bathroom door: "I know you are,"

In her mind, she feels them having a different conversation and she thinks he does too:

"J, I might not come back,"

"I know,"

So, dropping the towel, she rushes to him

now, cheeks wet with tears. He barely stands before she throws her arms around his neck and kisses him. She savours every part of him until they lie exhausted, complete, naked in each other's arms, on their bed.

* * *

"I think I need to go and see my mum and dad before I go," Lucy says, walking back from taking another shower.

James is sitting up in bed, looking at his phone, his hand over his mouth.

"What is it?" she asks.

He turns the phone around so she comes close to see what's on the screen. To her horror, she sees her own face, in her white mask, saying things she doesn't remember—things she should never have said.

"It's all over Youtube," he says.

She thought she had escaped. *How stupid.* She thought she would never have to go back to that time again. Here it is, facing her as starkly as the whole world now sees it, and sees her. There is no going back from this. Her heart drops into the pit of her stomach and she wants to curl up in a ball until she disappears. Not only did he film her as he tortured her and made her say things that feel totally alien to her, but he used her as a sign to his followers. He made her denounce everything.

He made her give up on the world. Now she understands.

It all happened this way because of her. Agent Bryce told her all that time ago back in David's garage that they knew McAvoy's followers were losing faith in him, because of her. When she stopped the missiles on 3/19, she showed them that maybe McAvoy's plan for them wasn't their destiny, and that maybe, instead of the world being out to get them, there's someone looking out for them. McAvoy needed her for something—he needed to break her and show them he's more powerful, that she is a powerless *worm*, and now she sees that he wanted her to take his side too. And she did. For that brief moment that he captured and spread.

The feeling of all being lost is a familiar one.

"I've lost!" the little girl, little Lucy, threw her hands up in despondence above the chess board, "It's over!"

"What are you talking about?" asked Grangran.

"I can see it, you've got me trapped," she felt like crying, "There's nothing I can do. I really wanted to win this time,"

"You've still got eight pieces on the board, young lady," said Grangran, putting a hand on her hip, the one with the tissue between the thumb and her palm.

"Yes but I'm going to move this pawn here," said little Lucy pointing at the board, "and then you'll move your knight here, so I'll have to put my bishop there and then you'll have my queen,"

"But I need your king,"

"Yeah but, I can see—it's too late --" she trailed off.

"Don't be so sure you've thought of all the moves, young one. Take your go and see what happens. I might have thought of something different to your imagined plan of mine,"

She'd always wondered whether Grangran was planning on letting her win. In the end, Lucy doesn't remember who won that game, only that it went on for a lot longer than she thought it would after that, as she chipped away at the board and new opportunity after opportunity became visible.

"Are you okay?" asks James.

She stands up straight.

"It's not too late," she says, turning to the wardrobe, "If I gave them hope once, I can do it again,"

She lifts the lid of the wide shallow box at the bottom of the wardrobe. Inside is her spare costume, all cleanly white and red, still with its red cape attached at the shoulders.

"The video says, *'The time will be today 12:00 GMT'*," says James, "What's that mean?"

* * *

"This is it!" Tim says, jabbing his finger at the screen, "That's Carol Wimberley's car,"

Cassandra stands over Tim's shoulder as he sits at his desk, where they've been scrolling through the CCTV of vehicles leaving Peninsula Heights. He clicks his mouse a few times, bringing up multiple video feeds of roads, of varying quality, where they now trace the car as it progresses disorientingly around the screen, from one video feed to the next like an Escher staircase illusion.

"Where's he going?"

"I'll speed it up, hold on,"

Takei and the team gather around as they collectively anticipate where McAvoy went the night Sentinel escaped. But he didn't go far. Out of nowhere, he stops the car on Waterloo Road at 01:13 and abandons it.

"Got the bastard," whispers Cassandra, as they watch Terrence McAvoy, skeletal though he appears, step out of the car and hobble down the pavement.

As he walks into the Travelodge as bold as brass, the phone on Tim's desk rings. Cassandra picks up, to be told that the flying woman is waiting for her in the lobby.

"Watch that hotel," she orders Tim, hoping McAvoy hasn't gone anywhere since last night, "Don't lose him," Then she says to Takei, "Get the strike team,"

When she gets upstairs to the lobby and sees Sentinel in her shining white and red costume, regal cape draped over her shoulders, she almost forgets how angry she is with her.

"You said you would stay at the flat," she says as she strides up to her. She's trying to believe that this is the same young woman she found lying in a hospital bed unable to stand, just a couple of hours ago. "But you're here just in time," Cassandra says, "We've got his last location,"

Takei arrives behind her, wearing an armoured vest, holding one for her.

"The car's going to meet us out front," he says as she slips it on and he passes her an earpiece.

"Travelodge on Waterloo Road," she says to Sentinel, the three of them walking towards the main entrance, "You know it?"

"No but I'll meet you there,"

"No," Cassandra says firmly, "We go in first. You wait,"

As Takei and Cassandra ride in the car, her in the front passenger seat, him in the back and a field agent driving, Tim's voice crackles into the earpiece.

"Team leader, the target left on foot and got into a black cab on Waterloo Road, about five minutes ago,"

"Where are they going, Tim?"

"They're in traffic on Westminster Bridge going East,"

"Parliament," she says gravely to Takei.

Of course.

"It's Wednesday today," says Takei looking at his watch, "Prime Minister's Questions are coming up,"

"Jones?" she asks into the earpiece.

"Yes, Ma'ame,"

"Low key evac of the Houses of Parliament. Get MPs into quarantine, filter the public audience into a side room as they come in. Alert Parliament security to McAvoy, delay him until we get there. He can't know anything is amiss. When I say so, get him into the Commons Chamber so we can meet him there. Understood?"

"Copy that, Ma'ame,"

"Strike team, divert to Westminster Palace and hold position there. Sentinel, do you copy?"

The line fuzzes.

"I'm here," says Sentinel, "Lost signal while I was going fast but I'm on the roof of the Houses of Parliament, out of sight,"

There's still time to get this right as long as

he doesn't release the virus before he gets inside. Hilton, Jones and Papa will be watching their every move back at Vauxhall, at a wall of screens, sipping their coffee and waiting.

* * *

Lucy hovers five feet off the floor in front of the Speaker's chair, with rows of green leather benches and wood panelling stretching out ahead of her. Despite seeing this place so many times on the news, she never realised how many cameras there are, hanging below the galleries on either side—large TV cameras and several CCTV cameras blended into the wooden surroundings. Every few feet, microphones hang suspended on wires from the high, vaulted roof.

At the other end of the chamber, above the entrance, is the public viewing gallery, separated from the main chamber by a thick wall of glass or perspex. She's terrified of seeing him appearing in that room, behind that screen. Now, hearing his voice echoing indecipherably in her head, she fears most what the monster might say. Somewhere, hiding in the wings, are men and women with guns, following Agent Bryce's orders, ready to kill McAvoy, but first, Lucy has to take apart his scheme and stop his followers. She has no idea how, but that will come.

McAvoy hobbles in through a door at the

back of the gallery, and an usher closes the door behind him. At first, he looks shocked and maybe even a little afraid—not of her, but to find himself in there all alone, rumbled—but he quickly composes himself. He looks twenty years older than when she first saw him on that balcony and so frail it's a wonder he's standing.

He addresses her. He has to shout through the clear barrier between them.

"Did you know the ventilation system here is all connected? I can put my little vial by one of these vents and all I have to do is use my little electric fan to send millions of little pathogens to be carried to every nook and cranny of every seedy and corrupt politician's hiding hole,"

Suddenly, the doors at the back of the gallery burst open and six armed men storm in, covered head-to-toe in black, wearing gas masks, pointing big guns at the back of McAvoy's head.

"ON YOUR KNEES!"

She can see that he's going to struggle to get onto his knees, but officers on either side of him push him down—the pain on his face is real. Lucy finds that she's moved through the air of the chamber halfway towards the gallery.

"I've already sent my sign to my apostles, *little worm*," he shouts, "It's too late,"

"One of them uploaded it to Youtube," she says, the microphones relaying her voice to him inside the gallery, "He's being arrested right now and, if any of your other followers are on his contact list, they'll follow within minutes,"

"Don't try that with me, *little worm*," he shouts, "I know that's not true,"

A TV monitor on either side of the chamber displays the time: it's 11:43. Less than seventeen minutes until his followers release the virus around the world. She needs to try something else.

"Tell me, Professor McAvoy," she says, trying to see him for the frail human that he is and not that monster in her head, "I understand that manipulating people, distorting their reality, their lives is your thing, but do you really believe anyone will be fooled by that video of me being drugged and tortured?"

"You're about to find out,"

"You know," she presses on, "You really got in my head. I couldn't resist. Maybe I know what it feels like now for your victims. You call them your apostles, right? But do you know what pulled me through?"

He doesn't answer. His beady eyes seem to be trying to bore into her, through bulletproof glass and bulletproof skin.

"I realised you were rushing. I felt your desperation because I know you're running out of time. Your victims haven't had that benefit. You've spent a lot of time with them, tearing them apart so slowly they couldn't feel it. But your victims started to lose faith in you because they saw a glimmer of the truth, a reminder of life, and one edited video, one sound bite, isn't going to undo that,"

"And what is this truth?" he demands, finally goaded into speaking.

"That life is uncertain, and hard, and full of hurt, but in that uncertainty there's also hope. That's just how it is and nothing will change that. You can't make people who you want them to be. You can't know what's going to happen or how people are going to react. You're looking for a utopia? You could be creating Hell,"

"This is Hell," he shouts, "And you are a naive little girl,"

"This is the real world," she says, "Maybe it's Hell for you but there's always hope as long as there are still chess pieces on the board, as long as there are still people trying to make it better. That's what people saw on 3/19. All is never lost,"

"Time's up,"

One of the two soldiers at McAvoy's shoulder is Agent Bryce. She nods her signal to Lucy from behind him. Bryce holds a credit card sized device and a mobile phone. Lucy can't tell for certain through Agent Bryce's gas mask, but Lucy thinks she sees her eyes smiling.

"You're right," Lucy says to McAvoy's surprise, "The person behind you has just sent a link to a live feed, to all your phone's contacts. She can see them all watching the feed. They've just seen the real you, in there. And the real me. And, I hope, maybe a reminder of the truth," McAvoy's face finally drops. He must know it's over. "You can't fix something or make it better if you wipe it out every time it starts going wrong, Professor. You'll just keep repeating the same mistakes,"

Before anyone can do anything, the professor throws a vial of clear liquid at the glass, smashing the vial to pieces.

* * *

Once McAvoy's contacts started following the link and Sentinel had said her piece, Cassandra thought that was it for Professor Terrence McAvoy, for Ibrahim Muhammad Al-Nasser. As she'd been told time and time again, he was beyond threats. But then, he surprised them all: in prison, for the first time since he became ill, he accepted cancer treatment. It may have been too late—it was already Stage IV—but he did it anyway.

"All is never lost," Takei said knowingly when he heard.

The contacts in McAvoy's phone, cloned to hers while she held him on his knees, were all unlisted, but when the recipients followed the link to the live stream of the Commons, Ben and his team could track their locations.

Those that didn't click the link took longer to find. Some had destroyed their phones after they watched McAvoy's first video and others just put them away. Ben pulled historical phone records for each number and cell tower data to triangulate their most likely last position.

In total, twenty-six of his followers were found in their homes, wondering what to do next; three had already handed themselves in to local police; seven had called their mental health services; and only one had released the virus, not including Ashley Kindle, or Otto Fleischaker. The virus was released into St Peter's Square in the Vatican. Thanks to mobile phone records, and because MI6 was able to warn them, the gendarmerie quarantined the Square and found the spreader, Matteo Bianchi, as he was trying to leave. The Vatican has been under lockdown for the week since then and, so far, there have been no reported cases of the virus outside the city. One hundred and twenty-one people who were in the Square around Bianchi have died, alone, not allowed to see their families. Most national governments are expected to maintain lockdowns in the hometowns of McAvoy and his thirty-nine followers for one month. The home cities of Ashley and Otto—Helena and Munich—are also locked down, in a show of international solidarity.

Now, Cassandra sits at her desk at the agency's central office in Vauxhall. It's been one hell of a week. *One hell of a year*. In front of her is the manilla folder Hilton dropped on her desk before leaving. When she opens it, she is met with a familiar, fabricated lie; the lie she presented to her FBI captors to convince them they had leverage over Sentinel when they had none. The photo of the young woman that stares back at her with a neatly pressed blouse, blank, unassuming expression and immaculate weave is her younger self; the mother and father hers too; all of them, with only their names changed, to give the Americans an entirely fake identity for Sentinel. It doesn't matter now that the US intelligence services hadn't fallen for it. She drops it into the paper shredder, which whirrs automatically into motion and hungrily devours the paper and card. Still on her desk lies another manilla folder. While Cassandra was also the curator of this file, the difference is that its contents are real, and no-one else but her has seen them. Inside is Lucy Sequoia Hazel. Cassandra drops it into the shredder too.

There's just one more thing she needs to do, to deal with Jill Hanson.

* * *

If that day at Wall Street, the day she ran,

was the worst day of Jill's life since Danny died, the day she said "Fuck it" was best. It came just a few days after, out of cash and nowhere to turn, she hitch-hiked to nowhere, keeping moving and keeping ahead of the law. She was riding in the cabin of a huge truck, next to a huge trucker. It smelled of body odour and those pine-scented air fresheners that smell like nothing but chemicals, and a bacon sub she could swear was nestled somewhere too warm. Despite the depths of winter, he wore a flannel shirt, torn jeans and a beanie hat. His name was Jeb.

"Running from or running to?" he asked.

"What?" she said, shaken from her reflection in the window, still searching for someone she might recognise.

"Running *from,* or running *to?*" he asked with a smile this time, trying to show he meant it with warmth.

"A bit of both I suppose," she said. He nodded. After a while, she continued, "I guess I'm running to my family," Then she looked back out the window at the road running by, underneath them. "And from the law,"

"What you did serious?" He asked. "I'm not about to hand you in—I gotta make my schedule —your business is your business,"

"There's what I did and there's what they think I did. Both are pretty serious but what they say I did is the worst,"

"I got a bit of a history myself actually. Wanna play a bit of Bad Guy Top Trumps?"

Outwardly, she smiled at that; inwardly she hoped to God he wasn't a rapist.

"Resisting arrest," she began.

"Oh, yeah I got that, plus assaulting a police officer,"

"Try assaulting a federal officer plus grievous bodily harm,"

"Oh!" he laughed, "That's good! Hope you broke something precious!"

She went on: "Endangerment of public safety, perverting the course of justice, aiding and abetting foreign agents--"

"Spies?!" he exclaimed with glee.

And then Jill's tone shifted: "Absence without leave, dereliction of duty, going on a crazy, heartbroken manhunt," She felt the pain in her cheek where the gun burnt her and it threatened her eyes with water.

"And what they say you did is worse than all that?" He asked. She nodded, eyes fixed on the road. "Well at least you aren't that little bomber girl the feds shot dead a couple days ago,"

"The feds?"

That was when she found out the FBI had taken credit for executing Kindle. The feds don't just appear out of nowhere; they'd known about Kindle, they'd called off Helena PD's investigation of her, they'd let her get to New York City so they could publicly execute her, but they'd known about her. Her heart told her they knew about Kindle long before then. But they'd hunted Jill anyway, because she was trying to stop a terrorist, to do their jobs for them when they wouldn't and then they killed Kindle anyway. Danny had given his life for his country and no-one had protected him. Flt Cpt Blake, who'd been terrible at his job and didn't care a bit about the deaths of all their colleagues, was still in-post and doing fine, while she took a stand for justice and that made her a wanted criminal. The system to which she'd dedicated her life was bullshit.

And that's when Jill Hanson finally said, "Fuck it," In the cab of that truck with Jeb, on the highway to nowhere. Danny would have been proud of her. It felt good, like a suit of concrete had finally cracked and crumbled for her to shrug it all off. She was out of it. And that was the best day.

She didn't have cash for Christmas presents but a gas station clerk did give her a pencil and a few sheets of paper, since it was the season. She wrote a letter to everyone she was running to: Mom, Dad, Tom, and his girls. She was still a wanted felon and she knew the feds would be watching Tom's house, waiting for her, so instead of going *home* home, she dropped the letters at Bill's place. The letters told them that she loves them, that she can't see them for a while, she hopes they have a good Christmas, and that she misses them more than they can know. She was never one for lots of words or emotional outpouring. Folding the paper and dropping them into Bill's mail box, she wondered with bittersweet anticipation whether she'd ever be back.

Now, she sits in the driving seat of a new car, under a tall brick archway and the words: *For the Benefit and Enjoyment of the People*.

Suddenly, a gloved knuckle raps loudly at her window. She's been sitting here so long she hadn't realised there was someone waiting behind her. But then the tall man stoops down to the window and peers in at her. He's wearing an Army uniform. He's a Lieutenant General.

"Excuse me, Flight Lieutenant," he says through the window, which she hurriedly opens, "My name's Lieutenant General Clay Hilton," The crazy thing is, if it weren't for his rank, she might speed off. But she doesn't despite everything she's thought about the government and the military over the last month. She's been on the run for all this time and just when she's about to leave it all behind and achieve something, she's caught, and she can't bring herself to keep running. Her name badge scratches uncomfortably through her shirt. "You need my help," He says. "Can you step out of the car?"

She doesn't take much convincing to get in his black car behind hers. If there is a good way of avoiding rotting in a jail cell for the rest of her life, she's taking it.

And it doesn't take him long to get to the point.

"Why?" she asks, after he's explained what he is offering.

"Frankly, Jill," he says, "I think you should take the offer before I change my mind. But know this: it's more than you deserve. One wrong word, and I mean *one*, and it all disappears, and you go to jail, for a long time,"

As she gets out of the car and begins walking to hers, still none-the-wiser as to where this luck has come from, his last words are: "Cassandra Bryce sends her regards,"

Under the brick archway, the fresh spring breeze gusts through her open car window, bringing with it the smell of pine and possibility. The breeze through the trees sounds like she imagines the sea sounds, perhaps a distant tide. She earnt this, she created this new identity, but the Lieutenant General let her keep it. *A clean slate*, he called it. She takes one last look at herself in the rearview mirror and drives over the threshold, through the Roosevelt Arch, into Yellowstone National Park, into her new life and her new job: Ranger Jane Ellroy.

*   *   *

Steve doesn't know what he's doing here. He sits on the floorboards with his back to the wall, to the side of the basement door. He's lost the last few hours somehow. *What does it matter?* He thinks to himself. He considers how long he's been in this house, in this town, without a call from work; whether his dad would care much if he went over now; whether his mom, although she might be happy to see him, would feel true love for him or whether smothering him is the only form of love she understands. Again, he comes back to the thought of whether any of that actually matters if *he* doesn't matter. Whether he'd be missed.

The basement—the bunker—is just behind him and he thinks of all the times he remembers going down into it, the creaking wooden steps, the swinging cord, the smell of musty damp bricks and vinegar. Why he was going down, he doesn't remember, just like he still doesn't remember ever coming up again.

He has a growing feeling now; formless and wordless. A deep, draining, swelling sense of dread, of hopelessness, but also of desire—for comfort and peace. And he knows that resisting it is futile. Somehow, in his bones, he knows that to go down into that basement now means death. He would go down and he just wouldn't come back. And that's what he should do.

Already in front of him on the floor are his wallet and its contents laid out neatly in a grid, all his cards and a few dollar notes. He removes his watch and slowly places it to the side of his wallet, as if making a logical schematic of where these things would be on his body. Next, he removes his phone from his pocket and lays it down on the other side of the wallet and its contents. The final piece of the little display of his life. As he's staring at its inactive black screen, it lights up and rings.

He lets it ring. There's no-one he wants to talk to and he has nothing to say. But it keeps ringing. *Why doesn't it go to voicemail?* Annoyed and curious, he picks it up and answers.

"Hello?"

"Hi, Steve," says the male voice, "It's Neil Stanton, how are you?"

It takes a moment to realise: "Oh, Mr Stanton. Hi. Yeah, I'm fine, thanks," he lies, "You?"

"Good, thanks. Listen, I was watching the news just now, have you seen? It's showing the super woman and everything that went down in London. The video of her being held captive and then what she did and said in British Parliament," Steve has seen the same news. It felt like watching a world he was no longer part of, setting off on a new course, becoming more distant. "Anyway,

I don't know why that got me thinking but I remembered I needed to call you. I checked with the Principal and the offer is good—she agreed we should have you in to talk to the students as an inspirational speaker,"

As if standing over a dam that suddenly cracks and bursts, in an instant, tears pour from his eyes. Without understanding why or how, as if it is both his final confession and prayer for salvation, he says into the phone something he has never said to anyone, not even himself: "I killed Samantha," He feels like he's crying for his entire life, every moment he has lived, every moment he has not lived and every moment he is yet to live, crying with his whole body.

"I heard that," Mr Stanton says calmly, "I know. And I figure it's pretty clear that you were one of the surviving missile operators on 3/19. But that doesn't define who you are. The kids would really like to hear from you, and so would I,"

When the call ends and Steve hangs up, he puts the phone back down where it was, on the floor next to his driving licence and credit card. He feels the wall at his back, sitting on the hard floor of the old family home and the beckoning of the basement feels a little fainter. He thinks to himself: *I have somewhere to be.*

You've reached the end of this book but this doesn't have to be the end of the story. As self-published author, I can only continue to write books like The Fateful Few if people buy them. If you liked it, please spread the word and leave a good review wherever you buy your books.

My sincerest thanks.

Alan.

Printed in Great Britain
by Amazon

16094102R00281